D1807569

Frost Fair

Edith Layton

Untreed
Reads

Frost Fair
By Edith Layton
Copyright 2018 by Estate of Edith Felber
Cover Copyright 2018 by Untreed Reads Publishing
Cover Design by Ginny Glass

ISBN-13: 978-1-94544-738-9

Also available in ebook format.

Published by Untreed Reads, LLC
506 Kansas Street, San Francisco, CA 94107
www.untreedreads.com

Printed in the United States of America.

Without limiting the rights under copyright reserved above, no part of this publication may be reproduced, stored in or introduced into a retrieval system, or transmitted, in any form, or by any means (electronic, mechanical, photocopying, recording, or otherwise), without the prior written permission of both the copyright owner and the above publisher of this book.

If you purchased this book without a cover, you should be aware that this book is stolen property. It was reported as "unsold and destroyed" to the publisher and neither the author nor the publisher has received any payment for the "stripped book."

The scanning, uploading, and distribution of this book via the Internet or via any other means without the permission of the publisher is illegal and punishable by law. Please purchase only authorized electronic editions, and do not participate in or encourage electronic piracy of copyrighted materials. Your support of the author's rights is appreciated.

Publisher's Note

This is a work of fiction. Names, characters, places, and incidents either are the product of the author's imagination or are used fictitiously, and any resemblance to actual persons, living or dead, business establishments, events, or locales is entirely coincidental.

The publisher does not have any control over and does not assume any responsibility for author or third-party websites or their content.

Also by Edith Layton and Untreed Reads Publishing

The Duke's Wager
The Disdainful Marquis
The Mysterious Heir
Red Jack's Daughter
Lord of Dishonor
Peaches and the Queen
False Angel
The Indian Maiden
Lady of Spirit
The Wedding
A True Lady
Bound by Love
The Fire Flower

Prologue

The gentleman was blue with cold. And small wonder. It was the coldest night of the coldest winter in the recorded history of London town, and he was entirely naked. His face was literally blue, but so was his ample stomach; frost drew a scarcely decent veil of icy rime over the scant hair on his narrow chest and the graying bits on his privy parts. But he didn't mind. He was much too dead to care. And probably a great deal warmer where he'd gone — or at least, where he deserved to go.

Chapter One

"Uncle's gone missing," the young gentleman said as he came into the dining room in the butler's wake.

"Indeed?" the gentleman at breakfast said, after a sip of coffee. "Have you looked under a book?"

"I'm not joking, Maldon, he's gone missing."

"You're not joking, no," the man he'd called Maldon said with a slight frown. "What else but a family matter would have brought you out so early, and in such weather? Unless you were only just going home now, and stopped by on the way?"

"Aren't you going to invite me to breakfast?" the young man asked, ignoring the outrageous comment, since the sun was well up and it was almost noon. He eyed the several silver serving dishes filled with eggs, kippers, bacon, beefsteak and porridge that stood on the great polished mahogany sideboard.

"Bring a plate for my brother," Lucian Peregrine Gregory Maldon, fifth Viscount Maldon, told a footman, with a wave of one slender hand.

There was no way to guess they were brothers. They both wore casual but correct morning dress for gentlemen—tightly fitted jackets over gleaming white linen, carefully tied neckcloths to keep their shirtpoints high, waistcoats, snug knit breeches, highly polished half boots. But the young man who had just been announced was in his early twenties, though he looked more like a schoolboy. He was slight, of average height, his boyish face was ruddy from the cold. He had warm brown eyes and a winning smile.

Even seated, the man at the table could be seen to be taller by several inches and older by several years, and the smile he wore was faint, and mocking. He was pale, lean to the point of gaunt, his face all planes and cheekbones, his nose long and high bridged, his winged brows arched over long gray eyes. Fans of dark eyelashes

1

over those knowing eyes were the only things to soften that angular, clever face. There was no spare flesh anywhere else on the man, but tensile strength was apparent in his long frame. He kept fit, and dressed to show it. His light brown hair was brushed back, smooth, elegant and precise as the rest of him. The only thing the two brothers had in common was the color of their hair.

"Uncle, is it? Did you think to find him here?" Lucian asked.

"Last place he would be, true," the younger man answered with a quick smile. "When did you last see him?"

"I tend to forget unpleasant things."

"Coming it too strong, even for you!" his brother chided, busying himself filling his plate. "There's nothing wrong with him. He's staid, true, but there are worse bores—in our family, at least."

"Doubtless. Which is why you don't see them here either. Have another side of beef, why don't you, and then kindly tell me why you're really here?"

The younger man sat, and flashed his brother another grin. "Afraid I'll eat you out of house and home? I don't think I could. I doubt anyone could." He glanced around the room as though seeing it for the first time, letting his eyes pointedly linger on the painted pagan gods cavorting on the high ceiling, the intricately carved wooden panels of fruits and pheasants that hung at each side of the fireplace, the long windows overlooking the garden at the back of the elegant townhouse. "This house, two others in the country," he mused, "a hunting box, and now another new house in town for your...private needs? Not counting the family seat."

"Mama *has* been talking to you, hasn't she?" Lucian said, amused. "Yes, the new townhouse. An extravagance, true. My fortune is not limitless though alas, my appetites seem to be. But it wouldn't do to entertain an unmarried female in my bed here, much less a married one. After all, think of the Name. This house isn't soley mine, it's been in the family since it was built and went from our father to me, and will go to my son on that unhappy day I leave you. Not at all the thing for such liasions, and though I hate to

2

sully such innocent ears as yours, I confess I have been known to indulge. But not here, of course.

"So, needs must, when the devil drives, and one's appetites are the very devil. Exactly as the vicar always told us," he pointed his knife at his brother. "Mark my words, Arthur, no man's immune to them, even such a spotless youth as yourself. Be that as it may—the new house has a discreet address, and is well suited to my vile purposes." He gave his brother a grin. It was a face that didn't often show a genuine smile, and so the effect was curiously charming. "But the rest?" he asked, tilting his head to the side, "the properties and possessions? Simply the privilege of being born a decade before you. Unfair, I grant, but fortunate, for me. Keeps me from the gutter. I have no other virtues, you know. Don't begrudge me, dear brother, eat hearty—I don't stint at my table."

"You don't have to," Arthur said over a mouthful of biscuit.

"Is that it? You're in the suds again?" Lucian sighed. "What was it? A horse that ran too slow or a female who would only slow down for a glimpse at your wallet? No, don't look at me like that, I don't care. I'll advance you the blunt; you didn't have to enact a tragedy for me." His tone was light, but he gave his brother a keen assessing glance. Arthur might smile and smile, but he was not in the habit of dropping in for a visit of a morning. Theirs was not that kind of relationship.

"Nothing like that," Arthur said. "I'm solvent. I did come about Uncle, it's just that I'm half-frozen, and hungry. It's cold as Death out there, and I haven't had breakfast. You may have just got up but I've been out and about for hours. Louisa sent word to her mother, who fired off a note to ours, and here I am—looking for Uncle everywhere." He put down his fork, his face earnest and a little worried. "He's gone, without a trace, Maldon, it's no joke."

"How long has he been gone?"

"Since Friday night. His valet says he never came home."

"Is that all?" Lucian groaned. "Not even two full days? I've stayed longer at a gaming table."

3

"Yes, you have. So have I. But Uncle's regular as a clock and has been for years. He has his regular pattern, his books and his club and his cronies…"

"And now the fair Louisa too," Lucian commented wryly. "The prospect of marriage has unhinged many men. Perhaps he's changed his mind, set sail, and is in the tropics even now, with a dusky maiden or two fanning his fevered brow."

Arthur's pleasant face grew a frown. "You don't have to like it; Lord knows you made your point clear enough to Uncle himself. But the thing is he wants to be married, and eagerly looks forward to the day. Whatever happened, he did *not* run away. Aside from the fact that a man like him would never go back on his word. The wedding's set for next week. No, he didn't run, I'd bet my life on it."

"Very high on our dear Uncle, aren't you?" Lucian said thoughtfully. "The thought of a man of fifty-odd marrying—no— rather say, *buying* a spinster of thirty so he might breed on the way to the graveyard doesn't repel you?"

Arthur's face grew as stiff as such a pleasant one could. "A man wants heirs, Maldon. You have yours, it doesn't occur to you. When I'm fifty, I'd think I'd want to know I was leaving my fortune to my own blood too."

Lucian didn't seem to hear. "Very thick with Nuncle, aren't we?" he mused. "I detect Mama's hand in that too. Why should the undeserving prodigal son get all the inherited wealth? Why indeed? And why shouldn't you feather your nest? But still…*Uncle?* She's being a bit previous, don't you think? He's only five and fifty. He's got *years* to go on prosing people to death, and now there's sweet Louisa in the picture too. You'd be far better off cozying up with that ancient pinchpenny, Aunt Ethel—no, I forgot, she hates males."

Arthur put down his napkin and stood up, his mouth tight. "I'll just be leaving then, no use talking to you, is there?"

"Oh, stay," Lucian said wearily, with a negligent wave of his hand. "Never mind me, I haven't a particle of family feeling,

Mama's quite right about that. You're right too, I don't understand Uncle's passion for the holy state of matrimony. I was once a good child, you see. I can scarcely expect you to remember, you were only ten, and I had a full twenty years—and two days—in my cup on my wedding day, as I recall. As if I could forget. But I marched up the aisle like a good little soldier because Mama and Papa expected it of me. It was agreed long before I was born, after all. Matching estates, old friends and good neighbors, and a charming daughter, well, to tell the truth it wasn't that hard for me. Still, I wouldn't have married at all, had I a choice. But my only choice was to either be a good son or a disappointment to the Name. I did my duty, dutifully produced an heir, and would be married still if Fate hadn't intervened."

"But you have Nicholas to carry on that Name!"

Lucian's hard expression eased. "Yes," he said softly, "so I do. But then, how many such lads are there in this poor old world, do you think? And," he added in his usual bantering tones, "can you see *Uncle* producing such a boy? Oh, sit down, sit down, you're giving me a stiff neck! And forgive me. There, you've heard something few men ever have, an apology from me."

Arthur sat again, and picked up his cup of coffee. His brother leaned back, looked at him, and drummed his long fingers on the table. "Now, cut line. Why *have* you come to me?"

"Why do you so dislike Louisa?" Arthur asked.

"I don't. I pity her, actually. Not unintelligent, but plain as a pikestaff, and with no funds, so forced to wed an old bore for his money. It can't be easy."

"You're not married, you might have offered."

"*Me*? Lucian laughed, richly. "Were I to offer for all the sad spinsters in London, I'd have to be an Arabian! Polygamy *is* frowned upon in our circles. No, I'll take my women, serially—and out of wedlock from now on, thank you. I tried it once, and don't have to again. And again, why have you come to me?"

"Someone has to go to Bow Street, to ask after Uncle," Arthur answered seriously, his eyes grave. "Yes, it's come to that. No one

5

knows where he is, Maldon, and now we all fear the worst. Well, here's a fellow who never takes a step he hasn't taken at exactly the same time the day before—except for his engagement to Louisa, yes, don't say it. But where is he? His valet, butler, man at law, his fiancée—no one in the family and no one at his club seem to know.

"I was, in fact, the last to see him—so far as I know," Arthur said with a frown. "He dined with me Friday night. And you know, thinking back—he was strangely excited, almost agitated, couldn't wait to be gone that night. Not like him at all."

"Probably only anxious to get back to a book," Lucian drawled, as bored now as he usually was on the subject of his mother's brother. "But if you have to go to Bow Street—and the mind recoils at the thought—though I'll allow they've the resources to ask questions in more places than you—why are you here now?"

"*Someone* has to go to Bow Street, I said. And all agree you're the one who ought. No—hear me out. You're the head of the family, you have the Name. Who wouldn't hasten to help the Viscount Maldon?"

"Head? In name only—try the other direction. I'm the bad end the family's come to, just as Mama always says," Lucian said. "And you're an 'Honorable,' I remind you, and ten years younger than I am. It's cold out, you just said so. And it's snowing now too. You go. You're young, you can stand the exertion."

Arthur shut his eyes, summoning patience. His brother was only five and thirty, he belonged to the prestigious Four in Hand Club because he was such a skillful whip, and drove his coaches to an inch. He was also a brilliant fencer, expert with pistols, and everyone knew he sparred with the best of the bloods at Gentleman Jackson's boxing salon on a weekly basis. But in the family he was equally well known for his reluctance to involve himself in anything he didn't enjoy.

"But you're ten thousand times richer, and so you can put up the reward," Arthur persisted. "And if you do, they'll believe it."

"Reward?"

"Bow Street works harder if a reward is offered. Even though we know it's unusual for Uncle to be unaccounted for, I'm sure there are murders and thefts they consider more important than the matter of a gentleman gone missing a few days. A reward would make the matter more urgent. The *Viscount* Maldon would make it more urgent still."

"My dear boy..." Lucian said, and paused, and tapped his spoon on the table, and sighed. "I suppose you'll come along?"

"I have to talk to more of his cronies, and then there's Louisa to tell. Thank you, brother!" Arthur said, grinning like a boy. "You're a great gun!"

"A great fool," Lucian grumbled. After Arthur left him, he sat frowning at his plate. He put down his napkin, stood, and called for his phaeton to be made ready. He went to the outer hall, still frowning. A footman helped him with his many-caped driving coat and handed him his high beaver hat. He strode outside.

It was like being slapped across the face with a cold washcloth. He could feel the ice in his nostrils with every inhalation as he waited for his high-perched carriage to be brought around. He wondered if he should take the closed carriage instead, sit inside in comfort and let his coachman drive. But at least the fog had lifted—to reveal snow.

Weeks of wretched dank dismal fogs and still no sunlight. It was a murderous winter, begun with fogs so dense that coaches on the roads crashed into each other almost as often as the ships in the Thames did. Pedestrians had been no better off groping their way through London because even linkboys' torches couldn't illuminate streets that looked like curdled milk. Now the new year had come, and fog gave way to snow. But Lucian saw it was intermittent, and the street sweepers had been busy, and he hadn't been able to go out driving for weeks. He'd drive himself.

His curricle came out of the stables. Lucian climbed up to the high driver's seat and took the reins from his groom. The man clambered down, and the boy who acted as his lordship's tiger saluted him from where he stood on the back of the elegant, light carriage in order to add weight and balance it. Lucian was still frowning as he threaded the reins through his gloved hands. *Bow Street. On such a day. On such a fool's errand.* He sighed. He didn't see his brother often, he didn't want to see his uncle, and he didn't much care if he pleased his mother, because he knew he never could.

His mother didn't know him very well, and seemed to like him even less. She'd had four daughters before him; his birth had been a boon to her only because then her husband had left her alone. She'd left her son alone too, to be raised by nurses and governesses and then sent off to school in the manner of a man who would someday inherit titles and property. Ten years later, his brother Arthur had been born, a surprise and a mischance, the product of a strange night at their country estate when her husband had been away from his mistress too long.

Lucian had come home from school one term to find his recently widowed mother madly in love, at last, for the first time in her life. With his baby brother. Arthur had been well timed, and so, well loved. Born after his father died, after his sisters had married, and while his only brother Lucian was away at school. The viscountess was glad to lavish attention on the only soul who seemed to need her. And too, she found it delicious to have produced a baby at an age when her friends had only grandchildren and the grave to look forward to.

It was difficult to love someone so well loved by the one person who had never loved you, but the new Viscount Maldon had honestly tried to like his baby brother. But Arthur had been leery of him then, and when he'd grown, perhaps a little envious, and in some ways just as disapproving as his mother. And too, in all fairness, Lucian reckoned he himself was not a very loveable fellow.

After all, he'd never loved either, at least not in the way the poets sung about. The women he'd mentioned to Arthur, those he had affairs with, either the restless and bored married ones or the avaricious professional ones, were not of a class or temperament or type to inspire anything but lust. Lust was fine with him, though he did find himself wondering about love, from time to time. Perhaps he wasn't capable of it, Lucian mused now, thinking of his uncle, his brother, and the women in his life, as he held his team to a safe pace and set them trotting over the frosty cobbles.

He'd never loved his late wife, Clara, though he'd liked her well enough, and had felt genuinely sorry that she'd died, so young, so unexpectedly of a chill, then a fever, then a congestion, and then from the doctors called to cure her. But she hadn't loved him either. He'd hoped they might grow into it. Life hadn't given him a chance to find out.

He did love his son, but perhaps that was more adoration than love. Because he'd been enchanted by his infant son, and saddened when the wetnurse, nursemaids and nannies shooed him away, making him realize a father had no place in the nursery except for the filling of it. Then the lad had to be sent to school. *But when he did see him*, Lucian thought now. Surely that pang he felt, that welling of emotion that froze him entirely as he tried to master himself so he wouldn't show it—surely that was a kind of love?

He never found a way to know Arthur though, much less love him. A decade was a considerable span between brothers, too few years to let him act the father without feeling pompous, too many to act like Arthur's peer without feeling he was behaving like a fool. As it was, they seemed to have no commonality but family, Lucian thought now, frowning more.

Arthur liked to collect books, he liked to read them, he liked to make love to females, Arthur liked to court ladies. Arthur loved the beautiful things their family owned. Lucian didn't bother, knowing they weren't his but only in his keeping until he had to pass them on. Lucian sought a thousand diversions to keep boredom at bay. Arthur seemed content with his every day. Lucian was cynical, he knew it too well; his brother, earnest. They laughed at very different things. And so they were brothers merely, never friends.

Still, here he was, doing errands for the brother he didn't know, and the mother who didn't like him, and the uncle who annoyed him. And Lucian prided himself on being a man who did not allow himself to be imposed upon. But even so, as the horses drew him toward Bow Street, he was no longer frowning. He might not understand love, but he did know his responsibilties. And the air was brisk, the horses well rested, and he suddenly realized that whatever the bother, at least he was going someplace he'd never been before.

*

Lucian was pleasantly surprised. Bow Street's quarters were in a neat townhouse, and when he entered he saw the place was clean and orderly. Of course, most of the people he saw in the main room weren't the sort he usually noticed: clerks, solicitors, people lodging complaints who were obviously common tradesmen or their ilk, seedy looking persons who could only be felons, and *runners*, who apart from their red waistcoats, looked just like the felons. But his name made a stir when he gave it, and caused a hurried conference.

The runner they summoned to deal with him was a surprise to Lucian too. He came swaggering out of some inner office, and seemed, at first glance, to be gentleman enough—if one ignored the traces of hard living in his face and his hard assessing eyes.

Lucian weighed the runner in turn. He judged the man to be about his own age and height, but there the similarity ended. The runner was a big man, tall and powerfully built, brutally handsome, with an air about him that made Lucian suspect he knew and traded on it. He exuded a pleased awareness of himself and his body. He'd be an able opponent in the ring, but Lucian thought he might have a weakness, wondering if he'd guard that handsome face too closely.

His Indian black hair was tied at the nape of his thick neck, in the old style men wore before the current fashion of cropped hair. Lucian thought it was deliberate; this was a man who liked a pose. He probably thought it made him look romantic, picturesque, the thief-taker as pirate. It did. His eyes were liquid, dark and watchful. He dressed as a gentleman, with clean linen, a tight fitted blue jacket and dun breeches, half boots, and a gaudy waistcoat, which marked him as a peacock. Not because it was red, he was a runner, after all. But because it was silk, embroidered, and likely cost as much as Lucian's own.

He had a smooth bronze complexion, with a hint of earthy red in it, either from a touch of foreign blood or a workingman's tan, neither of which any gentleman would admit or aspire to. That was the clue. Lucian knew his name even before he spoke, and was pleased. Bow Street had sent him one of their best, or at least, most famous runners.

"Spanish Will Corby at your service, my lord," the runner said, confirming it, as he bowed, but only slightly.

"I've heard of you," Lucian said, nodding. "Seen you in the caricatures too, now and then. In the newspapers more often. You've a reputation, a good one, in spite of all the fun they have with your name, and your popularity with the ladies. You're less popular with the villains."

Smiling, Spanish Will sketched another bow. "I'm not the celebrated Mr. Townsend, my lord, but I do my best."

"No, and you're not a royal pet either," Lucian said, "nor do I need such. But then, I hardly know what I need—I suppose you'll find my errand a waste of time. God knows I do."

"Then he knows more'n me, my lord, for I never waste my time. Want to tell me about it?"

The voice was deep, the accent almost refined. A rough and tough sort of gentleman, Lucian thought, and so, of course, no gentleman at all. But at least he listened to his problem with great interest. "Gone since Friday, you say?" the runner asked when he was done, his eyes still evaluating his visitor. Lucian saw a strange excitement kindling them, and was pleased. It might be that the man could help.

"Friday night was when he was last seen," Lucian said. "My uncle, the Baron St. Cloud, is a middle-aged gentleman, lightly built, though he's grown himself a stomach, well lined with capon, as Shakespeare recommended." He paused in thought. "Unexceptional face, at least I can't think of a way to describe it that would make him instantly recognizable. Brown eyes, and what's left of his hair is gray. Soberly, but well-dressed, I'd say. A bookish man with no reason to be gone from his home for days, and no history of it either. He is, in fact, expected at his own wedding this coming Sunday, and the bride is younger by a score of years than he. So it's not a day he'd want to miss or delay."

"Where was he last seen?" the runner asked absently, his mind obviously racing. Lucian grew a little alarmed in spite of himself.

"At dinner, at my brother's rooms, in Montague Square. And not since. My brother said Uncle was strangely excited, and that in itself is unusual. The only thing that excites him is scholarly argument. The family is naturally quite perturbed at his absence, this is unlike him. They've commissioned me to post a reward for information leading to his whereabouts. I'll add extra to ensure everyone's silence all 'round…"

Lucian paid the runner the courtesy of honesty. "That is because I'm more worldly perhaps than the rest of my family," he said softly, "or more evil minded. I believe that whatever takes a man like Uncle from his appointed rounds may be…the sort of thing we wouldn't want bruited about."

"Extra?" Spanish Will said. "Which would be how much altogether then?"

"Twenty pounds, we thought generous."

"P'raps it is, but not here, my lord. Our docket is full. But never fear, we'll get to it by and by."

Lucian sighed. Now he understood the excitement in the runner's eyes. "Thirty then, and an extra ten for speed if it's resolved quickly. Come, man, some men don't make that in a year!"

"Aye, some. Ragpickers and such. But it'll do. For now."

"Then here's my card, contact me when you've news," Lucian said, turning to go.

"My lord!" Spanish Will said quickly. "Before you leave… There's something I'd like you to see. A body. I doubt he's your uncle, but still…he hasn't been identified. This bloke was found Saturday morning, on a tasty young widow's doorstep. Her fish shop's doorstep, to be exact, in a market street near to Spitalfields, Whitechapel and St. Giles. Not the best district, but he was in no condition to care. He was found dead there, with his head stove in. Hard to say if he was a gentleman though, being he was found stark naked. But the fishwife, she said the fact he was so clean where no one could see it proved it."

"I'm quite sure it's not he," Lucian said with a thin smile. He was curiously disappointed. The trouble with lying down with dogs, even well-combed ones, is that you did get fleas. Uncle would doubtless soon appear, flushed with success at finding some new old book to add to his library, with a tale of staying over at a friend's house while he negotiated for it to explain his absence. Men like Uncle did not show up dead in the slums, after a tryst with a widow, or a fishmonger. But that was what one got for dealing with thief-takers. Their world was not Uncle's; they'd have a hard time even imagining it. A fool's errand, certainly, and now Lucian felt more than foolish, he felt slightly dirtied by having had to run it.

"Maybe not. Can't hurt to look though, can it?" Spanish Will asked with a white-toothed smile. "No one in the neighborhood recognizes the corpse. And rich men's clothes have been known to go walking off after their owner's sudden death, especially in places like that, in a winter such as this. Don't worry, my lord. I'll cover all but the good side of his face for you, if you like, and have salts ready if you find yourself feeling faint."

The Viscount Maldon seemed carved of ice. Then a snarl of a smile appeared on his thin lips. "Lead on," he said through clenched teeth, "and you may forget the salts."

But he didn't smile, or snarl, after the runner whipped the sheet off the body in the room in the back. Lucian's bony face went white and very still. Spanish Will watched him closely. Death himself would look like that, the runner mused, or at least, he would if he had the money.

It took a moment for Lucian to realize that his boring old uncle actually lay on a table before him, stiff and very dead, his head caved in. It almost seemed a worse violation to see him embarrassingly, obscenely naked. It was a sorry sight. He was very white—or rather, blue—now. A middle-aged man, who was aging badly. Who'd *been* aging badly, Lucian reminded himself, his eyes skimming over him, disbelieving. Uncle's arms and legs were spindly. Expensive tailoring had hidden his pathetic little paunch and the little shriveled privates that Lucian hated himself for looking at now.

Uncle lay on his back, one side of his balding head crushed. There was bone and bits there Lucian couldn't look at or away from. The Baron St. Cloud looked frozen in shock as well as death, but his nephew couldn't really judge his expression because he was so horrified at his condition. Hard to see him dead. And so brutally used.

"Yes," Lucian said simply, "it is he. My uncle." He cleared his throat, took in a deep breath and let it out before he looked at Spanish Will again, his eyes hard and chilly. His voice lacked its usual mocking tones. "He was found thus, on a doorstep, naked, you said? *Whose* doorstep, pray tell?"

"Ah, my lord," Spanish Will said, "best that you leave it to us, who are used to such."

"For my own edification then. You said a widow? Perhaps I know her."

"I doubt that, my lord, I do doubt it sincerely. But her name is Maggie Pushkin, Mrs. Maggie Pushkin."

"I never heard the name."

"I'm not too surprised," the runner said with a laugh.

"But a *tasty* young widow, you said?"

"Aye, if a man don't mind keeping it all in the dark. She's severely red."

"Red?"

"Red-haired and freckled, a bran-faced wonder, though if you could wash off the red she'd look a treat. A neat little package, with her own thriving fish shop, courtesy of her late husband. Perhaps your uncle fancied a taste of fine firm white—breams? Or a crab or two, in the night?" The runner's voice was innocent, but his eyes weren't as they watched Lucian's reaction to the insolence.

"My uncle would not find himself fancying even a case of crabs," Lucian said as lightly as the runner had, so firmly in control that he could feel his fingertips digging into his fisted palms. "No, he wasn't known for wanting anything but books."

"But he was to be legally leg shackled in a week, you said?"

"Precisely," Lucian said.

"And so then maybe saying good-bye to a charming little baggage he was bent on being rid of, not needing her anymore?"

Lucian paused, struck by the idea, considering it, turning it in his mind before seeing the impossibility of it. He shook his head, "No. Never. Not he. But why do you ask? What did she say?"

"Not much, especially after she had a look at him on her doorstep. She was sleeping when the body was discovered. Pounding on her door rousted her servants, and they had to wake her. She lives over her shop. I saw her when she first came down, she was so white and scared her freckles stood out like pox."

"Well, there you are," Lucian said, feeling a surge of anger that surprised him, because it had been so long since he'd felt anything that strongly, "and did she confess?"

"Only to being afraid it was a fire causing all the rumpus, and that I do understand," the runner said, "such houses going up like tinder if one in the row catches, you see. The shop is the sum and substance of her fortune; of course she'd be edgy as a cat. She, and her servants, claim to have never seen the dead…your uncle, before. Nor did she have any visitors that night. And her neighbors do say to a man—and woman—that her late husband put her off men for eternity."

"Was there blood in her shop?" Lucian asked. "Did you see?"

"Not gouts of it, no. But what's a fish shop without traces of blood?"

"He was found, naked, on her doorstep," Lucian said impatiently. "She had to have a hand in it somewhere."

"Maybe," the runner said.

"Maybe? She's a *fishwife*, man," Lucian said, letting his temper show. "I've seen them at Billingsgate, drunk, swearing, hauling baskets bigger than their heads, fighting with each other, brawling like cats in heat. They're violent and vulgar. Gads! It's a rite of passage for any young buck out on the town to go down to the fish market to watch their antics. Such women are used to blood and guts, and use force to settle every argument."

The runner laughed, "Oh, not she, my lord. But you're right about one thing. She might have done for him."

"But why?' Lucian asked, almost talking to himself. "And what on earth was he doing there? And why in God's name *kill* him? He was a bore, but that was the worst that could be said of him."

"Is it? I don't know," Spanish Will said slyly. "Maybe because I know too many things other folk don't. You're sure of his virtue. I'm not. Her neighbors are sure of hers. I'm not. He could be a stranger to them because he always came and left by night. He could've been naked because she threw him out without a stitch. Her coloring isn't in style, my lord, but her figure is, and if a female's got everything in order, who cares what colors they may be? A nice warm widow, a lonely old gent? Nothing more natural. A visit at night, when all's asleep and none's the wiser and where's the harm, eh?

"But then, maybe a quarrel because he's casting her off, growing hotter than she could handle with words. She's got a hot head, her hair tells me that. So they fight, she loses her head and goes for his, coshes him a good one with one of those nice big mallets I saw hanging on the wall in her shop. Then she pushes him out and sends him reeling into the night. Good riddance. Maybe she thought he wasn't hurt that bad. Maybe she thought he deserved to be sent out naked on the coldest night of the year to find his way home. Ice on his ballocks and frost on his rump and a good laugh to anyone who saw him, and she's revenged. Maybe that's all she wanted. Maybe she misread it and didn't know he was dying there on her doorstep whilst she went to bed. Comes the dawn, and he's stone dead. Aye, that may be."

"Then why not arrest her?" Lucian demanded.

The runner looked shocked, pious, secretly amused. "Why, my lord, this is *England*. I've got to prove it first. And that takes time, and effort, and..."

"I'll up the reward," Lucian said. "I'll double...no, triple it."

"I'll get to work," Spanish Will said.

"I'll go with you," the viscount said.

And now the runner only looked shocked. But not so much as the Viscount Maldon himself was when he realized that was exactly what he meant to do.

Chapter Two

"It's dangerous, difficult, touchy," Spanish Will said again.

"Understood, but I can take care of myself, you don't have to worry about me," Lucian repeated.

The runner's smile was chilly. "I wasn't. I'm not famous for working with others, nor do I know how you'll react if we do find a likely villain. I don't want anything getting in my way, do you see?"

"I understand," Lucian said curtly. "I won't interfere."

The runner shook his head and sighed. "I've met head colds that were less persistent. So anxious to come down to the dregs of London town with me? And you an aristocrat? You surprise me, my lord, you honestly do."

"Tenacity is in my blood. How do you think my family held on to their property all these years?" Lucian said with a tight smile that quickly slid away. "I want to find who killed my uncle, and why."

"So do I. But half the time my inquiries are only that," Spanish Will said patiently. "There's much walking, some talking and few answers. I can report to you. Come, my lord—why not go home now? This is my job. You must have other things to do."

"I've sent word to my brother," Lucian said tersely. "He'll tell the family, and as he was my uncle's favorite, he can arrange the funeral to suit his memory. What else should I do in any case? This is a terrible crime, Mr. Corby. A wrong against my family that must be righted. That's my job too. I wish to go with you. Now."

"Very well, on your head it is then," Will said resignedly as he hauled on his greatcoat.

Lucian nodded, and began to walk to the door with him.

"Hold!" Will said, turning to stare at him, astonished. "You're never going like that, are you?"

Lucian cocked his head to the side. "And why not?"

"Well, look at you," Will said, "dressed like a nob, and no mistake. Your shirt cost more than most people I'll be chatting up earn in a month! The villains I have to talk to will clam up like mice at the cat's picnic if I walk into a room with you by my side."

"But you're dressed similarly," Lucian said.

"Indeed, and I thank you for noticing it," Will said, "but all know who I am. You're a stranger. A richly dressed one. If you don't draw every rogue in Whitechapel to your shadow, I'll be blest. Even those that don't wish to treat you as your uncle was treated will never breathe a word of interest to me with you looking like that. They'll nose on their friends, even their mothers, for the right price. But not in front of some strange gentry cove."

"I won't take off my coat," Lucian said through gritted teeth.

"What difference does that make?" Will asked, amazed, "You're wearing a driving coat any flat can recognize from five paces. What would I be doing waltzing about with a member of the Four in Hand Club, I ask you? Be sure, they'll ask themselves that."

"I suppose you suggest I go home to change clothes? Into something less distinctive, perhaps?" Lucian asked.

"Why, that would be a prime idea," Will said enthusiastically.

"And when I was ready, why, I suppose you'd already be gone on your rounds, wouldn't you?" Lucian said just as pleasantly.

Will shrugged and grinned. "It is a possibility."

"Then suppose I borrow a suitable coat from someone here?" Lucian said with some force.

The runner's dark eyes gleamed, as he glanced around the room. "Well, if you insist. Mr. Reardon's coat's about your size. Hey there—John! Your ear for a minute, eh?"

A rat-faced wizened man came sidling across the room to them, his prominent ears fairly wagging with interest as he stared at Lucian. "Aye, Will, what's to do?"

"I was wondering if my friend, the viscount here, could have the loan of your coat for a few hours," Will said.

"Surely it wouldn't fit," Lucian said.

"Nah, t'would," the rat-faced runner said, as his eyes roved up and down the viscount's long frame. "I likes my clothing roomy-like. Lots of places to keep things, if you know what I mean."

The viscount's blank face showed clearly he didn't.

"I mean to say, a runner's coat be his office, sometimes, when he's on a case," Mr. Reardon said, "and handy for storing evidence, or dinner, and weapons or things a body be better off concealing." He looked at Spanish Will worriedly, "but what sort of surety, Will? I mean, against the return of my coat?"

"My word, Mr. Reardon," Will said, with affront.

"Good enough," the other runner said quickly.

"And my coat," Lucian said. "If I don't bring back yours, you may keep mine."

"Well then!" Mr. Reardon said more happily. "Hang on a tick, I'll get it for you."

"And now we may have Mr. Reardon wishful of doing you in too," Will told Lucian, on a long-suffering sigh, as Lucian began removing his fine driving coat. "Men have been killed for less."

"Ha, as if I ain't giving him as good or better," Mr. Reardon scoffed, hurrying back to hand Lucian his coat. He nevertheless tenderly folded Lucian's greatcoat over his arm before quickly carrying it off with him.

The runner's coat fit Lucian, with room to spare. It was old, long, and lumpy, and had obviously often housed far more than Mr. Reardon's scrawny body, and it smelled like it looked. "You can always cry off," Will suggested, when Lucian's nose came up.

"I can always get flea powders," Lucian said icily.

"No, John isn't lousy," Will commmented as Lucian drew the collar of the ancient coat up and tipped his hat to shade his face against the unlikelihood of encountering anyone he knew. "He bathes enough to prevent it—but only just. Sir Nathaniel Conant, our new Chief Magistrate, insists on his runners bathing every now and then. He's trying to improve us in the eyes of the gentry. But there's washing by the book, and bathing for one's own pleasure. And John goes by the rules. You'll grow accustomed, my lord."

"Doubtless," Lucian said, though he doubted it, and hoped he would not. "Here's my carriage," he said with satisfaction when they went out the door. "There should be room for us both."

"There should not be," Will said, amused. "We walk, my lord."

"But it's freezing, and we can travel swiftly and safely in my curricle. I know it looks flimsy, but I've never had an accident in it, nor will I, not even on the ice."

"Oh, doubtless," Spanish Will said mockingly, winding his scarf against his neck, "and congratulations to you, my lord. But a runner walks. At least, this one does, even if it's a long way, as it is today. He don't take a currricle, or a hack, or a sedan chair, even in a blizzard. Because what will the villains who'll be watching be thinking of a runner who worries about his boots or his health, eh? No, I walk. And it's a ways from here. I'm going places you've never imagined, my lord, much less been to."

"I visited such places in my salad days," Lucian said.

"Nah, they don't make such salads for the aristocracy," Will laughed. "These aren't colorful playgrounds for young gentry, quaint low taverns where you can laugh at the antics of the lower classes, and maybe pick out a cheap whore or two to cap the night. No. This is where real people live and work, my lord. Real people without much money. I also insist that you say nothing no matter where we go, unless I ask it of you. No doubt you'll have questions, but you'll have to ask them of me—later. For one word from you and they'll scatter like pigeons with a hawk in the sky. Agreed?"

Lucian bit back sarcasm. The man was only right. "Done," he agreed tersely. "My purpose walks before my vanity in this case, Mr. Corby. I'm wise enough to leave the Captain of the boat to the fishing grounds he knows best...for now."

"Good. And I remind you it's a long walk. Still coming?"

"Still," Lucian said tightly. He told his tiger to drive the curricle home, and began walking with the runner. "We're going to see the widow?" he remarked after they'd gone a few streets, heading east.

"No, best to let her simmer in her own fears for a spell, so she'll be nice and tender by the time I talk to her again," Will said. "I'm going to talk to those who know her, and of her, so I'll have more to ask when I do see her again."

There was no further conversation between them; a freshening, cold and cutting wind literally took their breath away and they needed it for walking. The snow began to fall more steadily, slanting in from off the river with a taste of cruel damp in it. Lucian noticed carriage traffic dwindling because of it, and as the streets grew meaner, he saw fewer people on foot. But he trudged on beside the runner. Spanish Will might enjoy a joke at a nobleman's expense, but he didn't look like a man who exerted himself for nothing. As for himself, rage against whomever had killed his uncle kept him warm enough. And the mystery of it kept churning in his mind, making him ignore mere bodily discomforts.

Spanish Will picked up his pace, and saw the viscount match it. Well, if the nob wanted to come along, no harm in it, if he kept his mouth shut. It would be pleasant reprimanding him if he didn't. He strode on, noticing how the snow filled the streets and emptied them of people. It even banished the ever-present wandering tribe of gleaners, pickers and grubbers who eked out their livelihoods by finding cast-off horseshoe nails, unused bits of coal, and other gutter treasures to clean and resell. The usual contingent of beggars had limped or staggered off the streets as well, leaving only the heartiest or unluckiest of their number to wait for something besides snow to fill their tin cups. They'd dine on snow soup and naught else tonight, he thought. Only a fool would be out on such a day. He didn't count himself as such.

He smelled money, and his nose seldom failed him. The man at his side was high in the instep but rich as Croesus. He'd ante up a treat for his uncle's murderer. Will hummed under his breath. It was a long walk on a freezing day, but it was Sunday, so he'd nothing else to do. He could start snooping for an easy answer and a rich purse. Any rate, he told himself as he kept plodding against the wind, heading towards the river, he was nicely numbed now and if there was any day to nose around Billingsgate, this was the one. Sunday silenced the clamor for a few hours, and the snow could cleanse even Billingsgate of its stink. *Some of it*, he thought, inhaling ice, letting his nose tell him what the sheets of falling snow still hid from his eyes.

Fish, brine, salt and spray, a brackish iodine sting filled his nostrils although the Thames, only a street away, was sweet water here—or what passed for sweet. The main arcades lay dead ahead, the rows of shops and stalls where most of London's fish were brought and sold daily. Will could just make out the profiles of the masts of those ships that lay at anchor near the wharf where most Billingsgate traffic was—most days. But never at this hour, and not today. Today the fishermen were home, if they were lucky. And as for the fishwives...he hoped to find some. They might know things he needed to know. They'd surely say things that might convice the bony nobleman at his side to go home and let a man who knew what he was about do his job in peace. And get paid more for the difficulty of it.

Will passed the first gin shop he saw, and paused at the second. The viscount stopped too, standing grim, cold and silent as Death at his side, waiting for him to enter. Will shook his head, and went on. He went into the third tavern he saw, because it was his lucky number. He ducked his head and stepped inside.

Lucian followed. His head came up and his nose stung at the stink. Thick fumes from many glowing pipes and a smoking peat fire made the air heavy, and the heat from both fires brought up the stench of fish, fish blood and guts and gills. He didn't want to think what the other smells might be, but as he eyed the ragged patrons of THE DOG AND DOLPHIN, he thought he could guess what they were.

The place was small, dark with age and aged dirt, like all the many taverns in the district. Its smell was remarkable, even so, though it didn't seem to have discouraged the dozen or more customers Lucian could barely make out in the haze. At least the air was warm enough, if you could stand to breath it. He followed Spanish Will to the tap.

"Yours?" the barkeep asked, as they approached.

"Something to keep off the cold—and some advice," Will said, peeling off his gloves. He laid some coins down on the scarred wood between them.

"Take more'n that to keep off this cold," the man said, eyeing the men with more interest than the coins.

Will sighed. He slowly squeezed a larger coin from his waistcoat and put it with the others. "Maybe," he agreed, "but we've places to go today. Two pints of never fear and some advice will do us fine."

Lucian's face stayed blank. He'd no idea of what the runner had ordered, or if he was actually supposed to drink it. He supposed that if the runner could, then he would as well.

"Aye. Well?" the man asked, scooping up all the coins, and then turning to draw two tankards of beer.

"We need some kindly folk to chat with," Will said, "folk who know them that do business in the market. The sort that don't mind talking to some interested strangers."

"There's many o' that sort," the barkeep said sourly, slapping two tankards down. "Too many, for my money. But ain't my money is it? Still—I dunno 'ow many'd be 'appy talking wi' redbreasts, y'see."

"Oho," said Will.

"Well, but I knowed *ye* fer a runner right off," the barkeep said with a thin smile. "Don't know yer friend, but yer face ain't easily forgot. I were there when y' nabbed ol' Snab Morgan—'e that done poor Rob Reese in...wi' a knife, in the night, last spring," he added to prod Will's memory.

"Morgan? Oh, aye. Him that was turned off at Tyburn in July. And good riddance. Hempen ripe, he was," Will said, nodding, remembering, "and so said all, did they not?"

"All," the barkeep agreed.

"Or were you a friend of his, maybe?" Will asked gently.

The man hastily dropped his gaze. "Me? Not 'ardly! Just I remembered. I don't doubt most round 'ere do. But it's only talk yer after?"

"Just talk," Will nodded.

"Buy any o' them a glass o' blue ruin and they'll talk yer ear off," he said, indicating all his patrons, "be ye runners or rogues. But I won't swear to what you'll 'ear. Talk rubbish, most of 'em. But let's see… Aye. See them two there, in the corner? Aye, them what's already giving you the eye. Buy 'em a gin, give 'em a smile, and there ye be. No 'arm in 'em, though."

Will guessed not. Nor much indiscretion either. Whomever the barkeep recommended would be sharp as a knife and careful of what to say. But he was good at hearing what wasn't said. And besides, he wanted them to know he was asking. That kind of news got out, and it always got back to those he asked after. Sometimes that did him more good than the gossip he heard.

"Thanks," Will said. He took his pint and made his way through the fog to a corner where two enormous figures sat hunched over a small table, watching him approach. Lucian followed, silently, as amazed as appalled at what he saw.

The light was bad, smoky red and dim. But it was enough for Lucian to see the two women sitting there. They were hard to miss. They were covered by many layers of clothing, but none of the layers seemed clean, and not surprisingly, none seemed to fit. Few clothes would. The pair of women seated there were middle-aged, or old, it was hard to tell under the grime. And huge. Big-breasted, wide-shouldered, with ample bellies and bums, great mounds of womenflesh, capable of swinging heavy baskets of fish up on their heads and holding them there as they pushed their barrows, cursing all that got in their way. He'd seen such females, but only from afar before. Shrewd eyes assessed him from under tangles of hair not covered by their woolen caps. Fish market women, observing their Sabbath—and the strangers in their midst.

One seemed shorter, one seemed grayer, but there wasn't much to choose between them.

"Ladies," Will said, bowing, "may we join you?"

Raucous laughter greeted this. When one of the women subsided, she ran a hand across her eyes and toed an empty chair toward him with one rag-wrapped and booted foot. She patted the seat with a plump mittened hand and sighed. "Gawd love ya!" she chortled. "*Ladies*, is it? Is it me purse or me person yer after, after a fine greeting like that?"

"Take 'er purse! Don't be daft, take 'er purse!" the other woman shouted, and the pair of them started roaring again.

"Gawd!" the first woman breathed, "you are a one, Mrs. Gow! What can we do fer ye and yer friend, redbreast?" she asked Will.

"You made me then," Will said with a show of surprised chagrin, seating himself as Lucian silently took another chair, trying to be invisible, wishing his nose was.

"*Made ye*? O'course! In a trice, and well ye know it," Mrs. Gow said on another laugh.

"As well as we know ye," her friend agreed, grinning over the pipe she held clenched in her surprisingly white teeth. "Spanish Will, hisownself. Come to see us, and bringing an 'andsome friend so nobody got to dance alone. We're that honored. Ain't that many gents with such pretty faces dressed so fine 'round here that we'd forget one, would we, Mrs. Gow? Beside which, ain't no *real* gents going to swill their rag water at this place, is there? It's about that cully what got topped front of Pushkin's establishment, ain't it?"

Will smiled. "It is. Not much escapes you, does it?"

"Oh flattery will do," the woman said, "but a bottle of Strip Me Naked would do better. You'll do the honors, lad?"

"With pleasure," Will said. He turned to signal the barkeep, only to see he'd already started to cross the room, bearing a bottle of gin. Mrs. Gow's hand snaked out and she poured herself and her friend both a full glass. The glasses were downed in a gulp and sighed over before the first woman spoke again.

"We'll tell you everything we knows," she said. "But we diddled you fair, 'cause it ain't worth so much as a glass of this cat's water. We don't know the gent, nor the one what scragged him."

"No, how should you?" Will asked. "When even I don't."

"'E *is* a one, Mrs. Gudge," Mrs. Gow said, laughing with relief before she poured herself another glass.

"Naked as well as stone dead, weren't he?" Mrs. Gudge commented. "Considerate of him, saves the undertaker a bit of work...or the resurrection man, eh?" she added, with a dig of her elbow into Mrs. Gow's ample side.

"He might have a family to claim him, bury him in Westminister Abbey, for all we know," Will said, choosing to ignore the insinuation he might stoop to the illegal, lucrative practice of selling unclaimed bodies to the resurrection men for the use of medical students. He didn't like the viscount even thinking about such things, but wanted the women's good will too much to make an issue of it. "What I'd like to know is what you know about Mrs. Pushkin, the female the corpse was dying to see," he said instead.

The women stopped drinking. Their expressions grew closed.

"Were he?" Mrs. Gudge asked slowly. "Ain't what we hears. We heared he was dead afore she woke, nor was we surprised. That one don't bother with men, y'see."

"Ever?" Will asked.

"Well, she did when she were married to old Pushkin," Mrs. Gow said seriously, "'cause she couldn't 'elp it, could she? There ain't a woman born would blame 'er fer not wanting to touch a man after 'im! Dirty as a barge bottom," she said scornfully, as though she were immaculate, "and with a mouth that was worse. Gawd! 'E had a mouth like a 'orn, 'e 'ad, and nary a good word fer no one ever come out of it, and damned to all else but 'is work. A real rusty guts! So who could blame 'er?"

"And her married to him when she were only a bit of a girl. All eyes and red hair. Gawd she were a sight, remember Mrs. Gow?" Mrs. Gudge asked softly. "Scart of him hollering, scart of us, scart of everything. But she worked hard, and dealt fair. She ain't the murdering kind, redbreast."

"Why should she be?" Mrs. Gow asked. "Got a good business, money, peace and quiet now, she don't need no man, nor nothing else. And good luck to 'er, says I!"

They drank to that.

Will sat back then and talked to them a while just for the pleasure of it, because they'd told him all they cared to about the crime he'd come to ask about. They liked the freckled widow. He was wise enough to know he'd get no more out of them on that head. But he liked them. He liked their honesty and their humor, and the fact that they weren't afraid of him. He didn't run into that often. The viscount sat in shadow and wisely held his tongue. They ignored him, taking him for an assistant or some underling. Will liked that too.

"And so who *would* know more about the bran-faced widow?" he finally asked out of the blue, when they stopped chuckling over a story they told him. "You know I'll ask more," he chided when they glared at him. "Not like me to give up so easy. The widow's prime with you, I see that. So who's got the gossip, piping hot? We'll hear it sooner or later. Best you tell me who to ask so I hear it right, eh?"

They looked at each other. Mrs. Gow sighed. "You could nip round to Petticoat Lane, I s'pose," she said grudgingly, "and chat up Roger Bell, him that's got the fish market there."

"*Bell*?" Mrs. Gudge shrieked, "that auld woman? That Jessamy? What can ye be thinking of, Mrs. Gow?"

"'E's a regular man milliner, I know that," her friend answered. "'is tongue runs on wheels, I know it too. But 'e ain't cruel nor stupid, is 'e? 'E got no knife to grind neither. Gives 'isself airs, but there's no 'arm in 'im. Anyways, we owe 'im a treat. 'E'll be that glad to have such two such brave, 'andsome cullys as Spanish Will and his friend in 'is shop, won't 'e? Be sure and say we sent you, Dearie," she told Will coyly.

Mrs. Gudge began to laugh so hard she choked. Mrs. Gow thumped her on the back as she flung her hands in the air and gasped and coughed and laughed all the harder, sputtering gin. "Oh *Gawd!*" she finally said on a wheezy sigh. "Won't he though? Aye, he lives to talk, does Roger Bell. Oh, you'll like 'im, lad," she told Will as he eyed her suspiciously. "But maybe not half so much as 'e'll like you. Don't know why 'e sells fish," she cackled, "seeing as how they smell like what 'e don't *never* want to use."

This set both women into gales of laughter.

"I take it he's a Molly mop," Will said sourly.

"Why, lad, how could we say? We don't never look in the back of 'is shop," Mrs. Gudge said piously, making it Mrs. Gow's turn to choke with laughter. "One thing sure, though, all fun aside," she added, "'e knows everything, and be sure, 'e'll tell it too."

"*If* you ask 'im *nice!*" Mrs. Gow crowed.

Will and Lucian left the tavern to the sound of the two fishwives' merriment.

"You did well to hold your tongue in there," Will commented when they stepped outside again.

"I'd no choice. I scarce understood two words in three they spoke," Lucian said wryly. "Did you learn anythng to the purpose?"

"I might have. I have another long walk to take now to find out. Still interested in coming along?"

"More than ever," Lucian said. It was absolute truth. He'd lived in London most of his life and was considered a man about town. But he'd never seen this side of it. He felt stimulated, enthralled. He hadn't felt so awake in years. He was fascinated. Both by the denizens Spanish Will mingled with, and the fact that he could mingle with them. It was very like being bilingual, he realized, more impressed with the runner now than before.

"You'd do well to remain silent then," Will grunted, and lowering their heads against the cutting wind, they made their way along the deserted streets to Petticoat Lane.

*

It was snowing just as hard there, and it was Sunday there as well. But Lucian was surprised to see the pavements thronged with shoppers buying at a jumble of shops, each fronted by a bawling crier, shouting merchandise of every sort to be found in London.

"Aye," Will said, reading his confusion. "It never sleeps, not even on the Sabbath. Here's Jews, whose Sabbath it is not, and Christians who only worship a good bargain. Bargains, and all—if neither new nor first quality, then cheap, and sold no questions asked or answered—honestly, at least." He interrupted a hawker trying to hook in customers with a lively spiel outside a men's clothing shop. "Bell's Fish Market?" Will asked him.

"Down the street, left, it's on the right... *Quality, Quality! Nice warm coats marked down and down! Special today,*" he sang.

Bell's was a hovel of a shop, the front window a bleak square, but the fish in it had been laid end to end with care and precision. The ones that were left, that was. The place did a thriving business. Inside, it was blistering cold in spite of the customers crowded in. Two boys in aprons and a lean man dressed like a gentlemen were bundling fish into papers, handing them out and pocketing change.

"Your pleasure, Sirs?" the man asked the moment he saw them, giving them a brilliant smile, "I've *lovely* smelts. So tender. And such a nice bit of plaice put away. I have it! *Lobster*. Costs the earth, because of how cold the sea is these days, but you're obviously men of taste. It's yours—for a good price," he promised, his light eyes dancing from Will to Lucian, eager and bright. He had a thin face and his fair thinning hair was tortured into a semblance of a Brutus cut. He was dressed as elegantly as a man in his club on St. James Place, Lucian thought, but the effect was ruined by the blood-stained gloves he wore, the many fobs on his waistcoat, and the huge pearl gleaming on his carefully tied cravat.

"Here!" a tiny old woman in front of Lucian cried indignantly. "*Oim* next, they just come in!"

"So they did, so they did," the lean man said, his smile still brilliant. "You see my dilemma?" He apologized to Will, his gaze never leaving his. "If you'd just wait a moment, Sirs? If you please? Just a bit?"

"A bit or two, certainly," Will said. "It's information we've come for—not fish. Are you the proprietor, Roger Bell? Well, then," he said to the man's quick confused nod, "we've some inquiries when you have a moment..." He took a small notebook from his inner pocket and glanced down into it.

Lucian saw Roger Bell's color change, and his smile fade to a sick grimace. "Our Jim here will take care of you, Mum," he told the old woman. "Sir?" he asked Will, blinking rapidly.

"Hardly needful to call a runner, '*Sir*'," Will said jovially. Lucian didn't think Roger Bell could grow more pale. He could. "'Mr. Corby' will do."

"And your associate?" Bell asked dazedly.

"*I'll* be doing the asking," Will said too gently. "He's just here to see all goes smoothly."

"To be sure, to be sure, if you'd care to step this way?"

They followed him to a next room where a boy slicing fish looked up at them curiously. Roger Bell waved him back to work and led Will and Lucian to a room in back, furnished like a parlor. A coal fire in the hearth made the air shimmer with the rumor of heat, though it couldn't dispel the terrible chill of the place.

"Would you like a seat?" he asked, and when Will shook his head, added quickly, licking his lips, "How may I help you?" He held his hands in front of him like a praying rabbit, all his former vivacity replaced by equally intense terror.

Well, but a man with his reputation should be terrified, Lucian realized. His rumored sin was punishable by death. Not if he had the money, rank, and sense to enjoy his pleasures on the quiet, of course, or the means and power to placate the right people if it became less quiet. He'd seen it done. But he supposed a man without a fortune or titled family could well end up hanging high for loving his fellow man and boy, and well they knew it. Sometimes, of course, as in the infamous case of the denizens of the White Swan that he'd read about in the *Times* a few years ago, they were more kindly used. Not hanged, but only pilloried, whipped, beaten and pelted with offal, dead cats and dung.

Will rocked back on his heels, pleased. Mrs. Gow had steered him right. It made getting information so much easier. He waited a few seconds so the fact of his presence could sink in, so that all the man's secret crimes could have time to roil in his brain before he asked his questions.

"We'd like to know what you know about a competitor of yours—Mrs. Maggie Pushkin," Will finally said.

The man deflated. He looked as if he'd had his backbone filleted as neatly as one of his fish. "Oh Lord!" he said as he slouched, one hand on his heart, "Is *that* all?"

"All for now—if I get the right answers."

"It's about the dead man on her doorstep, isn't it? Well, but I don't know anything about that," Roger said, slanting Will a roguish look, completely at odds with the pallor of his face. "I can't be expected to know *every* naked man in London, can I?" He gave Lucian a sidewise smile, in turn.

Will looked up from his notebook, amused and approving. The fellow had ballocks, even if he didn't know how to use them. "Aye, it's about him. And her."

"*Him,* I do not know. Her, I do. And I'm pleased to, I can tell you. She's a nice woman, not really my competitor, you know. Oh no. Her fish are...shall we say for a different market, price *and* quality? Well, but her late husband had *such* connections, a cousin on every fishing smack from here to Le Havre, so she's that well set up now. Not that I begrudge her, she worked hard enough for it. So what is it you wanted to know?"

"Who her friends are. And her enemies," Will said curtly, to discourage some of the charm the man was now attempting. He didn't seem to have a stop between terror and come-hither.

"Enemies? I couldn't say. Don't know of any. *Enviers*, though, Ah there, Mr. Corby—there you may have a full plate. And not just because she has so much. But she won't share it with a man, you see. You know how some men are, think they're cock of the walk and a gift to all women and get snarky when they're told they're not." He grinned at Will, as though that hard dark face were a challenge rather than a warning.

"Well, any event, she won't have a suitor, for none will suit her." He paused to see Will smile, and failing, glanced at Lucian, and seeing that cold face set in stone, still went on as cheerily. "And why not? Maggie has *breeding*, and few in our district do. I have some education, of course, but Maggie and I...ah, we would not suit either," he said coyly.

"Breeding?" Will asked stonily.

"*Oh yes*. Her mama was a lady's maid, which is why she speaks so charmingly. Her father had a barrow and sold what he could get his hands on, unlucky fellow. He bought from the wrong men and sold to the wrong man, because his goods turned out to be stolen and his customer was a runner. Still, the magistrate gave him a choice. The gallows or transportation, and last anyone heard he was on his way to the Antipodes. *After* marrying our poor Maggie off to ghastly Pushkin.

"Her mama died soon after..." Roger put a finger to his cheek, thinking. "She has some family in London, I believe, but they're not close. No consorts, if that's what you want to know. Only some urchins she takes in from the streets and trains to serve her. And there it is! Complete. More, I do not know, alas." He held up his hands to show they were empty.

"But if you hear more, you'll be sure to get word to me?"

"*Mister* Corby," Roger said with a die-away sigh of pure longing, "of course. I look for *any* excuse to see you again. And any friends you care to bring as well, of course," he added, with a winsome smile for Lucian.

Will was amused and annoyed in equal parts now. He was being sent up and put down, and there was just enough honesty in it to make him uneasy as well. "That's all I can ask," he said, snapping his notebook shut. Lucian almost grinned.

"Oh my *no!*" Roger said. "There's so much more *you* can ask..."

"Game's over," Will growled. "Do *not* take it further, I sincerely advise you not to." After noting how quiet Roger had gotten, he nodded, clapped his hat back on, and left.

"Edifying," Lucian said with laughter in his voice, when they reached the street.

"Indeed?" Will said. "How so?"

"I didn't know I could be so insignificant, of course," Lucian said, but the laughter was still there. "Nor be considered not half so attractive as yourself. I don't know whether to be wounded or not. And so, where to now?"

"Home. I live near Bow Street. Two rooms, one chair. Do you want to come there too?" Will said with annoyance.

"Such a graceful invitation, I quite see why Mr. Bell was so entranced with you," Lucian said, "but no, I fear not. My own hearth beckons. Will you let me know your next moves?"

"I'll let you know of any progress in the case," Spanish Will said stiffly. "If you want another tour of the lower classes, my lord, I suggest you get a map."

"As you will. I'll be in contact, Mr. Corby," Lucian said. "Ah. I see a hack." He waved an imperious hand, and the lonely hack driver's head came up. He didn't get that many fares in this district, but it was a cold night and he lived in hope. The coach came toward them at a trot. "I think I'll ride home, thank you," Lucian said. "May I take you up and leave you off? Bow Street is on my way."

"It is, but no, thank you, my lord. I have thinking to do, and I do that best on my feet."

"Then, adieu, I'm sure we'll met again. Tell Mr. Reardon I'll return his coat, or at least, set it on its feet. I'm sure it's fully capable of walking back to him on its own." And with a laugh, Lucian stepped up into the coach, and disappered within it.

Spanish Will watched him go, and then, ducking his head, started walking again. Leaving Lucian to wonder. Because as he sat back and the carriage carried him away, he glanced out the window and realized the runner was walking, quickly, in the wrong direction.

Chapter Three

The afternoon darkened to milky dusk as snow continued to fall. The elegant viscount had long since been borne away laughing, in his hackney carriage. But Will brooded as he trudged through the frozen streets, reviewing his last interview in his mind's eye. His best suspect had many friends, but he still had many tricks left up his sleeve. She had friends *and* wealth. The widow was altogether too privileged for him to feel a particle of sympathy for. And the reward was too rich for him to ignore.

Good breeding, that Nancy of a fishmonger had said of her, aye, he thought gloomily, as the cold set his dark face in even more rigid lines. The red-headed widow had that too, and good luck besides, whatever her late, unlamented husband had been. She'd had a mother who taught her, a father who provided for her before he left her, and now money and a good business as well? What right had anyone with such riches to rob a man of anything, much less his greatest treasure—his life?

He himself hadn't been half so lucky.

His mother was a memory, his father had been a mystery. They called him "Spanish Will" because he looked like a foreigner, so it was possible his father had been one, though his mother swore her lover had come from Wales as she had done, and not anywhere near the muddy banks of the Thames where Will was raised. She died when he was ten, but by then he was fierce and tough and clever enough to survive on his own, in a community of thievish children that lived by their wits in the streets. But it was a hard life. At thirteen his luck finally changed.

He met John James, and became his student, then his partner. All in a year, because John was clever as he could stare, but so foolish it was a wonder he'd lived to the great age of four and twenty he'd been when they'd met. He didn't live much longer.

But at least he'd taught Will to speak, read and write like a gent before he died, and how to do more than snatch and grab and run and hide. He taught him how to dress and act, how to talk in front of a lady and how to talk to a whore as though she was one, how to treat a friend and make one just by the power of his charm. He'd taught more practical things too, all sorts of rigs only a gentleman could run, frauds that paid more, with less risk. Or so he'd thought. He'd taught Will much before he was hanged at Tyburn for forging a five pound bank check. *Five pounds!* It staggered Will still although he knew far better by now, having seen them hang for half that. He shivered as he tramped the freezing streets, not because of present cold so much as how far back he was in his mind now to that April day. But the thought of John always took him there, and the thought was never that far away.

There he stood in the crowd, wanting a look, not wanting one, jumping up and staring down, trying to see and not see John on his cart as they drove him to Tyburn Hill. John, sitting on his empty coffin in the rocking cart, knowing he'd soon be borne back dead in it—and sobbing, sobbing like a babe.

It was a pitiful show, and some in the crowd cursed him for it. No stirring final declaration for the vendors to print up and sell. No show of defiance to titillate the crowd, no cursing, no vengeance sworn to make them shiver either. He just sat, long hands dangling useless between his bony knees, tears streaming down his face because it was his last hour and he so wanted to live.

"Poor soul," a woman had murmured near Will's ear. And he'd wanted to shout, *No! Don't just sit and blubber, John. No, don't hang him. No! and don't,* and caught between dismay and disdain and secret burning shame, he'd watched them bear John away to the scaffold. He'd resolved to stand close so he could leap up and hang on John's legs if he began choking, so he could have his neck snapped and die clean and easy. But he stood far away and there was some mercy in it. Because John died fast and silent—he saw that at least before he crept away that day.

38

Will rolled his shoulders, shedding the memory. He hadn't so easily then. A year passed, and he was still careful, watchful and worried. He thought long and hard about John's fate, because John had been the cleverest man he knew. So when the runner came to him one day to ask him to lay information about some other boy, he'd snarled his refusal...but struck up a conversation with the man anyway.

The runner wasn't the one who had done for John—Will had already seen to him, one night when the moon was low and there were so many other boys about no one ever knew who'd done for him, in turn. This runner was pleased at the interest shown, and more fortunately, he was at that age, and in that boozy, wistful frame of mind when a man needed to justify himself, even to a boy. He gave Will much to think about.

A runner made money off other's backs, just like a pimp, to be sure. But there were villains and there were villains, and didn't he know that firsthand? Of course a runner's stipend was meager, but rewards posted for crimes solved could make a man comfortable, and were he clever, then even better than that. And wasn't he clever? More than that, wasn't a thief-taker about as far from the hangman as a man could get, without being born to a Duke?

This time it took more than a year to equal his mentor, because of his youth. But Will went from apprentice, to taking a share of rewards, to runner himself, and then to a runner well known and well feared, and with good reason. He was not sentimental. It was a hard life and he meant to stay in it. And profit from it. So if it transpired that the speckled widow was responsible for the dead man on her doorstep he'd see her to the gallows. He'd even cheer as they topped her himself if the Viscount Maldon put his hand deep enough in his pocket. There were ways to insure him doing that too.

But first he had to get a scent of the way of it. Even the best criminal always left some sort of a trail. And Will doubted the widow was one of the best. Still, there were other paths to sniff along first. A hunter with only one thought in his head might catch his quarry faster, but it might be the wrong game he brought down.

Spanish Will had a long way to go before he slept tonight. He kept his eyes open, but hunched his broad shoulders, ducked his nose into his scarf, and marched onward. There was no heat in his body now and none in his loins, though that was an omnipresent itch. He knew many cheerful warm willing females who'd gladly share a bed with him of a frosty night. He thought about it to the point that he could feel a reluctant response—that he killed by thinking of the aftermath. He never took a female to his rooms, nor ever spent a whole night with one, and it looked to snow throughout the night. Which meant that when he rose and dressed after, he'd have to walk home in the cold. It was too frigid for such an expenditure of heat; the thought shriveled him. And so with all his appetite, he thought he could do without tonight. But some things he couldn't.

He stopped to buy a meat pasty at a shop about to close, so it cost half as much as it would have an hour before. The pasty was rich and hot and full of spicy gravy. He ate it quickly as he walked, because the night was trying to freeze it before he could finish it. No sooner had he swallowed the last bite than thirst set in. He thought after he'd done with this errand he might stop in at The Brown Bear, near his lodgings, it being the tavern runners frequented, and have a pint and some gossip there. But that too meant warming up and tramping home cold again. No. *Getting old*, he decided, laughing to himself at the thought, flexing his shoulders, feeling the muscles bunch, feeling the power humming through his body. But even so, so he was old, because three and thirty was older than he'd ever thought to be.

He longed for his bed, and groaned at the thought of the walk still ahead, because he had to veer farther east and south to reach his destination, and all of that before he finally headed west again to get to his own front door. But something he'd heard said was niggling at him and wouldn't let him rest yet. Something he couldn't investigate before because he didn't want the influential, fastidious viscount knowing about it, in any way. Unless it was the only way to get the reward, of course.

Will picked up his pace, taking detours down dark streets few men would have walked unless they were simple minded, truly lost, very drunk or deranged. Or else, a runner, with a name that ran in front of him, even on such a frigid night.

He reached the dark street in due time, and stood straight, so those watching from the alleys would see his face.

"*You*," the man said when he unbarred the door Will hammered on, and cracked it open. "To what do I owe this honor?"

"A question, or two," Will said, standing still as a standing stone as the snow covered his shoulders.

"Then, come in." The door creaked open slowly, reluctantly.

"No. Come out."

"In this? Are you mad? It's pissing down snow!"

"So it is. But why should I get warm only to get cold again? I'd have a word with you here."

"Hold on a moment," the man said after a pause. They both knew the game now. A cold man alone in the night with a runner was a man more likely to talk faster, and maybe less wisely, than a man snug in his own warm house. "There now," the man said, emerging quickly, with a greatcoat flung over his shoulders. "What can't wait, then?"

"About that corpse on the fishwife's doorstep."

"Oh! I might have known," the man sighed. He was middle-aged and corpulent, with an accent from a better district than his. But all knew he'd been born and educated to more and had worked his way down to less. "A waste," he said with a shrug. "You think he was mine? I am not so wasteful, Mr. Corby."

"Not usually," Will agreed, "but if someone was coming along the street unexpected? He might have been dropped when someone decided to cut and run."

"No. At least not one of my men, Mr. Corby; they're neat and discreet about their work. I'm surprised you even thought it."

"He was naked."

The man laughed, richly. "Oh but that should have told you. We do not transport the naked, Mr. Corby. Now, if you'd seen three men reeling down the street, one so drunk two had to hold him up—why then, it could have been one of ours. Or if a carriage stopped, and you peeped inside and saw a fellow dead to the world, with his head on another fellow's shoulder, but it was only poor old Uncle Jack sleeping—or so you would be assured—why then, that could be us too. But we'd never move a naked man, never."

He shifted his feet; he was wearing slippers. It was snowing hard and deadly cold, but Will didn't move, more and more he seemed a man of ice. His voice was colder now too. "Dead men have been known to be stripped naked. So it don't rule you out. He may have been dropped, even so. I'd like to know."

"It wasn't my coves," the man said quickly. "My word on it. I wasn't even expecting a delivery Friday, nor Saturday morning."

Will said nothing. The silence grew. "Frightful weather, cuts down on everyone's business," the man said, to say something, shifting his feet again.

"I'd think you'd have more trade out of it," Will finally said.

"Ah," the man said with an almost audible sigh of relief because it seemed the runner was inclined to small talk now. "Well, I didn't say they weren't dropping, for they are, of course. It's just harder to…resurrect them."

"Graveyards frozen too, eh? Too bad."

"Oh yes, and so…" the man lowered his voice, "if no one claims the poor fellow, and you didn't want the trouble of trying to take a pick ax to Potter's Field, there's always another alternative. We don't enjoy setting pick to earth in this weather either. So the price would be right, better than right this time, I promise you."

So, rumor hadn't got here yet, and the wily doctor didn't know the corpse was already spoken for, Will thought with pleasure.

"Early days," he said. "By the time we're done, he may be too far gone even for you."

"Hardly. The weather may be a blessing in this case. Just do remember me, Mr. Corby."

Will touched the brim of his hat. "I will, Dr. G. That I will."

Now it was time to go home. He'd done all he could this night. He hadn't learned much, but what he had pleased him. The field of suspects was narrowing, not grower wider, which was so often, so annoyingly the case at this stage of the game.

It could have been a random misadventure, Will mused as he headed west again. The baron could have simply been in the wrong place at the right time and been killed by mistake, or killed for his wealth, stripped of all the worldly possessions he had on him, and then dumped in sudden terror. That happened often enough in his part of the world. But it wasn't the baron's part of the world.

Why had he been there at all? And hadn't Will learned from the first that when there was a likely suspect there was often a likelier reason? It was just that he hadn't discovered it yet. He would.

There was already money in it. If he played it right, there'd certainly be more posted for reward. The rich wanted things done quick, and money meant nothing to them when they wanted something. But money meant everything to him. The more money he scraped together, the higher his hoard of gold grew, the further away from him the shadow of the hangman would lay. That shadow couldn't be far enough away for his comfort, not ever. Because it drifted across his every dream, and it always would.

*

"Good morning, Mama," Lucian said as he strolled into his mother's salon the next morning. "My condolences," he added with enough insincerity to let her know he knew very well that she'd scarcely exchanged two words with her brother in the past two years. "You sent for me? I've come, what can I do for you?"

The snow still fell, filling the morning with a clean bright light, but nothing so common as vagrant light from the streets was permitted in this room. Thick draperies were drawn against the cold. The enormous hearth was heaped high and burning brightly. The furniture was massive, of good wood and dark texture, covered by embroidery, and polished to a sheen. Ornately framed pictures hung on the walls, their colors subdued by the heavy elegance of the room. The aroma of woodsmoke and furniture oil was heavy, along with the indelible scent of money. The townhouse was old and rich and filled with history, and looked and smelled of it.

His mother sat on an antique sofa by a window, close to Arthur. They'd been in deep and murmurous conversation. Her companion, an elderly indigent cousin, sat behind them, knitting. Lucian nodded to her as he sketched a bow to his Mama. The dowager was dressed in black, and her dark eyes snapped with anger when she looked up to see her eldest son enter the room. She glowered at him.

An observer might think them unrelated. There was no physical resemblance. The widow of the fourth Viscount Maldon had been attractive in her youth, even winsome, or so her portrait over the mantle insisted. Now she settled for being imposing. It took all her considerable force of personality, as well as the sumptuousness of her jewelry. Because she was tiny, a little pouter pigeon of a woman, plump and broad breasted. She had too many jewels and too little neck, small even features in a smooth face, her eyes were brown, most of her jet hair was still dark, and her expression was darker still as she contemplated her firstborn son.

He knew what she was thinking. The spit and image of his Papa he was, and he'd never atoned for that with her.

"What can you do for me?" she echoed. "Your uncle is dead, and you ask me that?"

"True. But it's been a while since I resurrected anyone," Lucian said calmly, "and the last time it was a leper, remember? Or was that the other fellow I tended?"

"Insolence and impiety," she said with curious grudging satisfaction,."I expected no less."

44

"Then why did you send for me?" he asked, taking a seat, crossing his long legs carefully, contemplating the shining tip of his left boot with interest.

"You are the head of the family," she said sharply. "Arthur is doing his best, but he cannot do all."

"Indeed? You disappoint me, Brother," Lucian said.

Arthur looked embarrassed. "The thing of it is that Mama wanted to know how the investigation was coming, and I couldn't tell her. I said I'd go see you to find out and come back to tell her, but she wanted to know firsthand."

"Sensible," Lucian said, looking up. He frowned. "But where is everyone else? Why hasn't the family rallied round? I know Mary and Harriet live too far to have arrived in London yet, but where is Elizabeth? And Georgina?"

"Georgina is having her mourning clothes made," the dowager snapped. "She has nothing in black that suits her she says, silly gudgeon. As if death were a matter of fashion, but then, everything is to her. Elizabeth was here yesterday. I don't expect to see her again until this afternoon; she does not rise before noon. London could be set afire again, and she'd not leave her bed before then for fear of anyone seeing her and thinking her gauche. A pretty pair of clunches, my daughters are, are they not?"

She asked as though they weren't related, but Lucian didn't blink. He was used to it. They looked nothing alike, but the cut and thrust of their conversation was so similar, so ironic and derisive, that when they spoke it was clear they were kin. It was the one thing that linked them. They mightn't like each other, but each understood what the other said, and what they meant beneath it.

"Indeed," Lucian said. "But as to the investigation...there are many unanswered questions. If we could but know why Uncle was in such a squalid place, we might better understand why he was killed there."

His mother's eyes blazed. "A man of his stamp in such a place at night? Even an idiot could understand why he was killed. For his purse, of course. And his clothing. I understand they took all, including his shoes."

"All," Lucian said serenely, "including his small clothes. Which did not add to his dignity, I might add. But again, why was he there? The two facts can't be unconnected. He was killed in a common working class district, perilously close to the vilest slums. He was naked; it therefore, was not a simple accident of Fate, a matter of a gentleman gone walking for pleasure of a morning, accosted, struck dead and then robbed. No. Why was he impelled to visit such a place in the dead of the night in the first place? And was he stripped naked before or after the fact? The runner pursuing the matter says if he finds the answer to one, he'll know the other, and so I too believe."

"You have Mr. Townsend at work on it?" his mother demanded.

"Better, I have Spanish Will Corby."

"Spanish Will!" Arthur blurted, "But I've heard of him, Lucian. He's famous. I've read about him—seen caricatures of him too. Is he as clever as they say?"

"He thinks he is."

"Then he should be able to find Uncle's murderer."

"As easily find one particular grain of sand on a beach," Lucian said wryly, "There are so many villains in that district, and so few clues...unless...perhaps they'll find something the scoundrel pawns, and that will lead us to him."

"A runner named 'Spanish Will'?" their mother interrupted, clearly agitated, "but Mr. Townsend has been known to work for the Prince himself."

"Indeed," Lucian said. "I should think that would tell you his worth. However, if you want a courtier, a flatterer and a man about town, by all means, contact him. He's as well known to society as your daughters would wish, Ma'am, in that he works for Bow Street as well as at the opera on occasion, and the Bank of England, and other such perilous, crime-infested places. I hear the Prince has requested his presence at the palace too, and at Brighton. But then, such assignments pay well enough, I suppose, to make such terrible dangers acceptable to him."

He dropped his mocking tones to add, "Spanish Will patrols the gutters, and that is where your brother was found, Ma'am. He was found, to be precise, on a fishmonger's doorstep in a slum. Now, speaking of fish, I think if you wish to catch trout, you fish in a trout stream, no matter how pleasant the waters may be somewhere else. Spanish Will knows the district, and those even worse nearby. He's singular, however, in that though he knows the denizens of such places he nevertheless speaks well enough to talk to the Prince himself. I rather think I prefer to let him pursue the matter. But of course, you're free to do as you wish."

"Mama will, of course, be guided by you," Arthur said.

She nodded curtly. "Might as well be," she said ungraciously, "Elizabeth's George may be a baron himself, but he has no more brain than she. Georgina's Edward is a complete fool. Mary's husband is a sensible man, and a justice of the peace besides, but he needs must play the country squire and what use is that to us? And I will not discuss Harriet's husband, nor speak his name, he has only his title and fortune to recommend him."

"But this...Spanish Will..." Arthur said hesitantly. "I hear he's a rough sort of man, Maldon. Surely not the type to understand the workings of a man like Uncle's mind?"

"Can you, who were so close to him?" Lucian asked. "You were the last to see Uncle, after all. What the devil do you think he was thinking, going to such a place, so late at night?"

"I don't know. I've thought about little else," Arthur said unhappily. "He was excited, very much so, I told you that, and that was odd in him. He couldn't wait to be away that night. I wish I knew why."

"What did you talk about that night? Anything that might give us a hint as to his intentions?"

Arthur's pleasant face looked troubled. "We spoke of such things as men talk about at dinner, Maldon. We dined together, in my rooms. He was always taking me to his club. I thought it high time I invited him to my house."

Lucian laughed. "Quite the little maid of all work, are you? I didn't know you could cook, much less serve, in your rooms."

"I can't," Arthur said, growing ruddy-faced. "I had my man go out and bring in dinner from my favorite restaurant. He served. Uncle quite liked it, finished every bit. He's fond of game pie, kidneys... Lord! I can't stop saying 'is,' when I know it should be 'was.' This is hard to take in. Very hard."

"Yes," Lucian said, "understood. But did he say *anything* at all to the point?"

"Stop badgering the boy," his mother said angrily. "If he knew anything, he'd have told us, wouldn't he?"

"Would he?" Lucian asked silkily, looking at his brother.

It hardly seemed possible that Arthur could look more uncomfortable, but he did. "Well, but... Gads, Maldon, how you know such things is beyond me... I suppose I've always been an open book to you," Arthur said reluctantly, "but it's a thing I'd rather not discuss in front of Mama."

As his mother sputtered, Lucian said, "which means, of course, that now you've mentioned it, you must tell all. Well done, Arthur."

"Don't blame him," the dowager said. "He, at least, has my best interests at heart!"

"Whilst I, of course, am plotting your imminent demise. Go on, Arthur," Lucian said with a sigh.

"Well, but he was talking about his coming marriage," Arthur said, blushing. "I mean to say, the intimate side of it, that is. Asking my opinion, and such..."

"What?" the dowager thundered, as Lucian chuckled.

"Oh lord!" Lucian said wiping his eyes. "The lamb leading the bland. Whatever could he have been thinking, asking advice on sexual matters from such a man of the world as you?"

"You think he would have done better to ask someone as debauched as you?" his mother shouted so loudly her companion winced. Her sons didn't seem to notice.

"Well, were I inexperienced, I would have done," Lucian said, laughing.

"Of course *you* would have..." his mother said, and then, because she was not a fool, however prejudiced she was, she allowed herself a grin as well.

"Not about *that*," Arthur protested. "He never mentioned that part of marriage at all. I mean, he just spoke of how he knew how odd it looked to be marrying someone so much younger than he was, and so he asked me—as a younger man—what I thought might please a *'younger gel'* as he put it."

"And you said?" Lucian asked. "Behold me fascinated, what do the younger set expect these days?"

"As if you didn't know!" his mother shot back. "Your latest opera dancer, the one you've set up in your new townhouse, she's all of twenty, isn't she?"

"To the day," Lucian said calmly. "But far older in experience, I promise you. Still, you astonish me Mama."

"And you revolt me, Lucian," she said angrily. "You'd a different one just last month!"

"Had you been hoping I'd marry that one, then?" Lucian asked sweetly. "I do wish you'd said something sooner, Mama. She's gone to Lord Barrymore's protection by now, and is quite happy there, I hear, so it's much too late now for me. Odd, I hadn't thought you'd met."

"Yes, jest about it, I expect no less," his mother sneered.

"The truth then? How refreshing. It's simply that I tend to become bored easily," Lucian said lazily, "and I never have matrimony in mind, so be easy Mama. But it's comforting to know someone cares, and takes especial note of my adventures. So, speaking of matrimony, what did you tell him, Arthur?"

Arthur shifted in his seat. He lowered his eyes. "I told him that as I had no lady of my own as yet, I couldn't say. But that love and honesty, I should think, would always carry the day. I said a lady like Louisa was of an age and temperament to know what to expect from him, especially since she'd already pledged herself to him, and so he shouldn't get himself into a pother about it. I told him it would all work out most happily."

"As the nun told the virgin," Lucian sighed.

"I suppose you thought Arthur should discuss nasty details?" his mama cried. "He didn't expect *that* sort of advice, and Arthur was very right not to attempt it."

"Oh, certainly. But, on that head, there *is* one little thing," Lucian said casually, though his hard gray eyes glittered like sunlight on ice as he watched his mother and brother closely. "A tiny thing, but significant, I think. And so does the runner. You see, Spanish Will thinks the fact that Uncle was found on the doorstep of an attractive widow significant. Yes. The fishmonger is supposedly a comely young widow."

His mother gasped. Arthur looked amazed.

His mother recovered first. "*Never*," she said emphatically, shaking her head, "he didn't even *like* females. We all know he was marrying Louisa because she could give him an heir, and only that. So he himself said."

"Speaking of which," Lucian said, looking around the room, "where *is* the lovely Louisa?"

"Too overcome to attend us, she sent word," Arthur said.

"Too overcome to face his family's apparent glee," Lucian mused, "because now she gets naught. No wedding, no inheritance, nothing to show for all her troubles but a stack of wedding invitations, and a disappointed caterer. And Uncle was warm in the pocket. I suppose it all goes to you now, Arthur, does it?"

"I hadn't even thought..." Arthur said, biting his lip.

"I should think it would!" his mother said triumphantly. "You don't need it, Lucian. Arthur was his favorite, all know that, and it's only right. Although I regret his passing, better it should have happened now than next week."

"What a difference a week makes," Lucian sighed. "Poor Louisa. So near, and yet so far."

"Have you seen the widow?" Arthur asked. "I mean, the one whose doorstep—the one where Uncle was discovered."

Lucian looked startled. *"I?"* he asked.

"Yes, you," his mother said furiously. "She has no connection to my brother, we all know that. But even so, and still and all, someone from the family ought have a look at her."

"Go then, with my blessings," Lucian said, appalled. "I will do much for the Name, Mama, and well you know it. I will seek my uncle and identify his dead body, chat with a runner, and beggar myself by posting a too-generous reward, and do all sorts of unseemly things because my uncle was fool enough to get himself killed in an unseemly position in an unsavory place. And I have done. But now you expect *me* to interview a fishmonger? *My dear!"* he said with heartfelt amazement, the twin thin arcs of his brows rising as he sank back in his chair as though shot through the heart.

There was a grudging silence. "And so what do you intend to do now?" his mother finally asked.

"Exactly what the runner told me, of course," Lucian said serenely. "Wait for him to tell me what he's discovered. Why, what did you expect? Do you wish me to interview such a person? Go down to Bishopsgate and discuss my uncle with a *fishmonger?"*

Arthur remained still. Even his mother was silent.

Lucian smiled.

Chapter Four

Mrs. Maggie Pushkin woke, sat bolt upright and threw back her coverlet. She stepped from her bed and went straight to the window. It was still snowing. Neither of her serving girls had come to light the fire in her hearth yet and the floor was so cold it made her feet ache. But she couldn't go back to sleep. It wasn't just that it was Monday morning. She'd seen the face of the dead man in her mind's eye the moment she'd opened her own. Not surprising, since it had kept her up so long last night. His, and the hard, handsome, implacable face of the Bow Street runner, Spanish Will.

She hugged herself and shivered. She'd had a day and night to think about it, and now she was as frightened as she was angry. Leaving a dead man on her doorstep had been an act of cruelty. But in the night she'd had time to worry and now she wondered if it was worse—something personal. Could it have been a warning? She couldn't for the life of her think of anyone who'd have such a grudge against her. *For the life of her—exactly,* she thought, grimacing. Not knowing her enemy didn't mean it was impossible she had one.

The runner was one, for a certainty. He'd even said it.

"I'd deny it too," he'd told her after she swore she'd never known the dead man, never seen him before, never wanted to see him again, and would he please remove the body from her steps. She'd stood in her dressing gown, clutching it closed around her, holding her self control just as tightly together, trying so hard not to shake or shiver.

"But look, my girl," he'd said, his voice growing deeper, almost tender, loverlike, his dark eyes glowing like they were promising something delicious, instead of death and disgrace. "You're the most likely to have done it, and that's that. A man dead on your doorstep, naked as a babe—or a grown man in pursuit of pleasure? You're a pretty little package, I can't blame him. Nor will I blame you if you tell me what happened. Be honest with me, and I'll try to see it goes the easier for you."

"I do not know him," she'd said, biting off each word. "I am no man's mistress, and no man's joy. Find yourself a killer someplace else. And don't come back to plague me unless you have good reason, or I'll pay all my coins to get all the Magistrates in London after you. I did not do this thing. Now remove him—and yourself. Or must I call the Watch to do it?"

He'd stood looking down at her as she glared up at him. Neither blinked. Then he sighed. "You're saying his being here is a coincidence? I don't believe in coincidence, Mrs. Pushkin, that I do not. But there's no more I can do now. I'll take him, and find his name, and then I'll find his killer. Think on what I said. And if you change your mind, you know where Bow Street is. I'll be going— for now, and with him, to be sure. But never fear, not all the coins in London will keep me from coming back, do I think it needful. And I suspect I will."

She'd not dared speak. She'd nodded, spun on her heel and marched inside her shop, slamming the door so hard behind her that ice from the eaves fell on the dead man. She'd stood by the big front window, still as a statue, vibrating slightly, such a fine tremor that only the wisps of her wiry orange hair shivering like cat's whiskers showed it, watching as Spanish Will picked out four eager men from the watching crowd in front of her shop. They'd covered over the obscene blue corpse, hoisted it, and then marched it away down the street.

Maggie's rough freckled hands closed to little fists now. The runner thought she was a murderer. They hanged women for murder, they hanged men and women in pairs and three and fours every week on Tyburn Hill, for murder, for robbery, for stealing anything from hams to handkerchiefs. They hanged them at thirteen and thirty and seventy years of age, man, woman and child. They were hanged for a hundred crimes, because it was grand spectacle as well as justice. All London came to see and cheer and make merry at the hangings.

No more than the runner did she believe in coincidence. No. Someone had left the corpse there for her to find—or for the law to find for her. She thought hard. She had competitors, she had people who'd tried to cheat her, those she'd sent away with a flea in their ear for rudeness, for petty theft, for trying to make free with her person, of course, what living woman didn't? But she couldn't think of an *enemy*. Then again, she had friends, and anyone with friends must have enemies. And she had a thriving business she would leave and…

No! she thought now, looking wildly around her room. Her room. Her house. Her shop. Not after all her hard work and sacrifice. This was hers, and no random cadaver and eager runner or unseen enemy was going to bilk her of it. She'd worked too hard.

Her parents had married her off, at sixteen, to a man sixteen plus sixteen and half again over again, so that she could have a better life than they could offer, or any young lout they knew could provide her. It was necessary. They married off their girls and sent their boys to sea. Her father was going to be transported. Her mother knew it was death knocking, not just aggravation roiling her guts. They wed her to a hard-mouthed thick-set man with little breeding or humor, but a fair amount of money and a fine business. A man shopping for a healthy young creature to provide him with work and children, and nothing else. To be fair, he didn't think women were capable of much else. Or men either.

He was a decent enough husband, all told. He never had to raise his callused hand to her, because his voice was enough to terrify legions, and certainly enough to keep his young wife in line. He didn't drink or gamble or womanize. Or talk to her, or make conversation or friends, either. He lived to work. And wanted only the one thing that work couldn't give him.

She did her share, uncomplaining. Because complaining wouldn't help. He taught her to choose fish at the market, how to gut and slice and scale them too. She pushed his heavy barrow over the cobblestones through the streets of London, helping shout his wares, wrapping fish, taking coins, making change. She worked nights as well, concealing her distaste during those clumsy minutes three times a week, when he devoted himself to getting himself his fondest dream.

She worked hard. But brought no children forth. After a year, he began taking her to physicians, quacks and midwives. But her own Grandma had been a midwife and so she thought she already knew the answer. He'd been married before. And had no children. It wasn't a thing a man wanted to hear or know. So she listened to all the advice, drank all the potions, used all the salves and said all the prayers, and grew as tired of trying to beget as she did of trying to help him be rid of his fish every day.

It was a thing the one expensive doctor he finally took her to said that gave her the idea.

"Does she get ample food, and rest?" the physician at his awe-inspiring address asked, the physician whose usual lady patients never stirred from their couches, except to rise and dance. "She's healthy otherwise, you see, no structural disorder. But females are delicate creatures and need adequate nourishment, and ample rest in order to produce young, you see."

Bernard Pushkin nodded, paid his fee, and grumbled all the way home, feeling cheated for paying good coin for such nonsense.

"You know," Maggie told him in their marriage bed later, musing, as though she hadn't rehearsed the thing days and nights, "about what that physician said? The one that cost the earth? I wonder if there isn't something in it? I'm so tired every night I could cry, though I'd never tell him, of course. Do you think that might be it?"

He bridled. "My Ma had seven of us and worked like a horse all her days."

"But that was your Ma, and that was then," she said softly. "Now, if we were to get a shop, I could sell from there. A nice shop, in a good location, somewhere between the nobs and regular folk. That way I'd work and have my rest, even so. I have a way with words—and people, you know that. It might be the thing for both things we want..."

He'd snarled, turned on his side and gone to sleep.

But they began looking at shops. She'd been wildly excited, dreaming of the West End of town, of living far from the river, farther from her own home than she'd ever walked. She eventually got him to move away from his meager rooms in Billingsgate, at least, if not West, then North. It was a lovely house, the first such she'd ever known. It had once been a gentleman's townhouse, before the nobility had deserted the district.

They used the front room for their shop, the big bow window on the street level where the gentleman had once sat in powdered periwig, looking out haughtily at his fine neighbors, was filled with fish. Fine fish, fresh fish, laying on ice like gems on velvet, or hanging from the ceiling, their scales catching the sunlight and twinkling like diamonds. Or at least so Bernard Pushkin scoffed and said his young wife thought. But so she did. The back room was used for deliveries, work and storage. Blocks of ice stacked in sawdust kept that side of the house like January even in summer. The other side across the hall, with a kitchen and sitting rooms, was blocked off from the shop. They used the upstairs for their sleeping quarters.

She could scarcely believe she lived in such sumptuousness. Bernard Pushkin often reminded her of that too. With all it was, it wasn't far enough from the stews for her, but farther than he'd imagined himself going. He'd a fondness for her, perhaps in some part of his mind he already knew she was the only child he'd ever have. She turned a pretty profit for him too. She did have taking ways.

But he wouldn't give up the pushcart, and died behind it one afternoon of an apoplexy brought on by a shouting match with a surly footman who questioned the age of his oysters. Leaving Maggie alone, with only his fortune, his shop and his thriving business.

Which *no one*, she vowed now as she stood by the window, no one, not any man, alive or dead, was going to take from her. No matter what. Not even if she had to go out and find the murderer herself. She turned from the window and marched to her wardrobe, and dressed so hurriedly she shocked poor Alice when she went out the door just as Alice was coming in.

"Gawd!" Alice panted, her hand on her newly grown and ample breasts. "Missus! You scared me half to death! I was coming to light the fire. I got hot water for you too, never say you washed in cold?"

"It doesn't matter," Maggie said. "I couldn't lay abed. Too much on my mind."

"Us too!" Alice agreed eagerly. "I slept with a knife 'neath my pillow and a cleaver at my right hand. Dead men come calling, it's the only wise thing to do. But you could of asked. I'd have slept on the trundle at your bedside. They'd have to deal with me before they did for you. I'm that fast with a knife. I practiced in the kitchens and didn't Annie screech for fear I'd slice her ear off, thought she'd wake the dead... Oh, Gawd, what a thing to say, spit three times and send it away! But I'm good—I can skin a fish *or* a man in a minute. I could protect you, say the word and I'll do it tonight."

"Thank you, no. We'll have no more dead men come calling."

"Never say that, Missus!" Alice shrieked. "Once you say 'never' it's like asking for trouble!"

"Then say *'I doubt it,'* Maggie said as she went down the stair. "Come along, there's things to do."

Her staff greeted her in the kitchen. Annie curtsied, and wide-eyed little Davie looked frightened, but that was nothing new.

"It's a new day, so let's forget old fears," Maggie told them. "It will be all right. And so we may as well go on as if it never happened."

"Well, but we're not afeared," Alice said. "We're here to watch after you and each other, see if we don't." She looked to the others. They nodded solemn agreement.

"We'll help, you'll see," Annie vowed.

"Thank you," Maggie said, "but I think—I *expect*," she added, with a look to Alice, "that it's all over now."

She was touched and grateful. Alice was fifteen, Annie thirteen, little Davie was six or so, or so they guessed. They were little more than children, abandoned and ill-educated. She'd bought Alice's services to rescue her from a vicious mistress, Annie came from the workhouse, they'd found little Davie wandering the streets, with no memory of anything but that name. She gave them houseroom and board, a trade and wages. But still their loyalty moved her. She sat and had her breakfast quickly and in silence, because she didn't know what else to say, and didn't want them guessing how uneasy she was.

When she was done she put a long apron over her gown, dragged high heavy boots on, pulled on gloves, and then, finally warm enough to brave the shop, addressed her troops.

"Look sharp and work fast. Everyone will want to know what you know. You'll have to tell them, but be brief or we'll never be done. Business will be brisk today. Nothing brings in trade like exciting news, so we'll be dealing in gossip more than fish."

But she dealt in both. They came early and eager. Every customer crowding into the shop knew they'd never get her ear if they didn't buy something too. Bream, carp and wild surmises; Turbot, sole and speculation. Maggie had to verify the story with every sale. In turn, she had to listen to dozens of variations of how shocked each customer was to have heard the news, down to painstaking details of what they'd been doing when they'd been so shocked.

"*Stunned*, I was, *stunned!*" yet another woman gasped, clutching her forgotten parcel of fillet in one hand as the other thumped her breast for emphasis. "A dead man on that nice Mrs. Pushkin's doorstep? *'Never!'* says I, *'Why she's a lady, for all she sells fish,'* I tells him. But the Mister, he shakes his head, *'So 'tis, and none know who the cully is! And him naked as the day he was born.'* Well, I was that shocked, Mrs. Pushkin, I can't tell you..."

But she tried, as Maggie looked over her shoulder to see the line of other customers equally eager to tell her about their shock and surprise. She was relieved when Davie came to tell her that she'd a delivery to see to. With a nod to her waiting audience, she left the shop.

"Oh lass! Such news, poor girl," the coal carter said when she came to the back door.

"Yes, Tom, but if you've come to hear more, I tell you I've nothing more to add," she said wearily, because the warm sympathy in his voice almost undid her.

"Just as well. A female alone, with none to look after her? It's just luck that you've nothing more to tell, thank God! When I think of what could have been— Ah, it's a hard, lonely road you've chosen," he said, his voice tender, cajoling.

That made her head snap up. Tom was looking at her with something other than sympathy glowing in his bright blue eyes. He stood, legs apart, hands on narrow hips, smiling down at her, showing her all she'd missed, as usual. He was her own age, still looking young as the day they'd met, tall, lanky, the coal dust he was covered with only pointing up his white-toothed smile. Virile and eager, her first love, the answer to her maiden's prayer that she'd never had a prayer of getting.

He'd walked out with her once, never seeming to mind her hair and freckles. Still, if a female had it he wouldn't mind it—at least that's what they said back then. He'd walked out with dozens of girls. And it seemed to Maggie that he noticed her far more after she'd married, and even more after she'd been widowed. She allowed that might be unfair. What chance had he had, after all? His seeing her that once had made her father see the light. She'd been pledged to Bernard Pushkin soon after.

"For once, I wish it *were* lonelier out there," she told him, ignoring his insinuation, as usual.

"S'truth you didn't know the poor cove?"

"I wish I had done, then maybe I'd know why he was there. Did you hear anything? Does anyone know who he was?"

"It's all anyone's been talking of, but no. Ah, lass, what a fine kettle of fish... Sorry, don't doubt you've heard *that* all morning too, poor girl," he said with a warm soft laugh that made her long to rest her head on his wide shoulder, in spite of herself. He saw it, and stepped closer. "If you'd only married me," he said in low urgent tones. "But your parents were set on the fishmonger, and see what it's come to? There's naught we can do about that, that's yesterday. Today you need a man about the place. I can be that man, Maggie. You know I've longed to be. Now maybe you can see the wisdom of it?"

"Oh certainly. I'm sure your wife does too. And your four children. What can you be thinking of?" she said, stepping back.

"You know what I'm thinking," he said fervently. "Same thing all these years. Only now we got an excuse, a fine one. I can sleep here, stay here, protect you, be good to you..."

"Aye," she said angrily, "good as you are to poor Eleanor? God save me. She should have been buying beefsteak, not fish, last week to put on that eye you gave her. And not for the first time. You'll clout her once too often, Tom, and do her a terrible injury yet."

"Ah, but she's dim, Maggie, not quick like you. She makes her own trouble, she vexes me with her stupidity. But you! I'd never have to touch you, except to love you..."

"*Vexes* you? I'd do that too, Tom, I promise you. You'd have to kill me to quiet me, and there's truth," she snapped, glaring up at him. "You don't know how lucky you are to have married Eleanor and not me. Because if you ever laid a hand on me like you do to her—even once—I'd lay your head open for you."

"Like they say you did for that bloke?" he snarled.

"Oho! Now, *here's* the Tom poor Eleanor knows. So. Is that what they're saying?" she asked, arms crossed on her breast, voice chill as the room.

"Some," he said. "But they're saying everything, aren't they? Cod's heads, sapskulls. Maggie, forget what I said. You need a strong man about the place. Who you going to get? Flea, or some other shallow pate? Who else is there? I'll keep my hands off you. Let me stay."

"You won't, and you know it. And I don't mean just trying to get into my bed. With all he was and was not, Bernard never raised a hand to me."

"Nor could he raise anything else, it would seem," Tom said, accepting the inevitable. He swung his sack of coal up on his shoulder. "But I don't have that trouble. I've given that cow of mine four kids, and it'd be more if I could stand to get near to her more often. Think on that, Maggie Luv."

I do, idiot that I am, she thought sadly, watching him go. *Not you, Tom, half so much as those phantom children.* But people were thinking *she* bashed the dead gent? That was what stayed on her mind as she puttered in the back room, loathe to face customers until she could banish the worry about their gossip from her eyes.

"Missus?" A gentle voice intruded.

She looked up. A giant stood in her back doorway. Strong, robust, clad in simple clothing, looking like he stepped out of a child's tale of Robin Hood. Handsome too, with a genial face and a shy smile, his face as well as his enormous frame had all parts built to a mighty, but proportionate, pleasing scale. She'd met him when she'd first come to this house, and he'd become a friend.

"Flea!" she said with genuine pleasure. "What can I do for you today?" Here, at least, was one person who wouldn't spread cruel gossip about her. He couldn't.

Street toughs had named him "Flea" for his size, and after a time, it became his only name. Everyone said he'd been a busy, friendly, mischievous boy. But one day he came down with a fever, and by the end of the week they'd thought he'd die. He didn't. But part of his brain had, or else had been hidden or gone astray. He was never the same, and grew to be a huge man who spoke seldom and moved slowly. When he did speak it seemed as though he was choosing his words carefully, as if he were a normal man who didn't want to speak too soon and seem a fool. Because he appeared normal in every other way. He wasn't.

He was slow, not deliberate. Not an idiot, not a child, but also not a man you could have a conversation with. But he was gentle and kind, polite and obedient. In another age he would have been some nobleman's valued liege-man, or man at arms. But there were few jobs these days that called for strength, complete obedience and no wit. He'd found one, or rather, his mother had. She'd raised him well and then literally left him to a friend when she died.

He lived east of Maggie's shop, in Spitalfields, with "Auntie Jane," working in her house. He protected the girls there, throwing out those men Auntie Jane told him to, those who got nasty, or didn't pay. When he wasn't doing that by night, or errands by day, he wandered London looking for friendly faces. Maggie hated the way he earned his bread, but solaced herself by imagining he didn't understand the half of it.

"I suppose you heard about my dead man?" Maggie asked.

He lowered that massive head and nodded, looking guilty. But so he always looked when things went wrong. He'd look the same if she complained about the snow. "Did you know him?" she asked, on a wild, forlorn surmise.

He lowered his head further, in deep and painstaking thought. Then he shook it slowly. "No, Missus," he said.

"Then why have you come this morning? Auntie want a bit of fish? That would be a surprise. You usually come Fridays." She hoped he hadn't brought a dying sparrow or a crippled cat. She had herb lore from her Grandma, and everyone in the neighborhood knew it. Not much, but enough to cure a headache, ease a streaming cold, or pronounce an ankle strained or broken. Flea had brought her wounded creatures before. Some she saved. Some she left out with the rubbish. She tried, for his sake and hers. But today wasn't a good day for charity.

"No fish," he said, and thought a while as she waited, and then said, "Wanted to see you, Missus Maggie. You all right?"

She was touched. "I'm fine. Thank you for asking and caring."

"Wanted to be sure," he said, and smiled. A glorious child's smile, free of anything but pleasure. "You need me, you call me," he said, as he always did, and smiling, left.

He almost collided with Mrs. Gudge, who shouldered in through the doorway, carrying a huge basket. "Watch it, big 'un," she said jovially. "Don't want them flapping all over the floor, do we? Look what I got for you," she told Maggie proudly, planting her basket on a table. "Not only the best sole y'ever did see, but some nice fresh eels, lively as the grigs they be!" She whipped the wicker top off it, like a master chef displaying some incredible treat.

Maggie saw the writhing mass in the bottom of the basket and drew back. "I never take live goods, Mrs. Gudge, you know that."

"Getting as chicken hearted as the rattlepate that was just here, eh? Glad he didn't see 'em, he'd have 'em for pets! Nevermind. I knew, but I was wanting to do something extra for you. What with fog all them weeks, and snow now, these here will fetch double worth in any market. Not to worry," she said, clapping the top back on, "I'll sell them afore I go many more steps. But how are you keeping? I mean, with all this to-do?"

"I'm surviving, Mrs. Gudge," Magie said simply. "If no more dead men show up on my doorsill I'll be better still. As to that...Mrs. Gudge, you've known me so long... Have you heard anything at all? I don't mean just about the dead man, though I'd like to know more about him, certainly."

"I was hoping y'could give *me* something to dine out on," Mrs. Gudge laughed.

"Well, then, I mean to say," Maggie said, "have you heard, do you know—have I any enemies you know of?"

"Not a one—what would say it, leastways," Mrs. Gudge said, frowning fiercely, "save one...that runner, Spanish Will, was asking after you just yesterday. Aye, he come sniffing round me and Mrs. Gow. Run us down at our favorite spa the other night, whilst we was taking the waters," she said with a huge wink. "Him, and some stone-faced bloke who stood by him like Death waiting for his moment. We sent them straight to your friend, Roger Bell. Bet they got an earful, and Roger an eyefull, eh? Speaking of the devil—Spanish Will talks sweet and looks fine, but watch more than his handsome face, my girl, for it's reward money he's after, and truth be damned."

"I know. I know all about runners," Maggie said bitterly.

"We'll keep ears and eyes open too," Mrs. Gudge promised. "Never fret. If no one knows who the dead cove was, he could've been a nobody, and accident or no, *nobody* means no money for no one, and all your worry be for naught. After all, what sort of a man goes naked in the streets, eh? Nobody. So there y'are."

They laughed together, and for the first time since she'd got up Saturday morning, Maggie felt fine. Didn't she have wonderful protectors? she thought. Fishwives and men who were daintier than she was, simpletons and children, no wonder she felt so safe. That made her laugh even harder.

Mrs. Gudge heard the edge to her laughter. "He were nobody live, he be nobody dead," she said wisely. "You'll see, Dearie, I got this feeling about it."

*

By three in the afternoon, Maggie wondered if she'd run out of fish. It would be the first time. "If I'd known what it would do for business, I'd have hired dead men years ago," she muttered as she hurried to fill another order, after hearing yet another story of how shocked the buyer was.

"Never say!" Alice gasped, wrapping the flounder her flashing knife had just filleted, and handing it to Maggie.

"Just jesting," Maggie said. "Don't worry. No amount of money is worth this madness." *Or Death*, she thought, and didn't say, and not just to spare Alice's superstitious sensibilities.

She was glad when she had to go into the back room to see how much stock there was left. She could send to the market for more, she thought when she saw her depleted stores, or maybe it would be better for all to just close shop early and give the girls and everyone's tongues a rest. But that might start more talk. She stripped off her icy gloves and wiped her cold, damp hands, considering the matter.

"Missus?" Davie quavered, from her side. "Gent's here to talk to you."

"I'll be right back," she said absently. "He'll just have to wait. Everyone wants to talk with me today, Davie."

"But not perhaps, with the same urgency as I," a deep voice said in cultured accents.

She stopped, and looked up—and up. A tall gaunt gentleman stood in her doorway. He'd obviously followed Davie in from the shop. It was also obvious such a man had never set foot in a fish shop before. Although, Maggie thought numbly, gazing at him, just such a man might have once lived in this house, before it had fallen on hard times. That fellow would have worn velvet and silk, plumes and high-heeled shoes with silver buckles. This one wore a greatcoat open to show a blue superfine jacket over white linen, a gold waistcoat, and canary inexpressibles. His boots shone like black mirrors. He was quality top to toe. His face seemed to have more bones than most men's, and his eyes were gray and cold as sleet.

She'd never seen such a complete gentleman, at least not from so close. Because he was staring at her, and if that wasn't enough, he lifted a quizzing glass from his pocket and stared even harder. It made her lift her chin and stare back.

Lucian was so shocked he was temporarily speechless. This was the fishwife? He'd been expecting someone like Mrs. Gow or Mrs. Gudge. He'd been ready to duck a big red ham-sized fist for his insolence. Those little hands she was wiping were red, all right, but they were small and fragile. She was some thirty years younger than he'd imagined, easily forty pounds lighter, and trying to look directly at her was as hard as looking into the setting sun.

The runner had been right. She was severely red. Orange flaming red, her hair shouted. The countless freckles on her otherwise white face were blazing too. Beneath them, there was a pretty enough face, with small regular features, and a pair of blue-green eyes trying to cool off the vision she presented. To no avail.

Twenty and something then, with hideous unfashionable hair, a trim little body, a chilly voice that spoke in cultured accents, and eyes that spoke of cold murder. This creature—and *Uncle*? He might be able to imagine a woman with that sort of famous red-headed temper murdering someone, in fact, it looked as though she wanted to have at him right now. But as to the rest? Uncle was ambivalent about females. Whatever else this woman was, she was also profoundly female, and very attractive, in a bizarre way.

He always kept his head, he always knew what to say, but her appearance startled the comment from him. Although he knew her name, he still couldn't accept it, "*You* are Mrs. Pushkin? Surely not," he said.

She was insulted, though she couldn't say why. Perhaps it was his sneer, or the way he seemed to imply she wasn't good enough to be herself. She sought something cutting to say.

But was spared the effort. A shadow detached itself from the doorway behind her visitor and strolled into the room.

"Well," Spanish Will Corby said with great interest, looking from one of them to the other, his dark head to the side. "Well, well. I leave for a day, and see what happens? I'd say there was something smelled high as a dead fishie here, but I'll spare you the jest, because it's beneath me. Still, now the thing of it is, I'm wondering. Are you two getting acquainted? Or only just meeting again?"

Chapter Five

The runner walked into the room and circled the nobleman and the widow. They were so startled by his appearance they froze in place. The Viscount Maldon looked uncomfortable, if a man made of ice could seem so. But a ruddy flush suddenly bloomed on the bony ridges of his high cheekbones. Will noted the widow seemed miserably aware of the situation too. Probably because of her get-up. She was a female and they didn't like to be caught at a loss. Being rousted out of bed made wearing a dressing gown respectable, and she'd clutched a clean and pretty peach-colored one around herself that first time they'd met, he remembered.

She didn't look very respectable today, not in that blood-stained apron and those cracked oversized old boots. She made a swipe at an unruly strand of her shocking hair, looking nonplused. For once, the cool viscount looked just as uncomfortable. Spanish Will was very pleased with his catch in the fish shop this morning.

"Well," Will said again, gazing at one of them and then the other. "I had no idea. You two know each other?"

This shocked them both into speech.

"*Hardly,*" Lucian drawled.

The inference infuriated the widow as much as an outright insult. "I should think not!" she snapped, glowering at Lucian.

"Then may I ask why you're here, my lord?" Will asked, turning his attention to Lucian. "When last we met I told you I'd contact you if I'd any news, and so I would have done. But now I find you here? It makes me wonder, it does indeed."

"Wonder what?" Lucian asked, the flush on his cheekbones more hectic now. He had nothing to be embarrassed about, Lucian told himself, but somehow the fact that he'd gone ahead without telling the runner made him feel he had let down his side of the bargain. He had, of course, but he shouldn't feel as guilty about it as he did now. It was the runner's voice, he decided—Spanish Will acted as wounded as he did suspicious.

"Wonder what?"

Will raised one dark brow at the question. He smiled. "Like uncle, like nephew?"

The widow looked confused. Lucian did not. He inhaled sharply. "I do not know this young woman," he said grimly. "I am here precisely because I wanted to know if my uncle did."

"Uncle?" Maggie asked in a little voice.

"The dead man on your doorstep turns out to be the Baron St. Cloud, uncle to the Viscount Maldon here," Will explained, his eyes never leaving Lucian's. "But if you was wishful of knowing that, my lord, I'm wondering why you didn't just ask me? Instead of making me have to follow you all the way here so you could ask me the same thing? Seems wasteful."

"You followed me?"

"Oh aye. I didn't plan on seeing Mrs. Pushkin again 'til tomorrow. No reason to, just yet. Bitter cold out and snowing like fury for such a trek. I usually like to get all my ducks in a row before I take aim, but when I saw you leave your mother's house and head down here, I broke my own rule and called a hack in spite of…"

"You followed *me*?" Lucian said again, only his glittering eyes and tightened voice showing his rage. "But *I* am the fellow who put up the reward, as you said. Why would you follow me?"

"Oh, my lord," Will purred, shaking his dark head. "Had I tuppence for every murderer who posted a reward for his own crime so as to throw us off the scent, I'd quit my job tomorrow, I'd be that warm in the pocket. A gent thinking that if he offers money for a capture he won't be suspicioned? Nothing more common, I assure you. But it's useless. I'm Bow Street. We can be bought, in some ways, I'm sorry to say. A crime with gold in it tends to get seen to sooner, there's truth too. But some things can't be bought, no matter what the newspapers say. Murder is one of them."

The viscount's face went white as snow—or his dead uncle's— Maggie thought. "So you suspect *me*?" Lucian asked incredulously.

"My lord, I suspect everyone. It's my job," Will said simply.

Lucian was stunned into silence. He'd talked with the runner, and joked with him, laughed with the man too and respected him in a weird fashion, and in the end thought they'd achieved a sort of unity. And now to discover that all along he was being watched, weighed, considered as a suspect? In the murder of his own uncle? *He?* That was what one got for attempting anything like friendship with someone of the runner's class, Lucian thought furiously. He'd been duped and then betrayed by a Bow Street runner, and what was even worse, he found he was hurt by it.

"And so long as I'm here," Spanish Will went on, "and both of you are too, there's a few questions I may as well ask." He took out his notebook and looked around the storeroom. "But it's cold as death in here. There someplace warmer we can go?" he asked Maggie.

Not her own apartment, Maggie vowed. The rooms upstairs were hers, and hers alone, and not for the likes of the brutal runner and the nasty nobleman. The gentleman hadn't even bothered to introduce himself to her, and as for the runner—well... This place was as good as any for the likes of them. She almost smiled at the thought of these two big men suffering from the cold. Good. The colder they got the sooner they'd go. And the more wretched they'd be if they insisted on staying. The room was so frigid they all spoke puffs of white smoke every time they opened their mouths, even the icy nobleman.

Will answered himself before she could. "...there's always Bow Street, I suppose," he mused, his dark eyes malicious and bright.

"But I've a business to see to, right now," Maggie said, her chin jutting out.

"So have I," Will said, and waited.

Lucian crossed his arms on his chest. It was all he could do right now. He was so furious with the runner, and at himself, that it helped him ignore the cold. The fishwife could entertain them in a block of ice, for all he cared.

Maggie paused, then nodded, curtly. She was freezing and neither man cared. And her heart failed her at the thought of going to Bow Street. It would have to be the front room across the hall then. A private room, to be sure, but not hers alone. She shared it with the girls and little Davie. It was where they sat at night, reading and talking. A fire always burned in the hearth these days so it would be warm when they came in of an evening after work.

"I'll just tell the girls to carry on without me then," she said haughtily. "I'll be right back to take you someplace warmer." She marched out, but stumbled, mind and body, a step later. *A baron,* she thought as delayed shock set in and she felt her heart catch, *a baron,* no less, dead on her doorstep.

"Sell off the last and close early," she told Alice quickly. "We're done for the day. Then clean up. I've got to talk with the runner now." She looked at all the avid faces of her waiting customers. "They saw Spanish Will go in the back?"

Alice nodded, thrilled. "Aye, and the gentry cove too!"

"Then get word to Old Mack, the Guy brothers and Mrs. Gudge," Maggie said as she left. "Tell them to bring all they've got tomorrow morning. We'll need more than the usual then too."

Maggie returned quickly. She wordlessly led the runner and the nobleman down the hall, and opened the door to the front room opposite the shop. The two men stopped in the doorway, staring.

The walls of the salon were apple green, and there was an old Turkish carpet on the shining wood floor. A sofa and two comfortable chairs were arranged by the fireside. A polished walnut table bore a silver bowl filled with fruit and nuts. The mantel over the hearth had a china shepherd and shepherdess strolling along it. A few small landscapes hung on the walls, and the front window was covered by long rose draperies. There was a bookcase, well filled. It was a simple but colorful and inviting room, especially so on this snowy winter afternoon.

Davie was lighting the lamps in the room—lamps filled with good smokeless oil, Maggie thought proudly. It wasn't as elegant as her own salon upstairs. She'd furnished it for the children. It was comfortable and cozy as the homes they'd never had. It was also obviously not what the two men were expecting.

Lucian was shocked again. Cozy, warm, inviting, he raised his long nose, detecting a fresh and pleasant scent. Maggie noticed. Well, he could sniff 'til tomorrow morning, she sneered to herself, all he'd get was a snout full of lemon oil and beeswax. The fish stopped at the door, she made sure of that.

"Is this warm enough for you?" she asked Will sweetly. "We can move the fire screen so you can stand in the hearth, if you need."

That won a slash of a white smile from him. "Oh, it will do," he said, shucking off his greatcoat.

Lucian did the same, and took a step into the room—halting when he saw the runner didn't follow. Then he saw the widow looking pointedly at their boots. He looked down too. Curls of wood shavings and God knew what else from the street and her shop clung in clumps to their soles and shining sides. He had no idea of what to do. It wasn't a problem in his household—the staff would see to it if a visitor tracked in dirt. But his visitors seldom did. His street had sweepers who were always busy at work. His friends came in carriages and if their boots were wet, his servants saw to it after they'd gone. So far as he could recall, he'd never had to tramp through such muck before.

Spanish Will paused too. He looked around for the boot scraper. It was in the outer hall. A few swift slides along its iron blade with each foot and he got rid of most of the muck. When he was done, Lucian, with an inward shudder, did the same, wondering what his valet would think of the damage done to the perfection of his boots. Then they entered the salon.

They stood looking at each other in silence. Spanish Will spoke first. "My lord, this is Mrs. Maggie Pushkin, proprietress of this establishment. Mrs. Pushkin, this is the Viscount Maldon. We've come to talk about his uncle."

Lucian gave the barest suggestion of a bow, countered by Maggie's merely dipping her head in a mockery of a curtsey.

"What's there to talk about?" Maggie demanded, her face tight. "He had the bad fortune to die on my doorstep, and that's all I know about him. I wonder if I should ask Davie to take your coats at all."

"Oh, I'll carry mine," Will said, "and no harm done. But we do have to talk, Mrs. P. Because it just doesn't make sense that a fine gent like the Baron St. Cloud would come all the way from Montague Square on such a bitter night just to die at your door, and strip himself off before he did, at that. That makes no sense at all."

"Well, if you're still suggesting he had business with me, that makes no sense either," she said angrily, "unless he got a yearning in the middle of the night for some fresh flounder!"

"I'm thinking he got a yearning for something fresh, all right," Will agreed, leering at Maggie, "but not cold or scaly, neither."

"I most sincerely *doubt* that," Lucian said at the same time Maggie cried, "You're mad!"

An unlikely ally, and not one she appreciated, Maggie thought, eyeing Lucian as he turned to stare at her.

"Then maybe we ought sit and talk about what he did fancy," Will said patiently. "Middle of the night or no. Then we might yet make some sense of it."

The men gave Davie their coats, and then sat, gingerly. Maggie lowered herself to a chair—but stopped before she sat, in an awkward recover.

"If you'll wait a moment," she said calmly, though her face grew red. "I just have to show Davie where to hang your coats to dry them properly." She left the room as languidly as any grand lady. But once out of sight, she dashed down the hall. They'd flustered her, she'd almost sat on her good furniture in her working clothes!

Once in the kitchen, she whipped off her apron, peeled off the boots, and hurriedly rinsed her hands in lemon water, as she always did after work. There was only time to drag her hair back into a semblance of order. They might be deciding her fate out there, hanging her without hearing her, she thought frantically, panting as she rushed back down the hall. But when she neared the salon, flushed and lemon-scented, she heard nothing. The men were ignoring each other. The runner was jotting something in his notebook, the viscount was staring into the fire, his face as expressive as a rock.

"Now, then," she said, sitting on the edge of a chair near the fire, folding her hands in her lap, neatly as a tabby cat, "what must I tell you to convince you?"

"What you tell me makes no nevermind," Will said, not even looking up from his notebook. "Because I expect it'll be same as before: you didn't know him, never saw him before and don't know what I'm talking about. Right? But I was thinking that if we three sat a spell and talked about the baron, we might find out why he was here. Mrs. P.—you might remember more. My lord," he turned to Lucian as Maggie began to protest, "tell us something about your uncle, why don't you?"

Lucian looked at Maggie. He raised an arc of an eyebrow. "You really think it necessary to discuss him *here*?"

Maggie bridled. "You may take yourself off and discuss him on the roof for all *I* care!" He might be gentry, but she was her own mistress and didn't have to bend to any man except her king anymore.

Will nodded. "I do want to discuss him."

"Well then, let me think," Lucian said, sounding as bored as someone placating an annoying child. "What is there that you don't already know? He is—was—just turned five and fifty. And due to marry the Honorable Louisa Everley this Sunday. She's some years his junior, some *score* of years, though she's no dewy miss herself. She's got thirty years in her dish, an age the world would consider

75

youngish if she were a man, but not a woman. Life is unfair to females, is it not, Mrs. Pushkin?"

So much for reconciliation, he thought, as the widow glowered at him in response. He shrugged. "At any rate, it's an age that put her firmly on the shelf—until Uncle asked for her hand. Which surprised us all. He was a reclusive man. At least I saw him seldom, and never on the town. If we met it was at family affairs, which was rare too, because I'm not in the way of being a family man. My brother knew him better. I've no idea why he sought his company—but then I'm ten years my brother's senior, we aren't close either..."

"Your *uncle's* interests," Will cut in to say, "*his* diversions, his daily routine, my lord."

Maggie smiled at that, like a child who hears the teacher correcting a classmate she didn't like, Lucian thought, annoyed again. This time, because the image he conjured up was too uncomfortably apt. He'd been out of the schoolroom a long time, and didn't like feeling he'd been put back in it. Especially by a man *he'd* treated as an equal, in spite of all evidence to the contrary.

The nobleman's face was disciplined and hard, but his color betrayed him, Maggie thought with pleasure. And his eyes could speak violence while his face registered nothing but weariness. It must be a talent, she decided, cultivated by the very rich.

"He collected books," Lucian said, pinning the runner with his cold gray gaze, "on botany and biology. That was about the sum and substance of the man. He belonged to the Royal Society, the Alfred, clubs for scholarly men, but he seldom went to them. He had no interest in politics or parties, or fashion or anything else I can recall. He was wealthy, he was boring, he had absolutely no reason I can fathom for being in any part of London by night, much less being found murdered, and most especially not *here*.

And no," he went on as Maggie glared at him, "so far as I know he'd no interest in females—except for Louisa, of course. But that was necessity rather than ardor. He belatedly realized he had no heirs. That was all he wanted from a wife."

The widow's expression went from anger to rueful disgust. Both Lucian and the runner noted that with interest.

"Still no memories?" the runner asked her.

"No, but that's because I've so many barons buying up my fish, I can't place him," she snapped. "Give over. You heard it for yourself, he didn't fancy females. And as I'm not the sort most men would fancy, why not admit I've no part in this?"

"Then who'd fancy leaving him on your doorstep, do you think?" Will asked pleasantly, though he leaned forward and stared at her. "He was found here, and so here is where I must start."

"You might start with his family," Maggie snapped. "Most people who end up dead at someone's hands end up that way at the hands of someone they know."

"Ah. And so you are an expert on murder, Mrs. Pushkin, are you?" Lucian said mildly, though raising a brow.

Will was vastly pleased. The nobleman and the widow were trying to push each other up the steps to the scaffold. If they did know each other, all to the better. If they didn't, one might push the other to saying something unplanned anyway.

"I had nothing to profit from his murder," Maggie said with a tight little smile.

"Nor had I," Lucian said with a chilling one. "Not only have I an adequate fortune of my own, but I'm the last person he'd leave his to."

"Ah, but he won't be being wed this Sunday," Will said, his face smooth as his voice. "And since he had no children, and you're the head of your family now, my lord, you're now his heir. Or don't I correctly understand how the gentry does it?"

"No, you're right—or would be if he'd an entail on anything he owned, which he did not," Lucian said. "He didn't have any property of note. Only his townhouse and funds. He could leave those wherever he pleased, and I doubt it pleased him to leave them to me."

"You two didn't get on?" Will asked.

Lucian's eyes flashed. And this from a man who he'd thought understood him, if only a little! But the runner was looking for a villain, and was obviously not concerned where he found one. Lucian didn't need that kind of thinking interfering in his life.

An instant later Lucian wore the long suffering look of a man trying to explain himself to an idiot as he answered, "No. He disinterested me, merely. He had few sins, at least none that appealed to me, nor did his virtues. It was mutual. I didn't care a farthing for him and he knew it. It was my brother whose company he enjoyed, and Louisa he was to marry. Nor are they murderous souls either. I suggest you do exactly as you said—begin your investigation where the crime began."

"Crime begins at home, my lord!" Maggie cried, and was about to say more when the door opened.

Davie came into the room slowly, head lowered, biting his lips in concentration as he carefully carried a plate of seed cakes. Alice followed, smiling broadly. She wore her Sunday frock, and bore a tray with a steaming teapot on it. Annie brought up the rear, bright-eyed, bearing a tray with mugs and napery.

"Thought you'd like some tea, Missus," Alice said.

"Aye, 'tis a terrible cold night," Annie said, her eyes darting from Spanish Will to Lucian and back again.

The girls were so excited Maggie thought she might hear their hearts beating from where she sat. "Thank you," she said unhappily, accepting the inevitable. She'd taught them their company manners, after all. How could they know she'd sooner serve these guests rat poison? "Leave the trays on the table, please. Is the shop cleaned and closed tight?"

"'Tis, Missus," Alice said.

"Clean as can be," Annie echoed.

Davie nodded.

"Then, thank you. I'll speak with you later. You may go now. ...*Now*, girls," Maggie finally had to say, because the pair of them stood gaping at the two men in the salon. Well, but who could blame them? Maggie thought. The men looked fine as they could stare. She'd have to lecture the girls about fine feathers again, because these two were very black birds, indeed.

The Viscount Maldon looked elegant, sardonic and amused. He had just the sort of unobtainable glamour that would fascinate her poor slum-born and -bred girls. But Spanish Will, Maggie noted with horror, was not amused. It was much worse. His cruelly handsome face was intent, his eyes glowed with sudden interest as he gazed back at the girls. It was as though he'd turned on some inner force. Maggie could almost feel its pull. She was glad it wasn't focused on her—and then infuriated. Because it was centered on the girls. But they *were* girls!

Alice was buxom, but it was only puppy plumpness. Annie was still a girl in every sense. Only fifteen and thirteen...although some that age were mothers—but not her girls! Maggie bristled. "You may go *now*, girls," she said sharply, to break the runner's spell.

They ducked curtseys and fled, leaving the three adults alone again. Maggie turned to the runner, her eyes wild with anger. Lucian watched, bemused.

"I hadn't thought of it before," the runner mused, "but now...I do wonder. Would either of your girls care to walk out of an evening, I wonder? With a man, I mean to say?"

Maggie couldn't believe him. She drew a breath to blast him, even if it made him mad enough to invent evidence against her, even if he decided to drag her to the gallows by her hair for it. Even the viscount looked startled.

But the runner didn't seem to notice. "Some men like younger women," he mused, "some like young girls even more. Especially some older men. Your uncle," he told Lucian, "mightn't have been visiting Mrs. Pushkin, after all."

Lucian's distant amusement fled. His pale face grew ashen. "How *dare* you?" he asked, rising slowly to his feet, uncoiling like a cobra about to strike. "I'd offer any other man a chance to give me satisfaction for such a remark, but I expect your profession saves you from that."

"You mean a duel?" Spanish Will laughed. "No, don't wait for me under any oak trees, my lord. I'll be glad to meet you in the court of fives, with bare fists, but only after this is over."

"*My* girls do not walk out with men!" Maggie cried. She was afire with anger, as well as embarrassment for what she'd thought he'd wanted and almost damned him for. "The most they've ever done is simper at boys, they don't even look at men..." She realized the folly of saying that too late, especially after how they'd ogled the two men she was defending them to. "I know where they are all the time," she said quickly, "that at least, I can swear to!"

"A thought," Will said calmly, "just a thought."

"There have been too many of them tonight," Lucian said, his gray eyes glittering like frost on a windowpane. "Bad enough he was found dead here. I've better things to do than sit in a fishmonger's parlor and hear a Bow Street runner traduce my uncle's name."

Maggie gasped.

The runner laughed. "Then run along, my lord, do. But know this. I'm not done with the matter, not by a long shot. See, to my way of thinking, men of fortune have been known to lose them. Gentlemen being known for being demons for the gaming table, I'm sorry to say," he added with a sly look, "and Dame Fortune also so famous for being a wickedly fickle wench."

Will turned his gaze toward Maggie. "Lonely widows have been known to have callers of an evening, from every part of town too." He snapped his notebook shut. "Still, it may not have been someone he knew, that could be. One thing I do know," he said, very happy with himself now, even though he'd learned nothing new, "if I find the reason he was in this part of London the night he died—I'll find myself a murderer."

"He was *not* visiting me!" Maggie protested.

"Still, I suppose that's all there is to say tonight, my lord," Will went on, as though she hadn't spoken, "since you're not wishful of chatting with a runner or a purveyor of fish stuff, and seeing as how Mrs. Pushkin doesn't have much to contribute now either."

"This is ludicrous," Lucian said. "If you can't see further than your fingertips, Mr. Corby, perhaps we can have another runner see to the matter."

"Perhaps you will," Will said affably. "It's a fine reward you've offered, my lord, others will try. But I'm the best." He rose to his feet. "So, you've nothing more to say? I'd hoped you'd both be more agreeable."

"What more do you want of me?" Lucian asked.

"Facts, speculation, information," Will said, suddenly deadly serious, "something to go on. The less you tell me the more I think you have to say. It's the way of the world, my lord, think on!"

"And me? I've told you all I know," Maggie said. "Facts *and* information, and what good is my speculation when I didn't even know the man?"

"Aye," Will said, dismissing her, his eyes on Lucian, "agreed, Missus, your speculation is not what I'm after."

"And mine, of course, holds the key, I suppose?" Lucian said stonily, facing the runner, his hands knotted into fists at his sides.

Maggie clenched her own fists, trying to hold her anger in. It was *her* home, *her* house, and the two of them acted as though she wasn't even there. But then the viscount had already made it clear he thought she was about as consequential and attractive as a weevil in his porridge, and about as clever as one too. And the runner had promoted her from liar to fool? Before she could mull it over, she looked up and discovered she was the only one still seated. She shot to her feet as though scalded.

"The *fact*," Lucian was saying with a sneer, "is that my uncle was beaten to death at this doorstep. And now you're trying to lay it on mine? Oh, well done."

Maggie frowned, tilting her head as though she'd heard far-off music. Her forehead creased, she scowled and then her eyes flew wide. "That's it!" she cried, "No, he wasn't! He couldn't have been!"

The men turned to stare at her.

81

"He wasn't killed here," she said excitedly. "Think back, Mr. Corby, as I've just done. The viscount here, his saying that, it made me remember. I should have done on my own," she said in chagrin. "What was I thinking? But he looked so naked, so…dead. See, I had the girls clean the doorstep after…" She shook her head. "…I saw but I didn't see, what was I thinking? Oh, I should have known!"

Spanish Will stepped toward her and put his hands on her shoulders. They were big, warm, strong hands that gripped her firmly. Maggie went suddenly silent, as deadly quiet as though he'd slapped her. Her shoulders went rigid, her eyes widened, and she stared up at him, shocked at the intimacy. He let his hands drop.

She took a deep breath, steadying herself. "Yes, I was going on, wasn't I? But here it is. Think back. He was hit on the head, right? Hard—hard enough to…" she looked up at the viscount.

He nodded. "I saw him, I know, don't think to spare my feelings, he had his brains dashed in."

"Yes," she said in relief, "so he did. But that couldn't have been what killed him. The *blood*," she told the runner, "there wasn't enough. Remember? Only a bit, a patch, some, under his head, a stain, merely that, no matter he was hit hard enough to cave his skull in. Yes, it was freezing, but if you cut yourself that deep there'd be blood, lots of it, before you died! And there wasn't! It's like with…fish," she said defiantly, facing the viscount squarely, "you smack them with a mallet whilst their still living—they bleed, even cold-blooded fish will do. But after they're dead you can slice them and dice them and you'll only get scales on your hands for your trouble, do you see? He *wasn't* killed at my door. Someone just dropped him there, after."

The runner closed his eyes. When he opened them, he was smiling. "Mrs. P., you do surprise me. Yes. Of course."

"Yes," Lucian said ruminitively, gazing at Maggie as though seeing her for the first time, his eyes narrowing as he reassessed what he saw. "So it would be, I do see. But," he added wryly, "I don't see what difference it would make. At least to me."

"Well, it makes a world of difference to me," Maggie said gaily, smiling triumphantly, feeling for the first time, entirely free. "For if I'd coshed him, the place would be awelter of blood, wouldn't it, and it wasn't. I was sleeping when Annie woke me with the news."

"But," Lucian said too softly, "this place often is a welter, is it not? At least, you've all the trappings needed to be rid of blood: brushes and water and sawdust and so on?"

"No," Will said. "Her girls would've heard and their eyes tell me they're not in the murdering business. They're far too merry. Hauling him out would be too much for her alone, strong though she may be. And she may be. She doesn't look it but she's got muscles in those shoulders—I just felt them," he added with a hint of a glimmer in his eyes. "She's strong, but never enough to get a man your uncle's size out of doors and onto the step. He was dropped there. It was snowing, there'd have been a path made by his passage were he dragged."

"A path? It might have been covered by people milling about when he was discovered, there were a great many, no doubt," Lucian persisted.

"And how would *you* know that unless you were here to see it?" Maggie cried.

"I imagine..."

"Suppositions. Good," Will said, cutting them off impatiently, "but if we want to get anywhere they've got to be about more than the pair of you. I'll grant—for now, that it wasn't Mrs. P. who done for him, and allow it mightn't have been you, my lord. ...For now. But you've got to give me more to go on. Both of you."

"There *is* no more," Maggie said in vexation.

"Think on, think on, there will be," Will said. "Or ask around, Mrs. P. You've an ear where I don't. Aye, even me. Your friends, the lovely Mrs. Gudge and the beauteous Mrs. Gow, they won't give me the right time of day if it doesn't suit you, though they'll swear to. And as for you, my lord, there's more for you too. What exactly was the baron wearing when last seen?"

"Ask his valet."

"Oh, I will, I will, and all his servants besides. But you can ask even more. Your uncle was here. Why? You may find reason to seek me out before I find a need to see you again...though I doubt it," he added ominously.

"Maybe we three ought to meet again?" Maggie asked.

"'...*in thunder, lightning or in rain?*'" the viscount murmured to himself.

"Yes, or '*when the hurly burly's done*'!" Maggie quoted defiantly. "I can read, my lord," she said when she saw him check.

"My apologies," he said unapologetically, with one uplifted brow.

"Would you care for some tea?" Maggie asked, motioning to the table, so she wouldn't be tempted to hit him.

"Thank you, but I'm afraid I must take my leave now."

"Aye, me as well," Spanish Will said. "But there's something in what you said, Mrs. P. It may be we all will have to meet again."

"Perhaps," Lucian agreed impatiently. "Is that all for now?"

"Aye," the runner said, his thoughts already far away.

They said good-bye at the door, and went their separate ways. Lucian stepped up into his waiting carriage and took the reins from the youth who held his horses for him. He automatically threaded the reins through his gloved fingers, lost in thought. Meet again? *Cooperate with a fishwife?* Still, the woman was more intelligent than he'd suspected. But then—when had he ever had to contemplate a fishwife before? And the runner had acted like a friend, and then treated him like a common criminal. And yet, why should he not? There was something to be said for a man who believed nothing he couldn't prove.

He cracked his whip and drove off, deep in thought.

Will raised his shoulders against the snow as he began the long walk to his lodgings. *Trust those two? Ha! But there was that grand reward... But a runner cooperate with his two best suspects...?* Well, maybe. *If it helped to lull them...lulling was a powerful tool.*

He'd already lied to them. He'd laid his hands on the widow's shoulders for more than soothing her, and all he'd felt was the delicacy of her bone structure. She wasn't strong enough to lug the guts...*he'd been to the playhouse too*—he thought smugly, though he was better off with them not knowing that. And he never forgot a thing he heard. That was another powerful tool best kept to himself. But the Bard's plays were filled with murderous females, weren't they? So there was no saying she didn't have a hand in it, was there? And the viscount's finances needed looking into... Ignoring the cold, impervious to the cutting wind because of his busy mind, he trudged homeward.

And Maggie Pushkin stood in the doorway and watched them both go off into the snowy night, and wished with all her heart that she'd never see either of them again.

Chapter Six

It was a small but tasteful funeral. No one could say otherwise, even if the dead man had been sent to his maker in the most vulgar fashion, no one could say his funeral wasn't perfectly correct. The horses had been festooned in black, the hearse shone like a dark sun when it arrived at the churchyard, and the mourners assembled at the deceased's home now were the cream of society. But they weren't saying much and what they said showed how uncomfortable they were. They didn't know how to console the bereaved without risking mentioning the shocking reason they were there. That would come later, when they were elsewhere and could finally indulge in all the scandalous conjecture they were trying so hard to pretend wasn't consuming them now.

"Good of you to provide your own servants to serve here today," Arthur told his brother quietly, as the company accepted warming cups of tea, the gentlemen taking theirs laced with brandy. "Uncle's staff was pretty shaken. I should have thought of it. I'm glad you did. Nice to see you're already taking up the reins."

Lucian raised an eyebrow. "Hardly," he said. "It was merely that, or have this lot pretending to grieve at my house. It was simple self preservation; there are no reins to take up."

"What?" Arthur asked, his eyes widening. "What's this? You've talked to Uncle's lawyer already?"

"No need. Can you imagine Uncle leaving his precious moldering books to me, much less his house and fortune?" Lucian laughed without humor. "Come, my boy, don't be coy. Didn't you hear Mama? She was only right. You're the one he bored to bits of an evening, prosing on about his illustrated beetles or God knows what was in the latest book he bought. I don't expect or want any of it. It's all yours now, and welcome to it. Unless, of course, dear Louisa pretended a passion for those tomes filled with insects and fungi. It wouldn't have been the only passion she'd have had to pretend to with him."

"Don't be so hard on her," Arthur said, lowering his voice to a whisper, although their late uncle's fiancée was on the other side of the room. "She's a good woman, even you can't say otherwise."

"I don't," Lucian said lightly. "She has sense and manners. It's that as much as anything that made the idea of her marrying Uncle so repugnant. I'd thought there were some females who were above selling themselves. She proved me wrong. I hate being wrong."

"It's no time to joke. She seems genuinely upset."

They both gazed at the tall slender woman in black sitting by the fire, a throng of relatives surrounding her. "Upset? I should think so," Lucian said, with a thin smile. "If Uncle had only waited one more week before venturing into Spitalfields on his mysterious errand, she'd have been spared much, and gained more."

"Spitalfields!" Arthur gasped. "I thought you said he was found near Bishopsgate!"

"Bishopsgate, Spitalfields, Seven Dials, Whitechapel, that end of town is a garden of delights, isn't it? They're a stone's throw from each other," Lucian shrugged. "Well, perhaps a few stones. Who knows?" He gave a fastidious shudder. "I'm not in the habit of visiting such places. God knows why Uncle did."

"Have you heard anything from Bow Street? It's been days."

Lucian frowned. "No, but my staff certainly has. The runner in charge of the case spends more time in my kitchens than my dinners do these days."

"He's been investigating *you*?" Arthur asked in astonishment.

Arthur seldom saw his older brother looking uncomfortable. But now the older man rolled his shoulders as though his tightly fitted jacket was pinching. "He is, he has been," he admitted. "I think I'm going to have to increase the reward even more to get some other runners on the case. This one believes murder begins at home. Or at least, he thinks I'm the heir, and so his suspicions center on me. Men of that class often see relatives doing each other in for gain, I suppose," he muttered. "Too bad we can't have thief-takers who aren't so very nearly thieves themselves."

Lucian looked up at the ornate ceiling, then eyed the dark mahogany wainscoting lining the dim, heavily shadowed salon. "You'll have to have the place redone, of course," he commented. "It hasn't been touched since the last century. Put this heavy furniture in storage, get some new light pieces, in the Egyptian style that's all the rage since Wellington went there. Bring in some color." He waved a hand at the walls. "Paint it something bright, pleasant. Apple green, perhaps..." He paused, looking surprised at what he'd said. "Well, the thing is you can do wonders for the place," he went on briskly. "It could be made comfortable enough, more than enough for a young sprig like you."

"You're being premature," Arthur said, though his fresh face flushed with pleasure, or embarrassment. "We haven't heard the will yet. And—well, damme Lucian, but it doesn't feel right to be talking about acquiring a man's worldly goods when we've just laid him in his grave."

"Why? It's all *he* ever talked about," Lucian said callously— "justifying his autumn marriage, nattering on about the importance of begetting a male heir. What else is everyone here thinking about? Apart from the way he died, of course. I'm not the only one who found his forthcoming nuptials distasteful; others had better reason to resent it. Many are relieved the money's not leaving the family. Just look over there, in the corner—Cousin James. I've seen sadder faces at orgies. He must have hopes."

"Hopes?"

"Arthur, we must get you to listen to *some* gossip," Lucian sighed. "Yes. He's a gambler. He was born to a comfortable income, but not half enough to support his pleasure. One may see him at horse races all the time, unless he's at a boxing match, or cockfight or a gaming hell, that is. He's no great wit, and lives to wager... Now *there's* a fellow the runner ought to be questioning. That's a thought. I wonder if James saw Uncle often enough to wedge himself into a Last Will and Testament. I must remember to drop a word into Spanish Will's eager ear.

"On that head," Lucian said seriously, "have you been thinking about it? Any word recalled, any new ideas at all on where Uncle was bound that night?"

"Perhaps..." Arthur said hesitantly. "I've come to think that maybe he went to buy Louisa a bride present. He did ask me what young girls would want, and so it's the only thing that makes any sense at all. Because that might have been his errand, and if he'd just bought something expensive and someone had seen it and was following him, it might account for a sudden savage attack. I do listen to gossip sometimes, Lucian."

He leaned closer to his brother. "And I hear some people are saying he might have been buying something not quite legitimate down there. I mean, you know—sometimes one's barber or bootmaker says they know someone in the slums who can get their hands on a valuable they want to sell cheaply to be rid of fast. That could be. All Uncle knew how to buy was books. How would he know where to get something for a young woman? Jewels from Bond Street cost a fortune and he wasn't used to spending much. He always gloated when he got a good bargain on a valuable edition. I can't see him doing that in the normal way, but who knows? Love does strange things to men, they say."

"Coming it too strong!" Lucian said with a bark of laughter that made everyone in the room stare. Any other man might have looked abashed, Lucian merely stared back until they dropped their eyes and looked away. "*Love*—and *Uncle*? And in the same breath?" he chuckled. "Still, there may be something to it. Maybe Louisa's interest was waning, perhaps at the last minute she was thinking of calling it off. Maybe he thought diamonds would go a long way to mend matters...who knows? Interesting though..." he mused, staring across the room at the young woman in black.

His gaze sharpened. "Who is the gallant soldier at her shoulder?" he asked. "The one looking at her the way a dog looks at a bone?"

"I don't know, I've never seen him before."

"Past time to see him now, then," Lucian said, already moving toward the pair. "Again, I offer my condolences, my lady," he said, bending over Louisa's black-gloved hand, where she sat, by his mother's side.

"It is I who ought offer mine to you," she said, looking unflinchingly into his eyes. "After all, I'm not related to him, am I?"

"Alas, no," Lucian said, his face unreadable.

She wasn't an attractive woman, but she wasn't ugly. She looked like many another woman, and that was her tragedy. Tall, with a boyish figure that the new fashions showed to advantage, she had a face that was eminently forgettable. Her eyes were brown, her nose was straight, her lips well shaped, she had no deformity, but no grace notes either. Since she was also quiet and well mannered, she was the kind of woman men forgot about when some other female who was curvaceous and smiling came into the room. Or one who was slender and witty, or provocative with any kind of looks, for that matter. She was well liked but little noticed — until she'd become engaged to the Baron St. Cloud.

"She's holding up beautifully, Lucian," his mother said with a frown. "And I wish to say again that I think it doesn't look right for young Nicholas not to be here too. You were at your father's funeral when you were not much older than he."

"Rightly so, Mama, since he was my father," Lucian said coldly. "Your brother was Nick's great uncle. I sympathize with your loss, but now you suggest I take my son out of school and send him on such a journey in this weather for such a treat?"

She gasped as he went on. "Three weeks of fog with the roads closed half the time and the coaches crashing into each other the other half, and now this incessant snow. I'm sorry, Mama, but I don't aspire to attend two funerals this winter. Nick stays at school until spring unless I die before then, and Convention be damned."

His mother glared at him, but didn't argue. He was right; he was usually right, but that didn't endear him to her. Not much did. Why could he not be like Arthur? Child of her old age, and solace to her always. Even so, as she often told Arthur...she could almost wish Arthur had been the firstborn with all the rights, privileges and fortune. Because Arthur really liked her. Lucian tolerated her. He was very like his father.

At least, the dowager viscountess thought triumphantly, *Arthur would get her brother's estate now*. It wasn't a patch on what Lucian had, but at least it was something he wouldn't have. Lucian had too much as it was. Her brother had been a cold unfeeling man, but he'd listened to her and begun to cultivate Arthur a few years ago. And now he was dead before he could marry and leave it elsewhere. *The religious were right*, the viscountess thought happily, *the Lord did move in mysterious ways*.

"Such a pity, poor girl," she said again, patting Louisa's hand.

Louisa said nothing. Lucian noted it and approved. There was nothing for her to say. She was already an intruder in this house of mourning—if anyone was mourning the baron, that was. It wouldn't have been easy being his bride. It might be worse being the almost bride of a man found naked and dead in the gutter. But at least it was briefer. The gossip would fade in time. Left to his own devices Uncle might have lived on for years.

"A terrible misfortune," the soldier standing close to Louisa's side said, with a slight bow. "My condolences, my lord. It's a most unhappy circumstance."

He didn't look unhappy, Lucian thought, returning his bow. He looked proud, pleased and dashing in his Hussar uniform. He would have looked merely weedy in civilian clothes, Lucian thought, assessing him. Slight, with an ordinary face sporting a military mustache that tried to make up for his thinning blonde hair, his right arm was bound in a sling, clipped to his chest. But not so close as to obscure his medals.

"This is my cousin, Lieutenant Pascal, my lord," Louisa said. "Jonathan, here is Lord Maldon."

"Cousin *by marriage*," the lieutenant corrected in a murmur, bowing again.

Louisa ignored his comment. "My cousin just arrived in England, my lord. He's mending from wounds received when he was with the Marquess Wellington, at Nive, just a month ago. We're happy to have him still with us."

"No happier than I," the lieutenant said. "At least to be here, I mean to say. Not, of course, to be at this sad occasion, no, no. I'd thought to be at a wedding this week. Ah, well, that's life, isn't it?"

"No, it's death, actually," Lucian said.

The conversation faltered, as everyone tried to think of something fitting to say.

"My lord?" a meek hesitant voice behind Lucian asked. "Ah. Um. Lord Maldon? If you're not busy at the moment?"

Lucian turned to see a stout middle-aged man looking at him anxiously. "If you'd permit me to introduce myself? I'm your late uncle's man-at-law. If you could spare me a moment? If it's convenient?"

The room went deadly still.

"Of course," Lucian said. "The reading of the will?"

"Oh my no!" the lawyer said. "We can't probate with such speed, my lord, not even for you. But there are a few details that must be seen to immediately. So if you'd be so kind as to step into the library with me?"

"I see. Come along, Arthur, we may as well get things moving," Lucian said.

He turned, Arthur at his side. They were stopped by the lawyer's agonized whisper. "Oh, but that won't be necessary," he said apologetically. "Mr. Arthur doesn't have to come. His bequest can be handled in its time. It's the running of the household, the little matters—but quite large in the servant's eyes, of course—the disposition of their duties until such time as you make final arrangements as to their future in this house...."

Lucian sighed. "I *am* the head of the family now. But let's dispense with formalities. My brother, as my uncle's heir, can and should see to that."

The lawyer looked even more agitated. His whisper sank to a tortured croak. "But my lord!" he said miserably. "Such is not the case. You are your uncle's heir, and will get all—save for some bequests to his staff, and such."

"And my brother?" Lucian demanded, too surprised to care about all the enthralled listeners around them.

"Some volumes...some books," the lawyer stammered, looking from the viscount's angry face to Arthur's white one.

"But he was my uncle's favorite!"

"Yes, my lord, true...but you see, your uncle was a most conservative man. You must be aware of that. And so for all he enjoyed Mr. Arthur's company, 'Mr. Fisher,' said he, 'the lot goes to the elder, so it always is, and so it must be. I won't be the one to break with family tradition, nor should anyone expect me to.' He was going to change the will after he married, if he had a natural heir, of course, but..." The lawyer's voice faded into the silence in the room.

When Lucian finally spoke again his voice was clipped. "Yes, then certainly," he said crisply, "I'll be there—after a physician is called for my mother; she appears to be ill. See to her, Arthur," he snapped at his brother, who was standing stock still. Then he muttered, low, "Damn him, damn the old fool, anyway!"

"But you must have known, my lord," the lawyer protested, "for that was the one thing the baron knew about you. 'Whatever else he does, he does the right thing,' he told me, many a time he told me that."

Lucian shut his eyes. When he opened them again, everyone in the room was still staring at him. Except for his Mama, of course.

*

"What you need, lass, is a man about the place," Tom persisted. He still hadn't left Maggie's back room though he was done delivering his coal.

"Yes, so you've said," Maggie said impatiently, "and that's what I've got. And more. Men, women *and* children, everyone in

London, these days. I can't keep enough fish in stock. I thought it would pass. But they're still here. It's become a meeting place for everyone. They come, they buy, they gossip and wait."

"Good for you," he said.

"Well, if it was permanent... But even so, I can't be easy."

"Exactly!" he said triumphantly, stepping closer. "Days must be fine, the shop's filled. But nights... Oh Lass, I bet you can't close an eye. I bet you sit up at every sound you hear."

"Not likely," she said, laughing. "I'm so tired these nights, I could sleep through a herd of...but don't be getting any ideas. I've got the girls and Davie on alert, and safeguards too. So don't you think to come catting around of a night, because all you'll get for your troubles is a bucket of water in your face and enough screeching to raise the Watch *and* the dead."

"Then invite me in," he said with a bold smile.

"Don't hold your breath," she said, her smile gone, a warning clear in her voice and her eyes.

"There'll come a day," he said with a shrug. "Just remember I'm here, willing and able."

"And married," she said, as she turned her back on him, and went back to the shop, leaving him standing there.

But she was called to the back room often because deliveries kept coming. She'd put out the word and the cream of Billingsgate Market obliged her. Other fish sellers might have to go down to the docks at dawn to get the best selection. But Bernard's relatives remained loyal. Besides, she always paid cash, no arguments.

One had a particular fine delivery for her.

"Plump, fresh, I don't know how you get them, Mr. Hardy, what with the weather and all, but I'm that grateful," she said, looking at the box of shining silver mullet he'd just delivered.

"Aye, well, I'm thinking you'll be more so in a minute," he chuckled, fishing in the inner breast pocket of his heavy coat. He was an old man, or at least, he looked it; sun, wind and brine had practically pickled his face. He sailed out of London and fished in deeper waters than the Atlantic, or so rumor went. Bernard's family were seafaring men, and some had connections it was better not to ask about. They could deliver fish, or treasure whose origins were best left in ignorance, or so Bernard had said when she'd first gasped over some of her wedding presents. As she did now.

"Better than last time?" he asked, grinning.

"That vase was magnificent—but this! Oh Mr. Hardy! I'm almost afraid to touch it."

"Well, you needn't be!" he said indignantly. "If it were stolen, it were done a hundred years ago. Got it off Our Martin, what just come back from the Caribes, and he vows that's so. You know we've never landed suspect merchandise on you, nor will we ever."

"I know, that's not what I meant. But this!" She gazed at the perfect little jade figurine of some long dead Chinese lady.

"Well," he said smugly, "you got an eye for beauty, so when we see such oddments and pretties, we thinks of you. For Old Bernard's sake. And you pay prompt. So?"

"How much?"

He told her. It was more than reasonable and they both knew it. "I hadn't planned—but how can I pass it up?" she sighed again. "Done! But what's to become of my old age I don't know—what with me spending every spare penny on such beautiful things as you bring me."

"Ha! Got a great many extra pennies these days we hear! And no reason for a saucy, pretty wench like you to be worrying about your old age, is there? Not when you could get a husband by snapping your fingers. But after Bernard, may he rest in peace, who can blame you? As for the pretties? I vow, Maggie, you love them so, 'tis a wonder you don't open a shop and sell them 'stead of fish. We'd do for you, y'know. Keep you well stocked with all sorts of chinaware and gems, for only a small percent of the take."

"There's a thought—for another lifetime! I can hardly keep *this* shop running smooth. And how could I bear to part with them?

Cod's one thing, art's another. Still...I love this, and thank you kindly, I'll treasure it."

She paid him, said good-bye, and carried the figurine up to her own sitting room immediately. She put it on top of the bombe chest another of Bernard's relatives had sold her years before. But after giving it one last glance, she hurried downstairs again. There'd be time to gloat over it in privacy later. It would ease the long hours when she couldn't sleep, which were many these past nights, no matter what she'd told Tom.

When she got downstairs, she found she'd more company, and they'd made themselves at home.

"Davie brung us tea," Mrs. Gow said when Maggie came into the kitchens to see whose voices she'd heard. "'E's a good lad."

"Wouldn't trouble you or clutter up your kitchen,' Mrs. Gudge explained, "only we knows you always keeps a kettle on. Got a basket of mackerel for you today, sweet as peaches, swear on me life. Can you use them?"

"Absolutely," Maggie said, sitting down with them at the table.

"Well, you're still run off your feet, but it's all blown over now, 'asn't it?" Mrs. Gow asked, setting down her mug of tea. "It's as I said, didn't I, Mrs. Gudge? The nob was scragged and it's a fair pity—poor soul, what a turrible way to die—and 'im turning out to be a *baron*, no less, what got so much to live for! But it's over like a summer storm and good riddance, says I."

"Nice to be thinking about summer on a day like this, gone mad with the cold, dreaming of August, Mrs. Gow? Oh, she's a treat, ain't she?" Mrs. Gudge asked Maggie with a wink. "Oh cheer up, Mrs. Pushkin. Ain't seen sight nor sound of that dashing runner, have you? Nor his bony crony, eh?"

"You've a way with words, Mrs. Gudge," her friend hooted.

"It's only the truth," Mrs. Gudge said. "And we hear he was a nob too, that one, a viscount, no less, they all says, which goes to show you never can tell. Had I that much money, I'd be dining on lark's tongues and such, and be the size of a barrel in no time, not looking like a scarecrow like he was—and don't say a word about my girlish figger, Mrs. Gow, or I'll be that dismayed with you."

They both laughed, but saw Maggie did not.

"But you haven't seen a wink of them, I'll wager, my girl," Mrs. Gudge went on. "Well, neither have we."

"That's too bad," Mrs. Gow said with a hoot of laughter, "leastways fer us it is!"

"Aye, but it's good news for the lass. It's not on your plate anymore, to our way of thinking," Mrs. Gudge said, leaning forward as her chair creaked in protest. "We ain't seen so much as a grin out of you since that awful day, Mrs. Pushkin, and it's been over a week. We're here to say it's done. The poor cove's dead and buried, and there's an end to it."

"I wish I could be sure," Maggie said.

"But ain't it been a treat for business?" Mrs. Gudge said. "You been buying extra from us and lots more. Leastways, we hears lots of men been showing up at your back door."

This caused much laughter, amidst tea-scented snorts.

"The butcher, the baker—and the coal carter, for starters," Mrs. Gudge said. "And you're wise to send that one on his way! Were I poor Eleanor, I'd settle him, I would. Why, if Mr. Gudge ever raised a hand to me!"

"'E'd' 'ave it off at the wrist! Or *ye* would, I should say, Mrs. Gudge, yer that quick with yer gutting knife!" Mrs. Gow exclaimed, with a screech of laughter at the thought.

"Aye," Mrs. Gudge said, after wiping her eyes on her sleeve, "the butcher, the baker but not the runner no more, nor his silent noble partner, neither. So it's over, Luv, and done with, so give us a smile."

Maggie did. She was still smiling when she saw them out the door later, and found to her surprise she wasn't pretending anymore. Her expression was contagious. It made Flea happy when he saw her later, and he went away with a huge silly smile himself when she assured him she was just fine, the way she'd done every day since the dead man had landed at her door. But this time he really seemed to believe her. And why not? She began to believe herself. It was over. She kept smiling, and the girls wore big grins for the rest of the afternoon too. Even little Davie stopped frowning.

They laughed all through dinner, and after, when they sat in the front room together as usual. It was truly as if a storm had blown over them, and now they relaxed in the calm.

But when it grew late, the girls begged Maggie to read them yet another chapter, even though they knew they had to go to bed early to wake with first light. They were restless. With all their work in the shop, still they were young, and didn't get much exercise these wintry days. In spring and summer they had the parks to walk to together, and sometimes excursions on the river, or as a treat, a visit to a pleasure garden. But they'd only the shop and the street these days. It was too cold to venture farther. And too dangerous. They could never roam free in any weather. Not in London.

There were gangs of wild children and those who preyed on any sort of children everywhere. The sprawling Newgate Prison compound lay just to the west, and so did the sharps and barkers and shills who might lure the innocent inside and into crime there too. The docks with their dangers of thieving mudlarks, drunken sailors and human wharf rats lay to the south. People and places too terrible for Maggie to warn them about lay to the east and north, but that they knew. None of them were exactly innocents.

Annie had been with Maggie for six years now, but her only home before that had been the workhouse. Alice, a maid of all work, had been saved from a neighbor's beatings three years past. Davie had only been with them six months; they'd found him wandering, half out of his wits from fear. He didn't know where he'd come from or didn't want to remember. He couldn't read and couldn't learn, and still didn't speak much—and when he did he trembled.

Not good weather for her children, Maggie thought, and tried to remember spring.

"Well, that's the end of that chapter," she finally said, laying the book down, "and so to bed."

"Oh no, Missus!" Annie wailed. "How can we sleep not knowing what happens to the poor lady, what with a ghost in the castle and all?"

"It's only a story in a book, and well you know it," Maggie said. "Off to bed with you all. It's past time to sleep."

But she couldn't when she got to her own bed. There was only so long she could gloat over her new treasure. And only so long she could think of what she had to do tomorrow. She was still listening for noises a half hour after she'd turned down her lamp, and plumping her pillow and turning it to its cool side yet again, when she heard someone scratching at her door.

"Missus?" Alice whispered, when Maggie crept to the door, "there be someone outside, we seen him."

Maggie opened her door.

"Aye," Annie quavered, the two girls' shadows fantastical as they wavered in the candlelight, "by the side, in the alley, twixt the front and back."

A small shadow spoke from behind them. "I seen it," Davie whimpered.

"It's only a book, only a story, foolish to let it get you in such a bother," Maggie grumbled, trying to sound convinced of that as she flung her night robe on. She went downstairs with them and looked out their window.

But there was someone, or something, standing by the rubbish. She wouldn't have noticed, but she saw it shift as though from foot to foot. *So it was live,* she thought with relief, though if it were a few hours earlier she'd never have thought about it being dead at all. About five feet tall, and cold, from the look of things—if it were alive it would have to be. It was freezing out, and now a fitful moon wrought strange shadows on more newly fallen snow.

She could sit and wait until morning, like a mouse in a corner, waiting for the cat to walk away, Maggie thought. Or she could confront the thing and chase it. Or at least see what it was. It was like when you got a fish spine in your hand, she decided—you could pass agonizing moments easing it out, or you could yank it. It was sickening however you did it, but at least it was over faster that way. She didn't think of herself as courageous. But it was late, and she was frightened, and so were her children, and there was only one of it whatever it was, and there were four of them. And after all, no matter how hard she looked she could see it was only five feet tall.

She flung a coat on, picked up the bullseye lantern, lit and shuttered it before she could think better of it, and shushing the girls, stepped out the back door into the night. She placed her feet carefully so as not to make the frigid snow squeak, and crept up on the silent figure. When she got within two feet of it, she pulled back the shutter on the lantern, and ready to fling herself sideways if anything came hurtling towards her, and cried, "HOLD!"

The face that turned toward her in the sudden spear of light from her lantern was young, and even more terrified than she was.

"I've a pistol!" she lied, "don't move!"

The boy tensed, as if to run. But the mention of the pistol, and the blinding light in his eyes, froze him. He threw mittened hands in the air. "Don't shoot!" he yelled. "I ain't done nuffink, I swear!"

"Then what are you doing here?" Maggie demanded, and added, because power had gone to her head, "No lies, or I *will* shoot!"

"Spanish Will, he paid me half a crown, to keep watch, he did, you can ask him," the boy panted, trying to peer past the light to the figure who held it high. "Through the night, he said, to see who come in and went out of the fishmongers', that's all, I swear, don't shoot."

She didn't. She took him into the kitchen and gave him some hot tea instead. He said he was twelve, and looked ten. He lived by the river when he could find a place to sleep there, was dirty as a coal carter though whatever he was covered with didn't smell as good, and was frightened half to death. Whether it was of her, or what Spanish Will would do to him when he found he'd been discovered, Maggie couldn't say. She doubted the boy himself could.

"Well," she finally said, "I suppose it's not your fault. You can keep watch from in here as well as out there. It's too cold to breathe outside tonight, and I don't want two dead bodies laid at my door, do I? But you listen," she said shaking a finger at the starved-looking boy, "do you stir one step into my house or shop from where you sit tonight, you will regret it! And don't say one word to my girls, nor give so much as a look at our Davie. You sit by the fire, and don't stir a stump until I come down in the morning, or it will go hard with you, you hear? And Spanish Will won't hear a word of this *if* you mind your manners, understand?"

The boy shrank back in his chair, and nodded. She saw the girls into the room off the kitchen that they shared, and made sure they bolted their door. She took Davie to his cupboard and closed his door tight. She locked and bolted all the doors to the shop again, and then with one more threatening look to the boy, she left him near the hearth to keep his watch through the night.

As the boy drowsed in unaccustomed comfort in her kitchen, Maggie sat up in bed, thinking about how safe she really was now. She was protected by a starveling boy, her own three child servants, the knife by her bedside, the mallet on the table by her door, and the small knife she kept under her pillow. She'd have to buy a pistol, she decided, then turned down her lamp, and tried to go to sleep.

Chapter Seven

If he could learn to ignore the way his own Mama looked at him these days, Lucian thought, he would learn to tolerate the whispers in his wake at his club as well. He could deal with the way conversation stopped when he entered a room, pretend he didn't notice and ride that out too. He could, he supposed, even learn to ignore the way his usually plaint and complaint young mistress looked at him since the gossip had started, the way she jumped if he made a sudden movement, and grew round eyes if he merely raised his voice. But enough was enough.

The boy he spoke to at Bow Street raced ahead of him to show him into the small room Spanish Will used as an office, and bowed him inside. Lucian brushed past the boy and strode into the room. The boy kept staring at him. With good reason. He was dressed simply and casually, but even so, more magnificently than anyone the workers at Bow Street usually saw. His greatcoat was open to show he wore a fawn jacket, buckskins and top boots, the sum of which even the boy could tally in his head, and which made his eyes widen. But the runner didn't think the viscount looked well, even so. His face was white, grim. His eyes glittered and his mouth was held in a tight thin line. He looked like a man at the end of his rope, Will thought. Interesting.

Lucian tossed a sheet of paper on to Will's desk. "Have you seen this?" he asked tersely.

Will glanced at the caricature. It was a simple cartoon, not as elaborate as most. It showed a well-dressed gaunt man looking as much like Death as he did like a gentleman, lugging a sack of gold with the words "Last Will and Testament" printed on it. A trail of coins spilling from the sack lead to a comical-looking dead man, laying naked on the cobblestones, plump belly up. A fat fishwife was shrieking, and the balloon over her head read, *"Oh me! And I ordered flounder, I was sure!"* Some of the spilled coins tastefully covered the dead man's genitals.

"Oh, aye," Will said laconically, watching Lucian. "I saw it yesterday."

Lucian was taken aback. "You did?"

"It's my business to," Will shrugged, "and so? Your point, my lord?"

"My point," Lucian said through gritted teeth, "is that this was displayed in a printshop window in *St. James Street*, and it's vile slander!"

"It hasn't got your name on it," Will said mildly.

"It has that implication, and it's unconscionable!"

"Aye, likely it is," Will agreed calmly, "but that's how they make their money, my lord. The more scandalous they are the more they sell, the more they sell the more they eat. They hang them in the window and hope they catch on. It's all they can do, and they change them every day with the way the wind of gossip's blowing. The artist's a young one, not brilliant, like Gilray—Gawd, but I do miss that man! He had a way with a picture, he did. Remember his Napoleon? Little dwarf always hopping mad. Made you laugh just to see him.

"But the lad what's done this one?" Will tapped the picture, "he's not so good as Rowlandson, nor clever as Cruickshank neither, but he does what he can. You could wait 'til tomorrow, they'll probably be stale by then and out of the window. Or buy up the lot now and burn them. They're probably cheaper than firewood this winter, at that. It wasn't a big printing. I asked."

"I am aware of how they make their money," Lucian snarled. "The point is I want it stopped."

"Oh, I can't do that," Will said innocently. "Neither can you. my lord. It's a free press...unless you smear the King or the Prince too openly, of course."

"I know that! I mean I want the conjecture stopped, and the only way to do it is to find the murderer!"

"Oh, so you already bought up the lot?"

"I bought them, and told them that if they printed more they'd find themselves in court."

"But so would you, my lord, think on. Be sure, they will."

Lucian put two long hands on Will's desk, and from the way they flexed, it was clear he'd have preferred to put them around the runner's neck. He put his weight on them and leaned forward, glaring. "Look. Stop 'my lording' me to death. Stop being amusing. Stop playing with me. Find the murderer. That's what I'm here to say. I'll up the reward another one hundred pounds, do you hear? That's right, *one hundred* more. A fortune for most runners, although I suppose, not you. It doesn't matter. Just find the murderer."

"Hmm," Will hummed, not blinking in the furious face of the man whose own face almost touched his now. "Wouldn't I love to, though? Another hundred, plus the extra fifty your brother posted yesterday does make a tidy sum, my lord."

Lucian blinked. He straightened and stood back. His eyes went flat. Will had seen men look like that when they heard their own sentence of death pronounced. The viscount had obviously been dealt a stunning blow. Anguish shadowed that thin face, the man looked crushed... No, Will thought, if you put this man on a rack for a week, he'd only looked rumpled. But the pain was there now, in the back of those blinded gray eyes.

"My brother?" Lucian murmured. "But...I told him I'd taken care of it..."

"So you did, or so he said. But he was worried. Very worried."

"About me?" Lucian asked softly.

"About all of this," Will said with a shrug, "or so I gathered. Very devoted to your uncle, he was. And though he didn't say it, he knows you weren't. I think that's all it was, but then you know him better than I do."

"I don't," Lucian said, almost to himself. "The truth is, I do not. Difference in ages, difference in upbringings... But that's neither here nor there," he said more briskly. "It's getting out of proportion now. A tragedy, certainly. But now it's on its way to becoming a scandal. The thing is, Mr. Corby, I want to do all I can to get this resolved. Uncle's dead, killed in an unpleasant, unforeseen fashion. No one knows why, we don't even know why he was found dead where he was. Some think they might have a guess," he said with an ugly twist to his mouth, as though he'd bit on something even more bitter than his words, "but we both know otherwise." He paused and added, "or at least, *I* know otherwise."

He ran a hand through his neatly brushed hair, causing it to ripple and fall out of its precise style, and he didn't seem to notice or care. His voice held baffled pain, a rare thing for him, and it was a mark of the runner's knowledge of men that he knew it.

"I didn't do it, or know it was done," Lucian said. "I must discover who did. It's not just my reputation—I suppose it is. But I need an answer. Uncle behaved erratically and paid for his carelessness with his life. When a man acts so out of character there must be a reason, but for the life of me I can't figure it out."

"Neither can I—yet, that is to say," Will said. "From the look of things right now we may never find who done for him. But you're right. At least, we should be able to know why. Take a chair, if you will, my lord. There's some things we should talk about."

Lucian sat, and waited, watching as the runner tapped his pen against the desk a few times. A smooth, cruel face, Lucian thought, that gave nothing away. A very clever man, to be sure. The runner treated him with utmost civility, Lucian realized, and yet at the same time with no respect at all. He might well be as good as he said he was.

Spanish Will turned unreadable eyes on his visitor. "Your brother mentioned something about a bride gift your uncle might have been after buying at a bargain, in that part of town. That's a lively possibility."

"At a fish store?" Lucian said on a bitter laugh. "Hardly. Uncle was not the sort to buy his lady love oysters. I doubt he even knew what they're supposedly good for."

Will smiled more warmly than the jest deserved. It was a weak attempt at a joke, but he appreciated it for what it was. The nobleman was obviously, in his chilly way, trying to be congenial. Better and better.

"Well, he might not have been killed right there, as Mrs. Pushkin noted; he may have already been dead when he got there," Will said as affably. "He may have stumbled there, or been dropped when his murderer took alarm. But the thing of it is, my lord, that he might have been killed on the way there."

"On the way to a *fish shop*?"

"Ah well, I knew a fellow who opened an oyster for his lady and pretended to find a fine pearl necklace for her there," Will said. "Perhaps that was what he was after doing. Looking for something amusing to tickle her fancy."

"Uncle? No. He was not a fanciful man."

"Love makes a man do strange things, they say," Will mused.

Lucian frowned. "So my brother supposed. But I'm not my brother. I tell you my uncle was not in love. He didn't know the meaning of the word anymore than I do. He was a cold selfish man, who wanted a child and so he needed a wife, and he never pretended otherwise, not to us, or to her, and certainly not to himself."

"Can you be sure?"

"I was not privy to their private moments, of course. But I'd be shocked if it were otherwise."

Will hummed tunelessly for a moment before he spoke again, and when he did he sounded quizzical. "The baron was middle-aged, not handsome, nor did he cut a fine figure, I saw that for myself. He had no wit or charm, you say. Yet he got a young woman of good birth to agree to marry him. You're saying she was after his fortune?"

"She is of good birth but no funds, that's true. As for the rest—that's what I want you to discover."

"Ah. So you think the Honorable Louisa had reason? But surely not means?"

"No. But at the funeral she did suddenly have an ardent admirer we'd never seen before."

"Oh, Lieutenant Pascal?" Will asked, pleased at the almost imperceptible start he surprised from Lucian. "He's an admirer of hers, all right. So much so that he was otherwise occupied the night your uncle died. He was drowning his sorrows over her coming marriage, in fact. So he couldn't have bashed your uncle even if he wanted to, being drunk as a wheelbarrow all night. There are five fellow officers who'll swear to it. They had to put him to bed at dawn because he couldn't even fall down on his own by then. Drunk as a goat, and so say all."

"You knew about him?" Lucian asked in astonishment.

"I'm very good at my job, my lord. I never lied about that," Will said. "Now, if there's nothing else?"

Lucian frowned, but shook his head. "No, nothing, right now."

"Ah, but I've something else," Will said, looking thoughtfully at his visitor. "My lord, I've a proposition for you. I always work alone. I let you accompany me that first time because, to tell the truth…"

"The *truth*?" Lucian muttered with a hint of his usual mockery, "how refreshing."

"…that day I was interested in watching you as much as the others I talked to," Will went on blandly. "But now, and in this case…let me put it to you straightly. Your uncle moved in circles I can't. Bow Street doesn't appeal to the upper classes, you see. They think us not much better than thieves." Will was pleased to see betraying color bloom on those bony cheekbones as he continued. "So, I was thinking the ginger widow was more right than she knew. Working together sometimes might work to both our advantages. Meaning which, if you'd come along with me on some of my inquiries amongst your set, they'd be less likely to try to throw me into the gutter." He laughed, but his eyes didn't.

"Does that mean you don't suspect me anymore?" Lucian asked wryly.

"Oh no. I never stop suspecting anyone until I've got a confessed culprit with his head in the noose, and even then I wonder. But I will say I suspect you less, if that makes you happier."

"Infinitely," Lucian drawled, and discovered that it did seem that he felt better. At least something was going to be done.

"Well, then, so when I need you, I'll be sending for you, and thank you," Will said, rising to his feet.

"Where are you going now?"

"Now?" Will laughed. "So eager, are you? Well, I'm that sorry to disappoint you, my lord, but I don't need you now. I'm off to the fishmongers' again, and I don't think you want to go there."

"Why? Do you have any more evidence? Do you think she had some hand in it now?"

"Maybe. At least, there are some things I found out, and some things I don't understand, and so I have to speak with Mrs. Pushkin again. But I don't expect a man of your kidney to want to go to such a place, so adieu, my lord, for now."

But Lucian didn't move. His face became cold as it had been when he'd first entered the room. "Any fool with a title could help you gain entrée to someone's house," he said stiffly. "I would hope you wished for my reasoning abilities as well as my title, Mr. Corby."

"Aye, well, I do, of course, I do," Will said with a show of surprise. "If you want to come along with me now, I'd be honored, of course. It would be much easier today, at that, since it's cold enough to freeze a man's toes in his boots, and since the villains all know who you are by now they wouldn't be expecting you to walk with me. You do have your carriage at the curb?"

"Indeed," Lucian said, giving him a sidewise glance as they went to the door together. The runner looked monstrously pleased with himself. If he didn't know better, Lucian thought uneasily, he'd believe he'd been as neatly caught and landed as any fish for sale in the shop they were going to visit now. And not just because he had a warm coach at his disposal today.

*

This time Mrs. Pushkin received them in her front parlor, without making them wait in the cold. She had her little Davie bow them in and heap up the fire in the hearth, and after only a little wait, she joined them. Her hair was neatly bound, she wore an elegant blue gown, high at the neck and long at the wrist. She was calm and composed, and if they hadn't been across the hall from a fish shop filled with her customers, Lucian would have believed her to be any society hostess he knew. Any severely freckled haughty and hostile hostess, he corrected himself as she gave them a scant curtsey and motioned for them to be seated.

"To what do I owe this honor?" she asked, looking from one of them to the other.

"A few questions," Spanish Will said, taking out his notebook.

"I see. And is the Viscount Maldon now a runner too?"

"He is helping me with inquiries," Will said.

"Oh really?" she flashed, looking daggers at Lucian. "Things get boring down at Bethlehem Hospital, my lord? The inmates of Bedlam not up to snuff today, I suppose? No bear-baiting at the moment, nor any cockfights? And I suppose it's too cold to go down to Billingsgate and hope for some of the *other* fishwives there to do battle with each other, is it? The runner's doing his job. But you? I don't think this is amusing. Please go find your entertainment elsewhere!"

"I am not amused," Lucian retorted. "You perhaps forget that it was *my* uncle on *your* doorstep, and so whatever the runner does is of utmost interest to me."

"The runner is asking the Viscount Maldon to let him handle this," Will told Lucian sternly. "Look you, Mrs. Pushkin," he said abruptly, "it's a cold trail in more ways than one. The viscount is going to help me with inquiries, that's truth. There are some places

I can't go he can, so we've come to terms. He wanted to come along to other interviews as well. It seemed only fair. That's all it is, my word on it."

"So you no longer think he had anything to do with it?" Maggie asked incredulously.

"Never said that," Will said, "but I got to thinking about what you said last time. You were right. We three can do more together than alone. Now, at least, we have two cooperating."

"But you don't need my cooperation?" Maggie said angrily.

"Who said not?" Will asked in amazement.

"I do!" she spat, "and why should you, when you have me watched day and night!"

"Ha. The lad's doing more sleeping than watching these days," Will said disparagingly. "The one I employed to watch his lordship does a much better job."

Both Maggie and Lucian said, *"What?"* at once.

"I set a boy to watch the shop," Will told Lucian, "and what does she do but have him in for tea? *And* let him sleep by her kitchen fire like a tabby cat. You think he wouldn't tell me?" he asked Maggie. "My nose told me before he did. He smells like a rose now—she even sent him to the baths—well, who could blame her? He reeked. And tea gave way to bread and butter, and soon she's got him eating better than he has in his life. She could be murdering men every day and slicing them up by night and he wouldn't want to say, he thinks she's such a treat. Your lad freezes his skinny rump off in the alley, my lord, do you but sneeze and he'll tell me of it. I like uncomfortable servants much better, Mrs. Pushkin, 'deed I do."

They continued to stare. Will looked affronted. "Well," he said, "what sort of a runner would I be if I believed you straight off?"

"A boy watching my house?" Lucian muttered. "So much for your trust, Mr. Corby."

"I don't trust anyone," Will said simply, "that's why I'm still here. It's also why I'm such a good runner. But I do listen. That's why I'm here right now. It's in your own best interests to work with me, Mrs. Pushkin. The viscount can get me into some places, you can serve me in others. What do they say in the neighborhood? Who remembers seeing the baron that night?"

Maggie looked down at her reddened hands. "I haven't heard—well, but I haven't gone out and asked either. I think I was waiting for it all to go away. I see your point, Mr. Corby. I'll ask 'round tomorrow, I promise." She raised her head. "But you could have asked me that any time. That's not why you're here now, is it?"

"No, it isn't," he admitted. "*I* have been asking around. I heard something, then the viscount's brother suggested a thing, and I admit, it's been working at me. See, he suggested the baron was after buying his fiancée a bride present that night, and being a frugal sort, maybe he came down here to buy it cheaply, and that's how he brought himself troubles."

Maggie thought about it. "It makes sense," she said, "and so you want me to ask about that?"

"Absolutely," Will said. "But I've done that too. What I want to know right now, is if he came here that night to buy something?"

"*Here?*" Maggie squeaked. "Are you mad? The shop closes at dark, and what would he buy off me anyway? A hake? A cod's head?"

Will flipped open his notebook. "An antique silver dresser set," he read, "some French porcelain, a little China jade statue? A cloisonné urn, a crystal dagger, a snuffbox with a musical mechanism? Oh, there's much more he could have bought from you, Mrs. P., considering you bought all those things and more off your late husband's relatives. And what would a fishmonger be doing with such if not selling it off again? And so?"

Lucian's eyes widened almost as much as Maggie's did.

"Come on, Mrs. P.," Spanish Will said gently as Maggie sat horrified. "If you sold him aught, and then didn't tell for fear I'd find out and think you tried to take it back with interest, I can understand. But I've got to know. You do see that? And don't be vexed with your late husband's kin. They saw no harm in telling me. They're that proud of Bernard's widow has such taste, you see. They think you're collecting their treasures. But money's money. And what else would a fishmonger be doing with such fine and rare things?"

Lucian watched as the fishwife's face grew pale, and then flushed, and her little chapped hands curled into fists in her lap. He wondered if she'd fly at the runner, and braced himself so he could stop her. But she surprised him. She stood in one smooth movement, her hands remaining fisted at her sides.

"Come with me," she said in a cold tight voice.

Lucian hesitated, but Will followed her without a word. So then he did too. Stiff-backed, head high, she led them out of the room, and then up the stair in silence. She opened the first door off the hall on the second floor, and threw it wide.

"See for yourself," she said.

They stared. Her salon downstairs was a pleasant room. This one was not. It was magnificent. The dimmed late afternoon light could not diminish its grandeur. The walls were soft rose, picked out with green and gold, in the best Adam's colors. They only set off the wonders within. Outfitted in the latest style, the salon had all the fashionable Egyptian touches a modern room required, but much more. The furniture was graceful, original, and in some cases, obviously priceless.

There was a beautiful golden French bombe chest glowing in one corner, a small gem of a Jacobean table by a window, a graceful inlaid tea table, a gilded chaise-lounge covered in fine rose-embroidered silk near the hearth, and two intricately carved high-backed chairs near it that surely came from some Moroccan palace. Chinese silks were swagged over the long windows, and a fine red Turkey carpet lay on the gleaming wooden floors.

And everywhere, there were small and wondrous objects d'art. Statues, figurines, vases and bowls, all tastefully arranged so that the eye was as surprised to find them as it was enchanted by their discovery. It was the room of a connoisseur, of a collector, of a lady. The two men were speechless.

Will was the first to recover. "Well, you've dazzled me, Mrs. P.," he said, "and shamed me too, at that."

"It is not what one expects in a fishmong...*seller's* home," Lucian said.

"Indeed?" Maggie said icily, "are you sure? How can you be? After all, how many *fishmong—seller's* parlors have you been in, my lord?"

They were silenced, thinking about what she'd said. But so was Maggie. She blinked, coughed, but then it was too much for her and the cough turned into the giggle she couldn't suppress anymore. And then, all of them began to laugh.

"My apologies, Ma'am," Lucian said, when he was able.

"Aye, mine too," Will said.

"I never thought," Lucian added. "Doubtless Mrs. Gow and Mrs. Gudge have the very same in their front parlors." But that was too much for even him, and soon he, Maggie and Spanish Will were laughing together.

"Now," Maggie said, when she subsided, "do come in and please be seated. I can't offer tea, as my servants are downstairs serving up fish to my customers. But I have some very special brandy my late husband's relatives are also pleased to keep me supplied with. And yes, Mr. Corby, I do enjoy fine wines as well. And no," she added as the men seated themselves, "I do not resell them, or any of my treasures."

"So I see," Will said, "and thank you, brandy would be fine on such a day. This is one thing my lad never told me about," he commented as his eyes continued to make an inventory of the room.

"Don't blame him," Maggie said, as she poured, "he didn't know. This is my room. The children's is downstairs. I don't even let them clean here. The girls are careful, but they are only girls. I've been a widow six years, and in that time I've made this room my haven, mine alone, my escape from the shop and the street, and the world, I suppose."

Lucian stood. "Then we won't presume," he said.

"But it's my job to presume, my lord," Will said smoothly. "A runner can't afford to be such a grand gentleman, and if you want to help me you must remember that."

"Oh. But don't worry," Maggie said sweetly, as she handed them their brandy, "it's no presumption. After all, *I* asked you to stay. Now. How may I help you, gentlemen?"

She seated herself and looked at them expectantly. Her room was a fine setting, and now, at last, she realized, it had all the right accessories. The two gentlemen, one so dark and handsome, the other so impeccable and imperious, looked exactly right in it. That wasn't strictly true, she supposed. Spanish Will was about as far from a gentleman as a man could be. But he looked very gentlemanly, at least, and the Viscount Maldon was definitely top of the trees. She got a queer sense of pleasure seeing them there— when she could forget why there were there.

"Well," Will said, "it's as I said. Only now I've had to cross off one more promising lead, haven't I? I concede the baron wasn't on his way here to buy a bride gift from you. But from one of your husband's relatives, maybe?"

She shook her head. "I doubt it. They're very careful who they sell to. They don't deal with strangers."

"Then I suppose you'll ask around here, my lord will ask around there, and I'll do what I can," Will sighed. "I'll have to try talking to the baron's fiancée again."

Lucian looked up from contemplation of the excellent brandy. "You spoke to her already?" he asked in surprise.

"For all the good it did," Will admitted. "I wanted to know more about her soldier friend, more about all her doings, in fact. But she was cold enough to strike a match on. Maybe you can come along next time to help warm her up."

"Not I," Lucian said. "She's taken a distaste to me; I can't imagine why."

"Maybe she heard about how glad you were to have her in the family," Will murmured.

Lucian sipped his brandy, pretending not to have heard the comment.

"Is she normally reserved? I mean to say, with gentlemen?" Maggie asked.

"I can't say," Lucian drawled, "I never passed much time with her, before or after she became my uncle's bride to be. I saw her with him, of course. She stood at his side when he announced their engagement. Fortunately, for the sake of everyone's dinners that night, they did not cuddle, in the manner of those newly enamored, if that's what you're getting at."

"Well, no wonder she's cold with you," Maggie declared. "I can hear what you think of her in your voice when you talk about her."

"Grant me a bit more tact than that," Lucian said. "I am positively pleasant when we meet."

"I'm sure," Maggie said with a grimace.

"And I'm just a runner, so I suspect she doesn't look at me as an equal," Will said mildly, "which is right, as I'm not, after all."

"What kind of a woman is she, in all?" Maggie asked.

Will looked at Lucian, who shrugged. "She's been on the town any number of years, she's almost as old as I am, in fact. Good family, but no money there. Not pretty, not ugly, not a great conversationalist, but neither is she foolish when she does speak. She's thoughtful, or at least so she looks much of the time. I know why Uncle offered for her, but I'm surprised he even noticed her."

"Don't look so appalled," he told Maggie with a small smile, "I've never been actually cruel to her, at least not to her face. She has my pity rather than my scorn, but it was jarring to think of her marrying my uncle. I hadn't thought of it before but I suppose if she'd been young, silly and pretty, I'd have accepted it more easily. That is, admittedly, odd. But there it is. I respected her and one feels let down when someone one respects does something degrading, or desperate."

"There's no way either of you can talk to her," Maggie said with conviction. "If my fiancé was killed, and I had to talk to you two, especially feeling as you do—and certainly looking as you do—I wouldn't have two words to say to you either!"

"'Looking as we do'?" Lucian asked with interest, one brow raised, as Will put his head to the side.

Maggie felt her color betraying her. But she'd been admiring the sight of them in her special room, idly reflecting on the novelty of it, beginning to notice more than their fine feathers. The longer they stayed in her lovely salon, the less they fit in, because they dominated it. She almost felt the power emanating from the pair of them. Spanish Will, secret, dark and smooth; the viscount, lean, suave, vibrating with quick and supple strength... She'd been struck by the intensity of the masculine magnetism they both projected, and had spoken without thinking. And was paying for it now.

Damn the blushes, she thought, and said, feebly even to her own ears, "I mean, you're frightening. Well, you're both large, aren't you? And broad shouldered, and...Mr. Corby looks as though he'd enjoy pouncing on someone. And my lord looks as though he wouldn't care if he did!"

"*Pouncing*, eh?" Will asked, looking at her with renewed interest, his dark eyes roving over her. He wore a wicked grin that made Maggie wonder if he could read minds. The viscount's cool gaze now lingered on her too.

Maggie squirmed. She felt naked and hot. She strove for control. They were only men, after all. And it was her house. "I think she'd speak with a woman, though," she said quickly—and the more she thought about what she'd only said to save herself embarrassment, the more sense it made to her.

"I mean, women can speak more freely to each other," she went on eagerly, thinking out loud. "*I* wouldn't want to confide in a runner. Who'd want to confide in someone who was looking to find a neck to stretch? And you, my lord, well, the truth is that if she has known you for a long time, and you're still not friends, why should she imagine you have anything but disinterest—or worse—for her?

"No, you need to find a female to talk to her…*Me!*" she said in a burst of inspiration. "Yes! That would do it!"

"You? But you don't know her, my dear," Lucian said gently.

"Don't try to spare my feelings," she snapped. "I know exactly who I am, my lord. But the thing is—she don't! See? Listen," she said urgently. "I can speak as well as any lady if I wish to, for my mother was a lady's maid. And I get on well with people. I do, ask anyone. If I were to dress in style—and I can, I assure you—and visit with her… If I were to pay a sympathy call! Yes. Why, I'll wager I can find out more in a half hour than either of you in a day!"

Lucian's eyes narrowed. He was intrigued. Gentlemen were mad for wagers, she knew, and couldn't resist them anymore than a dog could pass up a bouncing ball.

"A sympathy call," Will said, considering the notion too, "but why? How would you know her?"

"She's lost her fiancé, a man much older than she is," Maggie invented quickly, "and I have a late husband—who was much older than me!"

"A late husband," Lucian said thoughtfully, "who knew Uncle…? No. Who *corresponded* with my uncle. Yes, better. That might do. Uncle had many far-flung correspondents. He was always sending off letters to journals, trying to correct them. But about what? Uncle lived for his books. Biology, botany…"

"Marine biology," Will said, grinning. "One thing the late Mr. P. knew, it was fish."

"Yes!" Maggie said excitedly. "I can say that. I can talk about that for hours. But I won't," she said quickly, "I'll only use my late husband's letters to her fiancé as an excuse, and then get around to discussing the crime. I can do it. I can dress like a lady, and act like one too. Oh, let me try!"

She sat on the edge of her seat, looking at them eagerly. The runner might be in it because it was his job, the viscount because it was his uncle, but she had pressing reasons of her own. It could free her of the runner's suspicions forever. It would be so much better than trawling around the neighborhood, trying to scoop up bits of leftover gossip. And it was a way into a new world, if only for a day.

Lucian looked at the runner. The runner was looking at Maggie thoughtfully, but he turned and caught Lucian's eye. The two men looked at each other. Slowly, they both began to nod.

Chapter Eight

"*This* way please, Madame," the butler said.

Maggie Pushkin picked up her skirt in one hand, clutched her reticule with the other, and followed him from the narrow hallway into the lion's den. *Lioness's den,* she corrected herself. It was a small townhouse, only adequately furnished, in a neighborhood just this side of respectable, but still she was awed. It was a real lady's home. The first she'd ever visited. She refused to tremble. She was a proper lady come to visit another, she told herself.

She looked the part. Even the viscount had said so, his eyes running down her gown and then up again as he circled her, quizzing glass to his eye, assessing her in a way that would have earned him a slap, nobleman or not, if things had been different. But they weren't.

He came to inspect her before she went to visit Lady Louisa at her elderly aunt's home. Maggie would pay her call alone, but the runner and the viscount had to approve her before they'd let her go. Spanish Will looked at her, and looked pleased, but his was only a man's opinion. The viscount's would be society's. It rankled. But she badly wanted to go.

"Very good," the viscount had finally said, "very, very good."

She'd beamed. And then quickly dropped her smile, lifted her head and inclined it, sketching a tiny bow. Ladies didn't beam at compliments. He'd smiled, as pleased with that as anything else about her today, and there was a lot to be pleased about in her humble opinion, she'd thought smugly.

Her gown was made of the finest wool, expensive as the pelt of some mythical beast, and got for a song on Petticoat Lane. It was black, as befitted a mourning call, and was fit to her frame by a master's hand, because if Mrs. Blum in Jewry Court didn't sew like an angel, no one did. A charming close-fitted little black bonnet covered most of her violently colored hair; there was no other way to make it look fashionable. Powder concealed most of her freckles, and black lace gloves made her work-worn hands look like they'd never known anything but rose water. Covered, perfumed and on her guard. "Mrs. Preston" rather than Mrs. Pushkin, so no one would ever guess her ruse. But whatever her name, a gentlewoman, if not born, then made. Carefully made.

"Mrs. Preston?" the tall young woman she'd called on asked, rising from her chair as Maggie was shown into the drawing room.

"My dear lady," Maggie trilled, "please accept my sincerest sympathies. I hope this is not an intrusion? I thought to write a note, I thought to write a letter, but in the end nothing would do but I come call on you in person. My poor late husband, Bernard, would have wanted it so."

The ladies curtsied to each other, and Louisa motioned Maggie to a chair. She was also dressed in black, but it didn't suit her. She was plain and sad, Maggie thought, no amount of style could lift her looks out of the ordinary, and mourning only made her look duller. But she had a wistful smile, and her eyes needed laughter. I could like her, Maggie thought.

"Thank you," Louisa said, as she sat again. "So kind of you to come. I'm afraid my dear Aunt is in bed with a chill; nothing serious, but I know she'd have wanted to meet you too. Your note said your late husband wrote to the baron about fish and marine animals? I'm sorry to admit I knew nothing about any of his correspondents, or much at all about his hobbies."

"But that makes two of us," Maggie said eagerly, "for I never understood dear Bernard's passion for fish, myself." *That*, she thought gloomily, was the biggest lie of all, so if she got through it without a stammer, the rest would be easy. Because Bernard's greatest passion had been money, everyone knew it, and fish meant only that to him.

"He wrote to the baron so often," Maggie went on, "and talked about him so much, that when I read of the baron's untimely death I knew I couldn't rest until I came to see you and offer my sympathies, and his. I expect you think that's foolish of me, since

Bernard's been dead these seven years. But I wouldn't have felt right otherwise."

"You must have been very devoted to him," Louisa said softly.

Maggie lowered her gaze. *I felt like dancing when I didn't feel so guilty about feeling so happy after he was gone,* she thought, and made herself sigh. "But that's past," she said, looking up into Louisa's sad and sympathetic eyes, "and now I've my own life to live, and that is what I've come to tell you! You see, I too was left alone when I least expected it, at an age when I scarcely knew how to cope alone, and yet I've thrived. You're still young, your life lies ahead of you—"

Louisa turned her head away as though she'd been slapped. Maggie's heart started beating faster, her mouth went dry. She could almost see Spanish Will and Maldon frowning. Or worse, laughing. She couldn't fail, at least not so soon! She went on quickly. "I know that seems harsh, and premature, or unfeeling, but I didn't mean it so. The reverse is true. Oh my dear lady, don't bury your heart with him, because you've life left over and he wouldn't want you to!"

"My dear Mrs. Preston..." Louisa said, and stopped, looking anguished.

"Maybe I ought to have come later, when my words wouldn't sound so heartless and cruel," Maggie said desperately, "but maybe that's why I came so soon, to prevent you from suffering needlessly. I had no children. We're of an age, I think, or as near as makes no difference, and I thought what I have learned about loss could be useful to you. I meant no disrespect, I didn't mean to belittle your grief, please understand I only meant the best."

"I do," Louisa said in a stifled voice, rising to her feet, and making Maggie leap to hers. "That's what makes it so difficult. Our cases are not the same, Mrs. Preston. You were married, you were obviously in love. I—I let my head decide my future; my heart was not involved in any way. It's one thing to listen to his family's sympathies," she said almost to herself as she paced, sounding goaded and as desperate as Maggie felt, "because they're either insincere or downright relieved. My own aunt genuinely mourns.

But that's because now I must remain here with her after all, and her means are as limited as my own. But my dear Mrs. Preston, you're the only one who seems to genuinely care, and that I can't bear."

She swung around to face Maggie. "I didn't love the baron, indeed, I didn't look to marry him. My relatives arranged the whole. I was tired of being unnecessary. The baron needed me—or rather, what I could offer him. And there's an end to it. In truth, you were the luckier, though you grieved more. Because all I've lost is my self-respect, because I cannot grieve. Do you see?"

"Oh," Maggie said, and sat, because she wasn't sure her legs could hold her. She took a deep breath. She wasn't a gambler, but she knew she had to dare all or loose all, and now. "My lady," she said simply, "I didn't marry for love either. I married for safety, or so my parents believed when they married me off. I had that. And nothing else. And that," she said, feeling her way and finding it easier as she got closer to the truth, "is part of what I came to tell you, truly.

"Bernard had his passions and they didn't include me," she said in all honesty. "He was more than twice my age, but that wasn't why. He had his fish, I had his name—and there was the beginning and end of it. It's how it would have been no matter what age he was. He died suddenly and left me well off. Better, in fact, than I'd ever been. But the guilt was terrible. So, you see, I do understand more than you know."

Louisa looked at her, and slowly, smiled. "Mrs. Preston," she said, "would you care for some tea?"

Louisa poured from a transparent china teapot Maggie coveted, but not half so much as she envied the smooth graceful white hands that served it. They chatted all through tea, and though Maggie had to watch her tongue and remember her role, she hadn't had such a good time in years. Louisa was charming and friendly, and seemed even lonelier than she was. That astonished Maggie.

After all, Maggie's friends from her youth were now matrons who could only talk babies and children and what to put on the table for their husbands of a night. Mrs. Gow and Mrs. Gudge were dears, but they couldn't discuss novels, not even the trifling romantic kind it turned out both she and Louisa loved. Roger Bell and Flea were friends, but Roger would only discuss gossip and fashion, and Flea couldn't talk about anything. Talking to her customers and her servants was pleasant, but it had been years since Maggie had a heart to heart with another woman as an equal. She liked Louisa, and had to keep reminding herself that she was here for more than that. But it was hard to bring death into their pleasant conversation.

She was trying to get around to it when the butler came into the room again. If her time was already up, Maggie thought unhappily, putting down her cup, she'd have to come back. She'd like that. But she'd bet Spanish Will and Maldon would sneer.

"Lieutenant Pascal has come to call, my lady," the butler said.

"Show him in," Louisa said on a sigh. A moment later, a dashing soldier entered the room on a gust of bracing air, looking jaunty and bright in his uniform, even in the cold winter light.

Louisa gave him her hand. He bowed low over it, and slid a glance at Maggie.

"Mrs. Preston," Louisa said, "here is my cousin Lieutenant Pascal. Jonathan, this is my friend, Margaret Preston."

"Cousin by marriage," the dragoon said, bending over Maggie's gloved hand. "Charmed. I came to ask if you'd like my company," he told Louisa, "but I see you're already occupied."

"Quite," Louisa said.

"Well, then," he said, fidgeting, "I suppose I'll be off, then?" He looked pointedly at the tray of tea and cakes.

"Mrs. Preston and I haven't seen each other for ages, Jonathan, I do hope you understand," Louisa said without regret.

"Well, then," he said, gazing at Louisa hungrily, and Maggie would swear it wasn't because of the cakes, "what do you think of a ride through the park later today then? I can hire a closed carriage. It's cold, but brisk, and at least it's stopped snowing."

"I think not," Louisa said.

"I see," he said in a suffocated voice. "And yesterday you had the headache, and the day before, an appointment with your dressmaker, and the day before that, with some childhood friend. I'm never going to be forgiven, am I?"

Maggie was fascinated. It was as though he'd forgotten she was there.

"Good afternoon, Jonathan," Louisa said.

He bowed. "I'll be back, Louisa," he said, never taking his eyes from her, "again and again. Before I'm off—perhaps for good. The war is still on, and I'm still a soldier, you know."

"I know," she said, "but I'm not responsible for that, am I, Jonathan?"

"More than you believe, obviously," he muttered, then bowed and left.

Maggie didn't know what to say. But it was too good an opportunity to pass up. "He wishes to be more than your cousin?" she dared ask, because the worst that could happen would be that she'd be ignored. But she was owed an explanation and she had the feeling Louisa needed someone to talk to.

She did.

*

"And so," Maggie said breathlessly, seconds after she got back in the carriage again, "the thing is, he courted her for years and years, but never actually asked the question. She waited for him. Lord knows what he was waiting for."

"Someone with more money, probably," Will said.

"Or more looks," Lucian commented from the other side of the coach. "Military men fancy dashing wives and mistresses."

"Anyway," Maggie said excitedly, "Lieutenant Pascal was furious when she got engaged to the baron, and he sent her stacks of letters protesting it. She showed me. He was wounded and sent

126

home, but still couldn't get her to change her mind. And now the baron's dead, he's all over her again—I mean, he'd like to be."

"But she rejects him?" Lucian asked.

"Absolutely. It seems once she made up her mind not to wait anymore she decided to never change it again. 'But he seems to adore you,' says I. 'Indeed,' she says, 'the more so since he knows I will be observing a year of mourning for the baron, and so wouldn't be able to marry him for yet another year.'"

The men exchanged smiles in the dim coach. Maggie's voice had changed for each part of her narration, sounding like a fine lady for Louisa, becoming gruff and coarser for her part.

"He said he bought his colors and went to war because he didn't have a fortune and wanted to establish himself for her sake," Maggie went on, "but she says now she sees he could have saved himself the money and set up with her right away. It costs a near fortune to buy yourself into a good regiment, she says, and he chose the best. She didn't want to marry and follow the drum, living on the edges of battlefields and dragging over the face of Europe with him. But she'd have done it, back then. He kept saying he didn't want to put her through such, but when she turned thirty, she realized he never meant to marry her at all, and decided she had to see to her own future."

"Thirty has that effect on women," Will commented.

"Fifty, obviously, on men," Lucian said, "at least, to judge from my uncle. And what does she say about my uncle's death? Did she pretend to heartbreak?"

"Not at all. She just said it was a bizarre thing to happen. But then she thought, and said that since she didn't know him that well, really, she doesn't know if it was bizarre or not."

"Think the dragoon did for your uncle?" Will asked Lucian.

"Possible," Lucian said.

"Well, I think he's paltry, and wouldn't have the courage," Maggie declared.

"He may not have treated your new friend fairly," Lucian told Maggie with amusement, "but he *is* a soldier in a crack regiment, not just a decoration at the palace gates, so he's used to dealing death."

"And if he's paltry," Will said, "remember, whoever coshed the baron could have come up from behind him with a club. It don't take courage for that, just determination, and enough strength to carry him off after."

The coach was silent a moment, except for the usual sounds of creaking leather and the steady distant hoof beats on the cobbles below. The viscount sat opposite Maggie, the runner, beside her. Her nostrils fluttered, picking up unaccustomed rich masculine scents of shaving soap, starched linen, leather, boot polish, and sandalwood. Rich men's scents. Or at least, she thought, those of men who didn't haul fish or push carts. The fainter aroma of her own rose perfume that she'd splurged on for this visit wasn't half as exciting.

They'd hired a carriage because they didn't want anyone seeing the viscount's crest on the door of anything she drove up in. The one Maldon had rented was warm and cushioned and well-sprung, the finest she'd ever been in. She was dressed in style, and surrounded by two powerful men. She felt like a real lady. But these two men had brought her here, waited for her to come out, and now they were waiting for her to go on. She knew what they wanted to hear.

"It wasn't Louisa," she said with decision, "it couldn't be. She wanted to marry him, Lord help her. I told her she was lucky to have escaped that."

"You two *did* get on, didn't you?" Lucian commented.

"Well, we'd much in common, after all," she said. "I was married off to Bernard for my own good, and she was going to marry your uncle for her good. Be sure, I told her not much good would have come from it. All he wanted was an heir, and if she thought children would have made her happy even if he didn't, what if they hadn't been blessed, eh? An empty cradle would have made her life even more of a misery, even if it wasn't her fault, for there's no man born who'd admit it was his fault, is there?"

The two men were silent. She'd showed them more of her own life than she'd meant to do. She flushed, glad it was too dim for them to see.

"Your pardon," she said, too gaily. "See? I'm dressed like a lady but talking like a fishwife after all. Ladies don't discuss such things, at least not with the gentlemen, do they? But it's almost all fishwives do talk about—their fertility. Oh no—now I've done it. I doubt ladies are even allowed to say the word, are they?" She laughed hollowly. Well, but it was what she was, and if she'd forgotten, her unruly tongue had reminded them, hadn't it?

"Any rate, she wanted to marry him. But the lieutenant didn't want her to, so that's where I'd go next were I you," she told Will. "He's still trying to get on her good side, but she don't trust him by half."

Will was silent, thinking. Not the lady then, he hadn't thought so, and still didn't think so, and that was a relief. The reward money was mounting, soon he'd have other runners poking their noses in. Nothing better than a fast arrest, a speedier conviction, and more money in his pocket. It would have been hard going, convicting a lady born. But a soldier now, even a decorated one....

Lucian sat deep in thought too. The little fishwife was surprisingly clever and observant. But even if she hadn't been blinded by her obvious fellow feeling for Louisa. He doubted Louisa had done anything to permanently postpone her wedding. He had wondered if she'd asked anyone to do it for her, though. He still did. His hopes, so high in the morning, were dim again. "So we're back where we started," he said quietly, "back to the gossip about me and conjecture about Mrs. Pushkin."

"No," Will said. "We've got a new player."

"Oh! *Play* reminds me!" Maggie said, sitting up as though she'd sat on a tack. "Do you know what else he did? He asked her to go out to a masquerade with him! A public masquerade. At the opera house, tomorrow night. She told me about it. You see, he told her that if she got into costume no one would know who she was, so they might as well take advantage of it and go dancing together. Not a week since he was buried and he asked her that!"

Lucian laughed. "Uncle asked from beyond the grave?"

"Oh, sorry," Maggie said. "Just the gall of the man got my mouth running before I could get the words straight! The lieutenant asked Louisa to go with him. Well, she gave him a flea in his ear, she said. He didn't turn a hair, just said that as she'd never loved your uncle, and didn't grieve for him, and no one would ever know—and so then why shouldn't she go out? Can you imagine?"

"Clever lad," Will said, nodding approval.

"Yes, very," Lucian agreed.

"But it didn't do him any good," Maggie said smugly. "She won't. He said he'd go anyway—and live in hope...." She stopped, and thought, and turned to Will.

"No," he said before she could open her mouth again. "If anyone goes to the masquerade to see what the dragoon's up to, it'll be me. It's one thing to have you chat up the lady for us, Mrs. P., and I grant you've done better than I could've hoped. But I'm not sending you to a public masquerade to play Cleopatra with the lieutenant."

"I can go anywhere I please," Maggie said boldly.

"Aye, alone, and be taken for a whore, is that what you're after?" Will asked.

Maggie gasped and Lucian blinked. It wasn't a word he would have used around a lady...but then, she wasn't one, he remembered. Maggie did too, and her face grew red.

"I'll take the girls with me then," she said angrily.

"Aye, and so then be taken for a procuress with your two chicks for sale," Will said. "I'm not just being mean, Mrs. P. Females have to be careful at public masquerades. They're prime places for the flesh trade. But you know...it isn't such a terrible idea, at that. No, I don't mean selling yourself, so don't puff up like an adder. I mean going to the masquerade. The lieutenant goes there, he drinks, as we know he's in the habit of doing, and he talks...maybe too much. I'll go, I think. You fancy coming along, my lord?"

"Me?" Lucian said, and thought *a public masquerade*? Obviously, there were dimensions to his sleuthing he hadn't fathomed yet. He wondered if he should. He decided of course he would. "But there is the fact that I'm in mourning..." he said, frowning.

"So might half the men there be, that's why masquerades are so popular," Will said. "The costume's not so important, the whole idea is the mask. But I do apologize if the suggestion offends, interfering with your grieving, I mean to say."

Lucian's bark of laughter was his only answer.

"So I thought," Will said, "and you don't have to unmask at midnight if you slip out before. You'd be surprised at how many of your friends will be there. Dukes dancing with housemaids, duchesses dallying with footmen, apprentices with sweeps—all will be sporting with whoever they please, whoever they are. Desire's the thing, and the game is everything else. The only danger is of some fellow seducing his own wife by mistake. There's drinking and carrying on, that's the whole idea. Didn't you ever go? I thought it customary for young gents to slum at such in their salad days."

"I married young," Lucian said, "and missed those sorts of treats, I'm afraid. Mrs. Pushkin is not the only one who wed to oblige her family. Only I was fortunate, I have a son to show for the experience. By the time my wife passed on, I'd passed the age for such sport."

"Ha," Will said, "were that the case, the place would be empty, instead of crowded to the doors—which it will be. Graybeard or stripling, they all go."

"But I thought noblemen could marry for love," Maggie blurted, and then was sorry she'd been so blunt with such a gentleman. She blamed it on a false sense of intimacy caused by the warmth, the dim light, the closeness of the three of them in the gently rocking coach. She tried to see the viscount's expression in the glow of the coach light. But all she saw were shadows shifting across that high-planed face.

"Indeed?" the viscount said, and she could imagine that eyebrow of his lifting. "Now, here I've always imagined love to be a pretty fiction, or at least, a luxury of the lower classes."

Maggie's back went up, but before she could retort, Spanish Will spoke. "No," he said, "love's a luxury of the unmarried, of any class."

The tension vanished in their laughter.

"Still, speaking of the masquerade, I really think I could do you a service, and we are in this together now, aren't we?" Maggie said, for the sake of argument. She'd already decided to go.

If they were going, so was she, and that was that, even if she had to resort to getting Flea to go with her. That wouldn't be too bad at that. He was slow, but loyal and very strong, and in a mask he could be a professor, for all anyone would know. The only problem would be getting him to leave off work for an evening. Auntie Jane did her business at night, and Flea was conscientious. But there was no need to think about it now.

"If Louisa went, I might be able to speak with her again," she said. "At least, I'd know her even in a disguise, and better than you, since I've passed more time with her."

"No, that you wouldn't, Mrs. P.," Will said, "for whatever she wore, I'd know first."

"Another boy keeping watch for you there?" Lucian asked.

"Two, one round the back as well as one out front," Will said without hesitation. "It's no problem, there are more hungry boys in London than there are dinners, my lord."

"You're spending your money freely," Lucian commented.

"Well, you have to spend some to earn some," Will replied. "And runner though I be, I'm warm enough in the pocket. I make money and plow it under again, and it grows like any crop. I make investments, and they do well enough for me, and for my old age — if I reach it."

"*Investments?*" Lucian said, as though he'd said "worms." "A risk, I'd think."

"Do you not risk, you can't gain," Will said. "I'm not speaking of blunders like the South Sea Bubble. No. Nice, steady investments in trade that grows—tobacco, sugar, rum, all the stuff of the New World. And the occasional flutter when I feel lucky. But money doesn't breed by itself any more than we do. It needs company."

Will thought a moment. The viscount and the fishmonger each had told something intimate about themselves tonight, whether by accident or on purpose. She'd spoke of her barren state, my lord had mentioned his loveless marriage. It was that kind of night, there was a queer air of intimacy in the carriage. He needed to work with the pair of them, and knew when a fellow wanted to gain confidence, he had to share confidences. And the most intimate, important thing Spanish Will could think of in his life was his money.

"Mrs. Pushkin has her works of art," he explained carefully, "but a good cracksman up her drainpipe could leave her a beggar sooner than you can wink, as could a fire or a flood. Even a bag of gold under the mattress can only grow dust. You've got your estates and your tenants, my lord, but a bad year or a bad manager, and there the money goes. No. Investments are the thing."

Maggie thought nervously about the hollow under the floorboards in her bedroom, just under the bed. Lucian thought of his estate manager, and couldn't remember the last time they'd talked.

"But I do put down the hire of my starving lads as an expense, and Bow Street does pony up for it," Will added slyly. "Because a penny saved is also a penny earned. And seeing as how the Lady Louisa has difficult sight lines from her front door to the back, you could say I'm on my way to helping Bow Street become a charitable institution."

"I wish *I* could see her again," Maggie said wistfully, thinking of her tea with the lady. "I mean to say, socially. But though I said I would, I know that can never be. She's a very nice lady," she told Lucian. "You've been too hard on her, you don't really know her."

"Match-making?" he asked languidly.

"No," she said honestly. She couldn't see the exquisite nobleman and the plain lady together, and found to her surprise that if she tried, she felt jealous, and that was so absurd that it disturbed her, and she fell silent.

"Then it's only a matter of getting costumes," Will said suddenly. "I can hire one from a shop at Covent Garden. No doubt you have one, my lord, being such a social fellow. And you can rent one too, Mrs. P."

Maggie gaped at the runner. "Well, you'd come anyway, wouldn't you?" Will asked her resignedly. "At least this way I can keep an eye on you."

Maggie was in high spirits when they got to her house. "Tomorrow evening, then," she told Will as he handed her out of the coach. She fairly danced up the steps to her doorstep, for all the world as though a dead man had never been discovered there. But if it weren't for him she wouldn't be so glad—she resolved not to think about that now. Joy wasn't that common a visitor to her door either.

Lucian walked her to the door, and waited for the girls to open it for her. Their faces, when they saw who had brought their mistress home, were studies in speculation, awe and envy. So too, Maggie imagined her neighbors' faces, behind all their curtains, to be. She was delighted.

"You made her very happy," Lucian told Will as he settled in his seat again and the coach drove away.

"I do like to leave women happy," Will agreed. "A happy lass is one who works harder for you, you can ask any procurer, do you doubt it. Or any lover," he added with a laugh.

"Indeed," Lucian said, but it was almost a question.

"Oh, indeed," Will said expansively. "A man who thinks only of his own pleasure gets only that, and it isn't half as much as a man gets when he gives pleasure. It's what any pimp worth his hire learns at his first lover's knee. But how would most men know that? *One, two, three, and here's your fee,* is how it is most of the time with them, and half of them with their own wives, at that. And she's left laying there, thinking murder, or mayhem, or at the least, how he'll look wearing a pair of horns. Or so I'm told."

Lucian's answer was silence as he mulled the thing over. He'd never had a complaint. But then, in all honesty, he reminded himself, he paid his mistresses handsomely. And the straying wives who bedded him were insatiable—for scoring social coups, rather than the act itself. Those he'd known, in the biblical sense, were more interested in keeping track of their illustrious lovers and so outshining the other roving ladies they knew, than taking any particular pleasure with the gentlemen they obliged. Clara hadn't liked it much at all. He hadn't expected her to, though he tried and she'd been very sweet about it. But they liked a man to take his time? He'd never heard that before. But who would he have heard it from? It made a man think.

"Being a runner teaches a man interesting things about females, my lord, never doubt it," Will went on as though he'd heard what wasn't said. "Speaking of which, we've other inquiries to make than at the masquerade, but I didn't want to mention them with the lass in the coach. She's too sharp by half, and not half enough afraid, to my way of thinking."

"She is indeed, unexpectedly so."

"No, not unexpected. She's smart and determined. More than that, she's had to do for herself for years now, which is why she was such a prime suspect for me. That's also why she's not half bad as a helper now. A rare treat is our little red-headed shrew, isn't she?"

"Indeed, she is that," Lucian said, and found himself smiling. Rarely quick and bright, there were moments in the coach just now when he'd forgotten she was a female. At her door, when she'd smiled up at him, he'd forgotten her hair color and her freckles too. And that she was no lady. But neither was she a slut, as he'd thought before. Whatever she was, she continually surprised him. And that was rare too.

"But cunning though she may be, she's no use for what I've in mind now," Will said. "What I need from you, my lord, is more in the nature of advice. I've a notion to start asking questions at knocking shops, and wondered if you've any suggestions as to where I should start first?"

"I beg your pardon?" Lucian said. "*'Knocking shops'?*"

"Aye. Pushing schools, brothels—whorehouses, my lord. That's the chiefest industry in this district, and the only other logical place an elderly gent might be after visiting after dark, you see."

"*My* uncle?"

"Aye, yours, mine and ours, my lord. You're telling me he was a monk?"

"Why, no, that is to say, I don't know, I never thought…"

"Well, think. He was healthy enough to want a wife, he must have been doing something about that itch before he thought about making it legal. Did he have a mistress?"

Lucian decided not to be insulted. What the runner said had shocked him, but thinking about it, distasteful as it was, it made sense. "A mistress? I doubt it," he said, after a minute, thinking about his own mistress. "Remember, he was a frugal man."

"Then he must have paid a visit to a house of accommodation every now and then," Will persisted, "or else he picked them off the street, which isn't the healthiest way to buy pleasure. So, what I'm asking is if he had any kind of preference, do you think? It'd make my job that much easier. If I have to go to every whore shop in Spitalfields and Whitechapel, I'll spend the rest of my life doing it. And that isn't even thinking about Seven Dials, which is also near where he was found. I was wondering if you could narrow it a bit for me. Do you think he might have fancied men or boys, or little girls, or being whipped, for example?"

The silence in the coach was palpable. The runner said it as easily as he might have asked if Uncle preferred wine or beer. But to him it was fact of life, Lucian supposed. And so it was. He cleared his throat. "I doubt he fancied men or boys. He was a bachelor because he was selfish, and preoccupied with books more than people, male *or* female. How should I know if he liked being whipped? And...little girls?"

"Aye, well, at least virgins, and there aren't any other kind for sale in London. It's a thriving business, my lord. There's some that think the only way to cure the clap is to have a virgin. They cost the earth, and the only way a man can be sure he's got one is to buy a child."

"They believe that works?" Lucian asked in astonishment.

"Some. But for myself, I think if it did, the rich would have made it legal by now, and in a year there wouldn't be any rich men with clap—nor one virgin—left in all London." Will laughed.

But Lucian didn't.

"So. I take it you won't be coming with me on these inquiries," Will said knowingly.

"No, I will," Lucian said. "The sooner we find an answer, the sooner I'll be free."

"Aye, of my company. I do understand," Will chuckled.

"That isn't what I meant," Lucian said, and was surprised to discover he meant it. His uncle's death had cast suspicion on him. Whatever anger and distress that had caused him, still there was no doubting that events since then had also made his life more interesting. Much more interesting. "No, that's not what I meant at all," Lucian said slowly, and with dawning wonder.

Chapter Nine

"I'm astonished. I wouldn't know you in a hundred years. It's a master of disguise you are and no mistake!" the runner said the moment he clapped eyes on the viscount.

"Amusing, I am so incredibly amused," Lucian said in a flat voice, somewhat muffled by his mask.

That was all he wore as a costume. The only incorrect thing about his scrupulous formal evening dress was that he wore a truncated domino over his head. He didn't wear the entire cloak, only the headpiece. It was almost a pillow slip, a fall of black silk hanging from the tricorne hat attached to the top, with a white mask over his eyes in the ancient Venetian style. The impressive nose was covered by the mask's even more impressive travesty of a nose, but there it stopped. His lips and chin were bare. Even so, silk billowed with each puff of air when he spoke.

"No one can recognize me. I believe you did say that's all that was needed," Lucian said, somewhat angrily.

He'd rejected all the costumes he'd seen at the shop he'd gone to, opting for an old domino mask he found in the back of his wardrobe instead. It was one he'd worn to fancy dress balls and masquerades in his youth. Even then, it had struck him as too much and he'd trimmed it. He felt silly enough in it as it was. But he told himself that at least it was a costume he could put on in the privacy of the carriage he'd rented. That way he could leave his house without his valet or any of his staff looking at him askance.

He was a man supposedly in mourning, after all. He mocked society, but hesitated to fly in its face. His uncle had been right in that at least, he did know the right thing to do, and when he could, he tried to do it. The world had a certain order, and no matter how he might scoff at it, order did make the world go round.

But now, perversely, he felt even more foolish because he hadn't tarted himself up. He loved a good jest but wasn't the sort of man who risked being made one himself. He hadn't known that before tonight. It did not endear the runner to him. Especially since Spanish Will had gone the whole hog, and looked surprisingly elegant, and somehow completely right.

The runner was a Spanish Grandee tonight. Black cloak, black suit and hose, black gloves, a dress sword at his side, complete to a white ruffle around his neck, and a false goatee. A simple black eye mask concealed his dark eyes. His smooth olive skin and shining black hair complemented the effect, but it was his arrogant air of command that completed it.

"They'll have a hard time guessing who *you* are, all right," Lucian muttered, eyeing Will as he settled into the coach.

"Don't care if they do," Will said smoothly. "It may be even better do I set them wondering. 'Is he making fun of the runner? What cheek!' '...Or could it be Spanish Will himself?' If they think it's me, fine. If they think I'm bold enough to mock big, bad Spanish Will, even better. The point is no one will know. That's the game within my game tonight. Can't be all work, can I? Though, I allow, I like my work so much I need no other play."

Lucian sat still, annoyed with himself and the runner, and feeling like a fool because he was. He wasn't used to that. He was a fashionable gentleman, and until recently he hadn't known how much that had pleased him. He was known as a Corinthian, a man devoted to sport, to the turf, the hunt and the chase. Not for him the fripperies of the Dandy set, or the dull and endless politics of the Reformer. He didn't attempt essays or poetry as so many other gentlemen did. He worked at play.

He gambled, he fenced, he was good with pistols. He drove his cattle and tried to set new coaching records for speed with them. He stripped at a gentlemen's boxing club once a week so he could spar. He competed for pleasure, never for applause or anything but his own approval. He minded his own business, and that business was simply to amuse himself.

But still and all, he was aware of who he was. He couldn't help knowing he was respected, admired, even envied. Now suddenly, he felt somewhat inadequate. But until now the game had always been to remain cool and amused, a man who was above wondering about how he was regarded.

His life certainly had changed since his uncle had died, he thought moodily.

Everything that had happened since then had been different. Remarkably different. And while not always pleasant, at least always enlightening. That was what fascinated him, and made him temper his tongue now. "I'll say I'm pretending to be a gentleman," he said.

Will laughed. "Do that, but say it different and you'll be a better success."

"Oim playin' at bein' a gent, don'cha see?"

Will turned to look at him. "Very, very good," he said in surprise.

"Well, but one must have some surprises up one's sleeve, mustn't one?" Lucian said, surprisingly pleased with himself.

But they were both surprised when they called for Maggie. Her serving girls opened the door, ushered them into her front parlor, then fled in a gust of giggles. Even little Davie looked as though he had a rare laugh hidden in him, and Will caught a glance of his street rat of a watchboy peeping in around the doorway, his narrow face brimming with suppressed smirks.

They forgot about that when Maggie walked into her parlor. Spanish Will had the audacity to dare the world by dressing as his namesake. Maggie Pushkin went him one better. She was a fishwife—dressed as a mermaid. And she made an exquisitely sensuous one.

She wore a shimmering gown of green, its long train cut out like a great fish tail. Her sleeves were long, her bodice was cut low, made decent only by a sparkling net of crystals sewn over the green net that covered her from her shoulders to the tops of her shapely breasts. The shawl she wore over all was a filmy green veil with more spangles dotting it. Green net gloves covered her reddened hands. She wore a small gold crown over her long black wig, and now, with all the blazing red of her concealed, even though she wore a tiny green eye mask, both men could clearly see those eyes were vividly blue and green and sparkling with mirth.

Her gown showed she had an excellent figure, her eyes showed how much she knew it, and her powdered skin glowed like a pearl. She was exotic and lovely, and fairly vibrated with the excitement and pleasure of it.

She seldom went out, and never to parties, and was so thrilled at the thought and then at the sight of herself transformed that she was actually short of breath now. Her customers, her neighbors, she'd wanted to show the world. But now she was glad the runner had warned her to keep it close. Mrs. Gow and Mrs. Gudge would have got the joke, but it was just as well. If Tom had seen her as she saw herself in her mirror, she'd never have got him out of her shop. Flea had seen her, by accident, while she was swanning around the kitchen, showing the girls her costume. He'd been awed. So was she. She swept her long veil around her, curtsying to the viscount and the runner.

Lucian gave her a deep bow in return. Spanish Will roared with laughter. "We're a fine trio," he said, "the three of us looking like we stepped right out of a caricature."

Lucian straightened, his back stiff. "There have been more?"

"No, but could they see us, there would be," Will answered, "and they'd sell out of the window faster than they could print them. That is if they could see us and know us for who we are. That's the whole idea. We're in costume. We could be Prinny and his mad father, *and* the old Queen herself, and no one would know—or care. And if they are there too, how should we know? There's the point." He chuckled. "My compliments, Mrs. P. You've outdone us all."

"My friend Mrs. Blum," she said, preening, "sews for the theater."

"You could step on to the stage in that, that's certain. Just be careful no one traps you offstage tonight," Will said gallantly. "A

142

fine masquerade. I don't know if I've ever seen better. A joke in a jest, and a beautiful thing besides. So what's your patter to be?"

Maggie and Lucian stared at him. Spanish Will sighed.

"See," he said patiently, "the costume sets the patter. Were you dressed like a shepherdess, Mrs. P., you'd talk broad, like a country girl. That's why the place will be filled with them, that's an easy voice to do. A fellow dressed like a Harlequin either says nothing or else he talks in rhyme—all the time. The girls who are Columbines will all be giggling. A man dressed like Death would stay silent as the tomb. Were you dressed like a Queen you'd command folks, telling them what to do instead of talking to them—and so on. See? It's the fashion at a masquerade, you act as you're dressed, and if you did different, you'd be noticed—at first, that is to say.

"They serve rack punch, and there's a full table of wines. They don't stint at the opera, you get worth for your money—and should at that price of admission. After a while it gets crowded and everyone gets drunk as owls, and then it makes no nevermind, though some stay in character all night, because the longer a man pretends to be something the harder it is to get out of it. Some have real trouble with that. I've heard tales of the woes they have…

"Remember that, young villain," he called to his watchboy still hiding behind the door in the hallway, "because this soft life is a game you're playing too. When you leave this place, you have to be yourself again. Be sweet-mannered and sweet-smelling when you're back in your own hole on the river bank and you'd be daft as some fellow still playing Harlequin as he's emptying his master's chamber pot the morning after a masquerade. Aye, I've heard of such, and so have the officers at Bedlam. You'd never get that far. You'll be at the bottom of the Thames with a hole in your head—if you forget the easy life you're leading now is nothing to do with your real life."

"Don't worry," Maggie said, "the boy's clever. And as for me? Why, if I stay in character it would only be that good for business." She giggled. "But I'll try, and so how should I speak? I'm a mermaid. I can't blow bubbles, and I don't want to be mute. So, you think if I hiss when I say something, it would be mermaidly enough?"

"Love," Spanish Will said, with a wink, "tonight, whatever you do will be fine."

"I'll thank you to remember my name," she snapped.

"You'll thank me not to!" Will said, suddenly serious. "From now on whoever speaks a name is an idiot, remember?"

"And what sort of voice for man in a domino?" Lucian asked thoughtfully.

"A man of mystery," Will replied. "No challenge at all. Disguise your voice, that's all you have to do. But don't expect any 'my lords' from us tonight, my lord, either, unless you don't mind giving your name away."

It was a warning more than an insult. "I'll do as you say," Lucian said in a deep hollow voice. "A man who doesn't listen to his guide is a fool, and I'm not dressed as one tonight."

"Very good," Will said approvingly. "But we have to call you something so you know if we need your attention. The trick is to stay as close to your own name as we can, so you can recognize the sound of it. That's how all the best rogues do it. So, not 'my lord,' but…'My…my…*Milo*'! Aye. Do you approve?"

"Perfect," Lucian said. "And Mrs. Pushkin?"

There was a thoughtful silence.

"Missus P. …'*Mystery*'—'Missus P.,' 'Mys-tery.' Get it?" Will's slum boy shouted, so carried away by the game he forgot to hide himself from Will.

"Got it, and well done," Will said, and added, "aye, it's a clever lad. Feed it and warm it and it comes up with ideas. Take care, Mystery, or you'll have yourself another boy in your kitchens, for his sort get under your skin like dirt under fingernails. Now, we'd best be going."

"But you, Mr. Corby?" Maggie asked. "How will you speak? And what should we call you?"

"Oh, I'm a Spanish gent tonight, though I can't speak a word of it. But I can murder English with a lisp with the best of them. And as for my name? Why, 'Spanish Will,' what else?" he laughed. "Half who hear you saying that will believe it, half the time, and the other half won't, and it's all the same to me."

"But you're never going out into the cold like that, Mrs....Mystery, are you?" Lucian asked Maggie when she walked toward the door with them. "It's clear at last, but it's freezing."

"Ice is good for keeping fish," Maggie said with a grin, pleased with him for thinking of her comfort, pleased with herself for looking like the kind of woman a gentleman might worry about. "But I've no wish to freeze. I have a good warm cape—or should I go wrapped in burlap like any other delivery of fresh fish?"

"*Very* fresh," Lucian said with an answering smile.

"And she's not the only one," Will cautioned sharply. "It's fine to be a gentleman, and Mystery looks like a lady, but a little gallantry goes a long way tonight. Remember, Milo, we go together, and keep an eye on each other, but don't forget why we're going. It's not to dance and drink and lark about together, much pleasure as that might be. We should do that, because not to would call attention to ourselves. But we have to keep our eyes open, mingle, talk to others when we can, if we want to discover who's there and what they're up to."

"I'll remember," Lucian said, smiling under his mask, delighted to have discovered what he already had tonight. Because it seemed the runner didn't at all care for him being charming to the fishwife. And she bloomed in the light of his praise, though she certainly deserved it. Who'd have thought she'd dress up to be such a charming baggage?

He helped Maggie on with her good woolen cloak, and then the three of them got into their hired coach and rode off together to the public masquerade.

But they were silent for several minutes after they got there. Maggie had never been to the opera, and so it took a while for her to get over her awe of the place itself, much less what was going on inside. It was so vast and bright and gilded, with so many tiers of seats and hanging boxes and its enormous stage, she thought it looked like a cathedral that had actually gone to Heaven.

Lucian had a box at the opera, but he'd only been there when there were performances. He'd certainly never seen it as it was tonight, or even imagined it so, with common folk in the audience, the aisles and on the stage itself.

Will was busily looking at the throng of people, trying to see around masks, under costumes and through disguises. A good runner could recognize a walk, a voice and a gesture. He tried, as Maggie gaped, and Lucian tried to pretend he wasn't there.

They'd done the place up as a Sylvan retreat, or so the program they got at the door with their tickets said. There were green trees, hedges in pots, arbors and urns and vases filled with hothouse flowers. It was frigid outside, but here it was some fanciful, mythical, eternal Spring. The orchestra played and the customers danced, posed, play-acted, prattled, gossiped, haggled and groped at each other.

"See," Will told Lucian in an undervoice, as Maggie stood staring. "As I said, whores and ladies, and you'll have to ask their price before you could tell them apart, and not even then, I'll wager."

But there were Turks and Egyptians and more Harlequins than she could count, Maggie thought, and princesses and dairymaids and a Satan or five, and gypsies and oh, my, look at those two—they weren't actually doing *that* there in the corner, were they? No, but it was close. And there were fairies and huntsmen, Amazons and Queens, nuns and witches, and more outrageous characters than she could recognize right off. Spanish Will had been right too. There was an old woman with three simpering shepherdesses at her side, and there was no doubt she was negotiating the price of them to a pair of ardent young Turks.

But that was only part of it, the way it was only part of life in London. Maggie was enthralled. It was an astonishing display, and everyone was having such a good time. But now she wondered how she could have been foolish and brazen enough to declare she could find the Lady Louisa here. She hated to be wrong. More so, when she thought of how both the runner and the viscount would react. They'd think she suggested this only because she'd wanted to go out for a night, and because it was such fun. But she hadn't known that before she'd come. And she didn't want to admit that either.

But the more she stared, the clearer the picture became. Soon she saw that the pattern could be pierced, an individual could be observed, and her heart slowed to a more bearable pace.

Lucian looked down at Maggie at his side. He could see her pink lips parting as she breathed in the atmosphere of the place. "Would you care for some punch, or wine?" he asked her, "or something to eat? As Mr. Cor...as Spanish Will here said, they do give value for their money."

She turned her head up toward him, and then looked up at Will. The runner nodded, and so then, did she, because she was too surprised to speak at once.

"Then, come along," Lucian said, offering her his arm.

She hesitated. He thought it was because she was unsure of him. But it was because with all she'd done in her short hard life, she'd never taken a gentleman's arm. Or been offered one. Did a lady grasp or grip, did her hand go under or over, it was such a simple thing, and so easy to get wrong. She faltered. She'd rather seem cold than stupid. A half-forgotten memory of her mother's lessons saved her. She remembered. She inclined her head, put one small hand lightly on his arm, and feeling like a gawk and a queen at the same time, went with him to one of the long buffet tables. Spanish Will looked after them, bemused.

No man had ever served her before either. That was more delicious to her than the taste of the little lobster patties, the shaved cuts of ham and beef, and the other tidbits Lucian put on her plate that she nibbled without tasting. He got her a glass of wine, and then another, and they ate and drank in silence, watching the kaleidoscope pattern of the revelers swirling around them, on the stage, in the aisles, in the boxes, mezzanines and seats.

"I dislike disputing your acumen, Mystery," Lucian finally commented in his false deep voice, "but I can't see how you'd recognize your own mother if she was here tonight."

"Be a miracle of some sort, if she were," Maggie sighed, "and a blessing to me, with her being gone these ten years and more. I thought that if you watched and listened, you could see something. But you may be right. See, the dragoons over there, the ones Spanish Will's with? I thought I recognized one of them as Lady Louisa's lieutenant, there—the weedy looking one, the one that's staggering. But that would be a costume, wouldn't it?"

"It might be the ardent lieutenant, at that," Lucian said, his eyes narrowing, "since it would be a crime to impersonate an officer, I'd think, even at a masquerade. This is wartime, after all. And since most military men are peacocks who'd rather die in battle than give up their uniforms, especially when there are so many females about. It could be. At least the usually astute Mr. Corby seems to be listening at his lips like a robin at a worm's hole."

"Speaking of listening…I know I'm nervous tonight," she said in a soft whisper, "but it seems like we're being watched too. Only I can't exactly say by who."

He glanced down at her. He'd noticed many men in the room doing the same. "By everyone," he said. "But who wouldn't watch you?" It was only truth. It wasn't just her clever costume. It was what it almost revealed. That was a neat little figure the netting barely covered. "Come to think on," he added, "do you think that little chap there is one of Mr. Corby's league of lurking boys, in disguise?" He gestured to a small man got up as the Emperor Napoleon himself. "Or is he a French spy wondering if he dares ask you how to circumnavigate the Channel? He's been staring at you with his tongue half out since you swam into his field of vision, little Mermaid."

She laughed. But so she was a dainty morsel, he mused. The long black wig made her look exotic, different, decidedly delicious. And this delectable little mermaid smelled of roses, not fish.

He didn't think he could recognize a soul in the crowd, and the longer he stayed, the less he wanted to. Who'd want to recognize his own valet or footman? He doubted anyone of birth would be here, no matter what the runner said. The murderer of his uncle had never seemed farther away, and the fact of it too. But that didn't mean he couldn't get something out of this strange evening.

"Would you care to dance?" he asked her. "It's a waltz. I'm tolerably good at that."

She turned her head and stared up at him. After a moment, she spoke, her voice low, embarrassed. "I can't dance," she said.

"Ah, but I can teach,' he said, and took her hand and led her toward the grand stage where dancers were twirling to the music.

"We're supposed to be looking…" she said, glancing back to see Spanish Will looking after them.

"And so we shall," Lucian said calmly, steering her with one hand at her back, "but first, we should establish ourselves as fellow revelers, don't you think?"

They didn't speak. He felt no need to, she was afraid to. She learned the steps quickly, and was soon moving in concert with him, buoyed by the music and her own daring. Once upon a time she'd loved to dance. Or so she thought; it had been so long ago she no longer knew if she'd dreamed the desire. She'd never danced with Bernard, of course. It had been seven years since she'd even been held by a man. It had been a lifetime since a strong fit male had held her.

Then, she'd been sixteen, and it had been Tom, and he'd been nothing like this. He'd clutched her close and taken hot open-mouthed kisses. The viscount didn't hold her close, or even look as though he wanted to kiss her. But he did. She knew by the way he bent his head to observe her, the way his shadowed eyes studied her, by the tensile strength in the steady hand at her waist, she

149

could almost touch the feeling he emanated, and it moved her more than she'd have believed it could.

She was right. He was intent and interested. She moved with him. He saw the way her eyes glittered and felt the way she swayed toward him, and thought, well then, an unexpected reward from this night's work, and wondered what freckles tasted like, and thought he might know before too long.

It was no trouble at all to dance her toward a flowery arbor. He'd glanced over the top of her head and seen other men doing the same with their willing partners. And no trouble at all to stop there, behind it, in a sheltering glade, his hand still at the neat little tuck in her curved waist. He let go of her hand and swept his domino up on top of his head. His face was suavely amused and smooth as ever, but his eyes were no longer cool, they were gentled and considering as he studied her face.

He brushed the back of one hand against her flushed cheek. It was warm and silken to the touch. Her eyes never left his. So sweet, so plaint, so willing now? He was enchanted.

"Well, then," he said.

"Well then," she echoed on a shaky breath. And as he began to lower his head, she said more stiffly, "Well, then, I think this won't get us anywhere, My—Milo. At least, anywhere but somewhere neither of us really want to be. I'm about as different from you as the mermaid I'm supposed to be."

"*Difference* is what this is all about," he said silkily.

"Oh, to be sure," she said. "And I'm sure all your friends marry fishwives, do they?"

That got the desired response. His head snapped back. She almost laughed. "*Marry*" was the word all right, it would sober any man of any class, and chase all thoughts of lechery. And coming from a fishwife? To a nobleman? It certainly chased all thoughts of nonsense from her own head. And his. His eyes narrowed.

"Not that I'd want to marry you, nor any man," she admitted, being completely honest with him. "That's the thing. I like being free, but not in the way you might take it to mean. For I won't bed a man I'm not wed to, nor will I marry any man. I'm done with that. And bedding is what comes from caresses, at least so I should think."

Or so at least so her mind had been running, she thought, marveling that she should have felt something she hadn't for so many years, shaking off the luxurious spell the dancing and his touch had caused. His cool veneer was only that, and it made a woman wonder how much heat he concealed. He'd almost showed her. He was immaculate, slender but sinewy strong, fragrant with good soap and expensive barbering, compelling and devastatingly attractive because of and in spite of his distant air. And about as real to her real life as any of the phantoms dancing around them, she reminded herself just in time.

"I ought to have come here tonight as a nun," she told him earnestly, "because that's how I live, you see. No man's wife, nor any man's mistress. And since there isn't any other thing I can be to you than your helper in this matter of your uncle, unless you want to be certain of a supply of fresh fish, I think we should stay with that, don't you?"

He was silent, then she heard him chuckle. He shook his head. She was as different as he'd imagined she'd be, if in a different fashion than the one he'd been hoping for. But he was a grown man and used to disappointment in matters beyond his control. Or at least, used to dealing with it. It had been a momentary fancy, after all. And she was only right. Clever chit. She hadn't acted affronted or insulted, or flattered either. She done it with just the right touch. He thought more of her, and no less of himself.

He took a step back. "Too right, Mystery," he said, grinning. "A pity. For me, that is. Still, yes, we've enough complications as it is. You are unusual though, you know."

"For a female, or for a fishwife?"

"Both, I think," he said, "but as you say, I wouldn't know. I don't know any other...females who deal in fish."

"Now that was nicely said," she said, and laughed.

"Would you care to go back and mingle with the other guests as Spanish Will suggested?" he asked, as he dropped his mask down again. "Or at least, before he thinks...?"

Her shoulders leaped, "Oh, yes!" she said, thinking of what the runner might be thinking.

They emerged from the greenery and stepped to the side of the great stage. They stood in companionable silence, each thinking of the narrow escape they'd just had, each regretting it just a little, watching the antics of the crowd. But after a while, when their eyes were less dazzled, and their regrets faded, they began to actually see the crowd. They were increasingly able to note those revelers who before seemed only to fill up space between the more outrageously costumed ones.

Maggie was the only mermaid there, and Lucian was the only one wearing an abbreviated domino. But he wasn't the only man wearing no costume but a mask. There were other gentlemen, or men dressed as gentlemen, wearing only eye masks as disguise. Some stood together in groups apart from the others, only watching, which made Lucian believe they might be gentlemen, after all. Some were negotiating with the obvious whores, and they were the ones Maggie took for real gentlemen. But neither saw anyone who looked remotely familiar, except for the dragoon across the vast room who was bending Spanish Will's ear.

They watched the crowd, wondering what to do next.

"I think we might as well merely eat, drink and be merry," Lucian finally commented, giving up his sepulchral voice for his usual deep rich tones, "because I don't think we can recognize anyone here. If you can find Louisa in this maelstrom, I'll eat my own domino, my dear."

She was about to agree.

"*Maldon?*" an astonished voice intruded. "Is that really your voice? I thought I recognized that antique moth-eaten domino. You wore it at Lady Fellow's masked ball last year and I wondered why you hadn't thrown it away years ago even then, and told you so, remember? But *you*, here?"

Lucian snapped to attention. *"Arthur?"* he asked incredulously, staring at the man who'd spoken. *"You,* here?"

Maggie almost giggled. She couldn't tell which of the two was more shocked. The one who'd spoken to Lord Maldon was a slight, boyish-looking young man, much younger than the viscount. She could see that much at least, because he only wore an eye mask. He was also well dressed, but not very well mannered, because he stood frankly gawking at the viscount.

"As you see," Lucian said, almost visibly recovering himself. Then he slowly looked Arthur up and down, and drawled, "And I see you are here as well. I suppose this means that your intense grief has quite turned your head, poor boy. A pretty place for a man in mourning, this. I salute your taste in mortuaries."

Maggie could see the other man's smooth cheeks grow a ruddy flush. "I got tired of sitting and wondering about it," he said, "sick, and tired. Not just about why it happened, but why he led me to believe he cared about me, and my future, when he obviously didn't give a rap."

"About that—I was going to tell you," Lucian said quickly, "I've no intention of keeping the house. I've no need for it, and it would suit you perfectly. I think he meant it for you all along. But the old fool was such a monster of propriety he couldn't change. Then too, he was going to marry and was looking toward a future neither of us could foresee."

They'd forgotten her, Maggie realized, feeling like a child listening to her parents quarrel, not saying a word lest they stop and she miss something that might be important to her.

"I don't want the house, damn you," Arthur said peevishly. "I don't want anything to do with anything he had. And how am I to support it if you *do* play Lord Bountiful? He didn't leave me enough to hire on even his meager staff. And no, I don't want your money, neither. I don't take charity, Brother. If you knew me better you'd know that. I liked Uncle, whatever you're thinking, but I can be disappointed in him, can't I? I'm only human, unlike you. You never turned a hair when he died. You didn't feel a moment's regret for your neglect of him even after you found out you'd inherited it all, did you? Yes, I'm supposed to be in mourning, but I'm out tonight, and I'm having a good time," he said, waving his glass of wine defiantly, "because I couldn't sit and think about it anymore."

Well, he was drunk and so that was his excuse, Maggie thought. But why did the viscount put up with such rudeness?

He didn't. His voice grew chilly. "I'd meet any other man, with his choice of weapons, for only one of the things you've just said to me. But I've no wish to play Cain to your Abel, even if this is a masquerade. I do wish you'd stop playing Bacchus, though. What say we go somewhere else and discuss all this?"

"But," Arthur said, weaving now, and squinting close at Maggie, "what about the lovely lady?" he leered. "You inviting me to share?"

"And she'd skewer any man for saying that," Lucian said quickly, seeing Maggie's skin growing red under all her pearly powder, "but as she *is* a lady, although I can't divulge her name, she will refrain from having her husband call you out, for my sake. Won't you, my dear?"

Maggie inclined her head. This was the viscount's world, she had to leave it to him now. His brother was studying her closely. She remained silent, only giving a slight nod of agreement.

"Thank you," Lucian said, taking her hand and bowing over it. "And so, my dear, I regretfully bid you adieu. Give my regards to your husband. I hope to see you both again soon. Come along, Arthur, let's be shut of this place; it's never as amusing as I thought it would be." Without another word to Maggie, he draped an arm around his brother's shoulders and steered him off into the crowd. Leaving Maggie standing staring after them, completely alone.

The viscount and his brother vanished into the throng. Maggie craned her neck but couldn't see Spanish Will anywhere. She wasn't on the stage anymore and didn't have the height to look over the heads of other people to see if he was still at the opera house at all.

The viscount had abandoned her. But she couldn't see how he could have done otherwise. He couldn't introduce her to his brother. And if the niggling thought came that he might have done, it went just as fast. She was a fishwife, he was a viscount, this was only a masquerade, in so many ways. He likely didn't want his family to know he was pursuing the hunt for his uncle's killer in the company of the very woman whose doorstep he'd been found dead on. It only made sense. They were banded together for both their sakes, and that was all. She told herself to ignore the little hurt she felt, because that was as foolish as any of the other illusions she might have indulged in.

She was seven and twenty, after all, and mistress of her own fate. And here she was, she told herself, dressed to the teeth, looking like her every dream, standing in the middle of a madly gay masquerade party in the heart of London. Alone. And deserted, and not knowing what to do.

He'd probably left the hired coach for her to use. She could turn tail and run home right now. Or stay, and try to do what she was here to do.

Maggie took a breath, raised her head, and looked around. One last time, she'd look for Lady Louisa, or whatever else she could see. Whatever the viscount had said about why she was being watched, the back of her neck had itched with more than the thought of being admired or desired. The moment she'd arrived she'd the eeriest feeling the murderer was here tonight. Well, but half of London was. Or at least the half she'd never seen. The viscount might have thought it was for the rabble, but she knew rabble, and no one in her neighborhood looked like this.

She stood tall as she could, and put a slight smile on her lips, as though she was just waiting for her escort to return to her. After all, the music was playing, and it was heavenly. There were flowers and candles, light and laughter. This was a world she might never see again. She might never have such a chance again—and not just to hunt for a criminal. She wouldn't waste it.

Chapter Ten

Maggie gaped.

"Oh Mistress fine, thou art divine, I only wish that thou wert mine!" the Harlequin crooned to her, both hands on his heart.

He was a scrawny fellow; his tightly fitted costume couldn't hide that. He wore classic checkered motley, tunic over tights. A white eye mask covered his upper face, a fitted hood covered all his hair. He capered as he danced to her side. Maggie had never seen a grown man actually caper before and was as shocked at that as by his skin-tight attire. But he was the essence of grace.

"I spy the Mermaid fair, she with moonbeams in her hair," he sang in a sweet voice. "Ah! Do I dare...ask her?"

"Ask her what?" Maggie asked, entranced.

"To dance with me, entrance with me, to lift a toe, to back and fro, to partner me delightfully?" He put a finger to his eye and whirled around. Then he dropped to one knee before her, and posed, both hands up, beseeching.

"Thank you," she said, so taken aback she actually took a step backward before she caught herself doing it. "But no, thank you. I—I'm waiting for my escort to return, you see."

She wanted to experience the masquerade, but he was a little too much for her. Any rate, she told herself sternly, he certainly wouldn't know a thing about the reason why she'd come. And however charming, he was obviously interested in more than she was willing to provide, now or later. But she felt badly about refusing him...until he leaped to his feet, and bowed.

Then he immediately whirled to her right and stared at the Shepherdess standing there. He danced over to her, crying, "Ah, I spy the Temptress fair, she with moonbeams in her hair!" Then he fell to one knee in front of the Shepherdess and sang, "O Mistress fine, thou art divine, I only wish thou wert mine!"

Maggie grinned. *So much for breaking hearts at a masquerade,* she thought, moving away from the pair of them. But it made her realize she was singularly alone and couldn't just stand by herself all night. She had to strike up a conversation, or leave. She hated to give up that easily. And too, the music kept playing.

She gazed across the room, hoping to catch sight of the soldier Spanish Will had been talking to. If Lieutenant Pascal was there he'd surely know if Lousia was. If the lady hadn't come, then maybe he'd be disappointed enough to talk to any attentive ear. Especially one belonging to a strange, flirtatious female. Maggie wasn't that certain of her powers of seduction but felt sure he'd be more forthcoming with her than with a man who looked like Spanish Will. If for no other reason than because he couldn't suspect her of spying on him. She was a mermaid tonight, a dark-haired, mysterious, appealing mermaid. Hadn't she attracted the Harlequin? And even more amazing, the aloof and usually discerning Viscount Maldon?

The thought gave her confidence and a feeling of power. She was alone, but she was well armed. She stood on tiptoe looking at the stage, the audience, up at the boxes, trying to get a glimpse of the lieutenant. She'd find out a thing or two. She'd surprise them all.

But she found her view was suddenly blocked.

"Well," said the gentleman who stopped in front of her, "well, well, well."

He hadn't bothered to put on a costume. He wore formal evening attire, black jacket, knee-length breeches, a black eyemask and a leer. He was tall and thickset and slightly drunk. And very confident.

"Nice rig," he said, looking her up and down. "Shows the goods but don't shout 'em. Been watching you. Your gent sheered off. Don't blame you for turning down the clown. But I'm blunt and I'm not mean with it, neither. Come along with me. If we suit, it'll be for more than tonight, and there's a promise. I like the look of you. Let's see if the touch equals it."

He reached out for her. She evaded him easily. He sounded like a gentleman, but also very drunk. She could handle this. "My escort's coming back," she said firmly. "He won't like this, not a bit. Good night, sir."

"So it will be a good night," he said happily, reaching for her again. This time, he managed to grab her wrist. "This won't up your price," he warned as she struggled to free herself. "Made your point. You ain't easy, aye, I see that. But a little of this goes a long way. Come along."

"I...am...not...going...with...you," Maggie panted, because although she said she wasn't going with him, she was. Because he was dragging her down an aisle. Her heart began pounding when she saw no one seemed to notice the struggle, or care, if they did. "Let go!" she demanded. She refused to believe she could be abducted in broad...lamplight, at any rate, beginning to fight in earnest when she realized he was actually successfully pulling her toward an exit.

She aimed a kick at his legs, and heard him laugh as she connected. She wore fashionable light slippers, her toe hurt more than his shin did. She drew back her free hand to slap him, and gasped when he captured that one too, and promptly pulled her up tight against himself. "So anxious?" he laughed, and bent his head to kiss her. She turned her head to escape his mouth, and opened her own to screech when his mouth followed.

And then she was free. And he was sitting on the floor, gaping up at her and the Spanish Grandee who flung his arm around her shaking shoulders, and pulled her to his side.

"No, no, Senor," said the Grandee, shaking one finger at the gentleman with coy caution, "theese one, she belongs to me. Unless, of course, you weesh to make a theeng of it? I have the sword. I have the pistol. And I have this fist. Remember it? Interested in any of them, eh? Ah. I thought not. Gracias, and good evening."

He laughed as he led Maggie away. But when he got her to the outer lobby of the opera house his arm came away from her shoulders and his laughter turned to ominous silence.

"Where's Milo?" he finally asked in a harsh undertone when he saw she'd got herself under control, and stopped shivering.

"Gone. With his brother. His brother—Arthur? Anyway, he, Arthur that is, recognized his voice, and the domino, and he was very drunk, and so my...Milo led him away."

"So why didn't you look for me?"

"I did! But I didn't see you anywhere."

"Then why didn't you leave?"

"I thought...well, I thought if I could talk to the lieutenant, I'd find out something. Or I could find Lady Louisa, or..."

"Or maybe see how the night side of London lives, eh? Well, I can't say I blame you, and I can't say I didn't warn you, so there's not much I *can* say, is there? But she isn't here, and the lieutenant has nothing to add, and this whole evening was a folly. So, come, I'll take you home. I told you a female alone was in danger here. But you didn't believe me, did you?"

"You just told me you couldn't say anything, and here you are saying it," she said, recovering her poise by getting angry at him. It was easier than being mad at herself for not listening to him. "But that's the wrong way...oh!" She gasped. Because he wasn't leading her toward the exit, but back into the auditorium and up the steps to the stage where the company was dancing.

"Well," he said, "since you were still wondering, I expect I'm the best one to show you. At least, the only one, since Milo's gone. He waltzed with you. And did tolerably well. I can do better. This is a country set. May I have this dance, Mystery? Just this one. Because then you do have to go home. Soon, masks will be coming off. There's already a lot more coming off in the boxes and at the side of the stage. Don't look. You're a lady tonight, remember?"

"So I am, so I won't be angry with you for saying it," she said loftily, inclining her head like any gracious lady.

A waltz with a viscount and a romp with a runner, Maggie thought as she took his hand. That was more dancing than she'd done in the whole of her life. It wasn't a wasted evening.

She was still humming to herself as she sat back in the coach and was carried home. Who'd have thought the runner could move with such supple timing, such easy grace, leading her through the intricate steps of the dance so deftly he covered her missteps? Who could have imagined he'd behave with such good humor? She might not find out who killed the man on her doorstep, but she was certainly learning more about life than she'd ever have known if he hadn't chosen her doorstep to die on.

"You're very quiet," Will remarked. "Still mad at me for reeling you in? That's odd, if that's so. I didn't think you'd had your heart set on taking up a new profession. That's all that you could find to do at the masquerade now. But selling fish is a much better calling than selling yourself. Think of the advantages. You can keep at it until you're old as the hills, and you don't have to pretend to like every customer you're selling to. And it don't matter if they ever bathe, neither. But maybe the best part is that in your present job, you catch the fish. You don't catch anything from them."

"I won't fight," Maggie said on a yawn. "I'm too tired tonight. Do you mind awfully if I put it off until tomorrow?"

He chuckled. "So sure of seeing me tomorrow, are you?"

She sat up. "But I thought you wanted my help!"

"So I do. But I have to get on with my own investigating. If you want to see me you have to come up with something new. I'm hoping you want to do both things. Ah, here we are."

He walked her to her door. "I've asked the fellow to wait, though usually I'd walk home," he said, a smile in his voice, "but even Spanish Will don't stroll through London town at midnight done up like Spanish Will. That's asking for too much trouble, even for me."

She let herself in her door, and looked around the darkened entry. "Good," she said, with satisfaction, "they're all sleeping. I told them not to wait up for me."

He checked. It could have been an innocent remark. But in Will's experience, women were not innocent. She certainly didn't look innocent. She still glowed, she was still as radiantly exotic and seductive as she'd been as they danced, as she'd been all evening. She smelled of roses, and he was acutely aware she came just to his shoulder. They'd fit well. She might be innocent of the crime she was involved in. She might not be. But what he found himself wanting to do wouldn't change that. If she thought it would, she was wrong. And if she was wrong, tonight he didn't care. She'd danced with the viscount, but the viscount had gone home alone. Had she sent him away? Had he sheered off? Will was made of stronger stuff. Or weaker. Tonight, he didn't care.

"Of course," he added, softly, bending to speak in her ear, "I could always send the fellow away. I *could* go home by dawn's light." He put his hand on her shoulder, lightly. "That's up to you to say."

She stared at him. He smiled down at her, his hand warm on her shoulder. Only that. But it was as though he'd turned on some inner force. She could swear she felt heat rising from him. She wore a good warm cape, but his big palm was warmer still. He cupped her shoulder and made it feel like a more intimate caress. His voice held deep and secret promises. She could feel the pull and allure of it. His eyes were on her, his total and complete attention was on her. She felt more than that.

She was fully dressed and so was he. And yet, and still, suddenly she could almost envision that powerful male body naked before her. It was as if he knew it and intended it. She closed her eyes. She could almost feel herself sliding her hands over big warm sleek muscles, smooth damp, heated skin...satiny... She stopped, in shock. She'd never seen such. She'd never done such. She'd never known she so wanted to do such.

He waited, his hand soft on her shoulder, and yet weighty, and suggestive as no words could be. And yet... She opened her eyes. She shook her head to clear it of the last echoes of his suggestion. She was suddenly appalled and alert, awakened to more than his suggestion.

"There must be something in the air tonight," she said in wonder. "You *and* the viscount! It can't be just me. Well, and if it is,

I suppose I should never take off this wig. But I will. Because I don't want that kind of complication in my life, thank you very much. I do thank you, but I don't want to play. I had a husband. I don't want another."

Ah, she thought on a sigh, as he snatched his hand away, so it works for nobles and runners alike. Well, good, it certainly works for me.

"Are you serious?" he asked, astonished.

"Are you?" she asked, amused.

He hesitated. And then smiled. And then laughed, and so then did she. "And since I don't take lovers," she went on, "there's no point to it now, is there?"

"Oh, there is," he said, "but you're right. Now isn't the time for it. The viscount too, eh? I thought so. I suppose you gave him the same answer or he wouldn't have run away."

"What do you think?" she asked pertly, because it wasn't tomorrow yet.

"I think we all had a good time," he said seriously, talking to himself as well as to her, "but that time is over. There's a man stone cold dead. Murdered. It's my job to find who done for him. *That* first, and last. That's the reason we're here together now, and the reason why we can't be together any other way, now. You're too right, whatever your reasons may be. It's like I told that wretch of a boy who should be sitting in your alley tonight watching over you and not snoring by your fireside. A masquerade is only that, and not a good thing to try to live. I should have remembered. Goodnight, Mrs. Pushkin, and say good-bye to 'Mystery' for me, will you?"

She smiled. He hesitated, and then abruptly left. She shut the door firmly behind him. Then she lay back on it, breathing as hard as if she'd run away from him. Because she had. And felt very lucky to have done it.

*

163

Will took the coach back to his rooms. He kept his eyes on the shadows, as always, as he mounted the long stair to the top floor. But he kept thinking of the little mermaid as he did, how her black wig had transformed her and beguiled him. He let himself into his rooms. They were under the roof, to the back, with a strong bolt on the door to them, and a rope ladder coiled near each window inside. There was no way any man could surprise him, and good ways to escape if he was wrong. He looked around quickly. His exhalation was a white cloud in the cold air when he sighed after taking his usual inventory, seeing nothing out of place.

He'd lied to the viscount. He had two rooms and two chairs. He also had a bed, a desk, a wardrobe and a table. Books and papers were their only ornaments. A fire would not leave him destitute. But there was no sense in having one lit when he wasn't home, and he seldom was. The place was neat and spare, and pleased him. He wasn't a man to waste his hard-earned money on creature comforts. But there wasn't much room for any creature to pace there, and since he had only one small hearth, little warmth on such a night for body or soul. Especially body.

That was why, late as it was, he dressed again after he stripped off his costume and went right back down the stair, two steps at a time.

He didn't get to bed for another hour, and when he did, it wasn't his own, and it wasn't to sleep. She had black hair, but there all similarity to the other woman he'd wanted tonight began and ended. She was tall and heavily built, with heavy breasts and wide hips, a strong back and light turn of mind. She worked at a tavern called The Blue Boar, and she worked hard. She dispensed ale and served food, and fended off pinches and served up slaps if the pinches became too persistent. Not that she was a prude. She earned her own way and made her own decisions, and if she didn't sell herself, she gave herself as freely as she desired. Because she was a woman on her own and had her own mind and desires. But her mind was never consulted when she met with Spanish Will. Only her desires.

"Gawd!" she whispered as she lay on her bed, waiting for him as he undressed for the second time that night. "Look at you! Will, if you ain't something! You don't call on me less'n you want me," she complained, never taking her eyes off him, watching the long muscular golden torso being revealed to her. "You don't never promise me nothing, nor never bring me presents. You got other women. Huh! Well, we both know that! Who don't? Still, no matter how I curse you, all you got to do is come to me and I follow you, Will, but I don't know what you do to me."

"But you do," he said as he bore her back on the bed with him. "I do this, and this, and yes, this...."

She met him move for move, twisting under him, giving no quarter, wanting no less, warm and damp and ready when he was, shuddering with pleasure as he made her and himself wait.

And if that pleasure was tainted for him because her hair smelled of bacon fat, ale and woodsmoke instead of roses, he managed to forget that. If it was diminished because she used him as eagerly as he used her, and didn't say a word of affection except to the sex he finally brought to hers, he didn't mind. Because he too gave nothing but what he took. So it was plain pound dealing. Yet for the first time, he felt cheated. Because there was nothing but their bodies in it, and because for the first time in a long time that bothered him. He didn't like the fact that there was something new clicking over in his head to ruin the fun his body was having.

Still, it was good, though he had to stop in time and finish alone, beside her. He never forgot to remember that. He wanted no ties beyond this night. He wasn't a man to leave a woman with his loose ends. He lay back, catching his breath, thinking of the work he had to do after he left her.

He dressed, ignoring how she tried to slide her hand along his back and buttocks and thighs as he did, ignoring how his body answered. Because it wasn't speaking for him tonight. He answered her pleas for him to stay with a final kiss and a caress. Then he went home to his own narrow bed to sleep at last.

165

It took him a while, even so. The sheets were cold, and his brain was still busy. He lay in the dark, as his body warmed his frigid sheets, musing about the other woman he'd dealt with tonight. A fishwife who spoke like a lady, could act like a temptress, and treated him like she was a nun. She could be an ally and might be a killer. A "mystery" indeed, in or out of costume. One he'd solve, one day, in due time. That was his job, after all. And he needed to be rested to do it. He closed his eyes, turned on his side, turned off his thoughts and slept.

*

Arthur staggered. Lucian frowned.

"An' I don' want your damned house, so don' ask me again, or I'll—I'll…" Arthur said wildly as his brother steered him out of the carriage and up the stair to his rooms.

"But I don't need it," Lucian said calmly. "We won't discuss it now, all right? You can't discuss *anything* now. Damnation, but what did you pour down your throat tonight? It seems to be getting you drunker as time goes by. Do give me the name, I could use a bottle or two myself."

Lucian propped his brother up with one hand as he thumped on his door with the other. "Your master has met with a slight accident," he told the manservant who opened the door. "He met up with some vile spirits. I advise putting his head under a tap. If he survives until morning, I salute you. …Do you need any help?" he asked more soberly, trying to keep Arthur from lurching into the wall as he tried to enter his rooms. The answer was evident. And so he held his brother upright, and with the scandalized valet on one side and himself on the other, they guided Arthur, weaving and muttering, to his bedchamber.

Once there, Arthur shook them off. "Don' need help. Don' wan' sympathy. Don' want your damned house neither!" he declared to his brother. "Place's *haunted* by Uncle. Don't wan' him neither! He didn't wan' me, did he? Ha!"

He shook a fist at the sky, and then stood stock still, growing pale, as though hearing some divine retribution for his insolence. His eyes rolled up in his head. Lucian managed to catch him as he began to fall, and rolled him to his bed, where he collapsed.

"Saved you a job of work," Lucian told the valet, looking at his unconscious brother. "Let him sleep in his clothes. But I'd keep a bucket by the bed, were I you. It'll save you cleaning the floor. On second thought, stay by him tonight. There should be someone near when he casts it all up. Good night, I'll let myself out."

Since the bedchamber was at the back he had to walk through Arthur's entire apartments to get to the door, looking around as he did—two bedchambers, a dining room with a small pantry adjacent, servant's room, sitting room and a study. High ceilings, decent woodwork, good floors and well kept. But not lavish, nor lavishly furnished. Lucian noted a familiar landscape, and a pair of chairs that had been part of his childhood landscape at his country estate, a settee and inlaid table from his Mama's house in London. It was very like his Mama to feather her fledgling's nest. He didn't care; she might be partial, but not blind to the entail specifying what was now his. Even if she was, he didn't begrudge his brother a few sticks of furniture, however fine.

His brother's rooms were in a respectable district. But not so established as Uncle's. His furniture was too elegant to be considered cast-off. But it was not new, and not of Arthur's own choosing, and might not legally be his. Lucian could understand his brother's disappointment. The place was comfortable, but not so comfortable as a whole house, and never as satisfying as something entirely, indisputably his, would be.

Arthur could serve dinner in his rooms, even if he did have to get his hot meals baked at a cookshop. He could bathe in an iron tub in his pantry if he didn't feel like going to the public baths. He could use a modern convenience at the end of the hall on the first floor, instead of going out to the yard or always using a chamberpot. He only had to take those stairs because water didn't rise to the second floor in this district. He lived better than most people in London did. But not so well as he could in the house Uncle left to his brother. Lucian resolved Arthur would have that house, one way or the other.

But that would have to wait until tomorrow, and that seemed very far off. It must have been the excitement of the masquerade, Lucian thought as he reached the pavements. Because he was wide awake now, and it was nearly midnight. Fortunately, this was London. A man didn't have to sleep his nights away here.

He paused on the pavement, undecided.

The theaters were closed now. But entertainment was just starting other places around town. He could go to St. James Street. The most distinguished clubs had gaming. But the most distinguished gentlemen gambled at such dens as the Two Sevens, the Pigeon Hole, and the well-named Mrs. Leach's house, or any of the new hells that kept opening there. He could sip champagne and dine on lobster patties as he tried his luck with the sheer luck of Faro, Baccarat, Rouge et Noir, or the dangerous illegal Hazard tables. Or try his skill with Piquet, Cribbage or Billiards.

He could take in a cockfight or a ratting and do his wagering there. Or go to a tavern, find friends, place bets on anything and spend hours gossiping about nothing. Sad stuff, he thought. He needed something more active.

He could drop in at several parties that were doubtless still going on. Balls in the best parts of town lasted until dawn. Whenever he arrived, he'd be welcomed. As a noble widower, he was eagerly sought. He had only to stop at his house and take an invitation from the stack on the table in the entry hall, where his butler left them for his consideration. There was always gaming at the most tonnish parties too, for the benefit of bored fathers, husbands, and gentlemen who weren't hanging after any one female. Or he could flirt and dance, perhaps meet up with an interesting woman. He frowned. He'd done that tonight. It had done nothing but unsettle him.

Lucian paused, testing his restive mood, measuring his needs. Still—a woman. There was a thought. It was cold and getting colder. The winter tightened its fist over a man's heart these nights. He didn't feel like dallying indoors or out. He made up his mind. He climbed back into the hackney he'd told to wait for him and gave the driver the direction of his newest townhouse, and his latest mistress.

She'd gone to bed, her maid said. But she threw on a dressing gown and welcomed him with delight. Well, but she had to, he thought as he removed his greatcoat and gloves. They both knew he paid for the maid who took his coat, the wardrobe it would be hung in, the room and the chair he sat in pretending polite chat before he got down to what they both knew he was here for tonight. But it would be vulgar to simply bear her immediately back to bed. He could, if he wanted. She wouldn't protest. But he wouldn't. The illusion of her choice in this was what he paid for too.

"I haven't seen you for *so* long," she pouted, and paused, prettily confused, because they both knew she shouldn't nag. That was for wives, or lovers. Not for the likes of her.

She was young, but not so young as his Mama thought. Fair and rounded, she had pretty doll-like good looks that made her seem almost innocent. She was far from that. She'd danced her way up from the slums to Drury Lane. After meeting some of the gentlemen who trolled for their mistresses in the Green Room backstage, she'd found private entertainment paid much better. She'd had several patrons. He was only her latest one. He provided her income, clothing, a servant, occasional jewels for good behavior, and a place to live and oblige him. She provided him exclusive use of her person. She was delighted to serve him. Or so he'd thought until he remembered Spanish Will's advice about lovemaking.

"How glad I am that you are *finally* here," she said, wriggling in her chair.

He gazed at her and was suddenly reminded of his horses, eating their heads off in the stables for all the weeks he couldn't take them driving. They too had been restive, uncomfortable, unused to not doing what he kept them for, and eager to be taken out and used again. He was appalled at his unbidden thought, and ashamed of it.

"Would you care for some tea?" she asked.

Enough was enough. He was bedeviled tonight. "I think we both know what I'd care for," he said in a deep voice, and winced inwardly. It was a thing a villain in the melodrama would say.

She didn't think so. She giggled, took his hand and led him to her bedchamber. She slipped off to her dressing room with a whispered promise to return soon. He didn't mind the delay. She used a sponge to prevent consequences of their act, and needed privacy to insert it. It pleased him, and marked her as a professional. So professional that she didn't remove her gown until she came back. Then she made a slow enchanting show of removing it for him. She sank to the bed and smiled as he came down to her level. He was lean and well made, and best of all to her, clean.

In the lamplight he could see she was all pink and gold, her lips and breasts sweetly swollen, ready for whatever he wished to do. He kissed her lightly, and touched her gently, and then less so. She slid down his body, using her hands and lips to drive him to the edge. He drew her back again, feeling her squirming with eagerness. But he paused at the last minute. He knelt on the high bed, looking down at her, his long eyes narrowed with thought. She looked at him questioningly.

"I was only wondering," he said, only slightly out of breath, because the wondering was cutting into the pleasure of it, "is there anything you'd like me to do?"

She looked as adorably puzzled as a naked woman could to an equally naked man in his position. It was a difficult question for him to ask, for that and other reasons. But he needed to know.

"*Do?*" she asked.

"For you," he said, and then more impatiently, "*to* you. To make it better for you. What," he finally ground out, "specifically, would give you pleasure now?"

"Oh," she said, very much relieved. "I'd like to make you happy, of course." She beamed, like a child who knew she'd given the right answer to her teacher.

"Apart from that. Aside from that. For you. What would feel good now?"

"To make you happy," she said a little nervously, puzzlement marring that fair brow.

"I mean," he tried again, "is there anything you'd like me to say, or do? Any place you'd like me to touch or caress you? Anything else that would give you more pleasure?"

She looked very worried. She was. She took her pleasure in knowing she pleased him. She didn't know what else he could be thinking about. She told him that.

He came to her then, as much in anger as in desire, and was instantly sorry for it. It wasn't her fault; he wasn't a man who used force. He too liked to think he made her happy. He did. It was over quickly. For the first time he felt vaguely cheated.

He patted her, and thanked her. She smiled, pleased with herself and him. When he came back from washing up in her dressing room, she was asleep. He gazed at her. But didn't join her again. It wasn't her fault. They'd nothing in common but their needs. His for sex, hers for money.

A woman he could talk to in bed would have to be one of his own class. Or so he'd thought until he'd met the little mermaid. But that was clearly an impossible liaison. An affair with a married woman of his own class was possible, but he wouldn't be able to speak freely with her. He couldn't expect a woman who cheated her husband to be faithful to him in any fashion. If she were a widow he couldn't fully open his mind to her either, lest he raise her hopes of marriage. If she were unwed it didn't matter how close they were, if he took her to bed he'd have to marry her—fast. So he was stranded with the likes of his mistress. Still, there were lightskirts who were less beautiful but more clever. He resolved to find one.

He dressed silently, and quietly let himself out.

He was frozen to the bone when he got home, and still restless. He kept thinking of too many things he could do nothing about tonight. Important things and foolish ones. Uncle's murder and all its consequences, Spanish Will's advice, the mermaid, and his mistress too. He read for a while. He drank a deal of brandy. Short of bludgeoning himself into unconsciousness, he could do no more. He didn't have to. He went to bed, closed his eyes and waited for morning. Astonishingly, he slept.

*

Maggie Pushkin pounded her pillow and spun it round again. It needed new feathers, it needed a new case, it needed a different head on it tonight. She couldn't sleep. Nor could she go down to the kitchens and make herself an infusion of anemone, or even take a snippet of valerian to put in hot tea to help matters. She'd wake Jack. He slept on a pallet by the hearth now, and young boys needed their sleep. She didn't want him wondering why she was waltzing around the house this hour of the night. He helped around the shop now, but still worked for Spanish Will, however nominally. But her legs twitched, and she stirred uncomfortably.

The dancing should have tired her instead of making her want to rise and dance some more. But it wasn't dancing she wanted. She wasn't sure exactly what it was. Her body tingled. Her skin thrummed. She prickled and pouted. She was restless and fidgety, as far from sleep as from peace in her own body, with yearnings in places she'd forgotten…

Was that it? Letting a man do that to her again? *She wanted that?* She sat straight up and locked her arms over her knees, scowling. But she hadn't liked what Bernard did. She never wanted anything like it again. The desire she'd felt for Tom was a distant memory. She suspected she liked seeing him now exactly because he was married and eager to cheat his poor wife and so the thought of doing *that* with him was repugnant. …*Desire?* For a *man?*

Desire for children, yes. Oh, yes. Every month she sorrowed at the loss of a child she hadn't begot, and felt her fruitful days passing, and grieved for it. But *that?* Bernard had made it brief, but it was never brief enough for her. Every Tuesday, Thursday and Saturday night, unless she was having her courses. Sometimes it hurt, and sometimes it ached after. But not if she prepared herself first. A dab of Jessamine or Tansy in slippery salve, as Grandmama had said, could ease the way for a woman and help them have a babe or a man. But she'd had to take care. Too much and he'd take too long.

He'd turn out the lamp, turn to her instead of turning on his side to go to sleep. He'd pull up his night shirt and ruck up her shift. He had a hairy chest and a flabby belly, and smelled of fish, of course. She'd hold her breath for as long as she could. He'd crawl over her, take himself in hand, part her, insert himself, and then push and puff. It was done before she could count to seventy one. Sometimes, she'd repeat that rhyme in her head if he took longer. Sometimes, he'd touch her breasts, to start himself. Sometimes, then, she'd be shocked to find she liked that. It never lasted long enough for her to wonder about. Then he'd go to sleep and she'd wash herself and be free for another two days.

But it would be different with a different man. The subversive thought surprised her. *A man like Spanish Will, say.... He was strong, tough and firm and yet his skin looked like it might be satin to the touch. And he was so proud of himself, he might even want her to touch him too...* Her cheeks flamed. She looked around the dark room guiltily, as though someone might hear her thoughts. She made herself change the subject. *Or a man like the viscount, who might say things to inflame her before he brought that lean body to hers, and smile down into her eyes, and kiss and stroke her, taking a long time with those long hands...*

Maggie was appalled at herself. Dreaming of such things with a Bow Street runner? And a Peer of the Realm? *And Maggie Pushkin?* As if she could do that with either man. Even if she ever let herself, which of course she never would. But *if?* Why, they'd scorn her as soon as they left her, and never want to see her again. The runner because he was too sure of females. So long as she remained chaste with him, he'd treat her well. And the viscount! He'd think her a drab, a slut, a common fishwife. Which last, at least, was exactly what she was. The other things too, if she ever crawled into bed with either man.

She saw the folly of it, and laughed to herself, albeit weakly. She settled back again. *But maybe, a man with Spanish Will's dark allure, his vitality. A man who also had the cool, easy grace and subtle humor of the viscount?*

Aye, a man who was two in one, and neither one. A dream fellow, made of the best parts of both men, and with no real male part at all. Now there was the fellow for her!

Desire evaporated as suddenly as night sweat from a bad dream, leaving only a residue of shame. And only a taste of regret. There were worse things than longing for things in the night. There was loss of independence. That came from having *that* with a man.

Maggie stretched luxuriously. The bed was wide and hers alone in all directions. As was her life and her future. No one suspected her of anything anymore. Except maybe of being easy prey because she was a widow. But that was nothing new. She yawned. Yearnings were like dreams. If you went on with your life, you forgot them in the morning. Her desire was not forgotten. But put where it belonged. She closed her eyes, and slept. Dreamlessly.

Chapter Eleven

"Not just yet, my lord," Spanish Will said.

Lucian cocked an eyebrow. He was ready to go out on inquiries with the runner again, but Spanish Will did not move from behind his desk. Instead, he leaned back, eyeing his visitor thoughtfully. "I've kept my end of the bargain. But now, as to yours...."

Lucian tilted his head to the side. "Behold me here before you, Mr. Corby. At nine in the morning, at Bow Street. An almost obscene hour of the morning, best viewed from the other side of night. I was up late last night because of the masquerade. Yet see? I make the sacrifice gladly. You said you were going to look into, ah...'knocking shops' next. I'm prepared to go with you. What part of the bargain could you be speaking of?"

"The part where I accompany you someplace I would feel as out of place in as you will in a 'ah...knocking shop,' my lord."

Lucian nodded. "I see. No knocking shops today then?"

The runner's expression grew serious. "I've been hearing rumors. Nothing I can act on, or believe me I would. No, what I keep hearing is the kind of rumor that's floated from person to person so that by the time it gets to me it's too watery to hold water, do you know what I mean? Enough to make me wonder, though. So what I'd like to do today, with your help, is interview a relative of yours."

Lucian's face grew still.

"I could take him on myself, of course," Will said, "but I wouldn't get far. I never do, not with the gentry or their servants. See, soon as I say 'Bow Street,' all know I work for His Majesty. But so does a hangman. And they'd no sooner invite me into their parlors than the Newgate hangman. I frighten the lower classes and shame the upper. I can talk to the lower fast and easier. All I have to do is make faces at them. The gentry have ways to hide from me, and when they do talk to me, it's down. I don't care about that. But

I care about how much cooperation I can get from them. You could help just by standing at my side, my lord."

"I said I'd help," Lucian said coldly. "Is it too much to ask just who you're talking about?"

"Did I not say it? Forgive me," Will said amiably. "Your cousin, Sir James St. Cloud."

Lucian relaxed, visibly. He shook his head. "Your sense of humor, Mr. Corby, is quite beyond me. I take it you enjoy terrifying your accomplices?"

"No. Why should I?" Will asked with interest. "Who were you afraid for? Oh. Your brother Arthur? No, I've only heard the usual rumors about motive there, and at that, they're fewer than the ones I hear about yours. Your sisters haven't got any motives I can see. Now, your Mama terrifies me. She could put down an earl fast as a sick cat, had she a reason to do it. But I doubt she'd slay a brother, even though she was vexed by the thought of his upcoming marriage...but so she was vexed, wasn't she?

"Oh, yes," he said, seeing Lucian's stunned expression, "I wasn't jesting, my lord. I suspect everyone. The thing of it is though, some I suspect more than others. Your cousin Sir James was spending money like it was going out of fashion. Leastways, until your uncle was done for. Since then, he's been prudent as a parson. Not a wager written in the books at his club nor placed at any of the hells where he was known to spend his time. He's least in sight these days and nights. Sudden changes after a sudden murder make me wonder. I must talk with him. You could make it easier. Will you?"

"Why should I not?"

Will fixed him with a steady gaze. "Well, my lord, gentry coves sometimes think their families are sacred, and above the law."

"Do they?" Lucian permitted himself a small smile, "But most men think their families are sacred, and if not above the law, then certainly beyond it. Don't they?"

"I wouldn't know," Will said simply, "I have no family. As for sacred? I don't hold much sacred, except the law—as I enforce it. I do know nobody's beyond it unless they're dead. I'd love to discuss philosophy all morning," he added, rising and reaching for his coat, "but I think we'd best be getting on our inquiries now. My lads tell me Sir James wasn't seen coming home last night. Where do you think he might be?"

"Out all night? Let me think... I doubt at any female's lodgings. He's not in the petticoat line. Dame Fortune is the only mistress he's ever had. Not at his club—not all night. Most hells have closed by now, unless he got into some game that's still running. Some go on for days."

"No," Will said, "he hasn't been seen at any hell. Not the lowest nor the highest. I'd have heard."

Lucian frowned. "His friends are all gamesters...wait. This hour of the morning? *Tats.* Yes. That is to say, Tattersalls. It's Monday morning? Monday and Thursday mornings they have auctions. He'll be there. He might have stayed late, wherever he was, and just gone there. He wouldn't miss an auction at Tats."

"I hadn't heard he was a whip or a bruising rider."

Lucian laughed. "Neither, you're right. But there's a betting book there. More important than that, he follows the men who buy horseflesh. It's worth money to him. You see, he wagers on more than horse races. He takes an active interest in carriage races. He bets on the hunt. Lord! He once wagered as to whether Old Carstairs would buy a team of chestnuts or grays, and won. But he knew Carstairs' preferences and what was for sale that week because he takes note of things like that. Not all gambling is luck, Mr. Corby. Much of it is observation."

"Then he should be a rich man instead of floating on the river Tick, as I hear he is," Will said. "The news is out, his pockets are to let. The duns are at his door. How observant can he be?"

"I said not *all* gambling is luck. If he limited his wagers to his observations, my cousin might well be a rich man. He's not exactly a fool. Unfortunately for him, he *is* a gamester. That means he tries his luck as well. He has little of that, I'm afraid."

"Then, Tattersalls," Will said, winding a scarf around his neck. "Nearer your part of town than mine, closer to Hyde Park than Bow Street, any rate. You've got your carriage?"

Lucian checked, then grinned. "Waiting just outside. But you surprise me. Getting spoiled, Mr. Corby?"

"Aye, but it isn't just that. A man arrives at a fine establishment like Tattersalls, he needs to step out of a carriage so as not to be unduly noted. When you come with me, you try to slip into my world. The same applies when I go with you."

"An excellent point," Lucian said. "I only wish I'd taken my high perch phaeton. Had I known where I was going, I would have. They appreciate such things at Tats. I can only offer another lumbering closed carriage today."

"Too bad," Will said as they walked to the outer door. "I suppose it's nicely warmed too? A pity. Not an invigorating ride, like going in your open phaeton, with wheels high as I am? That would have been a rare old treat, with the streets being cobbled with ice today. What a shame you don't get another chance to skate me around London town hanging on by my fingertips."

"There's always tomorrow," Lucian said pleasantly, "but I prefer saving my neck even above the joys of risking yours. The roads *are* glass. Now they're saying it will get worse before it gets better. Entrepreneurs are testing the ice on the Thames. They're thinking of holding another Frost Fair if it freezes solid enough. There hasn't been a really big one since Charles Second's day."

"Frost Fair?"

"Yes, a fair like St. Bartholomew's, or Smithfield, only right here, on the river. They had one when I was a boy, but it was only a matter of a few tents and a roasted ox. They're saying this could be big as the one in the olden times. Tents, amusements, music, dancing, fireworks, food and shops, the lot. All of it on the frozen Thames. Between London Bridge and Blackfriar's, they think."

"Wonderful idea," Will said approvingly. "Why freeze to death alone if you can get other people to do it with you, and charge them money for it too? Give a clever man a dead cat and he'll find a way to sell it. But God bless Londoners. They can take a block of ice in winter and profit from it."

The viscount's carriage was warmed by hot bricks, and so well padded and sprung that Will hardly felt the cobbles they were passing over. It was like gliding, he thought as he sat back against the fat leather squabs. "A body could get used to traveling like this," he remarked as they traveled westward.

"It's comfortable, but it takes no skill to drive this ark," Lucian commented.

"Aye," Will agreed, "but I believe a man should find comfort where he can, when he can. Life will bring him challenges enough."

Lucian bit back what he was about to say. He realized it was foolish to mention the pleasures of fending off boredom. He doubted Will knew the meaning of the word.

*

The horses were being paraded in the open courtyard outside the paddocks before the auction so that potential buyers could see them put through their paces. Will paid little attention to them. He was more interested in the crowd of men watching than the merchandise they were there to buy. All the horses looked prime to him anyway. They came in different colors and had different markings, but they all were glossy, sleek and bright-eyed, worthy of riding, pulling carriages or racing.

But he knew he wasn't seeing the same animals the viscount was. He thought of horses as beasts of burden, replaceable machines. Maldon knew them bone and blood. It was obvious from the way he stared, his eyes narrowing as he watched them trot by him. The usual blasé nobleman was rapt. He paused as a gleaming roan came close. Seeing that, so did the groom who led the horse. Almost as though he couldn't help it, the viscount put one hand on the animal's muscular shoulder and ran it along its sleek shining side.

Tattersalls was the most famous horse emporium in London, but like all things for sale in London, a man had to know what he was looking at. Will saw that the viscount knew what he was seeing, and lusted for it.

The stables were vast and well designed. They were fronted by long arcades where horse and man were kept dry in all weather by high vaulted roofs upheld by rows of white Grecian columns. It gave the place the look of an ancient temple. Tattersalls was built for the worship of horses, and flaunted it. There was actually a small open-air Grecian temple in the courtyard. The altar in its center had a marble statue of a horse mounted on it.

The barns were huge, clean and well ventilated. Nothing less would do for the exquisite steeds and the gentlemen who came to adore and bargain for them. Will had seen less desire on men's faces as they picked out women for a night at equally expensive brothels. He was impressed. Then annoyed. He knew too many people who would kill to live in a place half so fine. But then, none of them were worth two hundred guineas to anyone, alive or dead. And that was only for a passable mount, the viscount had said. A hunter would cost more, a good team for a fine carriage even more, and a racehorse more than that. There were over a hundred gentlemen there who looked like they could well afford it.

But that was only how they dressed. Will knew many might be debtors. The only difference between them and the poor souls he saw in debtors' prison was that the tradesmen they owed money accepted it as a fact of life. A man of fashion commonly owed his butcher, his baker and his candlestick maker, often not paying his bills for months. His name ensured they'd be paid one day. They had to be content with that. Unless word got out that he was about to lose everything. Then, and only then, would he be dunned, his debtors rightly fearing he'd sell up and leave the country forever.

The people Will knew wouldn't get away with owing a butcher three pence for three minutes, even though they'd no more think of flying for the Continent than they would of flying off a rooftop.

There were less than elegant gentlemen there too. Not all men who knew horses were rich enough to buy them. Will recognized plenty of sharpers and touts. They averted their faces when they saw him. But he wasn't interested in anything but murder today.

"See him?" Will finally asked, a trifle testily, irritated by the thought of so much money being wasted. And he saw the viscount was looking at the horses more than at the gentlemen.

"Hmm? Oh. James. No, nowhere in sight. Sorry, that roan caught my eye. Look at that gait! Still, let's go ask someone, shall we? Or else I'll wind up bidding and regretting it. I'm not a man to waste my money, Mr. Corby. But desire does ride me hard."

"You'd never catch me putting my hard-earned money on any living thing," Will muttered. "Bad enough I worry about my own health. I wouldn't put a guinea into anything that can pull up lame, get sick, or up and die on me."

"Easy to see why you've never wed," Lucian commented, and went in search of one of the salesmen.

The stables were warm and smelled of hay and horse, manure and moist earth. It was a curiously pleasant spring-like smell on a frigid day, Will thought. Lucian went up to a gentlemen holding the reins of a horse. He was so well dressed Will was surprised he turned out to be merely a salesman.

"Sir James? Haven't seen him in a while, now you come to mention it," the man told Lucian. "Not all last week. That's odd too. Hardly seems like the week's starting if he's not here. Is he ill, sir?"

"No, at least I think not. When did you last see him?"

"Let's see… Well, there it is!" the man said, his expression lightening as he was struck by an idea. Then it fell into lines of sorrow. "What a lummox I am not to think on it. The poor gentleman's grieving. I heard his uncle died, and then I didn't see him no more. There it is. If you see him, sir, tell him John Granger sends his condolences, as do we all. Poor Sir James must be all cut up. Not like him to miss the auctions."

Lucian was quiet as he and Will walked back to his carriage. "He was that fond of your uncle?" Will finally asked.

"No," Lucian said simply.

"Then if he's all cut up, it's because he's all to pieces. Maybe was expecting your uncle's will to remedy that? I really must speak with him. Now more than ever."

"I know you must," Lucian said in a troubled voice. "As must I. We'd best go to his house. It's not far. I'm surprised you lost track of him, Mr. Corby. I'd think you'd have all his entrances and exits watched."

"I did, and do," Will said as he climbed back into the coach, "it's just that no one's seen him for days."

"My cousin, Sir James, in Caroline Mews," Lucian told his driver, "and quickly."

Sir James St. Cloud's house was in a neat, quiet street, not far from his late uncle's. It was a narrow three-story house snugged in a row of similar ones. The door knocker was on, which meant, at least, that the owner of the house was still in London.

"Is my cousin in?" Lucian asked as soon as the door opened. "It's urgent I see him. Come man, if he's not here, at least give me his direction. You know me. His cousin, Maldon."

"It's you, my lord, forgive me," the butler said with obvious relief. "The light was in my eyes. It's that good you're here, my lord. For he won't go out, nor have anyone in. But I can't see how he can refuse you. It will be that good for him. Your coats? Then, this way, gentlemen, if you please. He's in the library. He has been for some time. We can get him out from time to time, but..."

They came to the library. The butler knocked and then opened the door. "Your cousin, Lord Maldon, sir. And a friend. Here to see you. Sir?"

The room was dim, the draperies pulled closed, but the fire in the hearth gave enough light for them to see the man slumped in a chair near it. His cravat was undone, he sat in shirtsleeves. His jaw showed at least two days' dark bristles. His hair was rumpled. Thickset and strong featured, Sir James wasn't a bad-looking fellow when dressed and combed. He was still attractive in a raffish sort of way. Especially when he looked up and greeted his cousin with a wide smile totally at odds with his woebegone appearance.

"Maldon! Come to solace me, have you? There's a good fellow."

"Come to find out what it is I must solace you about," Lucian said. "I'd no idea you were that fond of Uncle."

His cousin frowned. "Uncle? Oh. Aye. No, I didn't care a fig for the old bleater, thought you knew that. Who's your friend?"

"This is Mr. Corby, from Bow Street."

"Zounds!" Sir James said, "a redbreast! Wait—hold on a tick...Corby—that dark phiz—*Spanish Will*, is it? Pleased to meet you. Heard about you. Who hasn't? You caught that cully what slit throats over in St. Giles, didn't you? Aye, and the one what carved up that bit of Muslim at Mother Barrows place, right? And..."

"James," Lucian said repressively, "compare notes with Mr. Corby later. What I—we—would like to know is where you've been these past days."

James' pleasure faded. He looked down at his boots. "Well, when a chap's short of the ready rhino, 'specially if he owes a round sum, he don't want to show his phiz, does he?"

Lucian sighed. He thought his cousin too old for it, but James considered himself a dashing young man of fashion. It was the rage for such men to speak as though they were from the lowest slums. He thought Will would probably understand him better than he could. He did.

"Oh, too right," Will said pleasantly, "but the thing of it is, Sir James, that there ain't a bailiff nor a dun camped on your doorstep, nor one in sight. Now, it's my experience that when a fellow's lacking the ready, his creditors stand two in line on his front step and have three round the back in case he tries to give them the slip."

"Snapt!" Sir James said with admiration. "Damned if you ain't a downy one. No wonder you got yourself such a name. Come, have a seat. Some brandy? It's the best. I should know, been pulling on it all night."

"It's morning now, James," Lucian said coldly. "Do you mind telling me what's going on? And in English?

His cousin looked guilty. He was almost thirty and acted as though he were seven. He looked it now. "The whole of it?"

"All," Lucian said, removing newspapers from a chair and sitting. "But I should tell you Mr. Corby's interest in your explanation transcends the matter of your debts."

"Really?" James said with pleasure. "Famous cove like Spanish Will interested in *me*? Well, no sense holding back, is there? Only...I'd prefer if your Mama don't get her jaws on this, Maldon. I can talk my mother round, but not if yours gets to her first."

"Agreed," Lucian said.

"Well, the thing is I'd got myself to point non plus. Mean to say, I picked the wrong horse once too often. Played the wrong card. Backed the..."

"Yes. Understood," Lucian said impatiently.

"Had no money, in short," James said, "and didn't know where the next sou was coming from."

"Why didn't you apply to me?" Lucian asked.

"Well, damme, Maldon, had I done, you'd have come through, but you'd have given me a jaw-me-dead, wouldn't you?" James said irritably. "And I could get that from my Mama, couldn't I? Anyway, it was beyond that. Owed a *lot*, you see."

"Did you apply to your late uncle?" Will asked.

James looked astonished. "So that's what this is about? Lud, no! He was so stiff rumped he made Maldon here look like a merry Andrew! We didn't get on. Not to say a bad word about the deceased, but he didn't see anything in me."

"You didn't expect any legacy from him?" Will asked.

James laughed. "As soon expect one from the man in the moon! He thought me a wastrel. Well, so I am, I suppose. No, I had to find another way out. And I did."

"And that was...?" Lucian prompted.

"Getting married," James said. "Aye, wish me happy, Cousin. Made it official just last week. It ain't in the papers yet. They want me to tell my family first, well, only proper. They'll be a howdy-you-do as it is, worse if I don't break it to them myself. Only right. But I ain't got up the nerve, as yet."

"Lord, man, who are you marrying?" Lucian asked.

"Mary Williamson," James said. "No, don't go cudgeling your brain, you never heard of her. Father's a cit. Aye, a mushroom. Common as dirt. But rich as the Golden Ball. Owns a manufactory in the West and a Mill in the North. Thinks the world of his daughter and wants his grandchildren to be good blood. He needed an entry into the upper classes. I'm it. He paid off my debts. So there you are. Haven't gotten out much since the happy day. Well, trying to think of a way to tell m'friends. And the family. Bound to be problems. By the way, you going to ring a peal over me?"

"Lord, no!" Lucian said. But privately, he was shocked. He rallied quickly. James wasn't his heir, after all. James' estate was in the wilds of Derbyshire, where doubtless his new father-in-law would want him to settle down, and where he'd seldom run into him. And his debts would be his father-in-law's problem in future. "Is that why you're in hiding?"

"Not exactly. There's another small matter..." James looked down at his hands and mumbled, "Promised the old cit I wouldn't gamble no more. Aye, it came to that. But see, thing of it is, don't know how not to if I go to my old haunts. And don't know where else to go."

"A problem, certainly," Lucian agreed.

"So you weren't upset by your uncle's bequests?" Will persisted.

"Of course I was," James said in astonishment. "Wouldn't be getting married had he left the lot to me, would I? Didn't think he was ready to stick his spoon in the wall, though. Would have been nicer to him, had I," he said, brooding. "He was getting married himself, though. No way a man could have known."

"And where were you that night he died?" Will asked softly.

"Gaming," James said, "in the usual places, 'til dawn. Trying to get my own back, you know. Much good that did me."

Lucian looked at Will. Will shook his head. "So I heard. I've no more questions, Sir James. At the moment."

Lucian rose. "Then I wish you happy, James. I hope to see you on the town again soon. By the way, if you're looking for places to go, you might try the menagerie at the Strand. Nothing to bet on there, but plenty of interesting animals. Oh. And Miss Williamson? When shall I meet her?"

"You'll be invited. Her father will hold some sort of 'do.'" James said absently.

Lucian paused at the door. "Tell me, James," he asked curiously, "do you like her at all?"

"Like her?" James asked, surprised. "Aye, why not? Nice little thing. Pretty too, if you're in the petticoat line. Thing is, I'm not. Well, needs must, when the devil drives. The menagerie, you say? There may be something in that."

"Don't say it," Lucian said as he and Will got back into the carriage. "My sympathies are with Miss Williamson too."

"Mine aren't," Will said with a grunt. "Selling yourself is selling yourself, whether for bread, diamonds or a wedding ring. I don't give my sympathies to whores."

"But my cousin is selling himself as well."

"Aye, just so."

Lucian was silent a moment. "I see your point," he finally said. "But at least you've no more reason to suspect him."

"Don't I? He needed money. So much so he sold his birthright. Murder's easier than that, I think. Any rate," Will said, taking out his pocket watch, "the morning's almost gone. We'd best move smartly, do we wish to interview some bawds. They lay about mornings but get ready for the working day as afternoon comes on. We can see one or two if we go now. Or I can go alone. It's up to you."

"I'm at your disposal," Lucian said, "only let me stop at my house and leave my coach. I'm naturally fascinated at the prospect of visiting low houses of ill-repute in broad daylight, you understand. But just squeamish enough to not wish to advertise my presence there to the immediate world. You don't have to say it, Mr. Corby. Were they expensive ones in the heart of town, I might not be so reluctant. Grant me my idiosyncrasies. I have standards to uphold, even in dissipation. Since you're willing to laze about in carriages with dissipated gentlemen like me, we'll take a hired hack, I think."

"I never argue with a man who likes to spend his money on his comfort, my lord."

"Especially if it means his own?"

"Just so," Will said pleasantly.

Lucian went into his house to see if there were any messages for him before he left again. Will followed, idly, but his eyes missed nothing. It didn't seem to occur to the nobleman that the runner had never been in his house before. It occurred to Will.

"Well, that's it," Lucian said, after skimming a few notes and pocketing a few others. "We may as well go now."

But the door knocker sounded before they could leave the hall. And so when a footman opened the door, Lucian's visitor was startled to see him standing there as though he'd been expecting her.

Lucian recovered first, though he was equally surprised. "Louisa," he said, bowing, "to what do I owe this singular honor?"

The misty morning light became her. She wore a black cloak, but the voluminous hood had a lavender lining and it softened her face, emphasizing her best feature, her fine eyes. They looked past Lucian at Spanish Will.

"Good morning, my lady," Will said, bowing slightly.

"We've just returned from an errand," Lucian said. "Would you care to come in?"

She held herself stiffly and stood tall. "Thank you, but I can't. I too was on my morning rounds." She indicated her maidservant, standing on the step behind her. "I was only about to drop off a note for you. This makes it simpler." She looked down at her gloves before she went on, and then raised her eyes to his face. "I'd like to ask a favor. I realized that as your late uncle's heir, you have recourse to his correspondence. My...your uncle evidently had a lively correspondence with a Mr. Bernard Preston. His widow came to call on me the other week. I should like to see her again. But in my pleasure at making her acquaintance I never asked for her direction. So, if you'd be so kind as to find her late husband's address for me? When you've a chance, of course."

"Of course," Lucian said. "I'll see to it this very afternoon. Are you sure I can't offer you some tea, at least? It's a bitter day."

"So it is, and tea would be delicious, thank you. But I'd rather complete my errands and get home to my own hearth before this brief bit of sunshine is gone."

He bowed, she dropped a brief curtsey, and left.

"Well," Lucian said as soon as the door closed. "Here's a complication. And now what?"

"Here's a gift from the gods, you mean," Will said, thinking furiously.

"I think we'd better step into the library," Lucian said, acutely aware of the footman standing by the door. "What do you mean 'gift'?" Lucian asked as he closed the library door behind them.

But Will was looking at the walls of bookshelves. There was a sort of naked hunger on his dark face that Lucian had never seen before. In fact, Lucian thought, before this moment, he'd never seen any expression the runner didn't mean him to see. This must honestly be beyond concealment.

Will heard the silence. He shrugged his broad shoulders. He was nothing if not self-aware. "Aye," he said, "the house, the title— I envy you none of it, because such things are beyond my ken. But this..." He swept an arm to indicate the rows of volumes. "This, I can envy. And the money, of course."

"Of course," Lucian said lightly, because it was too intimate a confession to treat otherwise. "My life's ambition is to read them all. I don't think I'll live that long. They've accumulated, like dust on the shelves. They're legacy as much as the title, the house and the money. You're welcome to try to do what I haven't. I'd be delighted to give them an airing." He paused, wondering if he had misspoken. The runner's look of naked longing might have simply been his wish that he could read. Or be able to read more easily. "But as for our winsome fishwife," Lucian said quickly, "what are we to do?"

"Invent an address for her and take the wench to meet the lady again, of course," Will said promptly, the thought of business chasing everything else from his mind. Which was as well. He'd been tempted. Fine thing, he thought, to borrow books from a man who you might have to see swing, albeit from a silken rope.

Lucian smiled. The fishwife would like that. "But if Louisa wishes to call on her there?"

"She'll send a note round first. Ladies do, don't they? We'll be sure to get it. As for after that? Mrs. Preston is moveable. She lives in Maidstone and is only staying with a friend in London."

"Excellent. Where?"

"I don't know. A good address. But not too good. Far enough away to make a visit to her inconvenient. Something just this side of respectable, as befits a scholar's widow. What do you think?"

They mulled it over and talked it out. In the end, they settled on Hampstead. "I've someone there," Will said vaguely, "who owes me a favor or two. I'll let you know when you can send to the lady.

What say we broach the matter to Mrs. P. tomorrow? After our inquiries."

"Right," Lucian said, "now—to the knocking shops?"

"So eager?" Will laughed, "but no. Now it's too late, and getting later. I've got to see to my acquaintance in Hampstead and set things straight. I'll see you in the morning?"

"Fine. I'll come by and fetch you again, as it's on the way," Lucian said. "Oh, and give your lads a rest. I don't want to find them frozen stiff in my alley in the morning. I'm off to the theater tonight with friends."

"You've been hanging about with Mrs. P. too long, my lads are tough as boot leather. But—the theater? For a fellow in mourning? Or are the rules different for noblemen?"

Lucian winced, chagrined. "I'd forgot." He scowled. "A few weeks more and I'd go without hesitation," he muttered, thinking aloud. "We weren't close and so all know, and people's memories are short. But his murder isn't even solved yet. No sense setting people's backs up. I made my plans weeks ago. I'll send a note to my friends...no. Better tell them myself."

"Tomorrow then, earlier than today," Will said, clapped on his hat, and left.

*

Lucian left his house as evening fell. The temperature had plummeted again. He decided to have his footman call a hackney. No sense pulling his own horses out on such a night.

The streets leading to the theater were clogged with traffic. Day workers were heading home for the night, those seeking entertainment were heading out. The pavements were crammed with hurrying people too. This was a district for playhouses, supper rooms, gaming houses, brothels, taverns and other places for an evening's pleasure. Lucian paid the driver and left the coach a street away to avoid the crush of private carriages and hackneys delivering people to the playhouse. He hurried onward; it was getting late.

Here the night was bright with more than moon and starlight. Lanterns in front of the theater vied with the new gaslights, bright bonfires in ashcans blazed on each corner to keep the peddlers and beggars from freezing fast. They were beacons of warmth in defiance of the shatteringly cold night. Pennants in front of the theater blew in the brittle breeze. They spoke of putting up a fair on the Thames if it froze solid. But tonight this street had become an impromptu, unlikely Frost Fair.

The war was grinding on, and Londoners wanted diversion even on a frigid night. Clerks and gentlemen, ladies and shopgirls thronged the walkway. Grand gentlemen swept by in greatcoats and cloaks, their ladies wrapped to their elegant noses, their hoods or dashing hats in place. There were soldiers and sailors on leave, reminders the war still was grinding on. Too many walked with a halt, some were missing limbs, many had arms or legs bound. Criers standing in their midst waved programs, shouting the attractions of the play, the farce and the afterpiece shown tonight.

Barrow women stood fast in the crowd like rocks in a flowing river, crying the virtues of their oranges and apples, nuts and gingerbread, flowers for my lady's hair. Prostitutes lurked at the head of every alley, shifting from foot to foot, grabbing passing men by their sleeves, hoping to delay one long enough to make a few pence. It was too early for them to be out in such numbers, and they were too bold at such a respectable hour. But they were practical. It would be too cold for even the most desperate of sellers or customers by the time the theater let out.

They'd better work fast, Lucian thought. People were starting to stream into the playhouse as he approached. He kept his hand on his wallet as he paused, looking for his friends. He finally spied a tall gangling gentleman and his lady standing under a gaslight, also obviously looking around. The gentleman saw him and waved frantically. "There he is! Hey, Maldon! Here!"

Lucian shouldered his way to them. The gentleman had a long, homely, friendly face. His companion was almost too lovely to be seen with such an ill-favored fellow, Lucian thought, as he always did. But then, she knew her escort well, and like everyone who did, had long since forgotten his lack of looks.

Lucian took her gloved hand, "My lady Elizabeth. How comes it that you grow lovelier each time I see you, and yet you're still wed to this wretch?"

"And how comes it that you're still such a flatterer, my lord?" she asked, smiling.

"He never gives up," her husband laughed, "but the other thing he's not changed since school days is his tardiness. Come along, Maldon. You're late, and if you don't stir yourself we soon will be."

"That's what I've come to tell you," Lucian said, "I can't go at all, Ian. My uncle, you see..."

His friend's merriment fled. "I'd heard. I'm so sorry. My sincerest condolences. I'd forgot. No, damme, but I didn't. Who could? The thing is on everyone's lips. I simply thought you and he weren't close, but what a fool I am..."

"No, you're not," Lucian said quickly. "You're right. I don't grieve. But you see, dare I go to the theater before his murder is solved, at the very least, I think my Mama will murder me. So you go ahead and we'll meet after, perhaps for a late supper? Mourners are allowed to eat, you see." He said it with a self-mocking smile that explained why those few he called friend remained so for so many years.

"Nonsense," the lady said. "It's a tiresome play and a worse farce, and so say all I've heard talking about it tonight. You've saved us from a boring evening. We wanted to talk with you anyway. Let's go to dinner now, I vow I perish from starvation."

Her husband beamed at her. "It's your condition keeps you ravenous, but you're exactly right, my dear."

"No!" Lucian said with pleasure. "Is it so?" The lady ducked her head and blushed. "Now here's good news!" he said. He took her hand. "You're sure you'd rather dine?"

"I am sure I shall perish if I do not," she declared.

"Well then, it's freezing, and I doubt you'd want another carriage ride..." Lucian mused. "I know a place not a street away makes the most divine coq au vin. You must try their duckling as well. Come along. What a beast he is not to feed you. But didn't I warn you what would happen if you chose him instead of me?"

He took her arm and walked, his head bent to hers, talking low, pretending to rail at her husband for such mistreatment. The streets were emptying quickly as the last theater goers filed inside. Barrow mongers began to roll their merchandise away. The pavements were almost clear by the time Lucian led the lady across the road. There were no sweepers to clear a path for them. It had been too busy for them to ply their brooms before, and was too empty to be profitable now. Some stragglers stood on the sidewalks before going into the playhouse, a last few coaches rumbled by. A few frozen snowflakes drifted down.

Lucian waited until the way was clear and then led the lady carefully across the cobbles. Her husband ambled a few paces behind them, making fond, amusing comments about female fidelity.

Lucian heard the rumbling before he heard the horrified shouts. He saw it all in a split-second and acted in the next one. He lifted his head and saw the foaming horse running amuck. It appeared in an instant, and bore down on them inexorably, its cart swaying wildly side to side like a cobra's head behind it.

There was no time to run back. Lucian opened both arms and grabbed the surprised lady. Holding her tight, he flung himself as far as he could, setting them both spinning out into the street. His only thought was to keep her close, and to land—if he could— safely away with her atop him so he could absorb the impact. The noise was terrifying, the sound of drumming hooves and the wild clatter of the cart suddenly the only sounds in the world.

He felt the rush of air as the horse came crashing by. The cart thumped against his leg as he threw himself away from it. He felt himself going aloft, he felt himself begin to fall. He turned, tumbling over and over, clutching her tight, never letting her go—

193

even as his shoulder hit the ground, even as shocking pain sliced across his face as his head slid along the cobbles. Then there was a sudden clap of profound pain. And then he felt no more.

Chapter Twelve

He didn't want to open his eyes. Because he wasn't sure he could. And he was worried about what he'd see if he could see anything. He might not even have an eye anymore, Lucian thought groggily, as he tried to pry one open. But he still had his ears.

"Stand away," a voice demanded. "Stand back and let the doctor do his work."

Well, at least they hadn't said "let the coroner" have a look, Lucian thought. That was something. He cracked open an eye, saw nothing, and raised a hand to rub at it. His hand was dragged back.

"Here!" an unfamiliar voice said. "Don't touch it. Ah. Good. There's ice right here. It will work as well as water. Hand me your handkerchiefs, gentlemen. Now, let's clean this up. No, don't touch it, I said! Let me see. Good...good."

Lucian didn't know how such pain could be good. The snow pressed to his face felt like hot coals, the drag of cloth was like flames licking his cheek. But now he could at least see what had blocked his vision was only blood. His blood. The rest of his body was returning to him too, and it all hurt. His face, his leg, his..."Elizabeth!" he croaked as he struggled to sit up. "Elizabeth!"

"She's fine, old man," his friend's voice said from nearby. "Shocked, of course. But unhurt. Thanks to you."

"Unhurt?" Lucian said, trying to see for himself, pushing away the cloth his face was being swabbed with, "but the babe..."

"All's well. Miraculously. Because of you. Elizabeth rolled a fair way in your arms—and don't think I won't twit her about that for an eternity. But you held her fast. She's fine. She's waiting in the carriage. I'm taking her home as soon as we know how you'll do."

"I do fine. Have the doctor take a look at her," Lucian demanded.

"We'll have our own physician come round tonight. There's not a scratch on her, I promise you. She's shaken, but nothing hurts but her heart—for you," his friend Ian said soothingly, as though he was talking to a peevish child. He was kneeling on the cobbles next to Lucian. So was a portly man Lucian had never seen before. "Took you a long time to come around," Ian said. "Anything broken under all that blood, Doctor?" he asked the other man.

"No," the doctor said. Lucian winced as he prodded his cheekbone. "Not here, at least. Can you see my hand?" he asked Lucian. "How many fingers am I holding up?"

"Too many," Lucian said. "Let me up." He didn't know what was worse, the various pains calling in from all parts of his body or the fact that he was laying on the cobbles with a crowd of fascinating spectators gaping at him as though he were a raree show. But when the doctor put an arm around his shoulders and helped him sit, his ears began to buzz, the street tilted and he felt darkness rushing in from the edges of his vision.

"Put your head down," the doctor commanded, pushing on his neck. "We have to get him home," he told someone behind Lucian.

"I'll take care of that," Spanish Will's deep voice said. "First, tell me if there's anything needs tending to immediate."

"You!" Lucian exclaimed, trying to twist his neck to see the runner.

"Aye. I just happened to be passing by," Will said as Lucian struggled to stand, gave a strangled oath and sat again, "Ah. Something broken, then?"

"Difficult to say," the doctor said. "The light's no good here. We'll have to get him somewhere where I can work."

"We'll take him back to his house," Ian said. "My coach is ready, my wife's already in it. She'll want to thank him too."

"Good," the doctor said. "Speaking of wives, get word to mine, will you? She's waiting inside the theater. It won't be the first time I've had to desert her, but she does have to know my direction."

"I'll see to it," Will said.

Lucian began to rise to his feet, the runner at one side, his friend Ian, on the other. A keening cry interrupted them.

"He lives! Thank Gawd! He lives!" a new voice intruded. "Gawd have mercy upon us, he lives! She never did nuffin' like that before, good surs, on my life, never! She's a good lass, the best, I swear it on my Mother's grave!"

Lucian peered at a ragged-looking man who stood wringing his floppy hat between his hands, his dirty face set in an almost comic mask of despair. "I caught her at the end of the street, blowing hard, her eyes rolling in her head. But she stood still like a statcher fer me, she did. Good as gold, my Bess. She'd never. Some villain set her off is wot it is. Look for yerself, she's got a cruel wound on her poor rump. Aww, don't take her," he wailed, tears coursing down his seamed cheeks, "she never done nuffin' like. *Never!* She's all I got. But that ain't it. She's good, right as rain, she is. I've had her fifteen years! No, I lie. Sixteen, come next St. Swithin's Day! There ain't an ounce of meanness in her. She ain't sick, neither, why, she eats before I does every day. Oh, have *mercy*!"

"She's got a wound?" Will asked with interest. "I'll have a look."

"But she din't do nuffin'!" the peddler wailed. "One minute we's standin' there like we always does, gettin' ready to pack it in 'n go home. Next I know, she's off. But it ain't what she'd do on her own. It ain't like her a'tall. Oh 'ave pity!"

"What *is* he going on about?" Lucian said through gritted teeth as he was helped to his feet. He tested one leg. It hurt like blazes.

"It was his horse went wild," the runner said.

"Lost all my fine fruit," the old man gulped through his sobs. "Cart too. But that ain't nuffin'. Don't take my Bess, fine surs."

"Well who the devil wants your damned horse?" Lucian snarled, because try as he might, the leg didn't take much weight.

"They said as to how ye'd put her down!" the peddler grieved.

"Why would I do a thing like that?"

"He said as to how they needs to test her," the peddler whined, gesturing at Will. "Test her—*live or dead*, says he when I says I don't want to give her over to him, for how'm I to earn my bread if I do? I'm an old man. She's all I got!"

The peddler's keening made Lucian wince. "Tell you what," he said wearily, "take her round to my place. Give him my direction, Mr. Corby. Bring her to my stables and tell John James, my groom, that I said he should have a look at her. There's no better man for horses in London. Then you may take her home."

"Y'won't press charges 'gainst us?" the old man asked fearfully.

"I shudder at the thought of pressing anything at the moment," Lucian said as he began limping toward the carriage with the help of his friend and the runner.

"Well, sounds like you're yourself again," Ian said with relief.

"Unfortunately," Lucian said.

The ride to his home was an unpleasant blur to him. Elizabeth thanked him repeatedly. Ian thanked him whenever she paused for breath. Lucian tried not to groan because of that, and because he couldn't decide what part of his body hurt most.

"You kept me safe as an egg in a chicken," Elizabeth marveled for at least a third time. "Between your coat and your body, all I felt was a thump when we landed. But your poor head! I heard it hit. It sounded like a—I don't want to remember what it sounded like."

"Poor darling," her husband said. "You're the child's godfather, Maldon," he said fervently, "and you have my eternal gratitude."

"How brave!" Elizabeth said. "I cannot imagine how you had the courage."

"Nor can I," Lucian grunted, because the ride, smooth as it was, was making him sick to his stomach.

"The old man said someone hit his horse, he said there's actually a slash mark!" Ian marveled.

Elizabeth began to thank him again. But Lucian was trying not to empty his stomach, and so all he could do was nod. But not too vigorously, lest his head fall off.

The runner and the doctor saw him to his house and helped him inside. His valet came at a trot, all the servants were astir. Lucian waved them off, and refused to go to his bedchamber.

"If you don't, I'll let the doctor here have your pants down in your parlor," Will vowed. "I'm not leaving until we know the tally. You look green about the gills, my lord."

He looked far worse, the runner thought. One side of the viscount's face was badly abraded and already beginning to swell. He favored one shoulder, and limped, leaving bloody bootprints. His smile was crooked as he looked at Will. "Truth is," Lucian admitted, "I don't care to face the stairs. But you're right. Best sooner than later. Come along, Doctor, will you? I've ruined your evening at the theater, might as well let you to your work. Let's see what I've got left. Mr. Corby, you can entertain me as I crawl upstairs by telling me some long and pretty tales about why you were so close tonight."

"Can't a man go to the theater of an evening?" Will asked innocently, making Lucian realize it hurt to chuckle.

They helped him to his bedchamber. His valet helped him to undress. The doctor took inventory. Will stood by, taking a professional inventory of his own. The viscount wasn't a broad or heavily muscled man, but was well muscled, an entirely different thing. He was lean and sinewy strong, with not an ounce out of place. He'd do well in the ring, Will thought. He was stronger than he looked, and took pain well. He had to, tonight.

"I don't think the shoulder's broken," the doctor finally concluded. "A few ribs on the right, I'll strap them tight. I'll set some stitches to close the gash in the leg, and ask you to keep off it for a spell. If it putrefies, that's another matter. I've some salve for it and the face. I'd suggest a leech on that cheek tomorrow. Still, a few days rest and you should do well enough. Your head took quite a knock. If you begin seeing double, call me quick. Have your own physician call in the morning or I'll drop round if you like. You're a fortunate fellow, my lord."

Lucian smiled crookedly. "Indeed. I keep my teeth, my bones, and my lovely nose remains unbent."

"I'm not jesting," the doctor said. "A few inches more and you might have lost that leg, entirely. I've seen it happen."

"A few seconds more and you might have lost your *life* entirely," Will said. "That's what I thought would happen. You moved fast, and thought well."

"I didn't think at all," Lucian said ruefully.

"That fruit seller should have his noble beast in your stables by now," Will said, moving toward the door. "I think I'll have a look at it whilst you're being put together again."

"A charming excuse," Lucian commented, "since we all know it's because the sight of blood is so disturbing to you. I'm happy to spare your tender sensibilities."

Lucian was relieved to see the runner smile, and leave. He was fairly sure he could control his reaction to the pain of the doctor's ministrations, but preferred Spanish Will Corby to be far away if he couldn't. With good reason. By the time Will returned, Lucian was sitting back in his chair, exhausted and shaken. The doctor was putting his instruments away.

"Sewn, strapped, salved and settled," Lucian greeted him with a tired, lopsided smile. "You may safely enter, Mr. Corby." His voice grew harder. "I've been doing some thinking. I was too rattled to do much before. And so I'm very interested to know what state you found the so reliable Bess to be in."

"I almost asked the doctor here to have a look at her," Will said, "but your groom swears he can tend to it. Someone jabbed her right flank, my lord. Hard, and sudden. Too deep for a whip stroke. Now, why anyone would want to do that to a poor broken down old prad like her, I don't know. She'll take no lasting hurt, he says. Someone just wanted her attention, and fast. She's to pass the night in your stable so he can watch over her. Her owner will sleep nearby. He's so grateful he's vowing to keep you in oranges for the rest of your days."

"I prefer peaches," Lucian said, but he wasn't thinking of that. His eye had swollen halfway shut, and the bloodied scrape on his right cheek was turning black. But that wasn't the only reason his face grew dark and shuttered. He was remembering the sudden thunder of the horse bearing down on him. He doubted he'd ever forget it. He wondered if he'd have been able to do what he had done if he'd thought about it. That thought tormented him. As did another. He raised his eyes to Will. The runner nodded and answered the unspoken question.

"Aye," Will said, "it's possible. Like I said, I didn't think you could move out of the way that fast, myself. She was running mad. Straight for you. And you were the only ones in her path. All it took was a downward stroke of a knife or a sword stick. Could have been done by a passing horseman or a man on foot. It could have been an accident too. Or just some stray and random mischief. Such things happen in London. There was a crowd at the head of the street, barrows, pushcarts and horse-drawn carts. Vendors comparing notes at the end of the day. They were huddled together because of the cold, and it was dark outside the bonfires they made to keep from freezing to death. Even if I could talk to them all, I doubt anyone saw anything. But I'll ask around anyway, tomorrow night.

"As for now, I think you need to rest. Can you give him something for sleep?" Will asked the doctor.

"I could, but I won't," the doctor said. "Nor do I advise it. Sleep heals all but head wounds. It can deal eternal sleep in such cases. In fact, I'd have him wait a few hours before he sleeps at all. He won't have any trouble then."

"Care to sit up and try a hand at cards with me?" Lucian asked Will half-humorously.

"A fine idea," Will said, "but it's too easy playing cards with a man so mazed. No challenge. Let's make it Chess." He grinned like a wolf. "Stoke up the fire, get me some Scot's spirits or any good booze, and I'll win this house out from under you by morning."

201

Lucian raised an eyebrow. He winced at the pain, then laughed. "Chess?" he said. "But how will you be able to tell if I've dropped off to sleep? Still, yes. Certainly. I hope you're not too attached to your boots. Because you won't even own them by dawn."

They were settled down to their first game at a table set up by the hearth in the bedchamber, when Lucian's valet came in. He bore a tray with a decanter of spirits, and wore a worried expression.

"My lord," he said nervously, "there's a messenger from your lady mother to see you. He says your mother says it's urgent."

Lucian groaned. "Has rumor that many feet? Tell the fellow to tell her I do well, I am well, and she can see for herself in the morning. Your move, Mr. Corby."

"But it's not that…" the valet said hesitantly. "She wants you to come to her, you see."

"What's the trouble?" Lucian asked, and scowled. "Devil a bit, where are my wits? Send him up here, I'll ask him myself."

Neither man watched the chessboard, though both pretended to study it until the messenger, an unhappy looking young footman, arrived in the room. His eyes widened when he saw the viscount.

"What's toward?" Lucian asked immediately.

"My lord… Your mother requests your immediate attendance on her. See, it's young Mr. Arthur. Someone tried to kill him tonight."

They argued all the way down the stairs and into the viscount's coach.

"The fellow said your brother is mostly unharmed," Will said. "He said he lives. But you'll die if you career about like this. Look at you, man!" he thundered as Lucian let his head fall back against the leather padding in his coach.

"No, " Lucian groaned, "it would upset my stomach more. Listen, Mr. Corby." He paused to get his breath back. "I live. I will live. But I refuse to live in a state of apprehension, wondering what happened 'til dawn. Nor will I send messengers back and forth like badminton cocks all night. Nor have my mother come out at this hour, in this cold, even if she could pry herself from my brother's side. And what of him? I'll see for myself and hear the story first-hand. Someone tried to kill him? He was pushed in front of an oncoming hackney coach? He's hurt, but not mortally so? Bad enough my head rings like Christmas morning. I will not sit and wonder about that all night."

Will mumbled something bitter and vulgar under his breath. "I must be mad letting you go."

"The only way you could have stopped me is by flooring me, and that might well have killed me. Listen. I made up my mind. Think on, my Bow Street friend, if you'd made up your mind, do you think I could change it?"

Will grinned, until he looked at the viscount. It was a painful thing to do now, even by the meager unsteady light inside the coach. The flickering lantern was bright enough to show he was ashen and his bruises were beginning to darken. But his eyes burned. Will hoped it wasn't fever. He nodded. "Lay on MacDuff," he sighed.

Chess *and* Shakespeare? Lucian thought, amused. Then he sat back, hanging on to consciousness, hoping he wouldn't lose it before he got to his mother's house.

Will helped him limp in the door. By the time they arrived at the salon where the viscountess was waiting, Will was half holding him up. Lucian shook himself free, and straightened. He stood in the doorway looking at the scene by the fireside.

He sighed in relief. Arthur was there, looking whole, at least from what he could see. But he was wrapped in a blanket, holding a cup of something to his lips. His mother, in a dressing gown, sat beside him. They both stared when Lucian and Will walked in.

"Good God, Maldon!" Arthur said in a strangled voice.

Even his mother looked shaken. "What have you done to yourself, Lucian?" she asked in astonishment.

"An accident," he said, tilting one shoulder in a shrug, and immediately wincing for it.

Her face grew tight. She sneered. "I see. An accident with a bottle too many, I don't doubt. I knew something of the sort would come of your constantly associating with fist fighters. *Bruisers*, you call them. Ruffians, I say. *Sparring*? *Science*? Going to a *mill* is not like going to a horserace. It is watching two grown men battering each other with their bare fists. Bear baiting is more seemly, because at least you are wagering on animals. Champions or not, fashion or no, it is not a thing a *gentleman* ought to be doing."

Will stared. But Lucian only said smoothly, "Just so. But what of my brother? Don't tell me you were indulging as well, Arthur?"

Arthur began to speak, but his mother cut him off. "Before we get into that," she said acidly, "might one inquire as to why you've brought Mr. Corby to my home, at this hour of the night? Or is he perhaps one of the boon companions associated with your 'accident'?"

"Your pardon, Mama," Lucian said, as Will bowed, perfunctorily. "But surely, if Arthur was attacked, Mr. Corby should know of it immediately, you'll agree?"

The dowager huffed, accepting the logic with a nod. But she drew her voluminous dressing gown around herself, as though she expected the sight of an inch of her flesh would drive the runner to transports of lust.

"In spite of the hour, I felt we might have need of him," Lucian went on, "at least from what I understood of the message you sent to me. May I sit down, do you think?"

She waved him to a chair, and Lucian sank into it gratefully. Will sat next to him, and took out his notebook.

"Yes," the dowager said approvingly, "so you ought write down what happened. Someone tried to murder my son tonight."

Will bit back words that would tell her how she was more right than she knew. His first impulse had been to defend the viscount. That was new for him, and that was not good for his investigation. He firmly quashed his sympathies, and looked at the lady with polite inquiry.

"Tell them, Arthur," his mother commanded.

"I was out for the evening," Arthur explained, "going to a supper room. I wanted to be among people, you see, but didn't care to wish my mood on anyone I knew. Well, but I wasn't even good company for myself. I was going to Offley's, you know where it is, Maldon. Maldon can tell you, Mama, it's quite respectable really, even if it is in Covent Garden. A fellow in mourning can go there without setting anyone's back up. It's not a theater or anything like. They do have singing, sometimes, along with the food, which is plain, but good. I hoped it might cheer me up. The streets were crowded, so I was waiting on the curb for a chance to cross over. I suppose I was distracted, thinking about so many dismal things. But I felt two hands on my back, and before I knew it I was on my knees in the street. Luckily, the hackney stopped in time...."

"Show them!" his mother interrupted.

Arthur drew back the blanket with slightly shaking hands to show his tightly knitted pantaloons torn at both knees. The knees that poked through were scraped and reddened. A moment later, he twitched the blanket back, his youthful face pink with embarrassment. "There's only a scuff or two," he said apologetically. "It only stings. I oughtn't to be upset. But I suppose I am, if only because I've been thinking about what could have happened if that driver hadn't been watchful. Now I'm wondering why it happened. First Uncle. Now me. But why?"

"What time was this?" Will asked, his dark eyes locked on Arthur.

"Around seven, I can't say. I didn't look at my watch..."

"Are there any witnesses?" Will asked.

"Yes, yes, I did remember about that," Arthur said, fumbling in his pocket. "I got the name and the direction of the hackney driver, he was so shaken, poor fellow. And a Mr. Greenwood, who happened to be passing by and came to my assistance. Here's his address. But neither saw who pushed me. I asked. I went straight home. I confess I wouldn't have told Mama," he added sheepishly, avoiding Lucian's eyes, "but my valet did. She insisted I come here immediately so she could reassure herself."

"Without changing your britches?" Will asked, his eyebrows high.

"I sent to him not to do so," the dowager said. "I wanted to see all, and have the authorities see it too. I believe you call that 'evidence'?"

"I actually had to put them back on," Arthur said with an embarrassed shrug.

"Someone is after the men of my family," the dowager said angrily, sitting up straight, her hands clenched. "First my brother, now my son. Even Lucian is not safe. That is to say, if he doesn't manage to break his own neck first. I grant my brother behaved foolishly in going where he did, when he did, for whatever reasons he did so. But this puts an entirely different complexion on the matter of his death, does it not, Mr. Corby?"

"Aye, it would, if it's not the young gentleman's purse someone was after and not his life," Will said, pocketing the papers Arthur gave him. "The streets in that district are crowded of an evening, my lady. It could have just been some bungnippers at work."

"What?"

"Begging your pardon, Ma'am," Will said sweetly. "Thieves cant and not a word I'd use in front of a lady like yourself, but I'm not used to speaking in front of the gentry, do you see? I was speaking of pickpockets. See, they usually work in threes. There's the file, who does the forking, a bulker, whose job it is to push the mark—in this case, Mr. Arthur here. And then there's the adam tiler, he's the cully what flies with the goods before the pigeon can sing. That's three for the show—one to distract, and I guess there ain't a better distraction than shoving a fellow on his face, is there? One to nab, and one to snag the prize and flee."

"I'm not such a flat as that, Mr. Corby," Arthur said reproachfully. "I looked right off. But my wallet was untouched."

"P'raps they were a bit too eager," Will shrugged. "Only meant to make you stumble, but pushed too hard, then cut line before someone could sing beef on them." He cast a glance over to the viscount to see what he thought of his sudden descent into the sort of slang the dowager seemed to expect of him.

The man had been very quiet. One look showed Will why. Lucian's face was deathly white, his high forehead was dewed with moisture, his long eyes half closed against his pain.

Will stood, putting his notebook away. "I think that's all we can do tonight. I'll follow the matter further, tomorrow. Do you remember more, or hear or see anything unusual, let me know at once. My lord, I'm done here now. Are you leaving as well? It's grown very late."

Lucian heard Will's voice as though from afar, through an overlay of humming in his ears. He looked around the room and saw Arthur watching him with puzzlement. His mother frowned as she studied him. He shook himself, and managed to drag himself to a standing position. "Indeed, Mr. Corby is right. It is very late, and I find myself exhausted. Tomorrow, then."

He strode to the door, holding himself erect as he could, thinking only, *one foot in front of the other, one foot in front of the other,* until he got into his coach again. Then he sank back. "Lord," he said with a soft groan. "I thought I might have to stay in that chair all night, and think of a reason why in the morning."

"Any reason you don't want them to know what happened to you tonight?"

"Any reason they should?" Lucian asked as answer. "They're frightened enough as it is. As am I. I can't wait to get home."

Will frowned. That didn't sound like the Viscount Maldon he had come to know. Perhaps he didn't know the man that well after all. Or maybe the man was more in pain than he looked to be, though that was hard to imagine.

But the moment the carriage drew up at his door, the viscount was out of it and up his front step as though nothing was bothering him but a pebble in his boot. "Come along," he told Will as he went into the house. He made straight for his study, and motioned Will to a chair. "I won't be a moment," he muttered, taking out a sheet of paper. "Then, we must talk."

Lucian swiftly wrote one note, took another sheet and dashed off another. Will waited, relaxing in the unaccustomed comfort. The room was luxurious as every other one in this house. The fire in the spacious hearth made it pleasantly warm, the furniture was old...no, his own furniture was old, Will thought. The value of each item here made "antique" a better word, he decided without envy. Because it was about as far from his life as a room on the moon would be. The pop and crackle of the fire and the scratch of the viscount's quill were the only sounds to intrude on the quiet night until he put down his pen, and rang for a servant.

"These must go out at once," Lucian told his butler when he arrived. "Send to the stables, and have someone who is a swift, sure rider set out at first light. If some daring lad wants to go sooner, I'll make it worth his while. Speed is of the essence. Have him come back and tell me when it was delivered. It will take a day at least, both ways, please give him money for the journey. Thank you. Oh, blast," he muttered, one hand to his head. "Mr. Clower," he called to the butler, "a moment more, if you please."

He wrote out two more notes, and handed them to the butler. "There's no such immediacy about these. But they are to go out in the morning. Please see to it, will you?"

"Of course, my lord," the butler said.

When he left, Lucian relaxed at last. He loosened his neckcloth, and then with a muffled oath, unwound it and pulled it off entirely. He lay his head against the high wooden back of his chair. All the frantic tension that had kept him upright was gone. He looked drained, but easier in his mind. Will looked his question at him.

"A note to my son's headmaster," Lucian explained softly, closing his eyes, "instructing him to keep the boy close, under his observation at all times, and not allow him any visitors. I said there might be a problem with someone who had a grudge against the family. He's a wise man, he'll be careful. Another note told Nick to

208

be on his guard until I wrote to tell him otherwise. I feared he might revolt against being so restrained if I did not. He's a steady lad. But he has spirit. After what I wrote, I don't doubt he'll find the mystery more intriguing than frightening, and hold to my directions."

"So that was what you were afraid of," Will exclaimed, almost with relief.

Lucian opened his good eye and tilted his swollen mouth in a smile. "My dear Mr. Corby, that is the *only* thing I am afraid of, now or ever. ...That, and of wearing the wrong jacket, or a coat that is out of style, of course," he added in a burlesqued drawl.

"And the other two notes?"

"To my sisters," Lucian sighed. "The two that are still in London. My mother can inform the others, and doubtless will do. But they're back in the countryside now, and so I doubt in any imminent danger. I also doubt anyone will disturb the two who are here, but I had to be sure they knew at once, one never knows..."

He pulled himself up, and the eye Will could see stared back at him gravely. "My Mama was right about one thing. This puts a different complexion on everything, does it not?"

Will shook his head. "It might have been coincidence."

Lucian raised a brow. "You might as well say snow in winter is a coincidence, Mr. Corby."

"Who is your heir, my lord?" Will asked, not denying it.

"Nicholas, of course."

"After him?"

Lucian frowned. "Arthur... Ah. I anticipate you. After him? To tell the truth, I don't know, precisely. I should, of course. But I don't consider myself to be tottering on the brink of the grave—or at least, I didn't until tonight. I'm not as involved with lineage as perhaps I ought to be. All I know is that I seem to have enough family. Sometimes, too much. I'll have to ask Mother, or work it out myself, on paper. My sisters have been astonishingly fruitful. My nephews however, have not fascinated me, nor have my cousins.

I'll find out the precise order of succession. But tonight I'm not up to it."

He opened his good eye. "Still...come to think on, that strains credulity, Mr. Corby. Why kill Uncle, and then me, and then Arthur too? To what purpose? Inheritance? No, that would be a sequence of killings that would surely alert the authorities. You can't dispose of a man's entire line so easily. The Tudors and Plantagenets had to go to war to try to do it and even they were not successful. No. Were that so, I'd be looking for a nobleman and a madman both. And in the family. Not that it is inconceivable, mind. It's just that the madmen in our family tend to be eccentric rather than lethal.

"Perhaps it *is* a grudge against the Name. But this is not fourteenth century Florence, and as I said, we are not exactly de Medicis. At least, there's no stain of blood insult I ever heard of." Lucian's hands fisted on the arms of his chair. "We must know more, Mr. Corby. We must."

"Your brother's accident wasn't far from where yours was. The times weren't that far apart, either. I'll talk to the witnesses, those your brother gave me and those I find. And find them I will. It might've been the same fellow that did it. And I remind you, it might have only been a drunken gent, at that. Someone out for mischief. Don't look at me like that, my lord. Your set have odd ideas of amusement. What about the way fashionable young blades delight in harassing the Watch, eh?

"Now there's a sport I don't understand any better than your Mama understands prize fighters," Will mused. "After all, how much of a lark is it to terrify some poor old pensioner? And him only trying to put bread in his mouth by sitting up in a little wooden booth all night, with barely room to scratch his leg without sticking it outside. There he sits, pinching himself to stay awake and on the lookout for crime or danger in his street. Which is a rare old jest. Because if he finds it, he has only his rattle to sound the alarm, because he's too old to fight and usually too toothless to shout. Why would anyone think it a treat to sneak up behind and tip the box over with the poor old cove in it? Yet it's so popular a sport they even named it. 'Boxing the Watch.' Aye, box him all right. Tip his box over and watch him scurry to get himself out before his lantern sets the thing ablaze with him in it. And then beat him soundly when he does crawl out."

Will's handsome face was set in an ugly sneer. "And what of the habit your young gentlemen have of setting on any young female alone in the night and raping her in a train, because if she were to be respected she'd not be alone? Or if she were alone and charging for it, it wouldn't be as much fun? No, I don't understand. So pushing the gentry into the street might just be a new sport."

"Like slashing a horse so it will trample a man crossing the street?" Lucian asked. "And pushing his brother into the street in front of an oncoming carriage? After murdering their uncle outright? All in the same month? No. I agree the ideas of recreation enjoyed by some of the gentry needs improving. But I think there's a pattern here. We have to think of every possible connection. And we know so few." His forehead creased with the ache of his wounds and his thoughts. "There's James, of course. I can't get him out of my mind. He'll be coming into money. But perhaps not fast enough?"

"It's also possible your uncle may have had connections we don't know about," Will said. "Then there are his servants, the tradesmen he dealt with, friends…"

"…Romans and countrymen, I know," Lucian said wearily. "Or rather, don't know. But first, oughtn't we weed out those we do? Wasn't it Mrs. Pushkin who said that murder begins at home? So I'm coming to believe. On that head—there's Lieutenant Pascal. I think we must hear what Louisa suddenly wants to tell our little mermaid. We'll call on her at her fish shop tomorrow. She's a saucy piece but clever and certainly willing to help. No, eager. Didn't she ask to be included in the inquiry?"

"You no longer think Mrs. Pushkin is involved herself?"

"Well, and if she is, who better to speak to now?"

Both men fell still, each thinking about all the possibilities involved with dealing with the red-headed fishmonger again.

"I'll take her to Louisa's house myself tomorrow, I think," Lucian finally said. "I'll tell Lousia a tale about how I looked up the widow's direction, found her, and chose to simply deliver her while I was at it."

"You? Tomorrow? My lord, better say, next week, I think."

Lucian opened both eyes, although only one obeyed him. His face was set and cold. His voice came out stronger, his head rose high. He seemed to be looking at Will down that impressive nose of his. It would have been more intimidating if it weren't the only thing on his face that wasn't bruised or battered.

"I think *tomorrow*, Mr. Corby. Didn't you say we had to make inquiries at brothels as well? Or have you changed your mind?"

"No, but someone changed your face, and your body tonight. Be reasonable. You're in no condition to go sleuthing right now."

"No, not right now," Lucian agreed, "but tomorrow? Yes. Expect me at Bow Street, as agreed. We must get moving. Tomorrow, I will be able to move myself. I guarantee it."

He sat with the hauteur of a gentleman born. In spite of his battered face and utter pallor, his expression was intense, his eye wild with light. It might have been fever, Will thought. But in that moment the runner believed that there wasn't even an infection that would dare defy the man's will.

"We must get on with things," Lucian said again. "Rumors, hints innuendoes, we have to investigate each one. It doesn't matter how remote the possibility, we have to go on. We must discover what's happening, Mr. Corby. No one else must die.'

"Oh, I wouldn't say that," Will growled, thinking of the hangman, and the unknown villain he yearned to deliver to him.

Chapter Thirteen

"I'm late," Will said. "Do you think you could spit out what you have for me? Playing at being coy don't up the price."

"I never thought it would," the slender young man said genially, "but though I hesitate to mention this, Mr. Corby, you have not named a price at all. And since my merchandise is merely words, I'd be an out and out flat if I uttered them without some assurance as to their worth, wouldn't I? Some snuff? It's my own blend," he said, taking a gold and enamel snuffbox from his pocket and offering it to the runner.

Will let out an audible sigh. They sat in the corner of a tavern not far from Bow Street, huddled over their morning ale. The man he sat with was neatly dressed, almost a gentleman—to the untrained eye. His neckcloth was white, high and intricately folded, his breeches were blue superfine. But his jacket, while well cut, did not bear the stamp of any of the great tailors of London. And his gleaming top boots were not made to his feet. He spoke like a gentleman too. He was about as far from one as a man could get.

He lived by his wits, which were considerable. He could speak like gentry and reason like a barrow monger, and liked to describe himself as a man who sold items for persons who had acquired them in interesting ways. The only reason Will sighed now instead of barking at him was that he reminded him of another young man he'd once known, a long time ago.

For that reason Will restrained himself. "No, thank you," he said, refusing the snuff. "Sneezing ain't a mark of quality in my book. Nor do I care about being took for such. As for you...I hope for your sake the damned thing hasn't got initials on it. You sail close to the wind. I'd hate to have to see you dangling in the sheriff's picture frame. You're an agile lad, but once you learn the Tyburn trot you never get a chance to dance it again. The price of your information is the same as always. Now, tell me."

The young man made a face. "But it's worth more, surely. The reward for the cully who done for the gentry cove you found on the fishmonger's doorstep is princely, you know."

Will forced himself to keep his face smooth. He hunkered over his ale, staring into its golden depths so the man he spoke with couldn't see his eyes. He'd never got the trick of hiding the emotions in them as well as he wanted to. But then, he'd have to be dead to do that. "Aye. And if what you got to say *is* worth my while, you'll get more—in time—if it leads to the capture of said individual. Now out with it. I'm late."

"Rumor has it that the old gent was topped after he paid a visit to a pushing shop."

"You hauled me here to hear such eyewash?" Will said in honest surprise. "There's no one in London who hasn't heard that."

"True, but has anyone the location and the name?"

"You'll earned your guinea if you keep talking," Will said, sitting up straight now.

"Double or my lips are sealed."

"The name," Will said adamantly.

"For such a paltry fee?"

"For more, *if* it puts me on the right road. But anyone with a grudge can name a name."

"This one is certain. See, as I hear it, and I can't divulge who I heard it from, on my oath... Don't smirk, Mr. Corby. In my line of work, if I can't keep my word I'd be out of it. And well you know it." He leaned low over the table and dropped his voice to an intimate whisper. "But see, there's a ladybird in a certain snoozing ken in Spitalfields who's mad as fire at her aunt. And so, she's willing to peach on her."

Will showed his white teeth in a curling smile. "That's news? If I'd even a ha'penny for every trull in Spitalfields wanting to get back at her bawd, I'd be a rich man."

"You are."

"A richer one, then. I'll buy the name for what it's worth. Which ain't much, and well you know it."

The young man leaned closer. "It begins with a *J*."

"What I most wanted with my breakfast, a riddle," Will said angrily. "Damn you, enough sauce. Give me the name."

"I can't," the young man shrugged, "the initial's all I have. But I have it on the highest authority. All right, here's the way the rig runs. The mort seen the gent, first in her aunt's shop—though she swears she wasn't the one who serviced him—and then dead on the fishmonger's doorstep. She heard he was there and ran all the way to join the crowd to be sure of it. She even saw you there. But she can't squeak for fear of retribution. The old bawd would skin her if she found out she'd blown the gab. The initial is all she dare peach. It ought to be enough."

"Enough?" Will laughed. It only means I've half a hundred brothels to see to instead of a hundred. *J?* That will bring me to Madame Jessop's. Or send me to Mrs. Janeway, or Auntie Jane or Auntie Jennings. Let me think… Aye, and Aunt Janet, Mother Juniper—and Mrs. Jinever. That's only off the topmost part of my brain. In that district? An abbess with a name starting with *J*? Ho! And that's if your informer can spell. It could start with a *G* as well, couldn't it?"

Will stood, fished a coin from his waistcoat pocket and put it on the table along with some small ones to pay for his ale. "But I'm a fair man. You gave up what you could. I'll pay the piper. If it leads to more, you know I'm good for more. At least everyone's saying it's a bawd who supplies females. That cuts down my inquiries—some. Though why the old fool had to trek all the way down to Spitalfeilds, I don't know, when there's so many nunneries closer to his home. Maybe that's why, at that.

"Give you good morning, Peter. Come to me if you hear more or can tell me the whole. But stay away in every other way. I've a fondness for you because you remind me of another man I once knew. A much less fortunate one. He was as clever as he could hold together too. But Jack Ketch was more clever. He always is, in the long run. So, in that spirit...a word of advice."

Will leaned over the table and lowered his voice. "There's a set of fine china, good silver, and a gold watch took from a grab at a house in Grafton Mews the other week. Little blue flowers and gold trim on the china. I wonder your fingers didn't get seared. There's a fine reward posted and our Mr. Hardcastle is on the trail. He's almost as good at his job as I am. I'd get myself as far away from little blue flowers and all that grew in that garden as fast as I could, lad."

"Thank you for the gardening advice," the young man said merrily, but his eyes were sober.

Will walked to Bow Street, deep in thought. He'd lied. There weren't half a hundred bawds with a name starting with *J* in Spitalfields. There were, so far as he knew, about thirty. And about the same number whose name began with *G*. But he'd visit each one if he had to, and listen for what wasn't said. Because there wasn't a Procurer alive who wanted to be involved with a murder. Rumor thrived in London, and no man wanted to go to a whorehouse where he might lose his life for a little pleasure. Except for certain ones—but even then, it was only the threat of it that those men sought. His shadow on the doorstep of a brothel would close mouths, he knew that. He'd have to watch as much as listen.

He arrived at Bow Street and went into his small room. And checked at his doorway, his head snapping up at what he saw.

Viscount Maldon was sitting by his desk, waiting for him. He was dressed neatly, as always. His legs were crossed negligently. He looked totally at ease. And half dead. A white plaster covered one side of his face. It was about as white as his face itself. His hair was brushed back from his forehead, showing up the purpling surrounding one eye. Beneath that half-closed slit there was the unmistakable round red circle left by the mouth of a leech, recently applied. If it had brought down the swelling, Will hated to think of what it had looked like before it had been used.

216

"Relatives usually give notice of a funeral," Will said, entering the room. "This is the first time the corpse himself has done it. When are the services to be held, my lord? And do you expect flowers?"

"Amusing," Lucian said. "Forgive me if I do not laugh. It is a trifle painful to do so."

"It looks painful to breathe," Will said. "What are you doing here, my lord? I doubt your sawbones advised it."

"Perspicacious, as ever," Lucian drawled. "He, in fact, told me he washes his hands of me. I only wish he'd done it before he treated me. Nevertheless, I am here and ready to go."

"Your sawbones may not care, but I'd think you would. Not about dying from your old wounds, maybe. But from new ones. Someone may have attempted your life last night. Is it clever to give them a chance to get it right today?"

Lucian patted his breast. "I've a pocket pistol. My walking stick is also a sword stick. My Mama has sent her stoutest footman to my brother, to play keeper. I do not need a nursemaid."

"You think you're quick enough with sword and pistol as you are now?"

"I think I will not cower in my house, Mr. Corby," Lucian said. "It is not my way. Shall we go? My face should make inquiries go more smoothly for you. We can always say you did this to me."

Will grinned. "Aye. There's that. A man bent on finding who did that to him will make a powerful impression on someone being asked information about it. And I feel a deal safer about your continuing to breath if I'm with you."

"Ah. You are invulnerable then? Interesting."

"I've lived this long, haven't I? Then let's to it. This is a good time. Whores and panders are not at their best in the morning. They're half-asleep and not up to snuff after their long night. But mind!" he said, holding up one finger as though the nobleman were a boy, and he, a schoolmaster, "do you feel faint, or ill, or in any

217

way discomposed, we leave. I can protect you from everyone but yourself. I don't want your death on my conscience."

"Gratifying," Lucian said, rising, with difficulty. "I didn't know you had one."

"I've new information," Will said, ignoring the comment. "I'll tell you about it on the way. Shall I get a hackney or have you one outside?"

"I've my own carriage. It will be easier on what's left of my bones," Lucian said through clenched teeth. He moved stiffly, trying to stand erect even though he had to lean on his walking stick. "I think it hardly matters now if the world sees me visiting whorehouses of any sort, high or low. They'll know it's not for pleasure. And the more who know I am involved in this now, the better."

"Aye," Will agreed. "But maybe first we should pay a call on Mrs. Pushkin and arrange for her meeting with the lady Louisa?"

The viscount began to smile at the thought, only stopping when he felt his skin stretch and his abrasions protesting. He hoped Will and the fishwife would be somber. Laughter was definitely a mixed blessing today. "Yes," he agreed, "certainly. I don't know how she'll feel about you, but she may yet be grateful for my appearance at her door. The sight of me may cause her to loose her freckles."

But Maggie's freckles only stood out in bolder relief when she saw him. What she lost was her breath. Her heart had picked up its pace when she saw the two elegantly dressed gentlemen enter her shop. But she actually gasped when she saw the viscount clearly. Her customers stood back, fascinated and appalled. Spanish Will himself was enough to create that effect. But the battered gentleman beside him eclipsed him this time.

"A word, Mrs. Pushkin?" Will asked.

She nodded, eyes wide. She recovered herself enough to tell Alice and Mary to mind the shop before she went out the side door with the two men. Once in the hall, she hauled her apron off and peeled off her gloves. Then she opened the door to the sitting room, all the while staring at the viscount.

"Please wait," she said distractedly, "my hands, the fish.... Oh dear, does it hurt? Can I get you something? How did it happen? Who did such a thing?"

Lucian gave her a tilted smile. "It does hurt. I need nothing but your sympathy, thank you. And it was either an accident or someone tried to kill me. We don't know which, which is why we're here now."

"Tried to kill you?" Maggie squeaked.

"A horse attempted to run me down. I doubt it was the one with murderous intent."

Maggie fled to scrub her hands.

Spanish Will settled himself in a chair. Lucian seated himself with exquisite care, muffling the inadvertent gasps of pain that threatened with every movement. He'd just got himself still, if not comfortable, when Maggie appeared again, scented of lemons, still flushed with surprise.

"Lady Louisa came by my house the other day," Lucian said without preamble. "She asked me to go through my uncle's correspondence to find your direction. It seems you made quite an impression on her. She wants to see you again."

"We're hoping she's got something to tell you she might not want to tell us," Will said, "so we'd like you to pay a call on her again, if you're willing."

"Well, of course," Maggie said, her eyes never leaving Lucian's face, "but..." She looked up suddenly, dismayed. "How am I to tell her where I live?"

"We'll give you an address in a respectable, but remote part of the kingdom," Lucian said. "You're only visiting a relative in Hampstead at the moment, you see. In fact, if you are willing, we— rather say, *I*, can take you to see her today. I'll say I contacted you, and nothing would do but you see her right away. I'm such an obliging fellow, I brought you instantly."

Maggie stared. "Begging your pardon, my lord, you'd have to be more than obliging. You'd have to be mad. You look far too ill to be tooling about London today. It's cold as death, and you look…"

"Like Death himself," Will supplied. "Aye, and so I told him."

"But we must know what it is she has to say," Lucian said through clenched teeth. "Someone may have tried to run me down like a dog in the street. I am naturally anxious to get to the bottom of this, and cold and bruises be damned! Begging *your* pardon, Mrs. Pushkin," he added more gently, "but this is a subject most naturally close to my heart. Someone may have also attempted my brother the same night. In any case, I think my injuries may work for us now. Perhaps Louisa, seeing me thus, will become more anxious to confide in you—if she has anything to confide. We're grasping at straws, Mrs. Pushkin. But at least, in this case, there may be a straw to grasp at."

"If you'll wait," Maggie said quickly, "I'll just change my clothes. I won't be long. But I can't pay a call dressed as I am."

Lucian inclined his head like a liege lord bestowing a boon. But only because it hurt too much to actually nod. All the things that had been singing with pain last night were aching and throbbing today. He'd never realized there were so many shades of pain.

Maggie rushed from the room. She hesitated only a moment, getting her priorities in order. Davie was too young to do anything outside the shop. The girls were too inexperienced to run the shop all day. But Jack, the runner's watchboy, *was* a boy, and knew his way around London's dangerous streets the way a small shark knew the darkest waters. Besides, he enjoyed running errands. She found him quickly. He was waiting in the hall, obviously hard at work eavesdropping.

"Go to Mrs. Gudge, in Billingsgate Market," she told him. "No, wait…she's started on her rounds. No, go. They can tell you where she is at any hour. Ask her if she or Mrs. Gow would mind coming to watch the shop for me for a while today. Tell her the runner and the viscount have an errand they want me to run. But be sure to tell her to come soon as she can, and that I'd appreciate it."

As he took to his heels, Maggie ran to tell the girls the same, adding, "Mrs. Gow or Mrs. Gudge can judge how much more fish we'll need, for I don't doubt the neighborhood will be developing a passion for our fish again. More than that, no one will dare take advantage of either of them. I'll be back soon as I may."

But first, she told herself as she ran up to her bedchamber, *I'll dress for another masquerade. For I'm to be a lady again.*

When she came downstairs, her hair was neatly bound and topped with a handsome round bonnet. Her gown was speedwell blue wool. The vivid color made the little of her shocking hair that was showing look almost charming.

"You look bright, pretty as a gypsy on fair day," Will commented.

"Yes, a perfect antidote to this wretched gray day," Lucian agreed. He took out his watch. "Good, we can be there in time for a decent morning call. I'll tell you more in the coach. Put on a warm coat. It's colder today than yesterday."

"Only your wounds talking," Will said, as he helped Maggie on with her heavy cloak. "It's just as cold as yesterday. If it got any colder London would crack in two."

They chatted about the birds dropping frozen from the trees as they went out to the waiting carriage, walking more slowly than they'd wish on such a frigid day. But the viscount could move no faster, and they didn't want him to try.

*

Louisa was smiling when she rose from her chair as they came into her sitting room. Her smile stiffened and her face grew white when she saw Lucian. "Maldon!" she exclaimed. "Whatever happened to you?"

"Lud! Here's a coil? A jealous husband? Or a rabid dog?" Lieutenant Pascal asked with a heavy attempt at humor as he rose from his chair. He filled the drab room, his jacket red as blood on the snow on this bare winter day.

Will stared. Maggie blinked. Lucian's good eye narrowed. He made a sketch of a bow to show his contempt for the jest. And because he couldn't do more even if he'd wanted to.

"I went through my uncle's papers," Lucian told Louisa, ignoring the jape and the lieutenant, "and discovered Mrs. Preston's late husband's correspondence. The address was in Maidstone. But in reading through the letters I discovered he'd a cousin he often visited in Hampstead. I went there yesterday to discover if they knew whether Mrs. Preston was still in London, as she obviously couldn't have paid a call from so far. As you can see, she was. I made arrangements for her to pay a visit to you. I thought it would be a charming surprise, my gift to you. I didn't know I'd have a slight misfortune later. But I refused to let that make me disappoint Mrs. Preston."

"But what happened?" Louisa asked.

Maggie was watching her closely. Of course, anyone with any sensibilities would be concerned for the viscount. But Louisa had wanted to see her and now she'd obviously entirely forgotten she was there. It seemed she'd forgot everything in the world as she stared at the viscount, her heart in her eyes, her hands twisting together in anxiety.

Oh dear, Maggie thought, seeing Louisa's shocked, and so, unguarded eyes. *So that was how the wind blew.* But to marry a man so you could see his nephew more often? *Perhaps*, she mused, *perhaps, if you were consumed with futile longing, and that was the only way you thought you'd ever get to see him.* Maggie nodded to herself. She was an expert on futile longing.

"This?" Lucian smiled the half smile he was capable of. "A horse and cart decided to try to run me down last night. It may have been an accident. Or someone may have wanted me to visit Uncle sooner than I'd planned."

Lieutenant Pascal exclaimed something under his breath, and then realized he'd drawn every eye to himself. "What makes you think that?" he asked Lucian, trying to sound merely interested.

"The old jade was stabbed in the flank to make her fly," Will said, looking hard at him. "She'd usually have trouble going above a mile an hour, I'd think. But she was thundering down the road like a thoroughbred heading for the flag when she made for the viscount here. Someone pushed his brother Arthur into the street last night as well."

"Luckily, the hackney coach bearing down on him was more reasonable than Old Bess, my adversary," Lucian said quickly. "He was merely upset by experience."

"Damn!" Lieutenant Pascal muttered. He raised his eyes and locked glances with Will. "I'm naturally concerned for his lordship. But might as well admit I'm also worried for myself." He squared his padded shoulders. "I'm not a fool, Mr. Corby, whatever you think of military men. You see, I met a chap at a masquerade the other night. He was dressed like a Spaniard. Quite like you in size and height, Mr. Corby. Quite like your nickname, too. I suppose there was a jest in that. I thought everything a jest that night. I'd had more than a drop to drink. Well, I've been doing that these days.

"There are things I'm trying to forget, though I cannot," he said with a significant look to Louisa. "But I never get so high in my attitudes that I forget what I did the next day. Now, this chap was not only friendly, but fascinated by what I had to say. He was interested in things even my own mates are bored with. My complaints about my misfortune in love, to be exact." He scaled another look toward Louisa. She was oblivious, still studying Lucian's face.

"Someone murdered the Baron St. Cloud," the lieutenant went on. "And obviously—I must say it, though I am astonished by it—I am suspect. To my way of thinking, if someone's trying to murder the viscount or his brother now, I ought to be no longer suspect. But I doubt your mind works that way, does it Mr. Corby?"

Will smiled. "My mind works, lieutenant. It's how I earn my bead."

"I suppose you want to know my whereabouts last night?" the lieutenant asked stiffly.

"I suppose I *might* ask why you think I'm still so interested in you? It's an interesting conclusion you've leapt to," Will mused. The lieutenant paled. "And I suppose you'll tell me you were with friends last night. Fellow officers who'll swear to a man jack of them that it was so?"

"Just so, for so it was," the lieutenant said.

"Give me their names and I'll talk to them. Again," Will said wearily. "Though I wonder if we'll ever nab old Boney, what with the way our troops are sucking up the rum here in London town. Good thing his lads are weaned on wine, evens the score somewhat."

No one smiled. The lieutenant pokered up, Lucian looked uncomfortable, mind and body. Lousia was trying to look away from him now, and Maggie's mind was working furiously.

Louisa recovered first. "Mrs. Preston," she said, turning to Maggie, "'how difficult this must be for you, to find yourself in the midst of such dire doings. And how rude I am not to offer you some tea, at least, for your troubles. Have you the time for a visit? The lieutenant was just leaving."

"But was he?" Will wondered aloud when he and Lucian got back into the coach. "Just leaving, I mean? Looked black as a storm cloud when he marched out. But so did the lady when you said you had an appointment and had to go, even though you did promise to be back later to retrieve Mrs. P. No, I take that back. She didn't look like a storm cloud as much as a rain cloud. Thought she'd commence weeping at the sight of you."

"I am not as attractive as usual," Lucian agreed.

"Turning a blind eye? Aye, well, I don't blame you. Ticklish situation, at best. Consider this, though. With the way she obviously feels about you, it would have been the worse for you if your uncle hadn't got himself topped and she *had* gone through with the wedding to him."

"Indeed," Lucian said, refusing to think or speak about the revelation the lady's reactions to him implied. "And we two wouldn't have met. Now, I don't know how you could have coped with such a loss, Mr. Corby, and I daresay you don't even like to think about it."

"I don't need a tree to fall on my, my lord. I'm mum. At least on that head. Now, we've time to interview a few buttock brokers before we have to pick up Mrs. P. But it's your turn to be mum. Just play the grieving nephew and look pained. Leave me to the rest."

"I can do no other," Lucian said.

But there was nothing he could have said at Auntie Janet's establishment, the first stop they made. In fact, he wondered if the usually acute runner was mistaken. The woman looked ordinary as any female Lucian had never particularly noticed standing behind a counter anywhere in London. Middle-aged, thickset, her graying hair still in curl papers, she was merely a dowd. The only thing that spoke to her profession was the fact that she wore a wrapper rather than a gown. But that might be because Will had rousted her from bed.

The house wasn't as shabby or tawdry as Lucian had imagined a brothel in Spitalfields might be, either. The sitting room was furnished simply. There was a comfortable coal fire, the chairs and carpets were plain, but not threadbare. It didn't look like a den of vice. But then, he hadn't seen that many, and those he had were for the upper classes. He'd visited a few after his wife died. They didn't amuse him, but he'd had to admire how sumptuous they were. Some had bathing pools, some had music rooms and libraries. Many had erotic art on the walls, or coy statues of Venus and Cupid in their well-polished halls.

Whores in those houses were not called that. They were "Demi-reps" or "Cyprians," "birds of paradise," "barques of fraility," "bits of muslin," "high fliers" and "ladybirds" instead. The gentry had dozens of names for their occupation, all somehow exotic and almost flattering. Most could converse with a man, some with wit. They dressed voluptuously and were scented like expensive flowers. It was hard to tell if they were really pretty, but they were certainly sensuous. Their hair came in astonishing shades of midnight, red or yellow. Paint accentuated eyelashes and lips, filmy gowns showed random hints of forbidden areas, carmined nipples, rounded thighs, rosy bottoms. Eyes and mouths, breasts and buttocks, a man didn't need more when he hungered to take a body to bed. A look at their painted faces told their occupation, and that fact alone was enough to stir a man's blood if that was the mood he was in. Decent women didn't paint—except for some old ladies of the *ton* who couldn't forget the habits of the past century, or used it in a misguided attempt to show they were still young.

The mistresses of those brothels were either still so attractive men vied for the right to buy them for a night, or else resembled nothing so much as Society matrons past their prime. This bawd was nothing like, nor were her women.

The sleepy girls Will had Auntie Janet turned from their beds looked like shopgirls or females who worked in a manufactory, rather than at pleasuring men. They weren't even tempting in the secret guilty fashion of whores who lurked in alleys. Lucian doubted any amount of paint could change that. They were ordinary, in every way. Their shifts showed spare bodies, or flabby or awkward ones. They were pale and sometimes spotty, and blinked in the early sunlight like owlets. They were most young, and all confused. Lucian didn't see one who was seductive, though a few tried artificial smiles that blinked on and off with Will's scowls.

Auntie Janet kept complaining. "I don't know why you come to me, Mr. Corby, I do not! I have no custom amongst the gentry. I run an honest establishment for men who work with hands and backs, not a nob amongst them. Perhaps a clerk, now and again, but no more than that. Isn't that so, girls?"

The girls all shook their sleepy heads, looking bemused.

"Your baron, well, who hasn't heard of him by now?" Auntie Janet said. "It isn't often such a nob comes to our part of town, nor to such an end, neither. But never to my establishment, right girls?"

Lucian wondered if Will had misunderstood. He began to feel uneasy, foolish, as if he'd accused a schoolmistress of pandering. Until she went on.

"It's straight in and out work we do, Mr. Corby," she said with an injured air, "with maybe a French trick like bagpipe work for a fellow who wants it, for there's many a lad who likes a girl to do the work, and a suck off's no trouble, to be sure. Or similar for a fellow who can't get the wind up to go at a real rogering. And a bit of back door work for those who enjoy such. But nothing fancy, no doubles, no pain...though if a chap likes a little horsewhip took to him now and again, we'll oblige, to be sure. Now, your baron was after some fancier than that. You can bet on it. Otherwise he'd go nearer home, wouldn't he? But if he came here... Try Mrs. Manion, down the street. Or that Byrant woman. Nothing she won't do, some things I wouldn't ask my girls to listen to, much less try!"

"I wonder what those things were," Lucian mused when they got back into the coach.

"You'll find out, do you make the rounds with me," Will said. "But I believe old Janet. Not just because she caters to a set of working coves who only like their once a week. But because there was no tension in the room."

"That, I must also leave to your expertise."

"No," Will said, "trust me. When we find it, you'll feel it."

What Lucian found at the next stop was repugnance. Mother Juniper looked a caricaturist's bawd. At least, he was sure Mr. Rowlandson must have once used her as a model. Obese, unkempt, with small mean eyes that estimated a man from his clothing to his desires, all at one contemptuous glance. Her house was shoddily furnished and filled with cheap gim-cracks.

The mistress of such a house obviously set the style of it. Because her "girls" were anything but, and more nearly resembled the whores to be seen in the streets in the worst parts of town. They smiled at Will, and stared at Lucian. One licked her lips as Lucian stared back. He forgot his various pains in his chagrin at her imagining he was interested in her.

"No, your baron din't come here, redbreast," Mother Juniper laughed. "Not that he mightn't of. We do gets the gentry, from time to time. Well, some like to slum, and some like to get even with their wives, thinking nothing could be lower than bedding one of my trollops. But we ain't had once in a while. Y'might recommend us to your friends, my lord," she said, winking at Lucian.

"Be quiet!" Will snarled. "Or speak truth. I heard you get lambs, from time to time, for those gents."

The old procuress's amusement abruptly faded. She looked outraged. "Not I!" she shouted. "Who says it is a liar! Never. Ask anyone. There's a few'd like to see their Mother swing, there's truth. But no one can lay that at my door. Not that I wouldn't like the coin, but I was once such myself—and that I will not have! Prove it or leave me, redbreast, is all's I'll say."

"For now," Will muttered, and walked out the door.

Lucian's raised eyebrow said it all. Will explained in the coach. "She denied supplying virgins. Little girls for men with clap or pox. I told you some think it cures it. It infected Mother Juniper with poison, that's sure. I knew her history, but thought an accusation of worse might make her admit to less. Well, time to pick up our fishmonger. I'll wager she seems more like a lady to you every minute, eh?"

"Not only because of how we spent the last hour."

"Still, you'll meet many a whore who acts like a lady," Will said moodily. "Men like to think whores are in it for the pleasure. Some may be, but they're few and half-crazed at that. At least, so I've found it to be. It's just work for most of them, the pleasure comes after, with their pimps or woman friends. Many are lazy sluts who'd rather lift their skirts than turn their hands at honest labor. But too many are just hungry. Times are hard and sometimes that's all a female can sell. Freeze to death in a doorway these nights, or stay warm beneath strange men and make it until morning. Some choice. Mrs. P. is lucky, for all she had a hard master in that husband of hers. When he died he left her freedom, in more ways than one."

They were silent until they called for Maggie. They refused Louisa's offer of tea, and watched as Maggie bid her hostess a sad farewell. When she returned to the coach she took a handkerchief and dabbed her eyes. She sniffed, "Forgive me. It's just so sad. She's so lonely. She was so pleased to see me. We talked without let-up. We spoke about the baron and she confessed... Oh. No! Don't look like that! She didn't confess to *that*. She only said she felt dreadfully because though she was shocked and saddened by his death, she confessed she was horrified to discover she was also relieved. She had no hand in it."

"That's as may be," Will rumbled.

"Well, I believe her," Maggie sighed. "I'd love to see her again. But of course, I can't."

"Of course you can," Lucian said. "Perhaps there's more to be learned, perhaps not. I'll take you again, if you wish."

"But I said I was going back to Maidstone, as we agreed."

"A woman is entitled to change her mind," Lucian said.

"If she tells us what's on it first," Will said impatiently. "What else did she say?"

"She don't want to marry the lieutenant. She wishes he'd leave her alone because she's tempted, even so. Because she's so lonely, you see, and knows she'll never get a better offer. Because..." she glanced up at Lucian and then away. "...she's lonely," she concluded weakly, having obviously changed her mind about what she was going to say. "I'd swear she knows nothing about the baron's death—but you know?" she added on an inspiration, "I got the impression she was worried that Lieutenant Pascal's love for her might have made him do something rash. Didn't he even say he worried you thought just that? If we could take her into our confidence, I'm sure she'd find out everything you want to know about the lieutenant!"

"I think not, Mrs. P.," Will said, amused. "Not all females are as prudent as you are."

They rode in silence for a while. Maggie, savoring the unexpected compliment. Lucian, in too much pain to speak. And Will, because he was thinking.

"We've more calls to make before we're done today," Will said as the coach rolled up in front of Maggie's shop. "Send to me if you think of anything else."

"We will meet again?" she asked, pausing at the coach door.

"Of course," Will said. When she left he gazed at Lucian, silent in his corner of the coach. "I can go on alone if you like."

"I do not like," Lucian said. "I must find the man who killed my uncle. It's the only way I can feel easy anymore."

"Then let's go. We'll find you some more terrifying thoughts to change that," Will promised as they drove to Spitalfields again.

They spoke to two more bawds, and learned nothing except that whoremongers were eager to implicate others of their trade. And that men must be blind when lust was upon them.

"I think you'll find this next place more to your taste," Will commented.

Lucian was too dispirited to answer. His energy was flagging and he knew he wouldn't be able to disguise it from the runner much longer. His spirits were lowering too. It wasn't just that they were interrogating the dregs of society, or that the tawdry locale and desperate women they spoke with were darkening even his dim view of his fellow man. Nor was it even the increasing physical discomfort he felt. His ribs ached, his leg throbbed. Even the plaster on his cheek was chafing, because as the day wore on his beard was growing and rubbing at it. But worst of all was the growing suspicion that this was a cold trail and a fruitless endeavor.

The light was slate and the cobbles rang with cold. There were few street vendors and fewer passersby every hour because of it. The coach stopped in front of a row of townhouses that had once been grand. The quiet of the afternoon gave them the false appearance of being quality again. The street was deserted except for two little girls, wrapped to their ears, playing with a shaggy white puppy on the steps of one of the houses. One girl was fair and one was dark, and for a moment the innocence of their laughter struck Lucian to the heart. It didn't seem fair that they had to grow up in a world that would try to degrade them. He'd heard too many ways mankind degraded their women today.

The children looked up as the two gentlemen descended from the elegant coach. One of the girls essayed a smile at them, but the other pulled at her, aghast. In a moment, they raced away, disappearing down the nearest alleyway, the white puppy at their heels.

Will nodded approval. "Their mothers taught them well. They'd have done better to keep them off this street entirely. It's quiet now. It won't be by dusk. Auntie Jane does a brisk business. She's a shrewd old sow. Runs a better house than you've seen today, almost too good for this district. She's cold and cunning. I've dealt with her before."

They were let in by a monster of a man who took Will's name and shambled into the house to get his mistress for him. Will and Lucian stood patiently, hearing voices, hearing laughter.

The giant returned. "Auntie says as to how you should come in," he said carefully. "This way please, sirs."

They followed him into a dim parlor, where two women were sitting near the hearth, talking. One was obviously "Auntie Jane." She was rouged and bejeweled, and wore a sly and curling smile. But she might only have been laughing at their expressions.

Because the other woman was Mrs. Maggie Pushkin.

Chapter Fourteen

Spanish Will glowered at Maggie. The viscount's good eye gazed at her with suspicion too.

She'd been wondering who it was at the door. Auntie Jane had looked too pleased when Flea bent to whisper in her ear after he'd gone to see who was there. Maggie was in a fever of anxiety, fearing Auntie's customers had begun to come round. She'd thought men didn't conduct their vile business at this hour. It was why she was here now. Flea had even said so when she'd asked. He'd been visiting and had walked back to Auntie Jane's with her.

It wasn't a man bent on vice. It was two men determined to find a murderer. Now they looked at her as though she was one.

"But you *asked* me to ask questions everywhere," Maggie said nervously, though neither of the men spoke.

"Indeed," the viscount said, and there was a world of distrust and disdain in the one word.

"Well, *indeed*, to be sure," Maggie sputtered. "Where was I to ask, I ask you? The House of Lords? I heard a rumor that your uncle had been to a...place like this, and since I'm a friend of Flea's and know Auntie Jane...in a manner of speaking, I came to ask her what she knew. Who better to ask? You're here. ...Unless, you've come for other reasons?"

Well, that made them blink. She knew this last was terribly unfair and untrue. But they seemed to suspect her motives and she wanted to give them some of their own back. Auntie Jane laughed, even if they didn't. But the laugh had an unpleasant sound.

"Seeking the baron's murderer?" Auntie Jane chortled. "He was your uncle, I hear, my lord. My sympathies. The word is someone had a try at you and your brother the other night too." She smiled at their expressions. "Oh, it wasn't Mrs. Pushkin who told me. I could have told her. Word gets around faster than you do, gentlemen. But why come here? My nights are too busy for such play. I didn't know your uncle, my lord. But everyone knows the reward, and so everyone with a grudge is giving up names. So would I, if I had one. The baron may have come to play and left to die. It may be so. But not here."

"I was given your name," Will said.

"Of course," Auntie Jane answered on a shrug. "I'm successful. There's many who hate me for that. Bad luck to them. If clean towels and fresh sheets make me more business, let it make me more enemies too. But I didn't entertain the baron. If you think I did—prove it." She sat back, smug and amused.

Will's eyes narrowed. He realized some men couldn't charm a leech into their beds and had to buy females, but he wished women's sweet gifts could always be exactly that—free and freely given. Or if they had to make money by selling themselves, then at least that they alone profited from the work they alone did. Some whoremongers were fair, some even kindly, in their fashion. But just like their customers, their own needs came first. Bawds like Auntie Jane used women the way the stage companies used horses, working them until they dropped or were no good for hire anymore.

"Be sure, I'll try," Will said, "but it's folly to now. Your women are afraid to cough around you."

"Get them alone if you want to talk to them private," Auntie Jane said, "but I'll have to charge you full fee for each one."

He stepped closer. The look in his eyes made her smile vanish. His voice was deadly, dark and cold. "I'll speak to them when I must, and where I will. Keep amusing yourself with me, and discover how much fun that can be." The silence was total until Will spoke again. "But not here, and not now. Soon, though. Remember that and maybe you'll remember more."

"Huh!" Auntie Jane said, but she said no more.

"I'll be going now," Maggie said, leaping to her feet.

"We'll escort you home," Lucian said. She was grateful until she looked up at him. He was still looking at her oddly.

She simmered until she stepped into the coach with the two men. "Well, if you think I ran down to Drury Lane last night and set a horse on you, fine!" she told Lucian the instant she sat down, "Then *he* can lock me up and throw away the key. Or send me to the Antipodes. Perhaps I'll finally find my father there." Her voice broke, she stopped and bowed her head.

Lucian silently passed her his handkerchief. She waved it away and dug into her own recticule, extracted her own rumpled handkerchief, and blew her nose with a defiant honk.

"I can't keep throwing away keys," Will complained. "I've been warned about it. There's no way to extract a felon if you do that, they say, and where are they to put the new ones?"

"A problem, certainly," Lucian said.

They heard Maggie's faint giggle. She sniffled, and looked up again. "But you did distrust me," she said.

"Of course," Will said. "I still do. But don't let that vex you."

"He distrusts me too," Lucian said cheerfully.

"He thinks you threw yourself in front of a maddened horse?"

"He wouldn't be the first," Will commented lazily. "Men—and women—have shot, stabbed and even set themselves afire to throw me off their trail. But I don't think he'd have jeopardized the lady he was with. The quality have odd ideas about females. They'll buy and sell them like cattle without blinking an eye, but dislike butchering other gentlemen's wives."

"Oh," Maggie said, because she hadn't known about the woman. She realized the viscount must have his diversions, but was oddly disappointed he took them with married females.

"My good friend's wife," Lucian said to her unspoken question. "A good friend, herself. We were only going to have dinner together, all three of us. She's enciente, as well. With *his* child, of course, I hasten to add."

Maggie felt more cheerful when they got back to her house. "Do come in," she urged them. "I've a friend helping look after the shop. It's not often I can have callers in to tea, and it is that time.

I've heard some things, I'm sure you have too. Maybe we can put our heads together and come up with something new?" she added a little desperately. It would be good for solving their mystery, and for herself too. She wanted their company. They made her feel safe as well as under suspicion. The contradictions didn't bother her. They made her feel alive.

"Perishing cold," Will said, after a moment, "and snowing again. Hot tea would be a pleasure, at that. If it isn't too much trouble, Mrs. P.? But the viscount looks a bit peaky. Maybe I'll stop by and we'll just let him go along home."

"The viscount could do with a nice cup of tea too," Lucian said.

"I know the very thing," Maggie said. "My grandmother was an herb woman, and I learned at her knee. Tea, with an infusion of valerian, a clove to cover the taste, a pinch of willow bark, and a scant drop of belladonna. It will ease the headache and soothe you, my lord, trust me."

Mrs. Gudge certainly did. She came rolling into the parlor after Maggie left her guests there, excusing herself to go make the tea. "Good day to you, gents. Gawd! They done for you all right, didn't they, m'lord? Heard about it, well, who ain't? But still, you look ready for the rubbish heap. Good thing you've got our Maggie brewing you something to take the sting out. Though, myself, I think a glass of mother's milk would do as well," she added, with a wink at Will.

Unlike their hostess, Mrs. Gudge didn't mind appearing before them in her working clothes. She stood in the doorway in high wide boots, wearing her long leather apron over her several layers of clothing. A kerchief tied in knots at each corner covered her hair. The afternoon light showed bits of her signature Billingsgate red petticoats peeking out here and there, wherever she'd rucked up her assortment of skirts to keep them from trailing on the floor. "Aye, a glass of gin would do him fine, don't you think, Mrs. Gow?"

Mrs. Gow stepped out of Mrs. Gudge's huge shadow. "Afternoon, gentlemen, I'm sure," she said, peering around her friend's bulky form. "I mean, m'lord and gent—g'wan! I don't chat with that many m'lords, y'see, can't get m'tongue 'round it. Begging yer pardon fer not coming in, but I've m'boots on and once't they're off it's a day's work getting 'em back on. Got bunions big as oysters, like barnacles on a brig's bottom they is, and that's the sad truth."

"Delighted to see you again," Lucian said, rising from the chair he'd just fallen into, and inclining his aching head. It was hard work, but he'd have done it for any lady and most women he knew. The two females he'd so honored were ravished by the gesture.

Mrs. Gudge grew pink-cheeked. Mrs. Gow actually tittered, and tried a little curtsey in turn. "Oh sit, afore ye fall!" she cried out in pleasure. Lucian gratefully sat again.

Maggie's tea time procession began. Davie brought a tray of cakes, Alice bore in one with cups and Annie followed with teapot and napery. When Maggie came in with another teapot, she ordered them back to work. "Thank you for your help," she said, "but the fish can't sell themselves."

"Aye," Mrs. Gudge said. "And there's them as will help them walk out the door on their own do you not look sharp." But she didn't budge from the doorway herself.

"Just try some of this, my lord," Maggie said, pouring amber-colored tea into a flowered cup, and handing it to him. "It smells odd, and tastes strange too. But not bad. I've sweetened it with honey. It will do wonders for your head and nerves. The very thing after such a shock as you've had."

"Maggie knows," Mrs. Gudge said wisely.

"Aye," Mrs. Gow said with enthusiasm. "Din't I have the wind something fierce t'other week, and din't she brew up something had it whistling out in jigtime?"

"Made you better company, Mrs. Gow, and that's a fact," Mrs. Gudge said merrily.

Lucian took a sip, glad the cup concealed the smile he could not. He winced, because the sticking plaster loosened every time he moved his face.

"She could set up shop for doctoring, did she choose," Mrs. Gudge said approvingly. "She helps all them who comes with a complaint. For it's too much gold to see a sawbones for something little, and no one wants to go to them with nothing big."

"Rightly so," Will muttered. His opinion of physicians was only slightly lower than bawds. Because at least most people left a bawdy house alive.

Maggie was studying Lucian's face. "My lord," she said softly, "I help here and there where I can, is all. But at least I can do that. The plaster on your cheek is coming off, and it must hurt. Would you like me to change the dressing for you? I'm sure it's a long ride back and the cold will make it feel worse."

It was snug in the little parlor, and Lucian didn't want to say anything to change the warm atmosphere in the room. Besides, it did hurt. "If you wish," he said.

She gave him a quick smile, and hurried to pour Will his tea. Mrs. Gow and Mrs. Gudge declined. They'd be more comfortable slurping theirs in the kitchen later, discussing the two men who were sitting there now.

"I just have to go to my closet and get my herbs and oils.," Maggie said. "I'll soak the plaster off to avoid hurting you by pulling at it. I'll just infuse some herbs for the water. Then a soothing salve so when you next dress the wound it won't hurt to remove the bandaging, and can heal faster. I won't be a moment."

But she was less than that, and when she did come back, she was apologetic. "I have vervain," she explained, "and the comfrey and lavender. But I need just a drop more belladonna, and my stores are gone."

"*More* belladonna?" Will joked. "Why, do you think my lord's eyes aren't bright enough? The doxies use it to make their eyes look bigger," he explained in answer to Lucian's puzzled glance.

"Bigger, and blinder," Mrs. Gudge put in with a chuckle.

"In their case, 'tis a blessing," Mrs. Gow said piously.

"In their trade it's more a necessity than a blessing," Will said.

"Too much *would* blind someone," Maggie admitted, "but this isn't for his eyes. A mite in tea aids headache. Less than half a drop in a poultice aids healing wonderfully too. But only that. More would undo all the good it does. It's strong stuff in or outside the body. Deadly poison, in fact."

"Aye," Mrs. Gudge said. "I once seen what happened to a poor slut drank a vial of it to get even with her man for running around on her. She was very merry for a while. Remember, Mrs. Gow?

"Never seen *no one* more so," Mrs. Gow said mournfully. "It were a rare treat, for a spell. She were like a trip to Bedlam."

"She saw folks who wasn't there and went 'round chatting to the air, just like our good King George, God bless the poor soul," Mrs. Gudge explained. "We gave her purges, but it was too late. She danced away. Holding her down didn't help, she was laughing too hard. Then she commenced nodding and bowing to nobody. It was a rare sight. She couldn't stop—until she up and died."

Maggie made a face. "My grandmother said the greatest harm can be done by the greatest good; it's all a matter of proportions. Every plant that heals can harm. Don't worry," she told Lucian, "I know my herbs and I'll take care. I've sent Jack down to Mr. Abernathy, the apothecary, to get the belladonna, then I'll set to work."

Will frowned. "Abernathy! That old rogue! I'm surprised you deal with him, Mrs. P."

"He may have a reputation," she said, "all apothecaries do. Because of the strong stuffs they use and the fact that not everyone uses it right. Even my poor grandmother, and a better woman you'd never meet, had gossip about her in her time. But he's always got fresh herbs in stock and a wide selection too."

"'*Wide*'? I'll say," Mrs. Gudge cackled. "He'll open at any or all hours for the right price—just like the lightskirts what buy from him."

Will smiled, but Mrs. Gow went into whoops of laughter.

"I suppose you can see virtue in him, Mrs. P.," Will said, "but not everyone has your morals. Mrs. Gudge is only right. He's famous in the brothels, and at Bow Street too, for selling potions to help a girl get rid of an unwanted burden. But sometimes it stops both the new life and the older one together. Too many a poor lass who just wants to stay at her job loses her life along with what she's trying to be shut of. That's when I see them. You don't, or you wouldn't be as pleased with him. He's not as free with good advice as he is with his herbs."

Maggie sniffed. She couldn't argue what she didn't know. She turned her attention to Lucian. "We'll have the decoction for the poultice and the salve in a trice."

"Thank you," he said, smiling gently. The tea was wonderful. The tea, and whatever she'd brewed in it, and the crackling fire in the hearth all were wonderful. He felt sleepy and stupid, and vastly content. These people weren't out to kill him. Or if they were, he was so drowsy and comfortable now he scarcely cared.

"Remind me to have you bottle some of whatever he's drinking, for me," Will remarked, seeing the viscount's slow satisfied smile.

Jack came back quickly. He stepped into the sitting room after a cautious glance at Will and handed a package to Maggie. "Lucky I run," he reported. "He's busy packing up. Says as to how he's going to set up a booth at the Frost Fair. They're really going to have one!"

"Really?" Maggie asked, diverted. Everyone who came into the shop spoke of it, but she'd been so occupied with thoughts of mayhem it hadn't seemed real to her.

"Aye, the lads went out to test the ice, and when they din't fall in, the men tried it too. Now everyone's prancing about on it, scores of 'em!" Jack said eagerly. "They're setting up tents, and all! They'll be roasting pigs and having rides 'n such. Do you think we could go?"

"You ask her, and not me?" Will growled.

"Aye, well, but I have to foller her, don't I?" Jack said with a cocky grin. It faded when he saw the look on Will's face, and he said quickly, "So, Old Abernathy, he's clearing his shelves and taking the lot with him. You should see! He's got new labels for his papers and bottles. He says they all say 'Frost Fair' somewheres on them. Says he'll make twice as much just for having that printed, for there's them that will want keepsakes from the Fair, and why not his herbs?"

"He told you that?" Maggie asked.

Jack grinned. "He was talking to some other cove, but I got ears. Anyway when I up and ask for the belladonna, he was that surprised you wanted it, and he asks me what's to do? He says he asks as this was the last he's got. Says there was a run on it and he's already had to look for more so's he'll have some at the Fair. He wondered why. So I says, I don't know."

"Maybe all the girls want to look good if a grand Frost Fair be coming," Mrs. Gudge commented.

"Now there's an idea," Mrs. Gow chortled. "Should we get us some, do y'think, Mrs. Gudge? Sell a sight more fish do we 'ave beautiful eyes, won't we?" she asked, batting her stubby eyelashes, as Mrs. Gudge roared with laughter.

"At least I have all I need," Maggie murmured, going into the kitchens to make up her soak and salve.

Jack disappeared with her. He didn't return. He still worked for Spanish Will, but was never at ease under his watchful eye. Lucian sat back, sipping his tea as the fishwives discussed the coming Frost Fair with Will.

"No sense us working there," Mrs. Gow decided, "'ot fish would be a treat, but who'd buy cold?"

"If it's there, I'm going," Mrs. Gudge declared, "if not for selling, then for seeing. A regular holiday right under my nose, and me not there? Never!"

"Here we are," Maggie said, returning with her supplies. She set a steaming basin of water on a small table in front of Lucian. "If I may?" she asked, showing him the tablecloth she also carried. She tucked it around his high white neckcloth, spreading it over his jacket, taking care not to touch him as she did. She'd do what she could to ease his pain, but never wanted him to think she was being anything but medicinal about it.

"This will keep your clothing dry," she said. "Now, if you just lean your head back? Yes. Now, this will feel warm, but only that. I'm going to hold this wet toweling over the plaster, and it will loosen presently. I'll do it two or three times until it comes off neat and easy. Just relax."

"It won't be a pleasant sight," Lucian murmured from out of his cocoon of comfort. The warm cloth on his face felt wonderful. The herbs made it smell clean and bitter, but her soft voice sounded sweet. Her outrageous hair filled his line of vision, and it smelled of soap, lemon and roses. Her fingertips were cool and light. And when she spoke she breathed on him, softly. He'd paid women to do much more for him, but couldn't remember feeling as tenderly used as he did now with the fishwife's concerned eyes on his face, her gentle hands tending to him.

Mrs. Gudge and Mrs. Gow watched with interest, commenting on the procedure as though it was a theatrical presentation. Will watched silently, and to his surprise, enviously. Maldon looked lulled, relaxed, his eyes fluttered shut, he sighed. Even when the plaster at last came off, he didn't stir. A look at the cheek that was exposed made Will a deal less envious, though.

Maggie clucked and "tsked" and fulminated under her breath, muttering about the villain who had done this, and the doctor who had done that. She used her poultice, then dabbed on a salve, and her patient didn't stir. When she was done there was a smaller, neater plaster on Lucian's cheek. And he was in no pain at all.

"There," she said, stepping away, pleased.

The moment she said it another voice spoke, as though it had been waiting for permission. "Missus?" a deep voice asked from the doorway behind Mrs. Gudge and Mrs. Gow. Even their portly frames couldn't conceal the speaker. They stepped apart, surprised. For such an enormous man, Flea moved with stealth. He stood there, his hair and shoulders covered with snow, a white puppy sheltered deep in his massive arms.

"Flea!" Maggie exclaimed. "Why are you here at this hour? Aren't you supposed to be at work? Won't Auntie Jane be angry with you?"

"That one!" Mrs. Gudge said on a sniff, as Mrs. Gow added something Maggie pretended not to hear.

"She said I should go," Flea said sadly, his large, handsome face set in lines of deepest sorrow.

"Oh no," Maggie gasped, "never say she dismissed you? Because you brought me to talk with her? Because she thinks I brought the runner?"

Flea looked confused. He hung his head.

"Flea, do you still work for Auntie?" Maggie asked.

He nodded, relieved, clearly happy to be able to understand enough to answer. "I still work for Auntie. She said I must get rid of Dog." He looked down at the puppy sorrowfully, "She says the girls spend too much time with her. She says the neighbors pay too much attention to her too, and so too much attention to her house." His forehead wrinkled as he struggled to remember what he'd obviously tried to commit to heart. He nodded and went on, "She says it gives the gentlemen the wrong idea too. They should be thinking of the girls and nothing else, she says. So I'm taking her to you, Missus."

It was the longest speech Maggie had ever heard from him. He looked at her with hope. "And it's surely meant as a punishment for you, for bringing me," Maggie said angrily. "Oh, I'm so sorry, Flea."

"She's a good dog," he said anxiously.

"Well, I'm sure she is," Maggie said. "We can use one too, what with all the people suddenly prowling around the district bent on harm." That reminded her. "Jack!" she called. Jack popped his head in the door. "You go with Flea here," she told him. "Have him tell you what the dog needs. We're keeping her. She can stay in the hall or the kitchen, we'll settle that later. The girls will love her, little Davie too. Don't worry, Flea, we'll take good care of her and you can visit whenever you want."

"Thank you, Missus," Flea said, but he didn't look that much happier when he walked out of the sitting room with Jack.

Will scowled. "Do you think it's a good idea to invite that great lumpkin to run tame in your house?"

"I trust him more than most people I know," Maggie said defiantly. "He's got a good heart, even if he thinks a bit slow."

"A bit slow?" Mrs. Gow chuckled. "I've met cockles think faster. But 'e's a good 'un, like she says."

"But a bitch?" Mrs. Gudge asked. "You'll be up to your knees in more puppies soon as you can spit."

"Not if she 'as Old Abernathy brew up a concoction for 'er too," Mrs. Gow laughed.

"She's got paws on her," Will warned. "Don't be surprised to find you've got yourself a horse in dog's clothing. Well, we'd best be going," he said, looking over at the viscount. "My lord? Lord Maldon? I believe he's dropped off. What was in that tea?"

"No," Lucian said dreamily, passing a hand over his eyes, "only resting my eyes. Time to go, yes."

"Will he be all right by himself?" Will asked Maggie.

Lucian chuckled. "I am never by myself, Mr. Corby. I pay too much money to insure my comfort for that. No need to worry, I'm just a bit drowsy. I heard everything. So. Everyone's going to a Frost Fair?"

Mrs. Gudge and Mrs. Gow had too much respect for the nobility to laugh outright. But Will did. Maggie shot him a quelling glance. "Indeed, we probably shall. Should you like to come with us?" she asked Lucian.

"Thank you," he said. "I just may."

"If it's there, I'll be there," Will said, though no one had asked, and maybe just because no one had. "Because if everyone else is there it's my job to be too. We don't want to find the viscount smiling up at us from under the ice, do we?"

Maggie took this very seriously. "If we go, I'll ask Flea to come. He'd make sure everyone's safe."

"If he isn't the one they should be looking out for," Will said, rising to his feet before Maggie could argue. "Thank you for the tea, Mrs. P. I'll get his lordship home."

"Here," she said, taking a small packet from her skirt and handing it to Lucian. "Have your servants brew half this in a pot of tea if you feel poorly this evening. No more than that, though, for you're sensitive to something in it, I think."

"Best give it to me, and I'll give it to them," Will said, taking the herbs. "His lordship might use it as snuff, the way he's reacting to it."

"I'm a two bottle a day man. But one cup of your tea has quite finished me," Lucian agreed, swimming up from the muzzy depths of content. "Thank you, Mrs. Pushkin. We shall meet again, under happier circumstances, I hope."

But Maggie was happy enough with her day. She'd been out of the shop, had tea with a lady, gone riding in an elegant carriage twice in the company of two dashing men, and had helped one of them too. It was more excitement than she usually had in a year. And no one had to turn up dead to provide it.

The two men bowed, and left. The cold air woke Lucian somewhat. He was sorry for it. Getting to his house took longer than usual because the falling snow made it heavy going for the horses. His leg started aching, and the ride home reminded him of his ribs. Will saw him to his door, and gave the packet to his butler. "If your master leaves the house this night, I won't bet on his being

245

able to come back," Will warned the man after he gave him instructions for the tea. "He's a bit muddled from the medication."

"So glad you said 'from the medication,'" Lucian laughed. "But never fear. It would take several armies to get me out tonight."

"I'll come round in the morning," Will said. "No need to play the hero and seek me out. Tell him I said that, later," he told the butler, setting Lucian laughing again.

*

Lucian sat in his dressing gown in front of the fireplace in his study that evening. His foot was propped on a pillow, and he held a book in his hand. But he couldn't read. Even half a packet of the fishwife's tea made the words on the pages take flight. They seemed to swim away to the margins of each page when he tried to make sense of them. He was drowsy and yet not enough to actually sleep. But again, he felt wonderfully well.

"My lord?" his butler asked softly.

"Yes? Speak up. I can hear, even if I can't seem to see the words in this book."

"Your brother is here, but I told him you were feeling poorly."

"If you're ill, Maldon," Arthur's voice said, "I'll come round another time, though I wanted to see you,"

Lucian cracked open one eye. "I'm not ill, Arthur, I'm dying. No, no, I jest. Come in. I can't read, but I can talk. Bring my brother some wine—or some of this marvelous tea. I've been sipping it all evening. Nothing hurts now, Arthur. Nothing."

"Nothing to drink, thank you," Arthur said, pulling up a chair as the butler left them. "You look terrible...but happy," he said curiously, studying his brother's pale, but serene face.

"Exactly," Lucian said, drifting.

"I wanted to know if you've discovered anything," Arthur said from farther away than Lucian thought he'd been. "I wondered what you two—you and Spanish Will—have come up with so far."

"We two are a multitude," Lucian said, and hearing himself, sat up straighter. He tried to focus on his brother. Arthur looked younger and paler tonight. But Lucian allowed that might be because he was incapable of seeing sharp edges now. "We think Uncle might have gone to a low brothel the night he died," he said quickly, trapping the words on his mind and forcing them out on his tongue before they melted away. "At least, so the rumor runs."

"Uncle at a low brothel!" Arthur gasped, astonished. "Any kind of brothel would be shocking, but a low one? *Uncle?*"

"Yes, in Spitalfields, not far from where he was found. Will and I spent the day chatting with bawds. That sort of thing could put a man off women for a lifetime...well, yes, exactly." He chuckled, vastly amused at his inadvertent joke.

Arthur watched him closely. Lucian sat up straighter, vaguely embarrassed, for a brief moment.

"What else did you do today?" Arthur asked.

"Louisa invited me to tea. Me, and a mermaid."

"I wish you'd stop joking. Or are you joking?" Arthur asked.

"It's a private jest," Lucian said with a smile.

"I've come to give you a warning," Arthur said, dropping his voice, even though the butler had left the room.

"Mama wants me to wear my boots, because it's going to snow," Lucian guessed, and frowned, because his words didn't even make sense to himself. He opened both eyes, forcing the fog from his brain. "The medicine I took for my aches makes me nonsensical. But I am sensible. Come, what's toward?"

"I think I've been followed today, even here, even though I came in the company of that footman Mama sent," Arthur said anxiously. "I can't be sure, because when I turn around there's no one there. I told Mama's butler someone seemed to be lurking in the park across the street from her house when I visited her today. He saw a shadow too, but whoever it was fled before the servants could catch him. But now you say Uncle died in a *brothel*? Or is that your medication talking? Tell me, I must know."

'No, not *died*' there," Lucian said peevishly, "was there that night, I said. Someone said."

"Where, exactly?"

"We don't know. Some bawd's house that start's with *J* or *G*."

"Who said?" Arthur persisted.

"Everyone."

"You know no more?"

"I will know more," Lucian murmured, "I will. Will and I will."

"But then why should we be in danger?" Arthur asked thoughtfully. Lucian began to doze in the long silence that followed. When Arthur exclaimed suddenly, it woke him. He frowned at his brother's obvious excitement.

"A woman of the slums!" Arthur gasped. "That's it! Don't you see? Uncle may have had a secret lover! Perhaps a hidden child by her. A bastard who wanted Uncle's money and seeks revenge. Or is she herself seeking vengeance? It fits. It makes sense, terrible sense." He sounded as gleeful as horrified by his conclusions. He leapt to his feet. "We must discuss this with the runner. Can you hear me?"

"I hear, and obey," Lucian said.

"No use talking to you now. I'm going. I'll see Spanish Will in the morning. Lucian, can you hear me?"

Lucian did, but barely, because the voice he heard kept fading away. He drowsed. His brother stood, prepared to leave.

Lucian's head lay back on his chair, eyes closed. Arthur paused, gazing at him curiously. He'd never seen that clever face so unguarded, bereft of personality, so utterly still. But not vulnerable, Maldon could never be that. Pallid, his long high-bridged nose tilted upward, Arthur thought his brother looked almost like an effigy of himself, like one of their ancestors on a crypt in the family fault. He was so accomplished, so distant, cool and complete, he was as far from his younger brother's reality as any one of those ancestors were. But now Arthur felt a queer and unfamiliar pang of emotion.

"You're my brother," Arthur finally said, low. Lucian heard the words from a distance, and yet felt his brother was near, his breath was warm on his ear. "It's my duty to warn you," Arthur said. "I must. If I can do nothing else, at least I can do that. Only listen. Be warned, beware. Trust no one. *No one.*"

After a time, Lucian opened his eyes to find he was alone. "Beware," he murmured. The thought penetrated his misty mind. But only until he fell asleep a moment later.

Chapter Fifteen

It wasn't what Maggie had expected. It was beyond anything she could have imagined. She'd made great concessions in order to go to the Frost Fair, closing her shop for the entire day. It was the first time she'd done such a rash thing since her husband's funeral. But the Fair had finally come to be, and had been up and running for two days now. Everyone was talking about it, the children were on fire to see it. She finally decided to sacrifice an entire day's earnings so they all could go.

It was worth every penny she lost. This was a once in a lifetime event, and she was only glad it had happened in her lifetime. She'd never experienced anything like the awe she felt as she gazed down at it, spread out on the breast of the frozen Thames before her.

There was a whole new city risen before her eyes. A city built on the frozen surface of the river itself, ephemeral as ice, as transient as the winter itself was. The mighty Thames was rigid, tamed and turned to solid land. It was almost frightening, the way such powerful inexplicable forces of nature always were. It was certainly ridiculous because of what people had done with it. Maggie was astonished and delighted. Her girls stood open mouthed in shock. Even the viscount Maldon said nothing for a moment.

The ice extended from the hastily constructed boardwalk covering the river stair where they stood, and stretched far as the eye could see. London Bridge rose high on her left, Blackfriar's loomed far to the right. But there was no need for either bridge today. Because there was no river. Only a vast tundra, populated by celebrants. In the distance, crowds of people on London Bridge gazed down on the festival too. Because it looked as though all the rest of the population of London was cavorting on the vast plateau.

There were tents, dozens of them in ragged lines. Smoke from fragrant cookfires rose from them. Bonfires burned right on the surface of the ice. It was as if nomads had crossed over from the northlands, as in days of old, and set up camp. There were actually streets created between the tents, clearly marked by hastily erected signs. Every vendor had a sign to show his wares, and brightly painted pictures of pigs and boots, hats and sheep and every kind of merchandise decorated the stalls. Music floated on the air, as did the smells from all those fires, filling the breeze with the scent of pork and chestnuts, pies and spices.

Pennants and flags streamed in that light mild breeze—and it *was* mild. The biting cold was gone. As though to complement the madness of the enterprise, for the first time in weeks it was almost balmy, with a taste of spring in the air. It made the scene all the more amazing.

People surged through the temporary streets. They hooted from merry-go-rounds and roundabouts as they spun in circles. Here and there, tripod tentpoles held up wooden gondolas shaped liked half moons, with tiers of seats on their inner walls, for riders. They were filled with merry makers waiting for donkeys to pull the ride this way, so they could go that way, rocking like pendulums and screaming with glee. There were donkeys to ride too, and fortune tellers, makeshift ale halls and high wooden platforms where dancers were reeling. And that was only what Maggie could see at a glance.

"I thought the river would be like a looking glass," she marveled. "They said it was frozen so I thought it would be like a pond, all smooth and clear. But it's white and heaped up. There are hillocks and valleys. It looks more like a mountaintop than the top of the Thames."

"Ice from upstream has been breaking off and floating down, they say," Lucian said. "I read it in the paper. It formed floes, you see, and they've collided with others, heaved up and frozen fast. The snow kept falling over them. It looks like the surface of the moon—or what I always thought it might be."

"It looks like we have to pay before we can even set foot on it," Will grumbled. "What this?" he asked the hefty bargeman standing on the ice below the walk before them, his hand out.

"It costs a coin to cross the water," the fellow said. "*Ice toll*, is what we calls it, and it's only fair. All them that crosses the Thames must pay the waterman, winter or summer, whether they use his barge or no. Aw, don't hang back. And no need to look like thunder. All are paying it, up and down the river. What? Would y'have our kiddies starve just 'cause Mother Nature played us a trick? Don't be a skint. And look," he added jovially, pointing to a thin rivulet of water sluggishly flowing in the narrow trench he'd dug, "you'll be a'crossing the waters anyways, see?"

It was clever, even if it was extortion. Lucian put his hand in his pocket. Before he could give the man a coin, another called out. "Ho! Is that *Maggie* I see? So it is! Let her pass, Samuel. Beautiful women pay nothing, or at least that one doesn't. I'll pay the reckoning for her."

"As if I'd ask it of you," the bargeman said, grinning.

"Tom?" Maggie asked, peering at the tall man who hurried up to her. "What are you doing here? Working as a riverman now?"

"No," he said, his white teeth gleaming in a smile as he offered his hand to help her down the stair and over the trickle of ice water, "there aren't enough bargemen to go 'round, not half enough to watch every stair and bank. So they have coal heavers working the game too. Well, all must pay, you see—except for you, of course," he added, looking into her eyes as he helped her onto the ice. "But some don't want to. So they need men with broad shoulders to collect the fare, and that goes with strong backs."

He flexed his shoulders and gave her another bright grin. Then lowered his head and whispered, "I see you brought the girls and little Davie, and that lumpkin, Flea. But, Luv," he said, glancing back at Spanish Will, "a Redbreast too? Or is it that you can't be rid of him? Give me the word, and I'll make him vanish."

"I don't need your help, Tom," Maggie said, snatching her hand out of his.

"Too good for old friends now? Now you've got a 'gentleman' to escort you?" Tom hissed, his eyes glinting blue as the heart of a flame as he watched Lucian paying the bargeman for Maggie's servants' passage. "Not just a gent, but a *nobleman*. Don't look so surprised, all know who he is. But you'll catch cold at that, Maggie, my girl. What are you thinking? A viscount and a fishmonger? Don't make me laugh. He's only after what his uncle got before they got him, Luv."

Her head went up. "And you're after more?"

"At least, I'm not slumming. I'm after you, and always have been, and well you know it. Not a thrill I can forget an hour after."

"He's not after me," Maggie said through gritted teeth, "and I am *not* after him."

"Ah, so he takes a pounding and comes right back for more—and for no more than a taste of your flounders? Don't try to gammon me, I cut my eyeteeth years ago. That's why I'm surprised at you."

"You think he was attacked because of *me*?" Maggie squeaked.

"Aye, and he'll get more if he interferes with you. Open your eyes, girl! There's only one man who's ready and willing to look after you."

"Did you do anything to him, Tom?" Maggie asked, appalled.

"No. But I would if he plagued you, depend on it. Just say the word."

"Well, I say you're mad, is what I say. He's never plaguing me."

"He's not up to any good neither, Lass."

"And you are?" Maggie demanded.

Lucian saw Maggie's face grow red and heard her raise her voice as she confronted the handsome man who had greeted her. He'd thought they were friends. Now, he wondered. He went to her and offered her his arm. "Are you coming, Mrs. Pushkin?" he asked, as she put her shaking hand on it..

"Indeed I am!" she said, glaring at Tom.

"Be warned, Maggie," Tom muttered, standing hands on hips as she walked off with Lucian.

"Be warned about what?" Lucian asked her.

Before she could frame an answer Spanish Will's long stride brought him up beside them. "He's an old friend of Mrs. P.'s," Will said, "and I believe he's jealous of you, my lord."

Maggie wished the ice would open up and swallow her. She saw the viscount's eyebrow go up and looked away from him, wondering what to say. She'd been so comfortable with him today. When he'd arrived this morning he'd immediately complimented her on her tea and her medications, saying he'd slept long and well, and healed amazingly quick. The bandaging was off his cheek. There was still purple bruising there, and the last traces of a scrape. But he was clean shaven and looked almost himself. He moved with only a hint of stiffness, whatever he felt. She'd been proud of her handiwork. Now she averted her face, waiting to hear scorn or mockery in his voice.

But there was none. "Jealous, is he? Well, who wouldn't be jealous of Mrs. Pushkin?" Lucian said smoothly, "it's only reasonable."

"But I neither want nor encourage him, my lord," she said quickly.

"You need not, he can't help it. It is simply that you are yourself," he said calmly, without a trace of a leer or a smirk. He said it as though it were fact and not flirtation.

Maggie beamed. He was a gentleman, top to toes. Now she could enjoy the Fair. But there was so much to enjoy she didn't know where to begin. First, she had to martial her forces. She stopped and doled out coins to Alice, Annie and little Davie. Then she gave some to Jack too.

"Spoiling that villain rotten," Will growled, but grew silent when he saw how the boy's thin face lit up.

"Now when it's tea time, be back at this gate, and all together, mind," she told them. She turned to Flea. He'd been there at first light when they opened the back door to let out the puppy. It was no surprise. He'd been there every morning since he'd brought the dog to them. It seemed Flea was theirs as much as the puppy now, at least for most of the day. It was painful to see how eager he was to see the pup every morning, and how reluctant to leave her each evening. Today, after he'd tenderly put her back in her basket in the kitchen, he'd followed them obediently. Because Maggie asked him to.

"Flea," she said, "you're to go with the girls and little Davie and see no harm comes to them. Here's money to buy something for yourself. Unless, of course," she said, looking up at Spanish Will, "you think he ought to stay with the viscount all day?"

"Of course not," Lucian said, appalled.

Will grinned. "I think I can watch him well enough myself."

"The viscount can watch over himself, thank you," Lucian said stiffly.

"Then, it's Mrs. P. I'll oversee," Will said agreeably enough. "If you take off on your own we'll just follow along. Seeing as how you're known for your taste, we'd be sure to want to see the same things, eh, Mrs. P.?"

"Exactly," she said. She took Lucian's proffered arm again. Although she was honored by his courtly gesture to a mere fishwife, she was grateful for purely practical reasons. She was dressed for a holiday. She wore her caped shouldered blue pelisse over her best walking dress, the rose one with a ruffle at the neck. Her best bonnet, trimmed with artificial blue roses, fit snugly on her head. It subdued her shocking curls, showing them only at her ears and in wisps at her forehead.

To complete her finery she carried the silk parasol she usually kept carefully wrapped in cloth on the highest shelf of her wardrobe. She'd have to use it as a walking stick if not for the viscount's arm to lean on, because she wore high wooden patens to save her silk shoes from the snow and ice, and they made walking difficult at the best of times. Even the men had to place their boots carefully. The ice was rough and full of unexpected pitfalls. And everywhere the tread of many feet had made uneven furrows and ruts in it.

They walked down the main avenue, the newly made and named "Freezeland Street," looking at the attractions. Nobleman, runner and fishwife were soon reduced to children by the marvels of the Fair. Still, Lucian watched over Maggie as they wandered. And Will kept watch to see who was looking at the viscount when he wasn't looking. The ice they walked on was rough. But the crowd was even more so, as gentry and commoner combined, milling through the impromptu streets, taking in the wonder of it all.

The merchants and vendors of London had thought of every conceivable way to make money from the spectacle. There were toys and trinkets, baked goods and broadsheets, butcher's shops and book stalls with articles for sale, all blazoned somewhere with the words "Frost Fair." If a man grew tired of buying, and few Londoners did, there were amusements everywhere. Skittle alleys, with hundreds of fairgoers playing at them. Swings and slides, and wheels of fortune, and everywhere, games of chance. Trained bears, dogs and monkeys danced through the aisles of ice as pipers, fiddlers, buglers and drummers accompanied them.

The taverns in tents sold spirits and touted "Frost Ales." Foodstuffs were everywhere, and everywhere too expensive and yet selling twice as fast as they ever did in the normal streets of London. Vendors prowled, crying hot oysters and meat pies and gingerbread, all sold with fantastical ice-related names. They even called plain mutton "Lapland Mutton" and charged more because of it, adding a sixpence fee for anyone wanting to watch the whole sheep being cooked over a charcoal fire. It was burnt rather than cooked, and all anyone got was one charred or raw slice, but no one complained. It was cooked on the ice that covered the Thames, after all.

Lucian bought Maggie a copy of the *Northland Times* as a souvenir. The papers were going fast as they were printed, and they were being printed right there on presses set up on the ice. They printed and sold ballads and poems too, all dedicated to the Fair.

"If they could label fleas with 'Frost Fair' on their arses, someone would buy them," Will scoffed. And yet all three agreed "Frost Fair Gingerbread" tasted better than the usual sort. "Frost Ale" was crisper, and even the piping hot "Frosty" meat pasties they stopped to sample tasted richer there on the Thames.

Not the least of the fun and thrill was that no one forgot what they were walking over. It was like dancing on the chest of a sleeping giant, wondering what would happen if he woke. It was audacious and daring but everyone was doing it so it couldn't be as dangerous as it seemed to flaunt the wrath of the imprisoned river.

It seemed almost sacrilege to some, superstitiously foolhardy to others. Men had sacrificed to this river in ancient days. It was still the main avenue and lifeline of London. Now, half London seemed to be standing on water, like prophets of old, just as one of the ballads said. It was something to tell their grandchildren about, some day. For now, Maggie, Will and Lucian walked a lot and spoke little. There was too much to see to discuss it just yet.

They didn't speak to other people either. If Mrs. Gow and Mrs. Gudge were there, they hadn't come near the unlikely trio. But there were over fifty tents and thousands of people, and so the chances of accidentally meeting with someone was small.

But the gentry, because of their fine clothing, stood out from the masses, as ever. From time to time Lucian saw people he knew. He nodded as they passed. Most gentlemen were clever enough to leave a fellow alone if he was seen in the company of persons he might not wish to acknowledge or introduce. All the ladies were with gentlemen. None were mad enough to go to such a romp as a Fair unescorted. Maggie and Spanish Will were well dressed today. But they were not mistaken for gentlepersons. Especially since they were not introduced as such. No one minded. Such fairs brought the population together, but only in one physical place.

Spanish Will saw many people he knew too. But for the most part, they tried to pretend he did not.

Maggie was too rapt to look at other fairgoers. She didn't know how much time had passed until she felt a chill. The sun was westering, the temperature dropping. She'd had the best time she could remember in a long time, but her day was ending.

"Do you know?" she told her two escorts, "I confess I'd like to buy some of my herbs in a Frost Fair packet after all. I thought maybe some lavender, so I can keep my closet fresh smelling and still have the package as a keepsake. Do you think we could look for Mr. Abernathy? He said he'd be here."

"I see no reason why not," Lucian said.

Will nodded his agreement. He'd only seen shadows pursuing the viscount today. It was true he wondered if some of those shadows were more persistent than they ought to be. But then, he told himself, he couldn't catch a rogue unless that rogue could come close enough to catch, could he? No reason not to let the man wander some more. And the fishwife hadn't brought anything for herself to mark the day, and females were peculiar about such.

The apothecary's tent was the last in its row, the last row at the outer edge of the Fair. He was furious about it, of course.

"Paid good money to be here, and what do I get?" Mr. Abernathy complained after Maggie entered his big brown tent. "Exiled. I should have had 'Siberian Wasteland' printed up on my papers instead of 'London's Great Frost Fair.'"

"Have you had no customers, then?" Maggie asked, looking around the dim recesses of the tent. She wouldn't be surprised if he hadn't. Other vendors attracted customers with fires or gay pennants, or threw bright rugs on the ice in front of their tents. The outside of his tent had only a small sign, the interior was gloomy, chilly and damp. There were boxes of herbs and bottles, and he'd brought himself a chair to sit at and a table to mix his potions. But even the bare ice on the floor seemed colder than outside.

"Well, I've had some," he conceded, "but most I knew, and they were looking for me, like you. Should have saved myself the time and money," he grumbled. "Well, but what can I do for you, Mrs. Pushkin? Got enough belladonna now? I went to the trouble of getting more for the Fair, and at an unfair price at that, since I was in such a hurry. Much good it does me."

"Well, no," she said, "I've enough, thank you. But some lavender? Three packets—no four—if you please, and all with your new labels, please. I think I'll give the girls some for their clothes too. And for me—perhaps a bottle of your excellent decoction of betony. It hasn't rid me of my freckles, but it gives me hope," she added with a grin.

He didn't smile back at her. He seldom did. He was a dour man, tall, loose limbed, with sallow skin and receding hair, although the amount of hair in his nose and ears seemed to be trying to make up for it.

"And a packet of cudweed," Maggie said, thinking hard, because she was suddenly afire to get as many labeled packets, bottles and vials as she could. The viscount had brought her food and the souvenir paper, Spanish Will had surprised her by buying her ale. But she hadn't bought herself anything. She found she desperately wanted to take away a bit of this day with her, to keep and remember. Having the excuse of needing something made it less frivolous. She always needed herbs for her stores.

"Some Good King Henry too..." she said, thinking hard. "I could use more wild clary, some syrup of hart's tongue—all with labels, if you please. And some elderflowers. Oh yes! A bottle of elderflowers with a label on it would be charming. I'll display it on a shelf. Why, you ought to try that, Mr. Abernathy. It might lure customers, you know, if you presented your wares already packaged."

"And if they didn't sell? Huh. Job of work soaking the labels off, for who'd want to buy something from a Frost Fair in May or June, I ask you? It would look stale. Not that it matters with most herbs, mind, but folks like fresh in everything."

"What would you recommend for a puppy?" Maggie asked quickly, to forestall more grumbling. "Because we have one now. Maybe some arssmart to strew in her basket to keep off fleas?"

He packed her bottles and did up her papers, and sold her three other herbs and a bottle of dried bilberries besides. Maggie was glowing as he walked her to the entrance of his tent. She couldn't wait to take her bounty back to her companions outside.

"Ah, good," Lucian said, smiling when he saw how big a parcel the apothecary handed her, "now I can throw myself in front of carriages all winter."

Spanish Will took the package from her without a word, and Lucian offered his arm again. The light was going, now torches began to flare on every ice street. The tide of people was changing too. Both the gentry and the lowest classes were arriving in greater numbers. Servants, clerks, merchants and common men and women of all types were hurrying home to eat dinner and go to bed so they could be at work the next day. Ladies, gentlemen and criminals didn't worry about such things as late nights or early mornings.

The trio began to stroll toward the heart of the Fair, Maggie on the viscount's arm, the runner walking slightly apart, his eyes watching everywhere. Then Maggie gasped. One moment the runner was there, in the next he'd whirled around and gone sprinting back down an aisle toward the end of the Fair again. Lucian grabbed her hand, stopping her as she tried to follow.

"You can only make him more work by following," he said sternly. "Because then he'll have you to look after too. Wait here."

"So you can go? I think not!"

He paused. "I'd forgot who I was dealing with. Come along then, but stand behind me."

"You can't take on a fight now," she said indignantly. "Not after how you've been hurt."

"My pistol was not," he said, gesturing with the weapon he'd taken from inside his coat.

But he didn't need any weapon. They turned down the aisle to see Will standing in front of the apothecary's tent again, talking closely with a pale, willowy gentleman. At first, they thought the pair were only chatting—until they saw the runner had the gentleman's arm locked tight behind his back.

"God!" the gentleman said as he saw them drawing close, closing his eyes, his pale face growing whiter until his scant mustache provided the only color in it. "It needed only this! I tell you I was only watching to see what you were doing."

"Then why did you run?" Will asked harshly.

"Because I was embarrassed. Good God man, I am not the sort to skulk. It's only that I know you suspect me of God knows what, and when I saw you here, behind me, I thought you were following *me*, and doubled back to see. Why did you chase me?"

"I chase whatever runs, like any good hunting dog," Will said grimly. "If you were only visiting the Fair, why are you out of uniform, then, eh?"

Maggie's hand flew to her lips. Lady Lousia's Lieutenant Pascal! She'd never have known him—his uniform more than made him, it defined him.

The lieutenant shook his head. "I'm not. I've just put on this coat. I borrowed it from a friend. I could hardly follow you in a scarlet coat, against all this snow. You've as much as accused me of murder!" he said a little wildly. "I had to do something!"

"How long have you been following me?" Will asked, releasing the man's arm. "I mean, apart from the past hour? I've been watching you from the corner of my eye since then. I gave you the benefit of the doubt, at first. But you kept up the game too long."

The lieutenant rubbed his arm, and looked down at his boots. "It's as I said. I thought you were following me." He looked up at Maggie and Lucian. "Mrs. Preston. My lord Maldon... I don't know what you're doing here, nor am I spying on you, I promise. But please... Pray do not tell Louisa... Damme! But there has to be an end to this," he muttered. "Nevermind," he said, holding his head high. "I shall tell her myself. Unless, of course, Mr. Corby has decided to detain me."

"No," Will said, "but follow me again, and you'll follow me to Bow Street, Sir. That, *I* can promise you."

They watched the shaken lieutenant bow, and then walk off into the crowd.

"Do you believe him?" Lucian asked.

"It don't matter," Will said. "Now I've bubbled him, he'll be in sight, for a while, at least. It gives me time to discover more about him. Come along, we've got to get Mrs. P. back to her chicks, or they'll freeze solid in place waiting for her."

But they were stopped before they went three more steps. "Maldon!" a voice called.

Lucian turned. His brother was trotting up to him as fast as he could on the uneven ice. "You never said you were going to the Fair," he panted as he came close. "Surely it's too soon for you to be out?" But though he spoke to his brother, his eyes were on Maggie. Then he saw Spanish Will. "Mr. Corby," Arthur said excitedly. "Are you looking for anyone here? Never say!" He looked around. "At an apothecary's tent? But I don't understand. Maldon told me about your new theory. I thought you were looking for a—ahm..." he hesitated, glancing at Maggie, "woman of ill repute?"

"I didn't know you were privy to our latest news," Will said smoothly, though he shot a look at Lucian, "but no, I'm not looking for anyone. I'm only here to make sure your brother doesn't land under any more coaches today."

"Hardly any fear of that, at least here," Lucian said, flustered. He only dimly recalled his conversation with Arthur, and now wondered if Will was angry he'd shared the information. "But I did run into Mr. Corby and his friend here today. Are you here alone, Arthur? I mean, apart from Mama's footman?"

"I'm alone. Entirely. I've sent him back to Mama. If you can brave the world alone, Lucian, so can I," Arthur said, sounding a little hurt. He paused, staring pointedly at Maggie.

Although Maggie remembered him from the night of the masquerade, she realized he didn't recognize her because he'd never seen her face, or natural hair. She looked up at the viscount to see how he'd introduce her. He smiled down at her in turn. And then disengaged himself, and bowed.

"I've had a lovely time," he told her lightly. "Pray excuse me," he told Will, "but I think I'll go along with my brother now. I'm safe enough with him—as he will be with me. They'll hardly attempt the two of us together and I don't think he should be alone now that evening is coming on. That is, if it's all right with you?"

He made it seem like he was under some sort of arrest, Maggie thought. He made it seem like he could hardly wait to leave. And so she supposed he couldn't. Because after Will nodded, the viscount bowed again. Then he was gone, his arm slung over his brother's shoulders, head bent so he could speak quietly and constantly to him as they walked away. So constantly, that after one last suspicious glance at Maggie, Arthur wouldn't, or couldn't, look back again.

"Well," Maggie said, feeling flat. Of course, he wouldn't acknowledge a fishmonger. She knew that. It was just that she didn't like being reminded of it.

"Here, take my arm," Will said. "Don't need you falling on your nose. It isn't just because of your trade, you know," he commented as they walked on. "It's because it might be difficult for him to explain what he was doing larking about with the woman whose doorstep it was that his uncle died on."

"He could have said just exactly what it was he was about," Maggie said, raising her head.

Will didn't argue that. She rather wished he would have.

The children were as merry as Maggie was subdued. Will called a hackney for them all, touched his hat, and walked off into the growing night. Maggie's child servants all piled into the coach with her, jabbering, telling her the wonders they'd seen, showing their purchases to her. She smiled and nodded, but was as silent as Flea, who seemed cast into deep sorrow to be leaving the Fair.

The children rushed out when they got home. They had to change from their good clothes, stow their precious purchases, and then set to help making dinner. Flea left the coach, head down and shoulders slumped. He didn't hurry, as he usually did, to walk the white puppy before he returned to Aunt Jane and his night's work. Maggie felt as deflated as he looked, but she marched up to her bedchamber, refusing to let one arrogant nobleman make her precious day go flat. She'd been to the Frost Fair, she'd had two fine gents as escorts there, and nobody could take that from her now.

But after she'd changed out of her finery and gone down to the kitchen she began to wonder if there was any point in seeking out the company of the viscount and the runner anymore. She stirred the kettle of soup she'd left to warm on the hearth, and pondered. After all, no one suspected her of doing in the gentleman's uncle now. And though taking tea with ladies and swanning forth with a nobleman and matching wits with a dashing runner had been exhilarating — there was really nothing in it for her anymore. Except for snubs, and insult, of course.

The cooking soup and kettle boiling on the hob soon made the windows frost over. And so she couldn't see who began tapping at her back door. Flea had gone to work at Auntie Jane's. The girls were setting the table, Jack had run down to the corner to pick up a fresh bread, and Davie was playing with the puppy on the floor. Maggie put down her wooden spoon, and then on second thought picked it up and took it with her, as though it could defend her from anyone bent on mischief. But it felt authoritative in her hand. She cracked open the back door.

The Viscount Maldon stood there. "A word, please,' he said.

Maggie blinked, and opened the door wide. He stepped into the warm kitchen, his high beaver hat in his hand now. "I'm sorry," he said. "It was damnably rude of me to leave you like that, I don't know what I was thinking — well, but I do. I didn't know how to explain your presence and so I simply let my brother think you were a friend of Will's. ...No," he said, looking straight into her astonished eyes, "I suppose I didn't want him to see I was with you." He shook his head. "I thought I was above such. I am not. If it makes you feel any better, I believe I will try to be in future."

She was taken aback. "But a viscount does not have to acknowledge a fishmonger. We both know that."

"That kind of thinking made Corporal Bonaparte the Emperor Napoleon, my dear," he said with a twisted smile, "One hates to think of tumbrels rolling through Picadilly." He raised his impressive nose. "That delicious aroma is surely not fish?"

"Beef soup, my lord. And I've roast hen and lamb cutlets. Not that there's anything wrong with my fish, but we don't eat it all the time. Would you care to join us for dinner?" She said it automatically. She never expected him to agree.

"If there's enough?" he asked.

He sat and listened to Alice marveling about the fire eaters, and ate his own hot dinner to the accompaniment of Annie chattering about the horse that could count, add and subtract numbers too. He buttered his bread to the sound of Annie bragging about her new "Frost Fairest Beads," never interrupting to mention how he was defending his boots from the puppy's jaws under the table. He dined to the accompaniment of Jack's pleas to return to the Fair tomorrow, as it would surely be the last day.

"They're saying that the daft plumber tried to take a barrow of lead across the river, near to Blackfriar's, for a wager?" Jack said eagerly. "They said he slipped in-between two big pieces of ice and never come to the surface again. Gawd! I wisht I'd seen that. But that means things is melting, can we go again before it does?"

"So we can sink too?" Maggie laughed.

"Nah, we ain't got a load of lead, do we?" Jack said.

"I feel as though I do," Lucian said, "after such a dinner! It's all my fault. I stuffed myself in most gluttonous fashion, but how could I help it? It was delicious, Mrs. Pushkin."

After dinner, they sat before the fire, listening to little Davie's efforts with his new Frost Fair Jew's harp. "This tea," Lucian leaned over to ask Maggie, "it *is* just tea this time? Or have you added something to it again?"

"No," Maggie said, confused, "it's just tea, though my best sort. Why do you ask?"

"Because I feel so content," he said, and smiled to see her blush. It was while he was sipping his tea that another visitor came to the door. Lucian left off complimenting Alice on her wise choice of a silver ring with what she vowed was "London's Greatest Frost Fair, a Natural Miracle" etched in tiny letters on its inner rim to look up at the new visitor.

"Such domesticity," Spanish Will said as he took off his coat.

He stayed, and they all laughed and talked, reliving the great day until it was unmistakably over. *Because nothing lasts forever, even such felicity*, Maggie thought when she locked up the shop later, bolted the doors, and went to her own bed at last.

She was right. Because when she went down to the back door the next morning, Flea was there again. But this time, he didn't rush to the puppy as usual. Instead, he stared at Maggie with haunted eyes and his great shoulders slumped. Then he hung his heavy head, clearly troubled, obviously suffering.

"Missus," he mumbled in a dark voice, "I got to tell you. I said I wouldn't. I promised I wouldn't. That's why I didn't tell you before. But my Mam told me a bad promise is no promise. I can't sleep and all, 'cause I was wrong. You've been so good to me. Taking in Dog. Taking me to the Fair. Being my friend. Being so nice and all. Auntie Jane will skin me. But I have got to tell you."

"What?" Maggie said, waking up fast, because in some small part of her mind, she already knew.

"The old man," Flea said mournfully. "The dead man. The one you asked me about? I saw it. I helped."

Chapter Sixteen

They arrived amazingly fast. Spanish Will left Bow Street as soon as Jack got there to tell him to, and they picked up the viscount on the way. Now only a few hours past sunrise, the two men sat in Maggie's sitting room again. Spanish Will had his incident book out, and his face was as empty of expression as the page he had opened to. The usually immaculate viscount was neatly dressed, but Maggie could see he hadn't been shaved yet. From his expression, it was clear he'd had more urgent things on his mind after he'd been woken. They all did. She closed the door firmly, and told Jack to be sure no one interrupted them. Then she sat beside Flea again.

"Tell them," she said simply.

He gave her another worried look.

"It's all right, remember what I said?"

Flea nodded and hung his head. He clasped his big hands in his lap, looking guilty as a boy who'd spilled his milk, as he began to tell them how he had helped kill the Baron St. Cloud.

"The man came to Auntie Jane," he said.

"What man?" Will asked him, his pencil poised.

"The dead man on Missus Maggie's doorstep," Flea said sadly. "The naked man. I put him there."

"Do you know his name?" Will asked.

Flea looked confused. He looked at Maggie.

"It doesn't matter," she assured him.

"Right," Will said. "Go on."

Flea bowed his head again. He went on in a low, slow hesitant voice, picking his simple words with exquisite care. "He came at night. He said hello to Auntie Jane. He said, 'Good evening.' He said, 'You have a girl for me?' He said, 'As we agreed?'"

"So, he had come before?" Will interrupted, schooling himself to keep his voice low and even. He shifted in his chair. The big man spoke so slowly it would be nightfall before he got to the germ of it.

"Yes," Flea said. "He came the other week. Then he talked to Auntie Jane a long time. But he didn't go upstairs with a girl then. He went home. He came back to Auntie Jane again. He was very happy to come back. He was laughing and very happy to be back," Flea said sadly. "He was so happy then."

"Did he go with a girl that night?" Will asked. Flea just looked at him. Will took a deep breath. He spoke softly, patiently. "I mean, did he go upstairs with a girl the second time?"

"Yes. He went upstairs with a girl then."

"What girl?"

"Millie."

"And then?" Will prompted.

"I heard a scream. So I ran upstairs. I'm not supposed to go upstairs, unless there's trouble. Then I'm supposed to go upstairs and stop the trouble. Millie was screaming and screaming. But Auntie Jane says that's all right. She says sometimes the girls scream for the fun of it. Auntie Jane says they don't mean it. I'm only to come upstairs if she says. Or if she screams. She was screaming."

"Auntie Jane?" Will frowned. "She was upstairs too?"

Flea nodded.

"I mean," Will said, barely repressed impatience in his voice, "did she go upstairs after the scream?"

"No. She was there."

"*With* Millie and the man?" Will's expression was growing dark.

"Yes."

Will's hand fisted over his book, his face grew tight. Lucian looked at him curiously, and then turned his attention back to Flea.

Maggie sat beside the huge man, her hand on his arm, her expression distraught, her eyes bleak.

"And then?" Will asked.

Flea's chest moved in a sigh. "He was sick," Flea said, still not meeting the runner's eyes. "He was very sick. He was laying on Millie's bed. On his back. She was crying. His face was all red. Then it was white. He was choking. He was…" Flea frowned, trying to find the words. "He was….moving like an eel in Mrs. Gudge's basket, like. This way and that. All the time. Up and down. And back and forth. His mouth was open. He was saying things. I don't know what. Just noise."

"Then, he stopped," Flea said. "He got quiet. He got stiff and quiet. We waited. But he didn't move again. Auntie Jane looked at him and said, 'Oh God, he's dead.' 'Oh God, that's all I need. The old bastard is dead.'"

Lucian could swear his blood was actually running cold. *Uncle,* dead of a fit in a whore's bed? There was so much he wanted to ask. He didn't dare. The dialogue was between Spanish Will and the giant. It was clear the monstrous childish man was afraid of them. Maggie's small hand on his arm seemed to be the only thing keeping him from fleeing. He seemed to suffer as he sat there, forcing out the agonizingly slow, damnable words.

"And then?" Will asked softly.

"Then Auntie Jane slapped Millie. To get her to stop screaming. She sent her to another room. Jenny's room. They're friends. Then she looked at the old man. 'Well, he's never dying here,' she says."

Flea quoted Auntie Jane more clearly than he himself could speak. Will suspected the giant could remember far better than he could frame speech. "And so?" Will asked again.

"And so Auntie Jane told me to take him away. She said, 'If he's dead he can be just as dead somewhere else. Take him away, Flea.'"

"So then you carried him away," Will said.

"No. Auntie Jane said, 'Wait.' She told me to help her take his clothes off. She said, 'He won't be needing these anymore. And the less they find the less chance they'll ever know what happened.'"

"He didn't remove his clothes?" Lucian blurted.

"Many men don't in such places, my lord," Will said, never taking his eyes off Flea. "They don't go there for the same kind of experience more worldly men do. It's a simple thing they're after, like taking a…" He looked at Maggie, and said, "like relieving their bladders. And so then you took him away from Auntie Jane's?" he asked Flea.

"No. First Auntie Jane told me to wrap him in a blanket," Flea reported faithfully, his brow furrowing with the effort. "She said, 'drop him off and bring the blanket back. I want nothing of us in this. And stay to the shadows. Take care no one sees you. If anyone asks what you've got, say it's old clothes.'"

"Did Auntie Jane ask you to leave him on Mrs. Pushkin's doorstep?"

"No," Flea said sadly. "She asked me to drop him in the river. She said, 'Take this cosh, and hit him a good one, and then drop him in the river, down by the bridge. Go now.'"

"Ah," Will said, nodding, "the lack of blood, of course. Clever Auntie Jane. If we'd found him naked, bashed and floating, and mind—we might not have done because the tide could have carried him to sea or he could have got caught under a bridge until it was too late to recognize him—there wouldn't have been such an investigation. Because any man could be set upon and murdered were he fool enough to walk by the river at night this far east. But a man with no wounds might have set us wondering. Clever. So, why didn't you do it, Flea? Why didn't you listen to Auntie Jane?"

"He started moving," Flea said. Lucian's jaw knotted over the exclamation he stifled. "I felt him moving a little. I was walking to the river. I had him over my shoulder. I felt him move. So I put him down. I unwrapped him and looked. I touched him. He wasn't cold. I put my ear on his chest. I felt his chest, like Missus did when I brought her that cat I found. I brought Missus a cat after a carriage ran over it. She fixed it. The man's chest went up and down a little. I thought Missus could fix him like she did the cat."

"Then why did you bash him?" Will asked, though he already knew.

Flea's face set in lines of deepest woe. "When I got here, I put him down. I looked again. He wasn't breathing anymore. He was cold. He was dead. So I picked him up to take him to the river. But people were coming out on the street. The sun was coming up too. So I hit him like Auntie Jane said I should. I left him. I ran away. I took the blanket, like Auntie Jane told me to. Can I go home now?"

The room was very still.

Maggie spoke first. She turned to Will, then Lucian, her voice angry, and pleading too. "He didn't kill the baron, surely you see that? If you take him, it's Tyburn for him. Because what can he say? What can he do? But he didn't kill the baron. I believe him, don't you?"

"Aye," Will said on a deep sigh. "But the law is the law, Mrs. P. And it isn't wrong, neither. If Auntie Jane told your big friend there to bash some stranger for no reason other than spite, he'd do it. So if he swings for this, it may save someone else's life someday."

Flea looked up. He tilted his head, his eyebrows came down until they almost met at the middle. "No," he said slowly. "No. I wouldn't. Ma said it's wrong for me to hit people. I'm too big. I..." He heaved a great sigh. He licked his lips and looked down, sorting through his store of words to say what he meant. His head came up. "I wouldn't kill anyone. Not if Auntie Jane said so. Not even if Missus told me to. It's *wrong*. I protect the girls. Because it's wrong for men to hurt them. I protect anyone smaller than me. Ma said I should. I don't kill anyone. It's wrong. That man was dead. So I did what Auntie Jane said."

"Did you also attack the viscount the other night?" Will demanded. He huffed at Flea's obvious confusion and said through gritted teeth, "This man, here. Did you stab or stick a horse to get it running toward him?"

"I like horses," Flea said, clearly horrified at the idea.

"Maybe you didn't hurt it then," Will said with utmost patience. "Grant you that. But did get one to gallop toward this man the other night?"

"I *work* at night," Flea said, amazed.

"Aye, just so," Will said. "Did you work for Auntie Jane, or anyone else, and push another man into the street then? Near Covent Garden?"

"I work in Auntie Jane's house," Flea said, frowning. "She lets me go out walking all day. I have to be back at night to work for her in the house. I wouldn't push anyone," Flea said reproachfully. "Sneaking up behind isn't fair."

Will dropped his head into his hand and rubbed his cheek. "Here's a coil," he muttered. And was surprised he did. Because he was not known for his sympathy and had forgotten he had any. But the giant was not guilty. Not of murder, nor of trying to murder anyone. Of that, he was sure. But the law required he find a villain. Or at least, the reward he'd worked so hard for did. "My lord?" he asked, looking up at Lucian. Because a burden passed would not be his own.

But Lucian was not really listening. He was still reeling. "My uncle died in a whore's bed," he murmured, "but why? He was going to marry a worthy young woman in a week's time. Why trifle with a whore the week before?"

Now it was Will who looked down at his hands. This case was toying with his guts. He hadn't known he could feel anything but rage in them anymore. He'd have to tell the viscount the reason, because he was sure he knew. Better it was he did that, he reassured himself, than letting it be Auntie Jane. But still, he didn't want to see the look in the nobleman's eyes when he did. He'd come to respect the man, and know him a little. The Viscount Maldon was cool, arrogant and self-serving. He was a nobleman, after all. He wasn't cruel though. In fact, the man had shown touches of a rare compassion, for his kind. And he had a sense of humor that more nearly matched his own than most men did.

"Why did he do such a thing?" Will asked. "We'll speak of it later, my lord."

"Oh, really?" Maggie said, her eyes snapping with rage. "I think you ought speak of it now. I'm in this as much as either of you. I told poor Flea he could trust you, I persuaded him to tell you, and I ought to know what it is you'll speak of later too, I think. I may only be a fish..."

"Cut line," Will said. "It's nothing to do with you, or even Flea here. It's something I think the viscount ought to hear by himself."

"No," Lucian said, "have done, Mr. Corby. She's right. Mrs. Pushkin brought us to her friend Flea. She's helped all along. I think she deserves to know. If it's something you think will upset me, well then, who better to hear it in front of?" He offered Maggie a weary smile. "Perhaps if it's terrible enough news I'll get another pot of that amazing tea from her. I think I could hear of my own utter ruin and grin at it, if I'd enough of that. Come, what is it, Mr. Corby? You think you know why Uncle was there? I'd hear it, if you please."

Will sighed. "So be it. Auntie Jane was there through the whole of it, Flea said. That told me, and believe me, I didn't want to hear it either. But truth is truth. Here, big 'un," he told Flea. "Tell us about Millie. Only one thing. How old is she?"

"Millie is eight," Flea said promptly, happy to have an answer. "We had cake and tea for her birthday."

"There it is," Will said gruffly.

Lucian turned ghastly pale, his long eyes closed in pain. Maggie put a hand to her heart.

"I don't think he fancied them that young usually, or I'd have heard of it," Will said, "but it's like I said. Some men think such doings cure the clap. Your uncle, my lord, was trying to cure himself before his wedding to that worthy woman—who's luckier than she'll ever know. We have to pay a call on Auntie Jane now. I'll close her down, and set her on the run. That, at least, I can do now. But as for murder? I can't prove it. I think excitement killed the baron. Your brother said he was excited before he even started.

So did Flea. And—begging your pardon, Mrs. P.—but attempting an eight-year-old must have been hard work for an old fellow. But he got rid of the clap at least."

*

"She was no innocent!" Auntie Jane raged. "The little slut's been working the trade for a year now, maybe more. I got her from Mrs. Cooper. Well, the old man asked for a virgin, I got two and let him choose."

"She was *not* an innocent?" Maggie breathed, not knowing whether to be more aghast because the child was, or was not.

"God, no!" Will said for Auntie Jane, his mouth twisting in a cynical smile. "Were she, he might have managed it. Bawds like Auntie Jane don't supply real virgins. You know your herbs, Mrs. P. These girls make a living being innocent. You'll find Auntie Jane likely paid a visit to your friend Mr. Abernathy first."

"Alum," Auntie Jane said, nodding, "an ointment made with alum, agrimony and some wolf's bane, he said. I'm not used to such. But Abernathy is. He deals with everyone, no questions asked and all questions answered. The baron needed a virgin. I could have got him a widow's daughter from down the street, thirty, fat as a flawn and with spots, but a virgin absolutely, and in need of money. But he wouldn't have believed anything but a child, would he? Men don't.

"He asked 'round the street, and come up with my name. A little late. If he'd come to me before, he wouldn't have got the clap. He offered whatever I asked, he was that desperate, well, but he'd just come from his physician. I didn't want to loose the money. The ointment cost the earth, but you only use a bit. I think we used too much. She must have closed tighter than a drum. The old man was excited before he started, and then he was at it hard, puffing and pant..."

"Be still!" Will demanded, if only because the viscount was growing pale again. "No. You can tell me something else." He paced the parlor's length, and then rounded on her. "Why did you set rogues on the viscount here? And his brother?"

"What?" Auntie asked. Her perpetual sneer faded. She looked genuinely confused.

"The men you set to run him down the other night. The one you sent to push his brother into the street the same night."

"Never!" Auntie said, shocked. "You think I'm mad? I deal with men's bodily needs, redbreast. Nothing else. If a *gentleman* wants something of me, I hurry to find it for him, of course. But tangle with the gentry for anything else? I'm sorry I ever met up with the baron, I rue the day I tried to help the old bastard. If he were a common man, I wouldn't be entertaining you now, would I?"

"You didn't have a score to settle?"

"I didn't have a score to keep," she insisted. "Listen. He came to me. He asked me for a virgin. I gave him what I thought would make him happy. He died at it. Going to put me in chains for cheating him? Think I should have found him a real one? As for running down the viscount—why should I?"

"Did he say anything before he died?" Lucian said, because he had to know.

"Just before he died? Nothing that made sense," Auntie said. "Before that? He was full of jests. Bad ones, good ones, he couldn't keep his mouth shut. I never saw a man so happy, so ready, willing and eager to roger anyone. He had himself a huge…"

Will raised his hand, threateningly. She fell still. "Your uncle killed himself, my lord," Will said, "and there's an end to it. This trull had no part in it other than supplying him the means."

"But is that not punishable?" Lucian asked.

Will smiled. It was not a pleasant sight. "By God, maybe. Few others care. My lord, you can buy or sell a child to push up your chimney to clean it and light a fire beneath to get him working faster do you choose. You can use them to muck out your stables, your Jerichos, in factories, for ornaments, if you like. Look around. What's more common than common children? Nothing comes cheaper. The lucky ones work. At anything that will keep them alive."

"Yes, and so you may go now," Auntie Jane said.

"Oh, may we?" Will laughed. "I think it's the other way round, Auntie dear." He rose and walked to where she was sitting. He came so close he didn't need to speak as loudly as he did. "I want you out," he said, "closed and gone by nightfall, except for the lingering stench. I can't prove you killed the old man, you say? Oh, but I don't have to prove it, dear Auntie. And well you know it. I have only to haul you before a magistrate, and have my lord point his noble finger at you. Flea will say the rest. Then all you'll have to worry about is who'll hang on your ankles for you when you drop so you don't dangle too long at the end of your rope before you strangle."

"I didn't kill him." She glared at him.

"He died here, that's enough. Don't think about the justice of it, that would be a laugh. I can have you in Newgate for any number of reasons, Auntie, and you know it. If not for your child whores then for any number of other offenses. I can name them. It would only take a little imagination to put you in the Sheriff's picture frame. You'd be put to bed with a shovel before nightfall—if you were lucky. Otherwise, you'd find yourself useful to some eager medical students. Your choice now. Or mine, after?"

"It will take more than a day," Auntie Jane said, rising from her chair in agitation.

"No," Will said, "it will not."

"I need Flea to help me..."

"No," Maggie said, "he's staying with me now. He won't be back. And you can't have the children, either. I mean the little girls. She can't take them with her, can she?" she asked Will.

"She might as well. It's that or the workhouse for them. They won't be better off without her."

"Only a man could say a thing like that!" Maggie said furiously. "I'll take them too."

"Take them in? Are you mad?" Lucian asked, revolted.

"Are you?" she retaliated, because now she was so outraged she didn't care if he was a nobleman or her king himself. "They aren't wicked, they're too young. And what's to become of them? Should they be used again and again, because men have already sullied them? No. They're children. Eight years old. What do they know of sin? If men could buy them as virgins when they aren't, then by God I'll teach them to act like virgins, though they are not."

But in the end, only one of the little girls went with them. It was the fair-haired girl the men had seen playing with the puppy on the steps when they'd first come to Auntie Jane. She took her scant belongings in a bundle and rode away in the coach with them. The other, the dark-haired one who smiled at them when they arrived, ran away when she heard her fate.

The little blond girl sat huddled in a corner of the carriage, silent, all the way back to Maggie's house. She didn't look at the men. But then, they both avoided her eye too.

*

They stood in Maggie's sitting room, saying their good-byes.

"Your house will be bulging at the seams, Mrs. P.," Will said when Alice and Annie took the silent child away with them to bathe her as Maggie demanded. "My young rogue Jack in the kitchen. God knows where you'll put Flea. And there's his dog. And now, another girl. Can you sell enough fish to feed them all?"

"I'll buy fewer treasures for myself," Maggie said on a shrug. "The children will help around the shop, and they'll grow and help more. Flea has a strong back, even if his mind is weak. He can be taught to help too. Even the dog will eventually work for me, guarding my shop." She smiled up at the runner, her first genuine grin in hours. "I think of it as a good investment," she said pertly. "You're the one who told me how important they are, aren't you?"

"I was speaking more of grain, ores and such. But I see your point."

279

"So. That's all there is?" Maggie said. "After all our questions? But—what of the attacks on the viscount and his brother?"

"Not attacks, then," Lucian murmured, "simply coincidence." His voice surprised them both. He'd been quiet since they'd left Auntie Jane's. It was as if he had already left them in his mind.

"I don't believe in coincidences like that," Will said. "It doesn't make sense. It doesn't fit."

"Life doesn't make sense. And it's seldom fitting," Lucian said, almost to himself. "How I shall tell my mother, I don't know. I shudder to think of my brother's reaction. He was Uncle's favorite, and for reasons I never understood, Uncle was a favorite of his. Until he discovered he hadn't been left any money, of course. But that was in the nature of a betrayal. And so he'll take this hard anyhow. But he must know. I wonder if we ought to tell Lousia at all. Good God!" he said, his eyes opening wide in sudden shock. "How can we tell anyone? We can't have something like this on everyone's lips. There's Nicholas. I don't want him to ever know of this."

"They have to know," Will said. "Your brother offered a reward for the answer. I can't cheat him. Your son never has to know, but your mother certainly can deal with it. As for the lady Louisa…that's your decision. But I think she ought to know. She had a narrow escape. It might make her think more deeply in future."

"Yes," Maggie said, "Lady Louisa deserves to know." She gasped, struck by a sudden thought. From the color of her face, Will guessed it before she spoke. "My lord," Maggie told Lucian in a small voice, "she might have to know for other reasons. He went to Auntie Jane to cure himself, but—but it is possible that he and Lady Lousia—I know it's not pleasant to think about—but they…"

"They may have anticipated their vows?" Lucian said with an ugly twist to his lips. "A month ago I'd have laughed at the idea. But now? I know nothing anymore. You're right. Perhaps, Mrs. Puskin, I could impose on you? Could you—would you be willing to tell her?"

"Of course!' Maggie said.

"But..." Lucian shook his head. His face was stark, his voice had a note of desperation in it. "May I ask both of you to tell no one else? Please. I've my family, my name to think of."

It was a hard thing for him to ask them, and they both knew it.

Will tilted a shoulder. "My lord, my lips are sealed. I think I can say Mrs. Pushkin will be discreet. But there's no sense lying. Auntie Jane *will* talk. Her girls will talk. The lower classes will know. It may percolate to the top."

"Rumor can't be helped," Lucian said. "But rumor dies. So long as it never becomes fact. Thank you."

"So then, it's over,' Maggie sighed. "And here I was going to ask you if you'd care to come to the Fair again with us." She laughed nervously. The matter of the Frost Fair was an inconsequential thing in light of all she'd heard today. But she couldn't bear to think or talk about the consequential things just now.

"I know it's foolish, but I've caught the fever," she said. "No one knows how much longer it will last. If the weather holds fine it will soon be gone, and gone forever. I doubt we'll see another such in our lifetime. Since everyone's there I thought there wouldn't be sense keeping the shop open. So, since I promised the children...well, to be honest, I promised myself one last look at it. I thought to ask you two as well, but now I see our adventures together are over."

"Do you?" Will asked. "I don't. One last one, I think. I'll go. As you say, if everyone is there, there'll be more trade for me there too. I'll join you. And you, my lord?"

"I think not," Lucian said.

Neither Maggie or Will were surprised. They were only secretly surprised to find themselves feeling a little wounded. Because the world was returning to normal, and so why would a viscount want to pass his time with a Bow Street runner or even an uncommon fishmonger?

"I have to talk to the family, think this out," Lucian said absently. "I will see you again though," he added quickly, as though hearing their thoughts. "I'll take you to Lady Louisa," he told Maggie. "If not tomorrow, then at your earliest convenience? And there's the matter of the reward I owe you," he told Will.

"Well, I didn't earn it by myself," Will said handsomely. "I think there'll be something in it for Mrs. Pushkin too. But if I'm to be paid soon, I think I'll have enough coin in my pockets to treat you to a fine luncheon," he told Maggie. "You say you want to make a day of it? I'll be here at nine,"

"I think not!" Maggie said with a wicked grin. "*Noon*! If it's to be a holiday, let's make it a grand one. I'll sip chocolate in bed like a lady, and spend the morning making myself magnificent for the Fair."

"With that pup, and all your charges?" Will laughed. "Lucky if you can keep your eyes closed until first light."

"Well," Maggie admitted, "I do want to have things in order so we can start work all the earlier the next day."

"Noon, then," Will said.

"I *will* be back," Lucian told her at the door, before he followed Will to their waiting coach.

"The thing is..." Will said as they drove back to Lucian's house, "it don't all add up."

"It does," Lucian said, staring out the window at nothing. "No one tried to kill me, Mr. Corby. I see that now. It's just that when one's mind's on murder, one sees it in every shadow. The horse was struck and made to gallop in my direction. No doubt Arthur was pushed too. The streets were crowded, and London is never easy. My uncle was a vile man and met a deserved end. My brother and I were merely unlucky. At the same time. It's unusual, but not unheard of. Uncle's blood was spilled through his own idiocy. No one is after ours. Send your lads home from my alley. Let them have a holiday too. It's over."

But Will fretted about it, even as he treated himself to a hackney ride back to Bow Street. It didn't *feel* over to him.

*

"*No!*" Arthur breathed.

His mother was so distressed she got to her feet, as though she could leave the subject where she'd been sitting when she'd heard it. A moment later, she sat again, as the information sank in. "*Vile, vile* man," she muttered. "To lower himself so—well, but he was always a selfish creature, caring for nothing but himself. But the family! If this gets out—and it will, filth bubbles to the top, no matter how deeply it's hidden... What shall we do?"

"Deny it," Lucian said wearily. "Simply deny it. No one can prove it. The girl he died attempting has fled. Mr. Corby says she'll seek the same employment elsewhere, but who'll believe such a slum rat even if she knew his name? The procuress lives in lively fear of the runner, she'll say nothing. The giant who did the deed? He has an infant's mind, and will obey the fishwife because he adores her."

"And she?" his mother demanded.

"She wants to forget the whole, as we do."

"She won't try to get money from us for her silence?" his mother sneered, "I doubt that!"

"Don't. She has more honor than most females I know. Far more than your brother, Ma'am."

"Bah. My brother," she spat. "I only wish he'd lived so I could tell him how disgusting he is. But what about the danger to Arthur? Someone's been following him, and there was that night he was pushed into the street. How do you account for that? And your *accident*, that you've never enlarged upon, at least to me? Arthur said my brother might have had a low female as a lover. What if she still seeks vengeance—no—what if she looks for more now because he infected her too?"

Lucian shook his head. "Mama, think about it. If Uncle contracted a disease, it was likely from that mythical female, not the reverse. Any rate, I doubt that story. I sincerely do."

"I do too," Arthur said suddenly. "I think we've been jumping at shadows, Mama. I might have merely been pushed by someone accidentally. It *was* crowded. Lucian may have just been unlucky too." He gave his mother a significant look. "He was out for a night on the town, you know, and that usually entails a bit to drink."

Lucian frowned. The boy still didn't understand him. But if it allayed their mother's fear, he wouldn't argue the point.

"What of the fellow you saw in the park across the street?" the viscountess asked Arthur.

"He may have had nothing to do with me."

"Don't worry," Lucian said. "We'll still take care. But the matter is over with and done. Although all may know, no one can prove a thing. Let it be buried with Uncle, and have done with it. But not a word of this to Nick. Never. Do you understand?"

"Do you think we've run mad?' his mother snapped.

"I'll leave now," Lucian said. "I'm going to go about my business as usual. I suggest you do the same. No sense prolonging the period of mourning. We don't mean it, and it will only remind people of the circumstances. Best forget and let it be forgotten."

"Thank God Louisa doesn't know," his mother said fervently. "She was going to marry him for his money, no telling what she would do to get some of ours if she got her jaws on this bit of news."

Lucian didn't argue the point. He knew better and had heard enough. He merely bowed himself out. Arthur appeared in the hall as a footman was helping him on with his greatcoat.

"I hope you don't mind what I said to Mama?" Arthur said when the footman left them. "About your accident? I was only trying to get her not to worry. This whole thing has got me thinking as never before. I was a fool to cultivate Uncle. You thought so. Don't deny it. You were right. I was trying to make Mama happy—

but well, dammit, Maldon, it's you and I who ought to be friends, isn't it? What was I doing trying to befriend that filthy old man? I feel soiled by the whole incident. Worse, because I was trying to be his intimate."

"Tell you what," Arthur said, dropping his voice. "Lord, but this is hard to say...but the thing of it is, Maldon, Mama never wanted me close to you and so I never tried. It should have been your company I sought, not Uncle's. Do you think you could find it in your heart to forgive me that, and start anew? I'd like to be your friend, if it's not too late."

"Of course I'd like that," Lucian said, "and there's no need to apologize."

"Yes there is," Arthur said in a rushed whisper. "The truth is she always says disparaging things about you, and frowned on us ever getting together, as brothers ought to do. I'm afraid I played right into that. It's pleasant being mother's favorite little lad," he said on a broken laugh, "until you see it's time to grow up. Maldon—let's make amends. Let me, at least. Will you?"

"No need to ask such a thing. We'll get together for dinner, soon. Or better yet," Lucian said on a happy inspiration, "why not come with me tomorrow? I've a mind to see the Frost Fair one more time. It can't last forever, you know."

"Yes! Absolutely. I'll come by and fetch you. About noon?"

"Yes, perfect," Lucian said. "That's when I was planning to go."

"No!" Arthur said in chagrin. "No, damn, but I can't. I'm promised to tea with Mama. Better still. Have dinner with me. In my rooms. I know you've a grander home. But I can entertain too. Let me show you. You mocked me for having Uncle to dinner. Help me take the curse off it by dining with me. But, Maldon... Only one favor? If you please, don't tell Mama. I'm trying to grow up, but there's no sense making it harder, is there?"

"None at all," Lucian laughed.

"One more thing," Arthur said. "I hardly know, and I'm embarrassed for it. But what *is* your favorite dish? Uncle liked kidneys—no, I refuse to think about him!"

"Don't," Lucian said, "because I won't either."

But he did, all the way home. It was over. But Lucian wished he could be sure of it. He was not. Something ticked at the corner of his mind, like a moth tapping at a window pane on a late summer's night. But it was too dark to see.

Chapter Seventeen

Lucian woke feeling lighter than he had in weeks. The wintry darkness that had gripped his soul since his uncle's death had vanished in the night. When his valet entered the room and drew back the curtains from his windows, the bedchamber filled with a pure white light. It had snowed again in the night, but now the sun was out again. Lucian sat up, realizing he was actually looking forward to the day.

His uncle was dead, but so was his concern and any lingering regret about it. The earth was well rid of the old villain. In time, with luck, he'd forget the man ever existed. He'd turn Uncle's properties over to Arthur, little by little by stealth and design if he had to. But it was over.

He no longer had to see the runner, or the fishwife. Still, as he sat in the weak sunlight and let his valet shave him, Lucian decided that he chose to see the pair again today anyway. The thought pleased him. The only thing that nagged at him—and that only in a peripheral way—was the thought that since they no longer needed each other he'd doubtless never see them again after today.

But then he remembered he had promised to take Mrs. Pushkin to see Lousia. And he had to make arrangements to see the runner again as well, didn't he? Because he certainly wouldn't bring his reward money to the Fair. Lucian smiled, thanked his valet, and began to dress for what looked to be a delightful day.

He had a hearty breakfast, and read the newspapers. Then he went into his study and wrote a letter to Nicholas, filled with jests and promises for the fine spring holiday they would have together. He dashed off some more correspondence, looking up to consult the case clock in the corner every so often. They were going to be leaving Mrs. Pushkin's at noon, Will had said.

When he put down his pen he saw he'd time and to spare. He'd tell them he'd decided to buy some gimcrack for Nicholas at the

Fair. He would, because Nicholas would like that. But he liked the thought of their surprise at seeing him come along to the Fair with them again almost as much.

He glanced out the window. The new fallen snow was already melting. It was mild again, so he could take his curricle today. But if he did, Mrs. Pushkin and her staff would have to take a separate hackney... Lucian asked for his coach to be made ready. He shrugged on his greatcoat and selected one of his stoutest walking sticks. The ice at the Fair was treacherous stuff. He pulled on his kid gloves, tilted his hat just so, and grinning at his footman, went out the door—and almost walked into Arthur on his top step.

"Lord!" Lucian said, his hand to his heart. "If it was night, I'd have screeched like an old lady."

"You're here, good!" Arthur said.

'Well, but I was just on my way out."

"Where?" Arthur asked.

Lucian hesitated. He hadn't introduced Mrs. Pushkin to Arthur at the Fair because he'd been ashamed to be seen with the fishwife involved in his uncle's death. Or perhaps, as a small voice insisted, because he'd been ashamed of being seen with a fishwife, no matter how they'd met. But she wasn't here now. There were no feelings to be hurt. And no reason to tell his brother about her, either.

Lucian didn't entirely understand the tenuous relationship he'd forged with the fishwife and the runner. And so he was suddenly relieved Arthur hadn't taken him up on his rash invitation to accompany him to the Fair. He must have been overset indeed, he thought, to have proffered it in the first place.

"I'm off to run errands and such," he said. "Now that I don't have to look for assailants under every hedge, I can go anywhere."

"So you've no set appointments? No one expecting you? Nowhere you must be?"

"No. That's exactly it. I need to breathe some fresh and free air. Now that the temperature's moderating and my wounds are healed, I'm eager to be off."

"Well, good," Arthur said happily, "because I've decided you're to dine with me this very day."

"Tell me the time, and I'll be there," Lucian said. He'd envisioned a different evening—but solaced himself by deciding that sharing Mrs. Pushkin's dinner two nights in a week was far too much.

"Nuncheon, and now," Arthur said. "I've breakfasted at your house often enough. And I decided dinner would bring back too many unhappy memories. That was for Uncle and me, and I *don't* want to remember that. So, for us—a nuncheon. Don't be disappointed. I've got into the habit of having a hearty one. Uncle was old-fashioned and country bred... No, not another word on that head. But I promise you a delicious meal. The first of many, I hope. The sooner the better, I thought. Since you've no other appointments, what better time than now?"

"Now?" Lucian said, thinking quickly. Well, but it could be done, after all. He'd meet them at the Fair later than he'd planned. He didn't want Arthur to go along, but he might suggest it if he knew his plans. But this was a farewell, in a sense. And Arthur was, after all a stranger to the pair. And he didn't know how Arthur would react to socializing with a fishmonger, did he? Why ruin things at the very last? And he certainly didn't care to hear their mother's opinion of it, and he would, if Arthur knew.

But that meant getting a message to Mrs. Pushkin and Will Corby. The Fair would be so thronged with people he'd have a hard time meeting his own shadow there if he didn't set a time and place to do it. "Send away your hackney, I'll just go round and get my curricle," Lucian said., "I won't be a moment."

"Why don't you send for it?"

"My dear boy, I don't play the grand seigneur," Lucian lied. "No reason I can't walk three steps to the stables. Wait here, no sense the two of us getting our boots filthied. I'll be back in a tick."

He gave Arthur no time to answer, but stepped off his front step and strode into the long alley that led to his stables, alongside his townhouse. From the side of his eye Lucian saw a shadow slip into deeper shadows as he did. As he'd hoped, Spanish Will hadn't yet retired his crew of watchful street urchins. The runner probably wouldn't call them off until he'd explored every last loophole and avenue—or at least, until he was paid his reward.

"Here, boy," Lucian said to the empty air in a low voice. "Come out. I know you're there, and I know Spanish Will set you there. You've had my sympathies these past freezing days. But listen, I need to get a message to Mr. Corby. Double quick. Good lord, boy! Do you think you're invisible? Come here, I said."

A ragged boy emerged from the shadows, and stood, poised to run.

"Good," Lucian said, now sorry he was seeing the lad clearly. Because this one was young, and rail thin. And though it was growing milder, it *had* snowed in the night. He could have invited the lad into his kitchens as Mrs. Pushkin had done...yes, he thought, with a wry smile, and have his cook commit suicide on his own knife if he did. A nobleman's staff was notoriously proud of place. He'd perhaps been hanging about eccentrics like the fishwife too long, Lucian thought, amused.

"Now listen," he said, smiling at his thoughts, "I judge Spanish Will to be at Mrs. Pushkin's house now. That's the fish shop in Little Buckle Street. He'll be leaving for the Frost Fair by noon. That should give you time to reach him. Listen. Tell him the Viscount Maldon said he was planning to go too, but has just been invited to his brother's rooms for nuncheon, and must go there instead. But tell him I said as I'm done I'll meet them at the Fair. At the apothecary's tent—that's Abernathy the apothecary—at four, at the latest, half past the hour. I'd like them to wait for me there. Now, can you remember all that?"

The boy nodded. "You says as to how you'll be at Old Abernathy's tent at four or half past and to wait for you there."

"Good. Now listen. If you get the message to him, I'll present you with a guinea for your pains. Aye, that's right. A golden boy. All for simply getting to him and telling him. All right?"

But the boy was gone and down the street too fast to answer.

*

"Devilish good to have you here at last," Arthur said as he waved off his man and poured his brother a glass of wine himself.

He was flustered and fidgety, fussing with the bottle and glasses, his earnest young face deeply concentrated on each simple task. He was nervous as a new bride showing off her household, Lucian thought guiltily. "I ought to have come long before," he said.

"No. I ought to have asked you," Arthur answered. "It's not that Mama frowned on our friendship, precisely. It's more that…well, the strange thing is that I feel guilty meeting you like this even now without her knowing. I don't think she'd approve. You know what I think, Maldon? I think she was afraid that if we two became friends there would be less room in my heart for her—which is nonsense of course."

"No, it's not," Lucian said. "At least not on my part. We're not close. To be honest, I don't know her very well. To be more honest, I know she don't care for me very much. I remind her of our papa. Theirs was not a blissful union."

"That's an understatement!" Arthur said. "Good. Everything's ready. Come, sit down. We'll dine. I've got ragout and shaved ham, fowl, fresh bread and a special treat. I don't want to mention Uncle, but he was mad about a kidney pie the shop round the corner makes. And just because he liked something oughtn't to damn it. You must try it. It's extraordinary!"

Lucian seated himself. He wasn't sharp set but hungry enough to do justice to a light repast. He raised his glass. "To a new friendship between brothers," he proposed. "Thank you for inviting me, Arthur."

"Thank you for coming, Maldon. Now, let's get on with what we missed all these years."

*

"They left," the boy Will set to watch Maggie's alley told the boy Lucian sent to find her and the runner. "You missed 'em, you did. Aye, Spanish Will, he come early, and the fishwife and her crew come piling out of the house like it were afire. They're gone. Even that lucky dog, Jack. But she never seen me, so I still got to work."

"Blow it!" Lucian's thin boy exclaimed. "Now I got to try'n find him at the Fair!"

"Well, luck to you. 'cause you're more likely to catch cold than Mr. Corby there. How you going to find him? All London's there. You're dreaming."

But there was a whole guinea in it for him. So the boy took to his heels again. He wasn't a fool or a dreamer. He was hungry, and had always been. Yes, he knew there were thousands of people at the Fair. But he also knew all the ones there who were watching everything but the Fair.

*

The pace of the Frost Fair was frantic. The moderating temperatures spelled doom for it. The Fair was going to melt like the last traces of the dreadful winter, and all knew and wanted one last thrill from it. Five days of jubilation soon to be ended sent the festivities to a fever pitch. Spring was on the air, the cruelest winter anyone could remember was finally dying. The rides were whirling, the vendors shouting themselves hoarse, even the music was brighter. The printing presses churned out farewells, even a ditty called *Madame Tabitha Thaw*. London was giving its greatest Frost Fair a riotous good-bye.

But Spanish Will wasn't enjoying himself. His expression softened now and again, when he saw the fun Maggie was having, just strolling and taking it all in. But something was niggling at him, something was nagging, and he couldn't relax.

"It's vexing you too, isn't it?" Maggie asked unexpectedly.

"What?" Surprised, he looked down into her upturned face.

She grimaced. "The baron's death. I can't get it off my mind. It's coloring everything today. It doesn't all fit. Oh, I believe Flea took him to my doorstep and left him there when he died. I know he was dead then too. Otherwise Flea wouldn't have hit him. That makes me feel some better. Flea's simple, but clever in unexpected ways. Be sure, he knows what dead is and is not. But the way of it puzzles me. My grandmother tended the sick, and I helped her. There's things I know."

Her rusty eyebrows came down, and she frowned as she thought aloud, ticking off her reasons on her gloved fingers.

"If a man's heart gives out, he feels pain before he falls. He clutches his chest or his arm, and he gasps. But he doesn't writhe. If his brain's struck, he seizes up. It's like he was thunderstruck. And if a man has a fit, he seldom dies of it. The baron was thrashing about, Flea said. Shouting too, which a man with a fit does not do." She frowned. "What the baron was doing when he was taken was so ugly I haven't wanted to think about it. But now I am, and now I wonder if that's what killed him after all."

"Aye," Will said, "I do too."

"You do?" she gasped. "What do you think it was?"

"I don't know," Will said, "but I'll find out."

"But if you don't think his heart gave out or he had a brain spsam…it might have been murder, after all."

"Aye. But 'might' isn't a word I can act on. I didn't come with you just for the Fair today, Mrs. P. I want a word with your friend Mr. Abernathy, and I want you there with me. You know him and you know herbs, and his name has come up once too often for me."

"Mr. Abernathy," Maggie said. Her face grew so pale her freckles faded to mauve. "*Poison?* You think it might be…? *It might*," she said in horror as she thought about it. "But, you let the viscount go home thinking he was safe!"

"He's safe enough for now," Will said, patting the hand she had on his arm. "I've got my lads watching his house, as usual. I know where everyone is, and they're all in place. In fact, his lordship's downstairs maid sent word that he went for a drive with his brother today, leaving the house at eleven. I knew that before I came to your shop. I'm not worried. I doubt anyone will attempt the two of them together, or by the broad light of day. But I did come here for more than the fun of the Fair, Mrs. P."

"Well, Mr. Abernathy's tent's at the end of the Fair," she said. "That's why I told the children to meet us there at five, when it's time to go. So you'll have your chance then."

"I want to speak to him now."

All Maggie's taste for the Fair fled. "You know," she said as they began to walk faster, "any number of herbs can cause such things."

"And he's been selling them all," Will said.

Then they walked even faster.

*

Mr. Abernathy had no customers in his lonely tent at the end of the row. But he wasn't happy to see the ones he'd just got. He scarcely looked at Maggie. He was too busy glaring at Spanish Will.

"I need to talk with you," Will said.

"Ho! Spanish Will himself. When you need to talk, I need to listen, is it?"

"It is. But settle yourself. I'm not looking into any crimes on your part—just yet. I need to know about herbs."

"Pull the other one whilst you're at it. Mrs. Pushkin could tell you about herbs. What is it you want from me?"

"Knowledge," Will said. "Any idea of what could kill a man after sending him into a fit of shouting and writhing first?"

"Ha," the apothecary said without humor, "shouting and writhing, is it? That's an easy one. Getting a bill from his physician, for a start."

"I am incredibly amused," Will said in dangerous tones. "Now again, what have you got for me?" He took out his occurrence book.

"Aye, well, 'writhing'?" Abernathy said sourly. "That would be your foxglove, your mistletoe…aconite, too. Then you have your…"

294

At the end of five minutes, Will had the names of fifteen deadly herbs entered in his book. When the apothecary finished describing them, Maggie shook her head.

Mr. Abernathy laughed sourly. "Aye, Mrs. Pushkin knows before I say it."

"They're common enough. It depends on how they're used. You could have asked me," she told him reproachfully.

"But now I can ask Mr. Abernathy another question," Will said smoothly. "Now, I want him to tell me how much of any of those he's sold lately. And perhaps, to a stranger?"

"Am I the only apothecary in London town?"

"No," Will said, "but you know what I'm asking about, you old devil. The baron died in Spitalfields and well you know it. Where he died is where I begin."

"It's never that," Abernathy scoffed. "Some poisons take hours. He could have dined with the king the night before and got it then, if he got it at all."

Will snapped his book shut. "Fine. If you like, you can test your memory whilst you kick your heels in Newgate, it's all the same to me."

"Hold, hold," the apothecary grumbled. "Lately, you say? Well, I haven't sold much at all lately, sitting freezing my ballocks off in this curst tent at the edge of nothing. But before? When the old man died? Wait. Hold. I did have a run on my belladonna. You remember, Mrs. Pushkin."

"I don't mean drops for prettifying whore's eyes," Will said in disgust.

"Nor do I," Mr. Abernathy said, "because now I think on, I sold the last of my stores to a young gentleman. Back at my shop it was, before this damned fiasco of a Frost Fair. I'd only a little left for Mrs. Pushkin, remember, Missus? Yes, and the gent was a stranger too. Now I think back, it was an odd thing. I told him it was deadly stuff and to have a care—you can ask anyone, I always say that. He said not to worry, his mistress wanted it for her eyes. But he bought enough for a Sultan's harem. Maybe he was more ambitious than he looked." He cackled.

"Still—there's a thought," Abernathy mused. "You want an herb to set a man writhing? Belladonna's the one, your lady. Set a man winding like a snake, though I hear he'll do a piece of bowing too before he goes. Odd thing that... Because they do bow like they're meeting the king, when all they're doing is getting acquainted with King Death himself. First, you see, they get all excited..."

"*Who* did you sell it to?" Will roared.

The apothecary's bony shoulders went up in a shrug. "Never saw him before. A young man, a gent."

"Would you know him again?"

"Oh, aye," Abernathy said with a slow, ugly smile, "'cause I saw him again, didn't I? He bought more just the day before yesterday. Said his mistress dropped the bottle and spilled the whole of it. But you know that. Or should. Because after he bought it, Mrs. Pushkin came in to see me. Then when she left I saw he was still here. More than that, he was hob-nobbing with you and her and another gentry cove, just outside my tent."

Will and Maggie startled the apothecary by their sudden flight. But Will stopped on the ice outside. He caught Maggie by the wrist. "It's bad enough as it is, there's no sense making it worse," he said. "No need to break an ankle on this damned ice. Stop running. We don't know for certain."

"He made dinner for his Uncle before he died!" Maggie gasped. "He spoke with us and the viscount the other day, just here, outside Mr. Abernathy's tent. We *do* know!"

"But not for certain. A young gent? Could be anyone. Think on! It could have been the lieutenant. He was here that day. Might even have been his lordshhip's cousin, Sir James. A fribble can become desperate too... No matter. We can stop the viscount before another dinner comes round, whoever it is. Calm yourself. We don't know he's in any danger at all. Misliking an old uncle, and one you think will leave you a fortune to boot, is never the same as going up against a brother. No, brothers are different. There's family loyalty and love, and suchlike involved. So us rushing off and acting crazed now won't do a thing but harm. We know nothing. We suspect everything. That's a different matter.

"We find the viscount. He should know first. Even if it's only what we suspect." Will began walking Maggie away from the tent toward the embankment as he spoke, his voice mild and reasonable. But he walked quickly, even so.

Maggie tried to still her wildly fluttering heartbeat by force of pure reason. But her pulse was racing so hard she felt as though she had taken the vile herb that killed the baron. "I have men here, everywhere," Will went on in his slow deep voice. "They're invisible to you, as they're meant to be. We've hours yet. It's only noon time. Now, let's find Maldon."

Will stopped to have a word with a starveling boy, another with a loutish man, an old woman and a man playing a tin trumpet. Then he helped Maggie across the ice, up the embankment stair. He spoke with another man loitering there and sent him running in another direction. Only then, he called a hackney cab.

But when they got to the viscount's house, they discovered he hadn't returned to his townhouse. His servants, those Will paid as well as those who remained loyal to their master, had no idea of where he and Mr. Arthur had gone.

"Little villain," Will swore, as they raced back to the hackney again. At Maggie's look of confusion, he added, "I pay a street rat to keep watch, usually the cleverest of the lot. But he's gone too. Where's the man got himself to? He went off with his brother in his phaeton. Where did they go? His *brother*! What a lobcock I am."

He shouted at the driver, directing him to Arthur's rooms. "If he's not there, we'll go to the mother's," he told Maggie.

"Then start making the round of his clubs? Gentlemen go to their clubs of an afternoon, Mr. Corby."

"No, not this one, not today. I've men watching. I'll pass by and ask anyway, in case he just got there. Gentlemen go everywhere of an afternoon. I've eyes and ears everywhere, never fear."

He began to think aloud, running through his options. "He might have left his brother off, he might had took him along. So I have to think of where he'd go in either case. Gents don't go to their convenients by day, and he isn't a man to gamble until the sun sets. He's not known for loving cockfights or ratting or dogfights. I'll ask if he was seen at his boxing salon, or shooting salon, or fencing... This is all folly, you know," he said more gently, seeing Maggie's wild-eyed look. "We'll find him before dinner. We don't even know if it's needful that we do."

The boy Will had set at Arthur's house was gone. But so was Arthur, so the lad must have followed him as he was supposed to do. Will had a moment to regret setting such a young one on the man's trail. The lad had been a good hound, following him to the Fair the other day. But Will had seen Arthur there too, for all the good it did him. The boy hadn't said exactly where else at the Fair the viscount's brother had been that day. And he hadn't thought to ask him, Will realized, a cold feeling in the pit of his stomach.

"My master is gone," Arthur's man said loftily, once he'd been sufficiently threatened by the name of the law—and Will's clenched fist. "As is his brother. I cannot say where, for they parted immediately after nuncheon."

"Nuncheon?" Maggie breathed.

"To be sure. Mr. Arthur entertained his brother this afternoon. Both seemed very pleased at the menu, if I do compliment myself by saying so. We had veal ragoo'd and chicken pie. Aspic, shaved ham, sliced beef, a kidney pie that their late uncle, the baron, was quite fond of, poor gentleman. A good claret, an excellent Rhone, a..."

"When did they leave?" Will interrupted.

"An hour past. As I was saying, the viscount was very content with his meal..."

"I believe you, did you hear nothing of his direction?" Will growled. "Come, man! Servants do few things better than listening, especially since their masters forget they have ears. Where was he bound? It would be to his benefit if you told me. He may be in danger."

The servant's nose went up. "I cannot say. I would, of course, if I could, given the circumstances. But I did not listen, nor could I hear. I was busy in the kitchen. Especially since my master specifically asked me to take away the dishes and wash them promptly today, as he'd heard there were vermin in the building again. He requested that I scour them most particularly. He is a fastidious man. The only thing I can tell you is that I saw the Viscount Maldon when he was leaving. He seemed pleased, as I said. And seemed, if I may venture to say, also extremely happy, almost excited, about wherever it was he was bound. He was smiling widely too. A good thing to see at last, especially in light of the unfortunate circumstance of his uncle's..."

But he was talking to air. Because the fierce runner and the red-haired woman were already gone from the doorway and running down the stair.

"Where?" Maggie wailed, "where can he be?"

"We'll go to his mother, it's on the way. Though I doubt he'd be excited to go there, unless..." Will didn't finish that sentence. The fishwife's eyes showed white all round. "I'll stop and ask my man near St. James Street on the way too. You may have to go back to the Fair and pick up the others. Then go home. I'll scour London— all night if I must. We'll find him. He might even have decided to go to the Fair. God knows it seems everyone else in London is there."

The coach clattered on the cobbles, hoofs and wheels pounding hard and fast as their heartbeats. They were both thinking what would happen if a man took ill at a mad scene like the Frost Fair.

He'd be mistaken for drunk...not that it mattered, Maggie thought. If he'd eaten what his uncle had, it didn't matter at all. There were specifics for it. There was nux vomica, purges of all sorts. But there was no cure. It would likely be too late. And no one would think to try to provide one even if it weren't.

But poisoned? The viscount? It was true the elegant, reserved nobleman was about as different from her as he was from Mrs. Gow and Mrs. Gudge. It was amazing that they'd even met. In the normal way of things they never would have done. But she'd come to know him. She appreciated him treating her as though she might be his equal in any way, even though they both knew the world would never expect it of him. She enjoyed his mocking humor and admired his courage under the whip of pain. She'd seen the look on his face when he'd heard his uncle had bought a child. Nor could she forget the look in his eyes that night at the masquerade—in fact, it warmed her many a night since. But to think of him cold, blue and lifeless as his uncle had been on her doorstep? Impossible. She would not. She could not. But she did.

"Will," she said, so panicked she forgot formality, "don't coddle me. Do you think he would try so soon after his uncle?"

She didn't have to explain who "he" was. Will was wondering the same. He had only questions as answer.

"I don't know. If he thought we believed his uncle died of a heart spasm at that brothel? If he was sure we didn't know about his connection to Abernathy? If that even *was* him at Abernathy's tent in the first place? But if he needed the money that badly, or hated his brother for reasons we don't know? Or if he's mad? How can I say? How can I know? It may be nothing. It may be all coincidence. We may laugh at this yet." But still, he yelled at the driver to go faster.

The viscount wasn't at his mother's house, nor was his brother. Nor was the viscountess herself. She'd gone to take tea with friends, her servants said. And neither of her sons had shown their noses, nor were they expected to today.

The Viscount Maldon had not set polished boot on the pavements of St. James Street either, Will's man reported when he stopped the coach and leaped out to ask him. Nor had his brother, Sir James or Lieutenant Pascal been seen there. Will told the man to spread the word. If anyone saw the viscount, they should tell him

Spanish Will said he was to go to a physician immediately, and send word to him from there.

The hackney raced on toward the Thames.

The Fair was more crowded than ever because the afternoon was so balmy. Everyone had come to see what might be its last day on earth. Will and Maggie reached the river stair and leaped over the improvised channel in the ice, ignoring the attendant bargeman's outstretched hand and outraged cry. Will's face was enough to make him stand back. The channels were wider today, the ice at the edges had a porous honeycombed look. All the ice on the river seemed to be sweating, making their passage harder. They slipped often, and slid if they tried to run.

They tried, though. They pushed aside revelers and shouldered their way through the dense crowds.

"Mr. Corby! *Mr. Corby*!" a voice kept piping, coming nearer until they could hear it clear over the drums, and music, whistles and laughter.

Will spun around. The sharp-faced boy he'd set to watch the viscount was racing up to him. When he stopped, so did the boy. The lad doubled over, putting both hands on the ragged knees of his britches, blowing hard, catching his breath. But he was young and excited, so he raised his head and spoke quickly.

"I run all the way—from his house," he panted. "He bubbled me...then he tole me...to find you at the fish shop...'n give you a message. But you was gone...when I got there. So," he gulped more air, "I caught on the back of a hack and rode the rest of the way...'til I dropped off here. I asked everyone where you was. I found Our Bill near the sword swallower...he said I should ask Wee Charlie...over near..."

"Stop telling me how you found me!" Will shouted so loud other fairgoers looked around. "The Viscount Maldon? You're talking of him?"

The boy nodded, his thin chest working like a bellows.

"What did he say? Where is he?"

"He said as to how he'd be going with his brother for to eat...his nuncheon...but he'll be at Old Abernathy's tent at four...or half past and that...you was to wait for him there. And he's gonna gimme a golden boy for telling you, he said!"

"Here's another," Will said, flipping the coin to him, so relieved he was incautious of his own money for the first time in years. He looked at Maggie, allowing himself a meager smile. "Well, one thing's working right. Come."

They went fast as they could, but it wasn't that fast. The throngs weren't easy to part, not even for an angry runner and a woman who knew how to use her elbows. When they finally neared the end of the last row of tents, they saw a little group waiting in the center of the ice aisle there. Flea's huge form was unmistakable even from afar. He and Maggie's servants were on time, waiting for them.

Maggie had a stitch in her side, but refused to tell Will, lest he slow up—or worse, leave her behind. The apothecary's tent flap was closed. She hoped he hadn't left. It wasn't likely. He'd spent good money on the Fair and wouldn't leave until all chance of profit was gone. It might only mean he had a customer inside.

As she neared, Alice and Annie turned, as did Davie and the little blond brothel girl, holding Flea's hand. Jack stood in their midst, interrupted while obviously telling them another story of his adventures. But there wasn't a sign of the viscount.

"Have you seen the viscount?" Will demanded.

"I thought I seen him!" Jack volunteered. "When I was on my way here. From a far piece back. I thought I seen Mr. Arthur too!"

"Were they together?"

"Nah. I thought I seen the viscount on my *way* here. Looked like he was standing, waiting. But when I got here he was gone. And I was early. So then I went on down the aisle, walking up and down to see what I could whilst I waited, but keeping an eye out all the same. That's when I thought I seen Mr. Arthur going to the apothecary's tent. But when I got back he was gone too. I guess they missed each other, and me. What a day."

"Hoy!" a strident voice called, splitting through the clamor of the Fair. They all turned.

Mrs. Gudge and Mrs. Gow waved as they came rolling over the ice with the shifting stride of sailors, looking like two animated bundles of clothing. "We seen the viscount," Mrs. Gudge puffed, as she came abreast. "He said as to how he'd be meeting you here. Well, I says to Mrs. Gow, why not say hello?"

"Where was the viscount?" Will demanded.

"And a good afternoon to you too, I'm sure, Mr. Redbreast," Mrs. Gow said with heavy sarcasm, "'E was over to the fire-eater's stall, saying as to 'ow 'e was weary of just standing waiting 'ere."

"Aye, he couldn't stand still," Mrs. Gudge said, "and he'd the right of it. It's mild-like, but you got to take care. Stand too long and you'll take a chill, it's February ain't it, after all? Didn't Mr. Burke catch his death doing just that last year? Merry as a grig on Monday, blue as Death which he was by Sunday. And all for taking off his jacket because it were such a mild morning for February."

"It were January," Mrs. Gow said meticulously, "not that you ain't right in all other particulars, Mrs. Gudge."

"Well, there you are," Mrs. Gudge said. "But so I told his lordship, and he thanked me kindly for it. Well, but he looked merry enough to thank me for nothing. Happier than *I* ever seen him, and there's a fact. Well, but who wouldn't be? Ain't this a fine Fair?"

"I'll ask Mr. Abernathy if he left a message," Maggie told Will, biting her lip, "and pick up some purges—in case."

"And antidotes," Will said as she went to the tent.

"None, for there are none," she said over her shoulder, drawing back the flap and disappearing inside.

Will stood, impatient, waiting, looking around for a glimpse of the nobleman or his brother. The Fair was in full swing, but it seemed frayed, tawdry, overused to him today. The streaming banners were ragged, their edges picked to fringes by the shifting breezes. The ice was pocked and filthy now, with strewn ashes and trash, all the charm of the thing was gone. The huge crowd taking advantage of the clement air made it less charming every minute.

Maggie seemed to be taking a long time, Will thought. But he knew he was experiencing time differently because of his growing unease. He too couldn't keep still, but he was set pacing by thinking of the reason the viscount might not have been able to. He didn't like waiting but couldn't go—not with the viscount supposedly so near. And perhaps in such danger. But he hated inaction. With an oath, Will finally strode to the tent, flung back the flap and marched in. He almost tripped over Maggie.

She stood just inside, frozen in place, her hand to her mouth. It was dim inside; the single lantern cloaked the perimeters in shadow. But it gave light enough to show Mr. Abernathy clear. He sat at the table in the center of the tent, with his bottles and packets of herbs. He would never rise again. The black and still sluggishly bleeding bullet wound in the center of his forehead made sure of that. The air was thick, acrid and blue with gunpowder smoke. It smelled like the devil himself had just arisen from the sulfurous air of hell to come and personally carry the apothecary's black soul away.

"I was screaming and screaming," Maggie whispered to Will without turning when he put his hand on her shoulder. "Why didn't you come?"

"You never made a sound," Will said gently.

But someone else did.

"There he is!" They heard Jack call from outside the tent. "He's coming. Hoy! My lord Maldon! Over here! Stop a minute. Spanish Will's here! He wants a word with you!"

Chapter Eighteen

"Come," Will told Maggie gently, "the viscount's here."

She spun round. "Is he well? Does he stagger or…"

"He seems well enough—so far. But come, see for yourself."

She glanced back into the tent. He wondered if he'd have to bodily carry her away. Shock took some females like that. When she finally spoke, he relaxed. He should have known her better.

"No," Maggie said, "I have to get herbs, elixirs." She turned an ashen face up to his. "I know it may be too late. But if there's any chance we must give it to him. Let me get an emetic. I won't touch *him*," she said, inclining a shuddering shoulder toward the dead man. "But if we can purge the viscount, it may make a difference. It might have helped his uncle, had someone known in time." She swallowed hard. "Well, even if not—at least I can try. I'm all right now. I can deal with it now. I'll be there quick as I can. I know what to look for. Hold him, if you must."

Will understood. He nodded, pulled back the flap and left the tent. He squinted at the westering sun to see Maldon coming toward him. The viscount was negotiating the ice smoothly enough, Will noted with relief. But he was troubled because he could see the man's broad smile even from afar.

Mrs. Gow gave the viscount a great "Halloo!" The nobleman was soon surrounded by the fishwives and Maggie's servants. Will shouldered his way through them.

"How do you feel?" he asked without preamble.

He got a grin as answer. "Very well, thank you, Mr. Corby. In point of fact, I feel most excellently. It's as though my cares have vanished with the cold."

Well, that wasn't babbling, Will thought. But he wished Mrs. P. would hurry. The viscount obviously wasn't in pain, nor was he bowing. In fact, the only unusual thing Will noticed was that the man had such strong even white teeth. He'd never seen them displayed so brilliantly before. He glanced back at the tent, and then at the viscount again.

"I heard you were here, then left," Will said. "Did you go in to see the apothecary before?"

"No. Was I supposed to?"

"No. *What in God's name is keeping her?*" Will muttered.

Maggie frantically rummaged through the apothecary's boxes on the table he still sat at. Her hands shook so badly she dropped packets and vials back into the box before she could read their labels clear, and had to pick them up again. But she couldn't find what she needed. All she found was senna and tincture of rhubarb. "Too slow, not enough, not enough," she muttered in frustration. Things that would readily sell at a Fair, not what she needed. Laxatives for costive old men. Nothing for a young man poisoned in his prime.

She looked around desperately, trying to blot out the sight of the apothecary and yet see all that was in his tent. She peered behind him into the shadowy recesses by the thick brown walls.

Her eyes adjusted to the dim light. There were boxes stacked there! He must have packed up most of his supplies in readiness to go. Nux vomica, she thought quickly…mustard, ipecac certainly, barberry, castor bean, there were so many she could use. She had only to find one or two. Whatever she gave the viscount had to be specific, and quick. She edged around Abernathy, avoiding his staring eyes, and ventured into the shadows. There was an open box, filled with medications. She rifled through and grasped a vial, looked some more…and stopped. Something was stirring in the dark behind the boxes.

She wasn't a missish woman, feminine vapors had been trained out of her. Bernard had boxed her ears whenever she'd been squeamish about her duties in the shop, and the streets of London soon cured a body of foolishness. She'd learned how to confront the unknown, not faint or flee it. She no longer had to kill sea turtles or skin live eels, and never would again. But she knew how to deal with fear. And that was not to show indecision. She stiffened, but didn't shriek.

"Ooh!" a man's voice moaned. "My head! Someone struck me...what's happened...?"

"Mr. Arthur?" Maggie said hesitantly, peering into the dim recesses, as he arose from the floor, *"You?* Here? Now?"

"I was consulting with the apothecary and this wildly angry man burst in..." he said as he emerged from the shadows. "He struck me...I just awoke..." He came closer. He wasn't that much taller than Maggie but he seemed to loom over her now.

She stepped back. Too late. He locked a hand around her wrist. They both realized how fragile it felt in his clasp. She swallowed hard. "Mr. Corby's just outside," she said eagerly. "Let's go tell him..."

"Yes, I know," he said. "I saw him. I heard him too. You're looking for purges for my brother? Or so at least I thought you said."

She nodded, her throat too dry to answer, her pulse racing hard.

"Whyever are you doing that, I wonder?"

"We heard...that is to say, we thought..."

"You somehow heard he ate his nuncheon with me, did you? You then decided my man was such a bad cook he needed a purge? I hardly think so. But my brother is here? Now? Who'd have guessed he'd leave me and go to the Frost Fair, of all places?" Arthur mused.

He was so calm Maggie took heart. He was after all, a pleasant, open-faced young gentleman. Her hopes rose—until he spoke again.

"He never said," Arthur sighed. "I should have asked. Still, he might not have told me... But you've put the two facts together, haven't you? Why else would you be speaking of purges, my brother and my unfortunate uncle, all in the same breath? I came back to deal with Mr. Abernathy when I happened on the same thought. Too late too, it seems."

Maggie's eyes widened. Now she saw Arthur held a long pistol in his other hand. The sight of it robbed her of speech. He didn't seem to care that she saw it. That frightened her even more.

"And you know me by sight," Arthur said, his hand tightening on her wrist. "Although we were never really introduced. It wasn't necessary. I knew you before we met the other day. I went to see you in your fetid little shop, did you know? No, I saw to that. I had to see what was toward. He visited with you too often and never said a word about it to me, or Mama. That certainly got my interest. My brother practically took up rooms in your wretched shop. And he is usually so fastidious. Yet attracted to you, a common fishwife with carrot hair, and freckled like a toad. When he has a mistress a man would give his eyes for? Madness.

"How could I have known you knew Abernathy too?" Arthur said bitterly. "When I found out, I acted. Too late. I ought to have spoken with Mr. Abernathy at greater length. I ought to have done the thing when I first saw you visit him here the other day, but I had to leave with Maldon then. I thought I'd time... Who knew you'd come back? You're a fishwife, not a woman of leisure. Damn it!"

"But we can't prove anything," Maggie blurted.

"And the '*we*' of it!" Arthur said, his voice breaking. "The runner and you, and Maldon! Oh, God!" Now for the first time he showed an emotion other than chagrin. He bit his lip, shook his head, and heaved a trembling sigh. "What a mad triumvirate! Who could have thought it? I'll have to go," he murmured as though to himself. "There's nothing for it. I'll just have to cut and run now."

"Yes," Maggie said eagerly.

"But you have to come with me. There's no help for it. They're all out there, aren't they? How else can I leave? I couldn't get out the back of the tent without sending it crashing down on my head or I'd have done right away. The thaw's made it freeze fast to the ice. But Fate stays with me. It's luck I ran into you. Once gone from here, I can go anywhere—especially with half London on holiday today. I don't want to go, but I must," he said in agitation, "and there's only one way out. The way you came in. You have to come with me now."

"I won't," Maggie said. She tried to pull back. He was surprisingly strong. And angry.

"Don't be stupid. I have a pistol. Do you think I care? Especially now?" He easily spun her around, locking one arm tight across her neck, pulling her back tight against himself. He pressed the pistol into her back as he pushed her forward. She went staggering out of the tent, blinking at the sudden light. ...And Spanish Will's shocked face. He and Lucian were coming into the tent as she came stumbling out. They paused, aghast, when they saw her—and Arthur, behind her.

"Stand away!" Arthur cried. "There's a pistol at her back."

"*Arthur?*" Lucian said. He was confused for a moment, until he saw Maggie's expression and realized she was being held. Cold rage lit his long narrowing eyes. But then sudden comprehension dawned. He gazed at his brother in horror—then sorrow.

"Yes," Arthur said. "I'm sorry. I really am, Maldon. Well, but you don't know how it is. How it was." He was almost pleading. Maggie could feel his heart thumping madly against her back. "Uncle had so much," his voice trembled with outrage and self pity. "All of it was to come to me. Then suddenly he was going to give it to Lousia? That was *not* fair. Mama said so too, and so it was not. There *is* such a thing as justice, and one must attain it any way one can. Do you think our ancestors would have stood silently by and let vandals take all from them?

"But what would you know of ancestors and family?" he said in despair. "Uncle left it all to you, after all. And you simply didn't care. You offered me bits of our history as though they were nothing. A house? 'Why here—take it, it's nothing to me,'" Arthur said mockingly. "It was everything to me!" he cried.

Maggie's little group stood transfixed. But Arthur was only speaking to his brother.

"You had it *all*," Arthur raged. "The name, the money, the houses, the treasures, the wonderful books with the stirring tales of our family. *Yours*, just because you breathed first! And the travesty is that you don't care. You never did. *I* cared. It's not right, it's never right. Mama said so, Uncle agreed. You know it too."

"Yes," Lucian said softly. "You're right about that, Arthur. But I'm still your brother, and I care about you. Let's sit and talk about it. The books? I don't read them. I don't need them. I can give them to you. Money matters can be arranged and…"

"Do you think I'm *mad*?" Arthur shouted.

Maggie's servants and the fishwives inched closer. But Arthur saw them. "Stand back!" he threatened them.

Will motioned them back sharply, never turning his gaze from Arthur. Alice and Annie wrapped their arms around each other, Jack frowned like thunder, watching warily. Flea stood like a stone, his big face a study in confusion as little Davie and the brothel girl cowered in his shadow. The fishwives, amazed, stood as though their thick legs were planted in the ice.

"I'm prudent. Not mad, brother," Arthur said more quietly. But Maggie could hear his breath sawing and felt the rise and fall of his chest against her back. "*Brother*? As to that—what's in a name, indeed? Ten years is a *generation*. Too long a time to make us anything but brothers in name. You don't know me. How can you care about me? Mama loves me. You never did. She won't grieve for you. Nor will I.

"You'll be gone before nightfall," he added. "The kidney pie. The strong taste covers all." Maggie stiffened. He prodded her with the pistol to warn her to be still. "I could have waited," he told Lucian, "but why? Once I heard everyone thought Uncle died of the vile thing he was attempting in that filthy brothel, there was no need. God! Had I known that before! How much easier all of this would have been. I wouldn't have felt badly for a moment. I did, you know, now and then. At first. Until I knew what he'd done. I'm not a monster. Only trying to get what is my due."

"You murdered a man," Spanish Will said, his voice steel under dark velvet, soothing yet threatening. "No—two men. And now, three? Come, leave off. Help us help your brother. There's no sense to this anymore."

"Is there not?" Arthur said. "I didn't do wrong. I did justice, my good man! God's hand was in mine all through this. I didn't see that before, but I see it clearly now. Uncle *should* have been punished for what he did to that child. I was merely the instrument of justice. Abernathy? He was a *criminal*, selling poison as though it were candy, to anyone who asked. But Maldon...?" He sighed. "I grant you that, perhaps. But it's needful. If I waited, I'd have felt worse. I was growing to like you, Maldon. The famous Maldon charm," Arthur said bitterly. "It was working on me too.

"It had to be done quickly," he said, his bright blue eyes sincere as they fixed on his brother, "before I lost my resolve. No one would have seen my hand in it. I was surprised at that myself. Who knew it would take so long for it to work on Uncle? How far he'd get, how normal—no how *happy* everyone would think he was before he died? I wouldn't have tried to get that horse to trample you had I known. I wouldn't have had to pitch myself into the street either. Why, my knees hurt still. As it was, it was ridiculously easy. No one so much as suspected. That's how I knew I hadn't lost all, even after the damned Judas will was read."

"We knew," Spanish Will said.

"Oh, did you?" Arthur laughed. "Only because of Abernathy and the coincidence of my brother's plaguey ginger slut being acquainted with him. Otherwise? I think not, runner. You didn't know what really happened with Uncle. I daresay you're still not sure, and he's dead and buried now, so you'll never prove it. If Maldon had wandered off and something happened to him later, you'd never have connected it to me either. Especially when everyone knew there was someone evil after both of us. It was perfect. And to be caught for *Abernathy*? And because of what he said? What a travesty."

"We knew," Will said again. "The blow to your uncle's head didn't kill him; we discovered that almost immediately. Then when we were told he was taken by a seizure we realized it wasn't a natural one soon enough. The path led to your door before you killed the apothecary. That was a waste. It's over."

"Arthur, he's right," Lucian said calmly, although Maggie saw him swallow with difficulty before he spoke. "Now you'll get nothing, after all. After all you've done. So why run? What's the point now?"

"Time," Arthur said reasonably. "Time heals everything. Except in your case, of course. Whatever they tell Mama, she loves me and will forget the bad, in time. I'll go to the Continent for a few years, or the Antipodes, the Americas, it hardly matters. When I finally return, who'll be able prove it? I'll be the Viscount Maldon then, after all. I just need time now."

Lucian's eyes grew wild, he opened his mouth to speak, but choked on whatever he was about to say.

"So now I must go," Arthur said. "You're not to follow. Or I'll kill your red-headed whore here." He laughed bitterly. "Uncle and nephew, both drawn to low sluts. Ye Gads! Am I the only moral one in this family?

"Now move away," he told Spanish Will. "Get the others to stand aside too. I'm going to take the fishwife for a walk to the embankment, and then you can have her back. In time. But don't follow me. I've a pistol in her back, and another in my pocket. She only has one heart."

They stood aside. Lucian's face twisted, agonized. Spanish Will had no expression, and it was terrible to see. Arthur began to walk, stiff legged, pushing Maggie forward. He went in lock step with her across the ice, in a vile parody of a game she'd seen parents play with their children, letting them stand on their feet so they could dance together as one. Maggie went across the ice with Arthur, thinking frantically.

She wondered if she'd faint now, for the first time in her life… She wondered if that might be the best thing to do. Would he cast her aside and run? Or shoot her as she fell? Or drag her along and keep going? Would it buy her time? Or end her life?

Then she frowned. She heard something apart from Arthur's harsh breathing in her ear. It was so subtle at first she thought it was only her own heart cracking. But it grew in intensity. It was vibration as much as sound—she could feel it through to her bones. A moaning, a deep groaning. A monstrous creaking that sounded like some enormous ogre straining to open a locked and rusted iron door.

She shuddered. The world shuddered. It seemed the ice itself shivered under her feet.

Apart from that strange thrumming, a sudden silence fell, a breathlessness like the hush before a thunderstorm. It seemed everyone at the Fair paused too. The music trailed off, discordant as it died. Laughter and song, the busy hubbub and conversation, all came to a halt. Arthur stopped moving. They all stood on the frozen river in the mild breeze, listening.

There was a sudden cracking sound. Maggie stared, disbelieving. A tent across from them suddenly vanished, as though the air had opened and snapped it up whole. But it was the ice. The ice on the Thames was parting like the waters of the Nile rushing back after Moses's safe passage. The sound that rose now was that of the ice crazing and splitting, and thousands of people shouting as they realized it.

It happened more quickly than anyone could have imagined. The sleeping giant awoke with a roar, shaking off its icy bonds. The crowd swung in all directions, looking to escape the very ground they were standing on. Becuase it wasn't ground and had never been, and was about to show them now. Long and crooked fissures were suddenly snaking open under their feet. The ice splintered as people ran screaming. Tents collapsed. Arcades shattered, torches and cookfires were suddenly doused. Streamers and banners and boarwalks fell to the ice and the ice fell into the water and floated away. The printing presses that had churned out the papers celebrating the captivity of the great river dropped into the Thames like coins into a wishing well.

Maggie and Arthur stood at the end of the last row of tents in frozen solitude, watching as widening streams grew between vanishing floes of ice. The waters separated people on ice islands that went spinning downstream. Fairgoers fell into the churning river. Some shot under the ice, others clung to debris. Maggie saw one poor soul in the distance, silently, desperately clinging to his shard of ice as it shot by. When his icy raft spun under, he clung tighter and went under with it. Another raised hands, screaming for help until the water silenced his cries.

The Great Frost Fair was all in motion again as it shattered into pieces. The Thames bubbled and seethed, fomenting like a scummy cauldron as it boiled downstream toward the bridge again.

Everyone who could run was scrambling for the embankments. Bargemen who had charged coin for passage over a joke grabbed their boat hooks and tried to catch people writhing in the water. Some ran for their boats to try the turbulent waters.

But Maggie's servants and the fishwives were suspended in time and place just as she herself was. Lucian and Spanish Will stayed still, watching Arthur. ...Who stood, thinking.

He looked at the pandemonium. He noted where the ice was, and was not. Then he suddenly shoved Maggie away, sending her sprawling. He ran then, leaping like a spring lamb over fissures and cracks, fleeing over the ice to the shore like a thousand others doing the same.

Spanish Will went after him, the viscount at his side.

Maggie lay on the ice, panting with pain and relief. Arthur was sprinting nimbly, far ahead of his pursuers. She saw him suddenly veer. He swung toward where Flea was standing, dumbfounded, with the children at his side. Arthur run straight toward the giant. And then Maggie saw Arthur, still running, bend and reach for the smallest of the onlookers—the little blond brothel girl—like a boy spreading his fingers to grab for the golden ring as he whirled by on the merry-go-round. Then Maggie knew he'd only exchanged hostages. He sought someone smaller, lighter, easier to carry.

"No!" she cried in anguish. *"Flea!* Don't let him. Flea! Stop him!"

But Flea didn't move. Maggie dropped her head in despair.

Flea stood rock still as Arthur ran up beside him. Then one thick arm shot out. He grabbed Arthur by his high white elaborately starched neckcloth, and jerked him off his still running feet. He held him aloft for one second. Arthur's bright blue eyes flew open in surprise, his mouth opened too, but he'd no time to speak. Flea's heavy handsome face was grim and determined. He raised his other ham-sized fist and hit Arthur's chin hard, and then again, and then once more before he released him and flung him away, sending him spinning, then skidding far out across the ice.

Arthur's pistol went flying, as he did. He landed, very still. And wearing his neck as no living man could.

All around them, people were running and screaming. But the little party that circled around Arthur was still as Arthur himself was in death.

Lucian was the first to speak. He swallowed hard, then dragged his eyes from Arthur. "My brother," he whispered hoarsely, looking at each of them in turn, "slipped under the ice at the Fair. Some of you saw him fall into the water when the ice broke. I'm only sorry I wasn't there at that moment, to help him. My mother will be deeply grieved. If we get the body back, it will ease her mind. If we don't...we don't. But that is all. There's really no point to more. Is there?" He stared at Will.

Will cleared his throat. "No, no point now."

Lucian looked at the other silent onlookers. "Is that understood?" he asked. "...Please?"

They nodded.

But no one moved until Maggie finally reached them. She came running, limping across the ice towards Lucian, weeping. She thrust a bottle to his lips. "Drink!" she cried. "For the love of God, drink."

Flea and Jack, combining strong body with strong mind, led the party to safety as Spanish Will slid Arthur's body into the torrent, with only a muttered curse as a benediction.

The others waited silently on the embankment for Will to return. The Viscount Maldon lay there too, retching up his horror and sorrow, doubled over gasping with pain, as Maggie kept crying and imploring him to live.

Chapter Nineteen

They were well dressed and strangely somber, if only because everyone else in London seemed to be smiling on such a glorious day. Even the sun seemed reluctant to set on the mild March afternoon. The tea shop was in the best part of town, the service discreet, the other customers of the highest *ton*. But Maggie's heart was heavy. And Spanish Will looked glum.

Even Lucian was subdued. It was a parting. They were never easy. This one was more difficult than most, perhaps, because they'd shared so much, and it was a final break. It was time.

They huddled around the small table, like conspirators.

"Look," Will finally said, his voice tuned low. "As I see it, no man can account for his relatives. Not even a King. Good Edward had his brother Richard, didn't he? He thought naught of strangling his nephews, did he?"

Lucian allowed himself a reluctant grin. "Shakespeare, Mr. Corby? But I have no Plantagenant blood, I fear."

"Well, but he's only right," Maggie said staunchly. "Don't I have sisters? Though you wouldn't know it, they stay so far from me. Unless they need money, of course. No one can account for blood relations. Nor even husbands nor wives, come right down to it, since half the time they're landed on you without your consent either."

She saw the sudden sympathy in their faces and added hastily, "Well, but even if you're lucky enough to pick them, who can swear for another person? Just look at Mr. and Mrs. Macbeth, for example."

That set them all to laughing. But not for long.

"It's kind of you both and I thank you for it," Lucian said, his face stark and sad again, "and you're both right so far as it goes. But he was my brother, and I can't forget. Not just because of what he did to Uncle, or even what he tried with me. What keeps me awake some nights is what might have been. There was yet another bar to his getting the title. He didn't seem to consider that, even at the last. Probably because he was already considering how to rid himself of it. When I think of my young Nicholas, unaware...

"With me gone, Nick would have been *his* ward. Even if not, had he escaped and gone abroad, he could have come back. He was right about that. The years change people's appearances. Perhaps opinions too. People have short memories; they're always rewriting history. Those who live on, sometimes win just because they *do* live on and there's no one left to refute them. And what he might have done then... *That 's* the thought that's hard for me."

"Then don't think it!" Maggie said. "I know that's easy to say, but sometimes we pick at evil thoughts the way a child picks at a scab on a knee—because it's there, because sometimes there's even a kind of pleasure in pain like that."

Lucian raised an eyebrow. It was that kind of statement that made their strange friendship so compelling. And so difficult to break off now that there was no longer any real need for it. He doubted he'd have confessed his problem to any other people. He didn't know any who could have comforted him so well either. Like survivors of a cataclysm, thrown together because of it, they shared a terrible history and a strange sympathy for each other now too. But it was over and there was really no tangible need for their continuing to meet. The longer the days stretched from that terrible last day of the Frost Fair, the more absurd their unlikely partnership appeared to be.

Lucian sighed at the truth of it. A viscount who kept dropping in for tea with a fishmonger? She might think he was courting. God knew what the rest of London would think. He liked her too well to offer her the role his brother thought she'd held. Besides, he had a lively suspicion she'd not only never accept it, but never speak to him again if he suggested it. Their paths were parting, but he didn't want to leave her with a distaste for him. A gentleman had women friends, certainly. But a fishwife? And a nobleman being friends with a runner? Where could they meet and to what purpose? No, it was time to end it, and they all knew it. And still and all, it was hard.

"It's over," Maggie said, looking into the dregs of her tea, "and done with. With no one the wiser. He was found and buried, and be done with him. His death is a sad fact of the Fair now—along with too many innocents." She raised her eyes to Lucian's. "But he was lucky in that. At least his name and yours can remain clean. And though it's sad, you must remember it's no reflection on you. It's not always bad blood. Don't you sometimes find one fish misshapen in a whole basket of sound ones? It's an act of God. Or some sort of disease. Or in a man, even how he was raised, perhaps."

"How does your mother do?" Will asked, reminded.

"She does well under the circumstances," Lucian said, frowning. "Too well, in fact. She asks few questions, and mourns more for the look of it than the feel of it. Or so I think. She's the sort of female who'd grieve like your Lady Macbeth might, Mrs. Pushkin. All wringing of hands and high theater. Instead, it seems to me there's more bottled rage than sorrow. It makes me wonder. But we don't talk about it. In any case, she asks more after Nicholas than she sighs for Arthur these days. She's already on fire for him to be home on holiday. Not that she doesn't dote on Nick. But Arthur was all to her, and that is strange."

"Maybe not," Will said. "She's a shrewd piece—if you'll forgive me saying, for I mean it as a compliment. Not much passes under her window she don't see. I wonder if she doesn't already guess the whole of it, somehow? No one would have known good or ill of him better than she, I think."

Lucian shrugged. "Nothing can any longer shock me."

"Well, you shocked me," Maggie said brightly, to change the subject and get that bleak fathoms deep look out of his eyes. "I can't thank you enough for finding a home for little Millie. I worried for her here in London. Even under my care, there'd be so many dangers, memories... But to find tenants at your country estate willing to take on a little girl and raise her as their own? Even knowing her sad history? It's the very thing for her. Maybe that way one day she'll forget. She never could here."

He smiled at her. She looked amazingly like a lady today. She wore a fashionable dark blue walking dress. Her brazen hair was neatly tucked into a stylish bonnet. Her reddened hands looked dainty in little gloves. The late afternoon light showed she'd dabbed some powder on her face, but it only muted her freckles. It was so subtly done he mightn't have noticed, except that he'd grown so used to them. Her pert nose tipped up, her green eyes shone, she was a pretty little creature, her masquerade this time as complete as it had been the night she was a mermaid.

"And you, Mr. Corby," Maggie said, beaming at Spanish Will. "To have Bow Street hire on Flea was surely a stroke of genius! He loves the work. The fact that you got him a room right there to live in makes him proud and happy. Well done!"

"Glad to help. As it turns out, he helps us too. He does his work well," Will said generously, visibly expanding under Maggie's praise. "A fellow that size commands respect. Once I saw that he does what's asked, when asked, without question, I realized we had ourselves a fine man. He keeps the peace, and God help the one who doesn't let him. And I don't doubt you can use the room now he's gone from your hearth."

"But he still comes to visit," Maggie said. "Bowdie waits for him each evening by the kitchen door. He comes to call on her as promptly as any suitor to take her for her evening walk."

"*Bowdie?*" Will asked.

"Well, but I named her Boadicea, after the warrior queen," Maggie said. "Davie can only manage 'Bowdie,' so that she is... Don't laugh. It's only fitting. She'll be a queenly dog, and is growing as protective as huge." She grinned as both men laughed.

The runner looked amazingly handsome today, she thought. It wasn't just the way he was dressed. His dark face was relaxed, his eyes gleamed and when they looked on her they became soft as his deep voice. Too bad, she thought on an inner sigh, that there was no reason for him to continue to visit her as Flea did. But then, not too bad, after all. Flea only wanted friendship. It was all too clear to read what Mr. Corby wanted in those intense eyes of his.

And the viscount, well, but he was always elegant. But who could expect a nobleman to keep calling on her? She wished he could, if only because she knew she could take that haunted look from out of his eyes, if only now and again. And it would be delightful to meet his beloved young Nicholas, if only for an hour.... *Of course*, she thought, snapping out of her reverie. *Take a nobleman's son to meet a fishwife? Oh, good thinking!* He might take her to see Lousia again, perhaps, or so he'd said before the tragedy had begun. She wouldn't depend on it. She was a realistic female. She had to be.

"You've both helped me," she said.

"Well, but you helped us," Will said.

And so she had, he thought. But she wouldn't help him to anything else. At least, not what he discovered he wanted now. And he wasn't a man to tarry for no reason. No more sense tempting himself with her than there would be in calling on his good friend, the Viscount Maldon, of an evening. He'd taken the reward money from the nobleman, and that had fairly well clarified their relationship so far as he was concerned. A man could never call himself friend to a man who paid him. Nor could he befriend a woman he couldn't sleep with. But as to that…

…*Well*, Will thought, as that villain Arthur had said, *time would tell*. It just was not time for such a thing now. Or perhaps, ever.

The three fell silent. Each thinking of endings, and Time.

"Timing," Will said at last. "We had all the facts, but timing can't be discounted. If that lad hadn't got to me in time at the Fair to tell me where to meet up with you.… And a handsome thing it was to give him a job of work in your kitchens, my lord, I might add."

"No, he deserved it," Lucian said. "He's resourceful. Plans to be a great chef now, actually," he smiled. It banished his haunted expression—for a moment. A moment later, he was brooding again.

"But it wasn't just timing. Much of it was luck. He didn't know I detested kidneys."

No one asked who "he" was. The viscount's expression said it all. "I had an ogre of a nurse when I was a boy," he said with a painful attempt at a smile. "As hard-hearted as she was hard-headed. She was fond of serving intestinal meats, kidneys, lights and livers. They were cheap and nourishing, and she was convinced that if a boy didn't like something it meant it was good for him. And so I learned early on how to spread food around my plate, artfully distributing it so she didn't know what I ate and what I did not. A strange skill, to be sure. I always thought it hard luck my own brother didn't know me. But it was luck he didn't, after all."

"Still, you'd eaten of it enough to set your heart fluttering," Maggie said indignantly.

"It was only the sight of you that set my heart fluttering, my dear."

"You were very white," she insisted, "and so though you protested, it was as well you drank all that was in the vial anyway."

"Protested?" Lucian laughed, honestly this time. "But how could I? I couldn't even speak to tell you it wasn't needful. I downed it like a good chap, and then I was lucky I didn't cast up my own kidneys at your feet."

She nodded. "That was good. Because you'd eaten some of those kidneys, you can't deny it."

"Aye," Will put in. "I hadn't seen you smiling that wide since she dosed you with her tea. You were grinning hard enough to terrify me. I didn't think all the purges in London would save you—though I didn't dare tell the Mrs. P. that," he added with a fond smile for Maggie, "because she terrifies me even more."

"I thought I was just happy," Lucian said almost wistfully. "The mystery of my uncle solved, the springlike air, I felt totally carefree. It may have been the belladonna, at that. You said I was sensitive to it. He kept a fashionable table, with everything put on my plate at the same time. Thank God for fashion. It gave me room to hide my preferences. Perhaps I did swallow more of that vile dish than I meant to because I was trying so hard to please him. I'm a monster of civility, I *must* learn to be less polite."

They chuckled, for want of anything else to say.

Outside the tea shop window, a pale early spring twilight was casting pastel shadows on the pavements. A lamplighter trundled down the street, carrying his ladder and pole, delighting the populace by igniting the dazzling new gaslights there.

They'd finished all their little cakes and buns. The tea was gone, there was nothing left in their cups but messages only fortune tellers could read. The other patrons had long since left. Their waiter shuffled his feet in the corner. But none of the three rose from the table. Instead, Lucian asked about Boadicea. Maggie laughed and told him the most cunning thing she'd done just the other morning. Then Will told them a humorous thing Flea had said, as well. And then Lucian spoke of his new kitchen boy again.

The streetlights outside the window flared on one by one, as one by one evening stars came out in the night sky above them. But none of the three moved from the table. Because no one wanted to be the first to leave.

* * *

For more information about Edith Layton's life and books, please visit http://www.facebook.com/authoredithlayton.

Ingram Content Group UK Ltd.
Milton Keynes UK
UKHW011944270323
419267UK00003B/62